TELL ME WHAT I AM

Una Mannion was born in Philadelphia and lives in County Sligo, Ireland. She has won numerous prizes for her poetry and short stories. Her work has been published in the *Irish Times* and *Winter Papers* and anthologised in story collections. Her debut novel, *A Crooked Tree*, was shortlisted for the An Post Irish Book Awards and the Dalkey Literary Awards and it won the 2022 Kate O'Brien Award.

UNA MANNION

Tell Me What I Am

faber

First published in the UK in 2023
by Faber & Faber Ltd
The Bindery, 51 Hatton Garden
London, EC1N 8HN

This export edition published in 2023

Typeset by Faber & Faber Ltd
Printed and bound in the UK by CPI Group (UK) Ltd, Croydon CR0 4YY

Extracts from Robert Frost's 'The Lesson for Today' and 'My November Guest'
from *Collected Poems* by Robert Frost, published by Henry Holt and Company,
New York, 1939, and by Penguin Random House in the UK

*This book is a work of fiction. Any references to historical events, real
people, or real places are used fictitiously. Other names, characters, places, and
events are products of the author's imagination, and any resemblance to actual
events or places or persons, living or dead, is entirely coincidental*

A CIP record for this book
is available from the British Library

ISBN 978-0-751-35878-6

Printed and bound in the UK on FSC® certified paper in line with our continuing
commitment to ethical business practices, sustainability and the environment.
For further information see faber.co.uk/environmental-policy

2 4 6 8 10 9 7 5 3

for Dúaltagh, Brónagh and Aoibhín

You have often
Begun to tell me what I am, but stopp'd
And left me to a bootless inquisition,
Concluding 'Stay: not yet.'

William Shakespeare, *The Tempest*

Everlasting layers of ideas, images, feelings,
have fallen upon your brain softly as light.
Each succession has seemed to bury all that
went before. And yet, in reality, not one has
been extinguished.

Thomas De Quincey,
'The Palimpsest of the Human Brain'

PART I

1

Ruby

May 2018, The Islands, Vermont

From the open door of the coop, a needle of light fell across the hen's egg – mute blue in a nest of pine shavings – a misshapen moon, or one of the pale-green pills the doctor prescribed for Clover. Ruby wrapped her fingers over it, turned her palm up. She considered the weight of the egg, how it moulded to the human grip so perfectly.

Outside the coop the hens murmured and clucked in their dust baths, old tyres Ruby had filled with sand and wood ash. A happy sound, even though it was mid-morning and she'd only just let them out. Yesterday she hadn't collected their eggs at all. Put it off, and off. Neglected them. Most nights now they took themselves to bed, a little assembly line heading up the ramp when the sun fell, a sad string of would-be mothers. She'd watch them from the porch, dragging herself down in the pitch dark to shut the coop door.

She squeezed her fingers, pressed the egg tighter: still enough calcium that it didn't break. That was good. She listened to the soft chatter outside and hated herself. Their beating flightless wings when they saw her coming, their dumb trust, following her around the yard, letting her reach in and take their brood. All that foraging and effort she'd been throwing into the trash or scrambling and feeding back to them. Lucas always said they should: scrambled eggs helped the hens regain nutrients lost while laying. He'd rattle out the list of benefits – protein, calcium, magnesium, vitamins A, E, B6 and 12 – and her thoughts would start to drift.

Every few days Ethan Puckett pulled up in his truck and left a few groceries, cartons of milk, loaves of bread, meals in baking dishes still warm that Adelaide made for Ruby and Clover. Lasagne,

3

macaroni and cheese, maple baked beans, venison. Ruby stacked the cleaned dishes on the bottom step for him to take. All of Clover's food had to be pureed now because of the stroke; the left side of her mouth still sagged. The blender left Adelaide's meals a bland lumpy grey. Neither Ruby nor Clover had much appetite. The hens ate Clover's pureed dinners, as well as their scrambled selves. Ruby had been back home for almost a week. She was so angry with Adelaide and Clover that her stomach stayed clenched.

Ruby stepped outside the dark coop and away from the heavy smell of bedding and manure. Maybe she should give the eggs to Ethan today. Instead of avoiding him when he pulled up, she could thank him for all he'd been doing, mention the heat, the fishing. And hand him a box of eggs. Adelaide could use them. Maybe Ethan could take the hens.

The house phone was ringing. Clover was there but she probably wouldn't answer. It was hard for her to stand and then she'd have to lumber across the kitchen because they still didn't have a cordless phone; the caller would have given up. It kept ringing. Ruby put the basket down at the bottom of the steps, stamped up to the porch and let the screen door slam behind her against its aluminium frame. Clover was slouched in her day chair, staring at the TV; her mug of tea had turned milky grey beside her. She didn't look up.

The phone shook on the wall when it rang, like in a cartoon. Hello, Ruby said, glaring at Clover, but Clover just shrugged her right shoulder, the way she did, up to the ear, which meant something defeated like So what about it, or I don't want to listen. She had *The Price Is Right* on loud, her housedress hiked to her knees, bare legs shocking white above inflamed ankles. A pair of pink plastic barrettes held her hair each side of her face, just above the ears. Ruby recognized them as her own, from years ago, and felt a slap of remorse. Clover's post-stroke fingers grappling with the child's

4

clasp. The slippers were Ruby's too: pink faux fur, matted and pilled and too tight on Clover's swollen feet.

Hello? she said again, the receiver on her shoulder, her hand against the vinyl wallpaper, the once-bright oranges sun-bleached into large spectral patches. There was a pause on the line, like whoever it was hadn't expected it to be answered after so many rings and was gathering themselves to speak. A woman said, Ruby? Is this Ruby?

Yes, she said, this is Ruby Chevalier. Who's calling, please? She used the don't-mess-with-me voice she'd rehearsed for journalists or investigators. Don't say anything, the lawyer had told her. To anyone. She'd spoken as if Ruby couldn't grasp how serious all this was. Ruby didn't even know what it was she might mistakenly say. It wasn't a journalist, though. Ruby could tell by the halting uncertainty, the out-breath like a sigh, the hesitation. When journalists called they spoke immediately and said things fast, like Hey Ruby, how've you been? Familiar, like they knew her, as if she'd be tricked into thinking they'd met before. Nathalie said they'd even waited outside the school, asking kids who she was, to point her out if she showed up. Ruby hadn't left the house since she'd come back.

The woman wasn't from around here, the way she said Ruby. The exaggerated vowel sound. She said it again: Ruby. Ruby, this is Nessa. Nessa Garvey. From Philadelphia? Your aunt. Ruby opened her mouth to speak but didn't really have anything to say.

Ruby's finger traced a faded petal on the wall. It was barely visible. One of the only times Nathalie had ever stepped inside their kitchen, she'd said to Ruby, Oh my God, *That '70s Show* – a phone with a cord, the vinyl, orange and brown, the Formica table.

The woman, Nessa Garvey, *Aunt Nessa*, started again. Please don't hang up, she said. Please. Hear me for a minute. Ruby wanted to burst into tears. She glanced over at Clover but Clover wasn't paying attention. She was writing possible prices for showroom merchandise on the back of an envelope with her right hand. She couldn't work the other one anymore.

Nessa. A name Ruby remembered on her own. She pushed open the screen door and stretched the cord to sit at the top of the steps. She balanced the phone between her cheek and shoulder to wipe her hand on her shirt because the receiver was slipping, and realized that in her other hand she was still holding the blue egg.

Yeah, she said, go ahead. Her voice didn't sound like her own.

I don't know if you remember. You used to live with me. You and your mother? Ruby didn't say anything. Nessa. Maybe she wanted Ruby to say things to get Lucas in more trouble. The voice wasn't rude or unkind, but it wasn't friendly either. She sounded like she was reading from a page. The tremor that had started in Ruby's lip moved up the muscles on her cheek. She couldn't still herself.

We're having a— She stopped, cleared her throat, kept going. We'd like you to come here. You were her whole world. We've waited. We had to, you know, at first, but now we've waited for you, so you could be here. I'm making this call for her. To ask you. We don't have to talk about—

Nessa broke off.

We don't have to talk about your father. We've made all the arrangements for you. If you'll come.

Ruby held the receiver in her lap and looked east toward the Green Mountains, squinting against all the blue – the bright morning, the glare of the lake. The day would be fine. She should move the run to a fresh patch. She'd do that today. Clean out the coop, give them a fresh start; it wouldn't take long. And she'd reseed the lawn from the sack of clover in the shed. The hens were foraging where the enclosure met the shale, pecking at the clawed brown earth and grey slates, the scratch grain gone and the morning dew long evaporated. One hen's golden feathers caught the sun, her comb still radiant red, healthy. Beside her a blue-black Ameraucana camouflaged against the shale; beech leaves stirred above them; a motorboat cut across the water, tracing a dark gash in its wake. Everything was still beautiful. The hens were hers. She should keep them.

2

Nessa

Nessa heard her sister moving through the house, the creak of floor-boards overhead, toilet flush, sink running, the front door clicking shut. Beside her Ronan slept, his lips parted, a soft snore on the breath in. Later she told the detectives she heard the car start on the street. The last sound that connected Deena to the world. Something could have happened right there outside as Nessa rolled back toward Ronan's warm body, burrowed deeper under the comforter and slept.

Maybe an hour after she heard the car, Nessa walked down toward the museum for the papers. She hadn't worn a scarf or hat and the wind blowing from the river was sharp, stinging her face. Afterward, every detail of that morning became crystallized, refined through repetitions into a series of stills. The naked trees. Her breath making small quick clouds in the air. The patch of ice at the corner of Aspen. The empty sidewalk. The blank grey of it all, everything bare, giving away nothing.

Back at the house she woke him. They drank coffee and read the papers. She repeated something Howard Dean had said about the war in Iraq. Ronan agreed. *The Da Vinci Code* was still number 1 on the bestseller list. Ronan handed her an article from the *New York Times* and tapped the headline. It was about the death of Kitty Genovese in Queens. Next month marked the fortieth anniversary. Nessa vaguely remembered the story from a college class. The bystander effect. Thirty-eight people had heard the woman being attacked and no one had done anything.

She watched Ronan dress and pack his bag. One of his socks was black, the other navy blue, his hair sleep-matted at the back. She wished he wasn't leaving. She listened to the sound of running water in the bathroom and was thinking about the word *ablutions* when her phone rang. It was Molly: Deena hadn't shown up for her 7 a.m. shift.

Nessa opened the curtains and looked out the window at the empty space below, where Deena parked her car.

Later the detectives would tell her that Molly McKenna first called her at eight forty-five. When Ronan came back in, ready to go, Nessa was standing in the middle of her room, still holding the phone.

They drove to the train and talked about the things that might have held Deena up – a flat tyre, an accident, an appointment she forgot. Getting out of the car at Suburban Station, Ronan gazed up at the art deco facade. Nessa smiled because she knew he was about to tell her how much he liked it, for maybe the hundredth time. His hair was still flattened and she'd forgotten to tell him his socks were mismatched. Later she would remember watching him look up, and would hold that moment: the last time she was seeing him or anyone before she could never see anything the same again.

Back at the house she tried to read the *New York Times* article. Kitty Genovese's brother said that he'd found it difficult to cope after her death and had enlisted in the Marines. All the time he was in Vietnam he had flashbacks about what had happened to his sister. He became obsessed with trying to save people.

The bare walls of Deena's room were painted brilliant white. Everything was in its place. When they'd shared a bedroom at home, Deena's side had been strewn with empty Coke cans, heaps of dirty clothes, stacks of books. Four years older but ten times messier. Nessa had had to patrol the demarcation line they'd agreed, kicking back wet towels and school kilts. But now Deena's space was immaculate. If you start arranging my cans in the cupboard by colour we're done, Nessa had joked when she'd moved in. On the bedside table, a black-and-white photograph of Ruby just after she was born softened the space. In it, Ruby's head rests on Deena's bare chest. It is their first moment together, Ruby's small hand clutching a handful of her mother's hair. Skin-to-skin, the midwife had said when she put Ruby on Deena's chest.

Deena's bookcase was organized by category. Nursing and anatomy on the bottom shelf; above were self-help guides on mental health, ways of rebuilding yourself, books about living with narcissistic men, books on motherhood. Neatly stacked beside them were the journals she'd endlessly scribbled in since high school. The month, the year recorded on the spine of each book, from the age of fourteen. Then the gap, 1999 to 2002, the years with Lucas. He'd taken those and Deena hadn't been able to get them back. The rest of the shelves were lined with novels and poetry. One volume was balanced horizontally on top: Adrienne Rich, *Dark Fields of the Republic* – paper strips slipped in to mark the poems she returned to.

Deena had painted the wooden floorboards white too. The order and blankness had initially bothered Nessa, as if Lucas was still bossing Deena around from a distance, making her think she was messy, making her shrink. But she was beginning to understand Deena's need to control her environment, to be hyper-structured about everything. Lucas had taken so much. The desperation to keep order was her resisting him and all the things he'd said to her about who she was: lazy, chaotic, crazy, whatever. Maybe having order was her way of telling herself she was not those things; maybe it was even a fuck-you. Standing in the emptiness of Deena's room, the possibility first occurred to Nessa that her sister might never come back.

Nessa counted the scrubs hanging in Deena's closet. She owned three – one wasn't there. She had gotten ready for work. In the bathroom the hamper was empty. Her toothbrush sat in its holder. There was a framed card their mother had given Deena for graduation. A Dickens quote with a stethoscope spiralled around it: *Have a heart that never hardens, and a temper that never tires, and a touch that never hurts.* Deena had hung it in the bathroom. Probably because it was where she got ready every day, a reminder from her mother before she went in to the NICU.

Sometimes their dad called Deena if he wasn't feeling well. She'd take his blood pressure. She'd bring her stethoscope and let Ruby listen too. Ruby would compare hearts. She'd place the chest piece against her own. Mine's quiet, Grandad. Yours is noisy. Another time she'd listened to their two hearts and said, Mine's winning. It's faster.

Something must have happened at home. Deena was there, looking after him. Nessa ran downstairs to the phone.

Joey answered. He was in a hurry, couldn't talk. But he said, No, Dad's asleep.

He stopped at the news that Deena hadn't shown up at work. He hadn't talked to her since Friday.

I'll come in, he said.

The *John Garvey* stencilled on the side of the truck was faded, nearly gone, the *& Son* slightly brighter. Plaster dust, wood shavings, paint, receipts stuffed between the windshield and dashboard; it was just like their dad's trucks growing up. The familiarity steadied Nessa. Her phone rang as they merged onto the Parkway. Molly. Deena still hadn't shown up. The parking garage near the hospital had four levels; they checked every one. The guy in the security booth scanned the camera footage. She hadn't arrived.

They sat in Joey's truck with the engine turning over, shivering, waiting for the air to blow hot. Nessa checked the time. One thirty.

Six hours until Ruby would need to be collected from her weekend with Lucas.

Back at the house they went upstairs to Deena's room. Joey stood in the middle of it, uncertain what to do. Nessa went into the bathroom and checked the medicine cabinet. Deena's medication was there; beside it a bottle of Children's Tylenol.

Joey, maybe something happened to Ruby. Why didn't I think of that already?

Ruby was sick and Deena had gone over there. Everything made sense.

They decided Nessa should call Lucas, ask to speak to Ruby.

Joey sat next to her, leaning in so he could listen. She exhaled slowly as she dialled, trying to calm herself.

This is Nessa, she said when he answered.

Oh, hi Nessa. How are you?

Joey shook his head slightly at her. This was off. She and Lucas were never polite.

Can I speak with Ruby?

She's a bit busy right now.

She made up something about Ruby's fish having babies. He said nothing.

Just let me talk to my niece, Lucas.

Nessa? Ruby's small voice.

Ruby! How are you?

Good. My grandmom's here.

What? Their mother had died over a year ago.

Grandma's there?

Not *our* grandma. Clover.

Nessa had never met Lucas's mother. She wasn't sure if Ruby had either. She didn't think so.

13

Did your mommy meet her too?

How?

You didn't see your mom today?

No. I'm at my dad's.

Nessa watched Joey as she spoke. She could see the worry.

After she hung up, she tried calling Deena's phone again.

When the Police Department started investigating Deena's disappearance, one of the detectives told Nessa she had made forty-eight calls to Deena's number before midnight that Sunday. How many hundreds did she make to Deena that week, that month? Sometimes she still dialled her number if she had too much to drink.

By the time Nessa arrived at the bookstore, Deena had been missing for thirteen hours. She waited in the dark doorway on Walnut Street. The window was full of bursting red hearts. Valentine's Day was coming. The temperature had fallen to the low twenties and her cheeks were raw. Calm down. Don't fuck this up. She stamped her feet. The sidewalk was empty, but the traffic was steady. Her eyes teared from the cold, the oncoming headlights dissolving to streaks of white. She squeezed them shut and opened them again, looking toward the corner of 18th.

Lucas and Ruby always came through the square. Nessa could feel a cold ache low in her back. Blocks of ice tightening in the depths of her, like she might never be warm again. Her mother had told her once that people felt fear in their kidneys. She pushed her hands deep into her pockets and counted backward from five. When she looked again, Ruby was there at the crossing, waving frantically as she and Lucas stepped onto the street. They reached the sidewalk and Ruby let go of his hand and hurtled toward Nessa, the pom-pom on her knitted hat bobbing. Lucas walked behind at a deliberate pace, carrying Ruby's little suitcase. Nessa crouched, arms out, and Ruby flew straight into her. Her neck smelled like them. Their house, their kitchen, the fabric softener Deena used.

Are all the babies okay?

What?

For a moment Nessa thought Ruby was asking about the babies in the hospital, the ones Deena took care of.

The new baby fish, Ruby said. Nessa remembered then the phone call and the phantom babies. She and Joey had gone to the pet store earlier – he'd said they'd better. Ruby would be excited. There were no little goldfish, so they'd bought a bag of minnows.

Oh, they're great. There's so many. They're excited to see you.

Lucas stepped into the doorway. Nessa's arms tightened around Ruby and she took a step back.

Nessa.

She didn't answer and avoided eye contact. Lucas's gaze had always unnerved her. The first time they'd met he'd reminded her of the replicant in *Blade Runner*, the one played by Rutger Hauer. The very blue eyes. The stare. He was dressed up, as if he was heading to a law firm or bank. On a Sunday evening? He usually wore flannel lumberjack-type tops and cargo pants. Nessa lowered her head, breathed in Ruby again.

Nessa, can we get ice cream? Ruby's cheeks were bright from the cold.

Yep. Two scoops even, to celebrate the baby fish.

I thought there was just one fish in the tank, Lucas said. He checked his watch.

Deena said she might be running behind. They've had a late admission and they're short-staffed, so I'll just go ahead with Ruby now.

Nessa couldn't hear her own voice, didn't know if she had squeaked or shouted out.

No. We'll wait for Deena.

Oh, didn't she call you?

No.

Nessa tried to think.

Hmm. She said she would. Did she call you at all today? She knew she might be running behind because this really sick baby was admitted late.

I haven't talked to Deena since Friday.

Yeah. Okay. But it's well below freezing, it's too cold for Ruby out here. We'll just head home now. You can talk to Deena later.

He spoke without looking at her. I told you. I'll give Ruby to her mother. No one else.

Ruby's face creased with worry.

Please, Dad. I need to see the fish babies. And Nemo. And we're getting ice cream. Please, please, please. I want to go with Nessa. She buried her face back into her aunt's neck. Her breath was warm.

Okay, Nessa said to Lucas, but she didn't let go of Ruby. There's about ten fish babies – you'll have to come up with a lot of names.

They're called larvae, said Lucas. She's an intelligent person. We don't dumb things down.

They both stared at the traffic as it travelled west. Across from them, old gas lamps lit up the oak and linden trees along Rittenhouse Square. Nessa's first job in the city had been in an Irish restaurant a few blocks over. She had just started college. Those autumn mornings, cutting through the square, the leaves changing colour, on the cusp of a whole new life. Ruby squirmed to get down and Nessa let her, but kept hold of Ruby's hand. Neither of them was wearing gloves or mittens and Nessa tried to warm the small hand in hers.

Deena wasn't coming. Lucas was going to take Ruby. It was happening.

It's cold, Nessa.

I know, sweetie. She stared east toward Center City as if she were expecting Deena.

We're going home, Lucas said. He put out his gloved hand, but Ruby didn't take it; she wrapped her arms around Nessa's legs.

Come on, Ruby. Your mom didn't come, so we have to go back home.

No, I'm going with Nessa. For ice cream and to see Nemo's baby larvae.

Ruby, we're going. His voice had tensed. Ruby's grip on Nessa's legs tightened. Nessa put her hand on Ruby's head. She could feel the sobs starting against her thigh.

I want my mom. And Nessa.

Please, Lucas. She's upset. I'll take her and you can talk to Deena later about what happened at work.

Stop lying.

He said it low and brutal under his breath. The shock of his words made her step back. How could he know?

Stop making excuses for her.

Ruby was crying. Please, Nessa.

Lucas raised his finger toward Nessa's face then pulled it back, a gesture she had seen him do with Deena, giving her a warning sign as if she were a disobedient child. He was struggling to control himself.

You're upsetting Ruby, he said. We're leaving now.

Lucas lifted Ruby from under the armpits, and she clenched the ends of Nessa's coat as he pulled. Ruby wailed and Nessa tried to speak but her throat blocked her words. Lucas swung Ruby away and walked down Walnut Street, anger radiating from his raised shoulders, the coat taut across his back. Nessa watched Ruby kick and wrench, calling her as they disappeared.

The precinct was a room, fluorescent-lit and grimy, with a walk-up window at the far end. There were no chairs, just a bench along a wall. A tiny woman in a heavy beige overcoat that nearly touched the floor was talking to a uniformed officer through the hatch. She was wearing slippers. Joey and Nessa sat and waited. The woman couldn't get somebody out of her apartment. Granddaughter's boyfriend? Someone was high on drugs. Nessa couldn't hear her. The woman had been pushed. When she turned to leave, her gaze met Nessa's, her eyes rheumy and tired. High cheekbones made her appear taller or somehow less defeated. She used a cane. Had she walked here by herself?

Nessa and Joey went up to the window. Without looking up, the officer reached to slide it shut, his head bent to the paperwork in front of him. After a few minutes Nessa went to knock but Joey put his hand on her arm and shook his head. They waited. How long had the woman in the beige coat been made to stand with her cane? The officer got up and left. In the background one cop was seated on a desk, telling a story, and a handful of others stood around listening, arms folded, laughing. Nessa wanted to bash the partition. None of them would make eye contact.

She gestured palms up, shoulders raised. Are you fucking kidding me?

Don't, Joey said.

There wasn't even counter space to lean on. Nessa pressed her forehead against the glass. The officer came back over and tapped the window, shaking his head.

Ma'am, don't touch the glass. He turned his back again.

Joey picked up a newspaper that had been left on the bench and leaned a shoulder against the wall. He ran his finger down the sports page, basketball scores, squinting at the small type. He was better at managing himself in situations like this. Nessa wanted to throttle someone. They waited. The red second hand on the wall clock jerked its way around. She lost count of how many times.

A small female officer, with large eyeglasses and hair pulled back into a tight bun, slid the window open.

How can I help you? She sat in the chair and didn't look at them.

We'd like to report a missing person, Nessa said. Our sister.

How long has she been missing?

Over fourteen hours.

She's an adult?

Yes.

The officer's eyes stayed fixed on the computer screen, her eyebrows lifting a fraction above the frame of the glasses.

So maybe she's just met with some people and hasn't come back yet.

She didn't show up for work today and left home like normal. And she didn't collect her daughter. She'd never do that. Not show up.

Is she on any mental health medication?

What? It wasn't a question Nessa had expected.

You know. Antipsychotics, antidepressants, medication for bipolar disorder?

Joey rubbed the wood grain on the counter, kept his head down.

Effexor. It's an antidepressant. She's fine, though. It has nothing to do with this. It's a small dosage.

How do you know she's not voluntarily missing?

Excuse me?

With friends. By choice.

I live with her. She left for work and didn't arrive. That's never happened. She didn't pick up her daughter from her estranged partner. She'd never do that. You'll have her in your system. She's had to file restraining orders. He's hurt her in the past.

The officer turned to them then, but her eyes were closed.

We'll have to fill out a 75-74A. She said it like a question, like Do you really want to do this?

Okay, said Nessa.

The window shut.

*

19

Name, gender and age of the person you are reporting?

Deena Garvey. Female. Thirty years old.

Height?

Five-eight.

Eyes?

Brown.

Hair?

Dark. But with auburn tones.

Okay, brown. She's white?

Yes.

Complexion?

Pale. With a spatter of freckles.

A what?

You know, they're scattered across her nose and cheeks. But more so in the summer.

Fair, the officer said, ticking a small box. Weight?

Nessa wasn't sure. Maybe 125. Deena had gotten thin.

No distinguishing features. No tattoos. A NICU nurse. One child. Estranged from partner who is child's father.

A stay-away order, Nessa added. Can you write that?

Blood type?

A-positive. Nessa knew. They all were.

The officer asked about her clothes, make of car, licence plate, time she left.

Do you have a photograph?

Nessa handed her a picture of Deena sitting on a swing in the park near the elementary school. She'd taken it the previous summer. The officer paperclipped it to the form.

Has the missing person ever been fingerprinted?

Next to her, Joey shifted his weight from one foot to the other and exhaled.

Yes, Nessa said.

By whom?

The cop clicked the pen while Nessa hesitated.

The Sixteenth District. Here in Philadelphia. A few years ago.

Black spots dissolved in the air between them. Nessa squeezed her eyes shut and opened them again. They were going to drag stuff up about Deena.

Probable reason for current absence?

Nessa glanced at Joey. Was this for real?

Like I said, we think something has happened to her. She would never not get her daughter—

Custody dispute?

There was a burst of laughter at the back of the room. Both Nessa and the female cop looked over. The cop on the desk was being funny.

Yes. No. I mean, there was. Not now. My sister has primary physical custody. He gets every other weekend. They share legal custody. But he isn't happy about the judgment.

Close contacts?

There were only eight. Her, Joey, Dad, Molly, Kate, Lucas, Ronan and Tina.

What relationship did they have with the missing person?

Molly was her best friend, Nessa explained, the one who called to say she hadn't arrived at work. Kate was Joey's fiancée and was like part of the family. They'd been together since tenth grade. Lucas was Deena's estranged partner and the father of their child. Ronan was Nessa's boyfriend, visiting from Ireland. She felt stupid, adding that detail. How was that relevant? Tina. Nessa didn't know what to call her.

A sort-of friend. She has a daughter the same age as my sister's.

I don't want to get caught in the middle, Tina had said to Nessa one afternoon, standing in her doorway. Ugg boots, designer faded jeans, tight ponytail, oversized sunglasses on top of her head. Tina had given Lucas a glowing character reference in the custody trial. Nessa hated her.

She's one of those women that's always on the side of men.

The officer looked up at her for the first time.

I know some Tinas, she said. For just a second she held Nessa's gaze, and then looked down again.

A divisional detective would be in touch. Within a day. Maybe two. In the meantime they would check county and state detention centres and the medical examiner's office. Nessa and Joey should call local hospitals. In most cases people are voluntarily missing. Don't forget to call the precinct if Deena returns. She spun the form around for Nessa to sign. *Absence reported by.* Nessa's hand was so cold the pen shook. *Nessa Garvey.* The officer signed her own name below: *S. Hernandez.*

In the truck they waited for the ice to melt on the windshield.

They're going to look her up, Joey said. They'll see the other stuff. They'll think she's gone off the rails again and done something to herself.

Well, that's just bullshit.

I'm just saying. That's what they'll think.

They didn't speak during the short drive home. Nessa hadn't been able to say what she needed to – about who Deena was, what had happened to her, how good a mother she was. That fucking form, diminishing Deena to ticked boxes and mental health history.

Do you want me to sleep here tonight? Joey asked when they pulled onto Parrish Street. Nessa willed there to be lights on, Deena at home and all of this a mistake.

No. Stay with Dad. I don't know how we're going to tell him.

I'll be back here first thing, Joey said. We'll find her. We'll get her.

Nessa opened the door and climbed down, reached in and dragged her purse across the seat. Okay, she said.

Her hand flew to her mouth.

Oh fuck, the fish, Joey! They must be frozen solid.

Joey reached under the driver's seat. He held the bag up to the light. The minnows were floating upside down at the top of the slushy water.

Here, give it to me, she said. I'll bury them in the back.

Give them the flush. It'll be easier.

I can't.

Joey waited while she walked up her front stoop, opened the door in the dark, keys in one hand, the bag of dead fish in the other, and stepped into the empty house.

3

Ruby

2008

Ruby handed the woman behind the counter of Middle Lake Post Office a tracking number on a slip of paper.

I hope you're Chevalier and that this is for those birds.

I'm Ruby Chevalier. She couldn't see over the counter but could hear the peeping.

Glad you're here. It's about time. Boy, are they noisy.

Ruby and Lucas had mail-ordered twenty chicks from a farm in Iowa. All different breeds. Ruby was going to be in charge of them. The woman came out from the back and handed Ruby a brown cardboard box with a grid of circular holes punched all over it.

They're loud and they smell. Can you manage by yourself?

Ruby hoisted the box against her chest, tilting it slightly, and an alarmed crescendo rose from within.

Yep, she said as she pushed open the doors with her back. The truck was waiting at the bottom of the steps.

Sounds like they made it, Lucas said. Well done.

He leaned over and rubbed her head. She hadn't done anything but collect them, but she felt proud.

She tried to see in through one of the holes but it was completely dark inside. Pushing a finger through one near the bottom, she touched a small body, could feel the fluff and the strange hollow bones beneath. She wanted to squeeze the box she was so happy, couldn't wait to hold a chick in her hand. Lucas took a fishing knife from his tackle kit at Ruby's feet and slit the yellow plastic straps. She parted the lid. Twenty little heads, brown, gold, black, grey, trilled together. Reaching in, she picked up a chick the colour of honey.

I think it's one of the Rhode Island Reds, she whispered.

I think you're right, he whispered back.

The next one she lifted up looked like a chick from an Easter card – pale yellow that faded down to white, and pitch-black eyes. Her finger touched a thread of crust on the underside.

There's something on her.

Lucas leaned over. That's the umbilical cord. Don't touch it. It will fall off itself.

In one corner a ball of blue-grey fluff lay flat and lifeless. Ruby knew it had died but, before she could ask, Lucas scooped it up with a piece of newspaper and put it in the pocket on the driver's-side door.

Forget about it. This can happen. Let's get them home.

He put the truck into gear.

Lucas had written out instructions for Ruby. The chicks would stay upstairs in the bathroom for the first week. He'd strung an infrared light over their brooder. It had to be 95 degrees. Even their water had to be warm. She had to take the temperature of the water with the thermometer, fill the dispensers, open the box and immediately bring each chick to drink. Chicks ingested the yolk in their eggs and could survive for seventy-two hours after hatching. But they could easily get dehydrated. That must be what had happened to the blue-grey chick in the box. That first day she lifted each of the nineteen chicks, tipped beaks toward the water drops and checked their vents.

In the mornings Ruby changed the bedding, filled the dispenser and scattered the starter feed. At night she snuck into the glowing red room just to be near them and listen to their small sounds. When they moved the brooder to the coop outside, she still went, careful always to lock it when she left so that nothing could take them from her.

By September they were pullets and had started to lay. Every morning Ruby sprinted down the track to the mailbox, then searched for eggs on the way back up. The day the Ameraucanas first laid, she had nothing to carry them in, and she cupped the eggs against her chest with the mail, a large yellow envelope and smaller white ones. She rushed back to the house.

There's blue ones! Look. She held out the tiny eggs in her hands.

Good news and bad news, said Lucas, taking the letters Ruby handed him. Eggs and bills. He flicked through the pile. And don't start getting hen shit on my mail.

At the sink, Clover showed Ruby how to clean the eggs. Clover's hands were large, her knuckles deformed and fingers stiffened by arthritis. She rolled the small egg in her palm under warm running water. Cold water makes the pores open and it might absorb bacteria. Always use warm running water. Ruby had the paper towels ready. Each egg had to be patted fully dry or salmonella might get through the shell.

Where did you get this?

Lucas was holding up the large yellow envelope.

From the mailbox. She stood stock-still. Was she in trouble?

Who sent this?

I don't know. Ruby hadn't even noticed it, she'd been running too hard to get to the coop.

Lucas tucked it quickly under his arm and left the kitchen, but as he went, for a flash of a second, Ruby saw her name in thick black marker on the front.

Lucas and Ruby were working on multiplication at the kitchen table. Clover was about to go out to the garden; she was talking about weeding when there was a knock at the door. Clover opened it and two women were standing there, both holding files. We're here from the Department of Education, said the taller woman. Clover didn't say anything. She picked up her gloves from the counter and went outside.

Lucas stayed sitting. Take a seat, he said, and gestured around the kitchen. Welcome to the third-grade classroom.

Neither of them sat. The taller woman gestured toward Ruby. Her eyebrows moved close together like she was worried, her mouth turned down. Can we speak alone, Mr Chevalier?

Lucas stared at her.

It's sensitive, the woman said.

Whatever you have to say about Ruby's education can be said in front of her.

The two women exchanged a look. The taller one pulled out a chair and sat down across from Lucas. She spread her elbows wide on the table, touching the corner of Ruby's math worksheet. Ruby moved it away.

Mr Chevalier, we have written you multiple letters. The compulsory education laws in Vermont say a child has to go to school from age six. You haven't submitted the curriculum for your home-schooling programme. It's required.

Lucas leaned forward, his elbows also on the table. My curriculum is based on experiential learning. Your curriculum form doesn't accommodate that. I can't predict when there might be a storm or weather event, an ecological change, a gyrfalcon visiting the lake, a screech owl outside. We have to drop tools and see those things. There's no section on your forms that allows for discovery, for Ruby to set goals for her own learning, there's no section for boredom, for being alone with her thoughts.

The tall woman leaned forward when Lucas was finished. Our job is to make sure that no child is excluded from educational opportunities, Mr Chevalier.

She used her right hand when she talked, fingers together, slicing the air between them.

We can't assess or sanction your curriculum if we don't know what it is.

Ruby is reading way ahead of her age level and the material I'm giving her is intellectually engaging, not the generic dumbed-down primers taught in your schools. Test her. In any area. She's doing the long division and pre-algebra that you require from students years ahead of her and she can do it in her head in applied situations, but she can also grow her own food, gut a fish and name every plant out there. Lucas pointed to the door.

I am sure your daughter is very bright, Mr Chevalier.

It helps that she escaped your curriculum in these formative years.

Ruby stared at the worksheet. She wondered if she should say Lucas was a really good teacher.

There's also the question of Ruby's socialization. Her opportunity to play with children her own age, Mr Chevalier. This has also been reported—

Reported? Lucas interrupted her. He was angry.

Ruby, said the smaller woman, why don't you show me the lake? We'll let your father and Ms Marshall talk in private.

Lucas nodded. Go, Ruby.

On the steps Ruby heard Lucas say, She's an interfering bitch. The smaller woman glanced back at Ruby. They both pretended they hadn't heard. Who was an interfering bitch? Someone had reported her not being in school. Clover was bent over in the vegetable garden, digging. She straightened up and watched them, her hand on the spade. They walked across the grass toward the shoreline. The woman kept sinking in her high shoes. Who was the interfering bitch? Not Clover. She never meddled. Who else was there? Only the Pucketts lived on their road, Ethan and Adelaide. They were old and didn't have children. They kept themselves to themselves and never said anything about her not going to school. Her mother? Ruby doubted it was her. She didn't know where her mother was, only that she had left a long time ago. It was the wrong thing to bring her up with Lucas. He got annoyed. She left us. She was disloyal. She betrayed us. She was messed-up.

I guess kitten heels was the wrong choice today.

Ruby had no idea what kitten heels were. The woman pointed to the mountains across the lake. What are those? she asked.

Mountains? Why didn't the woman know this?

Do you know which ones?

Ruby understood then that she and Lucas were being tested. She told the woman everything she knew about the Green Mountains: they were part of the Berkshires, part of the Appalachians, part of a chain which ran all the way from Quebec to Alabama, the state was named after them – *Vert Mont*, from the French for *green* and *mountain*. The Abenaki had taken refuge there. She told her what she knew about the Abenaki and how their name translated as *people of the dawnlands*.

The woman said she was impressed.

Would you like to see my pullets? Ruby asked.

A fisherman has a catch of ninety-six salmon and has just four crates to evenly distribute them. How many fish in each crate?

Ruby was barely listening. Packs of children were walking down the sidewalk, dragging Hannah Montana and Jonas Brothers backpacks, holding lunchboxes, getting out of cars and off buses. Everyone was in T-shirts. Girls had braided hair. She'd worn the wrong thing. Clover had said to wear the dress but hadn't been sure.

Ruby, pay attention, said Lucas, because she hadn't answered.

Twenty-four, she said, twenty-four salmon per crate.

Lucas parked the truck and they sat there for a moment, looking out at the other kids, running, talking, girls holding hands, as they filed toward the building. She didn't know anyone. She wanted to say to Lucas, What if no one likes me, but he would say it was a frivolous thought. It was important to be able to be by yourself. They waited. Ruby sat in the truck. This was her real test today, meeting other people. She wouldn't tell him that.

Weird fact? asked Lucas.

Yeah, she said.

He thought for a second. What's the only mammal that sees in ultraviolet light?

She knew straight away it was a trick question because they'd read an article last year in a nature magazine that claimed reindeer were the only mammals to see ultraviolet. Lucas had pointed out that it was wrong. Not one, Ruby said, at least three – rats, bats, reindeer.

Let's go do this, then, he said, and they got out of the truck. They walked past the flagpoles, up the steps and through the glass doors into the reception area of Middle Lake Elementary. She was in school. Lucas stood with her at the front desk. A woman with a big smile and glasses on a cord around her neck came out to meet them.

I'm Principal Clarke. You're very welcome, Ruby. Lucas was still standing there. We'll take it from here, Mr Chevalier. Thank you.

The principal led Ruby to a small room and before they stepped in she looked behind her. Lucas was gone. She was in school on her own. In the room she was given an exam to see what grade she'd be placed into. It seemed easy. There were no tricks like Lucas would give her to make sure every question was read correctly. When she'd finished, she pushed the sheets across the table to Principal Clarke, who gave her a cup of juice and two chocolate-chip cookies. She told Ruby that she had to mark the test, and Ruby was welcome to read any of the books on the shelves. Ruby drank the juice straight down and hid the cup in the trash can in the corner. Like getting rid of the evidence. Lucas said it wasn't just the sugar that caused tooth decay – the acid in the juice ate away at the enamel. So far she'd had zero cavities.

She searched the book covers and chose a hazy-blue one with a picture of a boy throwing his arms up in the air, a falcon overhead.

She sank into a beanbag in the corner of the room. The boy was alone in a home that he had made in the hollow of a tree while a blizzard blew outside. He had run away to the Catskill Mountains and wrote by the light of a candle he'd made from deer fat poured in a turtle shell.

Principal Clarke put down her pencil and took off her glasses. Congratulations, Ruby, it looks like you're going into the third grade. Ruby stood to put the book back on the shelf, but the principal said, You can take that home to read if you like.

The corridor walls were covered in sheets of construction paper and posters. Cut-out letters spelled *Welcome Back!* Lucas would hate the exclamation point. In computer coding an exclamation point is called a shriek, a sound no one likes.

They stopped at a door and Principal Clarke peered through the square window above Ruby's head. She tapped a few times and waved at someone.

This is Miss Bukowski's third-grade classroom. From now on this is where you'll come by yourself every morning. You can't be truant anymore.

In Miss Bukowski's room all the children looked up. Ruby counted ten of them. Principal Clarke said, I'll leave her with you, Miss Bukowski, and went back into the hallway. Miss Bukowski's dress had turquoise-and-green swirling patterns and nearly reached her ankles. She wore Converse high-tops. She had long brown hair with blonde streaks through it and she smiled, a good smile.

Everybody, she announced, this is Ruby Chevalier and she will be joining us in the third grade. The whole class said, Hi Ruby, holding up their hands to wave hello at her. Ruby lifted her hand slightly to wave back. There were five girls and five boys. She would unbalance them. They stared. She stared back. No one said anything until one of the boys said, *Awkward*, and all the others looked at Miss Bukowski. Ruby started to laugh. She couldn't help it, and they laughed, and she laughed harder, the relief spilling out of her. Miss Bukowski thought it was funny too. Then she stopped and said, Okay, Ruby, let's get started. You take the desk next to Nathalie. She pointed toward a girl with long dark hair and glasses. She was wearing a headscarf with beads hanging from it in braided bits of hair. Ruby had seen this before but couldn't remember where. She sat in the empty desk. Nathalie's school bag was at her feet and there was a picture of a pirate wearing the same headscarf as she was. Ruby remembered then. She'd seen it hundreds of times, on notebooks, lunch bags, T-shirts. It was everywhere. *Pirates of the Caribbean: The Case of the Black Pearl.* Ruby didn't know what to think. Lucas would say this girl was batshit crazy. Ruby forced a smile. Nathalie waited for Miss Bukowski to turn her back to the class and then leaned over and whispered, her eyes huge behind her glasses, I love your name. Ruby Chevalier. It sounds like a buccaneer.

While Clover cooked dinner, Ruby pulled down the dictionary to look up definitions because she had been told she was two words that she didn't know the meaning of. *Truant,* said the dictionary, is one who shirks duty, especially one who stays out of school. Also the Old Irish for *wretch.* She searched for *wretch.* The first definition said a miserable person: one who is profoundly unhappy or in great misfortune, and the second one said a despicable or vile person. Her cheeks burned and it took her a few moments to be brave enough to find the second word. *Buccaneer.*

She'd been called a pirate, a freebooter. An adventurer.

4

Ruby

Why's your mother an old woman? one of the boys asked Ruby on the playground, his elbows wide, thumbs hooked in the loops of his jeans like he was going to have an argument.

Ruby was still trying to understand the question when Nathalie answered for her.

That's her grandmother, you idiot.

The boy opened his mouth like a fish: Ohhhhhhh, he said, as if some great mystery had been solved.

It had never occurred to Ruby that people might think Clover was her mother.

At the end of the day when everyone ran to their moms or dads in their compact cars, SUVs or trucks, Ruby slid into the front seat of Clover's blue 1975 Pontiac Bonneville. Clover called it the Blue Boat. It smelled like cigarettes, her Jergens hand cream and air fresheners. Everyone knew Clover and her car because she never drove at more than twenty miles per hour and she parked haphazardly around the Islands wherever suited her, sideways across three pull-in spaces or right out in front of the post office, blocking a lane of traffic, instead of out back where there was a lot.

Lucas called the Pontiac a gas-guzzler and an embarrassment. When he drove just like her, parked wherever he wanted and ignored the rules, Ruby started repeating what he said – A Clover manoeuvre – and he would laugh; he loved her mimicking his phrases. Every Saturday morning Clover shuffled outside with a bottle of Windex and newspaper to clean the Blue Boat's windows, empty the ashtray and take a brush to the seats and floor mats.

Lucas would wink at Ruby and Ruby would wink back.

How does that idiot think your grandmother's your mother?

Nathalie was like her shadow. Every time Ruby turned, Nathalie was right there by her side. In line at lunch, attached to her at recess. Every day was the same. Ruby had never spent so much time with someone. And Nathalie never stopped talking. She chattered away full throttle about everything, shaking her head so that the beads in her braids clicked together. Miss Bukowski didn't even have to turn around when she was facing the whiteboard. She would just say *Nathalie* . . . in her warning voice. It occurred to Ruby that there had been an empty desk next to Nathalie for a reason. When Ruby told Lucas that Nathalie was always fastened to her he compared her to a sea lamprey, vampire fish that bit holes into the sides of other fish and sucked everything out of them. She stopped mentioning Nathalie to him after that. The devotion didn't confuse her anymore. Nathalie was her best friend.

Ruby told Nathalie about being on the lake, gutting fish, piloting boats. Nathalie was rapt. While she was definitely vegetarian, she rated all adventures highly, especially those on the water and anything to do with pirating. She invented plans every day and talked about their future: what we'll do when the snow comes, what we'll do next summer, what we'll be. Ruby loved her like she'd known her forever.

Nathalie asked her questions she had never considered before.

Why do you call your dad Lucas instead of Dad?

Ruby didn't know why. She thought maybe Lucas had tried to get her to say Dad but everyone around them that they'd ever met called him Lucas. Same with Clover.

Maybe because I'm an only child?

I'm one too, said Nathalie, but I say Dad and Grandmom.

*

36

Miss Bukowski assigned the class their first project. She said it would involve research. They were to look at the nature around them, select one thing – it could be a fish, a tree, a bird, an insect, waterfowl, mountains, rocks, whatever – and make a presentation to the class. Three projects from last year's third grade hung on the back wall of the classroom. The best was on the cormorant. It told the whole story: how it had nearly died out because DDT made its eggs brittle and unsustainable, but that it had come back, so much so that it was destroying parts of the lake, especially Young Island, which locals called Bird Island. The guano, or droppings, of the cormorant were acidic and had killed all the vegetation. Everything on that island had been stripped and other birds couldn't nest.

Ruby passed that island all the time in the boat with Lucas. Watching the birds with binoculars, she had seen all the dead trees, and the rocks covered in white droppings. They couldn't dock there because the smell was so bad. Sky-rats, Lucas would say. She'd seen it but had never known what was happening or why. The project showed how environmentalists were now oiling cormorant eggs, addling them, to control the population. The oil would suffocate the chicks, so they couldn't hatch. There were several names for a group of cormorants: a sunning, a swim, a gulp. Whoever had done the project had even written that some cultures believed the bird carried messages from the dead. That part made Ruby shiver. Sometimes there was a gulp of cormorants on the rocky outcrop along their shoreline, wings stretched wide to dry.

All the projects on the wall had pictures from the internet but Lucas always said that it was dangerous and slowed thinking, turned brains to mush. When the class was shown how to use search engines, Ruby had to be excused to Principal Clarke's reading room. Lucas was right about the internet but sometimes, like now, maybe it might be good to know how to use it. She couldn't ask him, she knew what he'd say. Her responsibility was to become *more* connected, not *dis*connected.

In the truck after school she was quiet. Lucas was listening to talk radio about the upcoming election. Vermont was going to vote for Obama. Ruby was thinking about the project and how to explain it to him. She wanted his help because he always knew interesting and unusual things and she needed to explain it right so he didn't think it was stupid. Then she just said it.

I need a really good science project idea. It has to be about something in our environment here on the Islands. Like geology, or the lake, or animals, or plants. Something we see and want to learn more about and can teach others. I don't know what to do.

Lucas leaned to turn off the radio. He tapped his fingers a few times on the steering wheel.

What ideas do you have so far?

None. I don't have any. She told him about the cormorant project.

Hmm, he said. She worried he was going to say something about the school's low standards. Keep thinking about it. And keep looking. It will come to you. It won't be yours if I come up with the idea.

The project was due the following Monday. She had five days left and thought about it constantly. But by the weekend she still hadn't chosen her subject. While they made sauerkraut on Saturday morning she asked Clover what in her opinion was most interesting about the lake. Clover was slicing the cabbage leaves into strips and salting them before Ruby pounded them to release the juices and then used the tamper to press them down into the crock.

The way it changes colour. There are so many shades of lake out there.

No, Ruby snapped. For my project.

They worked a few minutes in silence. Clover held up a finger: What about those fossils on Isle La Motte?

38

Ruby had been about a hundred times, and probably all the other kids had too. They'd know about it already. Every tourist went there. She was nearly in tears. There was no time left. She'd have to do the fossils, something the other kids wouldn't care about.

Lucas came into the kitchen to make coffee.

She mumbled about going over to Isle La Motte for the dumb project.

Lucas half-snorted. This project. How can kids use their imaginations when they're stuck at desks all day?

You're not helping, Ruby wanted to shout.

Tomorrow, Lucas said. Today we're going to do some foraging.

They took the boat north on the lake toward an island above Knight. Deciduous forest and teeming with mushrooms. Both she and Lucas wore long-sleeved shirts. There was a cooler breeze now on the lake; the red and white oak had started to brown, the sugar maple behind revealing bursts of red and blazing orange. The sun still held some heat and she leaned down to the water to feel the light spray on her face. Lucas, his hand on the tiller, was looking out across the lake. He didn't seem worried about anything. He never seemed uncertain. Ruby couldn't stop worrying about the project and how she was going to solve the problem of pictures. Maybe she could take rubbings of the fossils.

Ruby and Lucas both carried knives and bags. The forest was dank, the smell of leaf rot heavy in the air. Perfect for mushrooms. They walked into its darkest parts, slowing down, separating to look. Ruby kicked away leaf fall and moved close to the ground, knelt. It was one of her favourite things to do, scouring the earth, uncovering, finding. Hedgehog mushroom, lobster mushroom, golden chanterelle, black trumpet, blewit, chicken of the forest – she knew them all. There on the ground, her hands deep in the mulch, she knew exactly what her project should be. Lucas had taught her how to make spore prints with mushrooms. You could identify them not only by colour

39

and size and where you found them, but also by the trace of their spore patterns. She filled her bag, searching for wide caps and crowded gills, imagining their spooky effects on paper. The project would be good. Lucas had been right: you had to be out in nature to have ideas. Then she realized. He'd brought her up here to help her think. He'd known an idea for the project would come to her.

Coming back down toward the lake, Lucas held out his arm to stop her, silent, as if he had just spotted a dangerous animal, something living, that might hear them. He pointed to an area just off the trail, and there, in the midst of the rotting leaves, was a cluster of almost iridescent white mushrooms, *Amanita bisporigera*. The destroying angel. Usually they wouldn't touch them, but Ruby felt a sickly kind of thrill. This would be so good for the project: a deadly death mushroom. She pushed her hands into Lucas's too-large gloves and cut through the white flesh of the stalk just below the volva. It toppled onto the dark palm, glowing blue-white, like a ghost.

Very poisonous, Lucas said. Even an ounce can kill. Ruby took out a sandwich bag and put it inside to keep it separate from the others.

She couldn't ask Lucas to buy poster board or paper. He didn't like that kind of thing. It was a lot of buying and waste. At school the trash cans were always stuffed with old projects just thrown out. She'd have to figure it out with stuff they had. She found a piece of plywood in the shed and brushed off the dust and spiderwebs. Black cardboard boxes and white paper were perfect canvases. She cut the stems of the mushrooms and arranged the caps with their undersides facing down. The spores lie on the gill surface, Lucas had explained, so out in nature they fall to the ground to grow. She centred the black trumpet and hedgehog on squares of white paper and put a glass bowl over them. Others, like the lobster mushroom and the destroying angel, had white spores, so she placed them on squares of black cardboard and covered them for the night. The whole kitchen table was taken up with her project, so they had to eat in the living room, and Ruby worried that Lucas would complain about her school or her teacher or fake science, even though he was the one who'd taken her foraging. Clover put a metal TV tray in front of him, and shuffled back and forth from the kitchen, bringing him more fresh basil and seconds. She and Ruby held their plates on their laps. Clover had made a pie with blackberries and apples that Ruby had picked. Lucas didn't say a word about having to eat in the living room or about *that school*. Watching Clover, the quiet way she heaved herself up and down, back and forth, Ruby's throat tightened with gratitude. Clover was doing these things for her.

She woke in the dark on Sunday morning. In the kitchen she lifted the bowl from the destroying angel on the black cardboard and scooped up the mushroom cap using a sandwich bag like a glove, the way people picked up dog dirt in town. It had left a perfect white imprint, each line of the gills written onto the black surface. She lifted all the bowls, counted twelve prints in every shade, from white to black – the pale pink of the blewit and rust brown of the hedgehog. Under the sink in the bathroom she found Clover's hairspray, so old the can had tarnished, making it impossible to read the instructions. She sprayed the spore prints, fixing them in place, then glued each square to the plywood in tidy rows, as if displaying butterfly specimens. As the sun rose she sat on the porch, facing the propped-up board. It was good. It looked scientific. She labelled the prints, carefully writing out their Latin names and their common ones with Lucas's fountain pen, and glued these under each square. She combed through their books on mushrooms, writing brief descriptions, and then, like the cormorant project, the stories linked to them, how they'd got their names, the religious beliefs. In careful neat print she wrote across the top on white paper: *Fungi In Our Forests*.

On Monday morning, Ruby laid the plywood board flat in the trunk of the Blue Boat.

I told you this car was a good size, said Clover.

Ruby held a shoebox with all the real mushrooms in her lap. She could see her classmates making their way to the front doors. Sophie Dragan was carrying a bag. Nathalie had made a diorama in an old Amazon box. Nathan Le Blanc wasn't carrying anything and looked worried.

Miss Bukowski set up the room so that they gathered at the back of it in a semicircle of chairs. Facing them was a display easel where they could put their projects.

Sophie Dragan went first, pulling a long red cape out of her bag and putting it on. Sophie was thin, her skin so pale it looked see-through. Her presentation was on Cloak Island just off Isle La Motte. The island got its name from a woman hundreds of years ago who tried to leave her husband who was horrible to her. She'd had enough, said Sophie. She hitched her wagon and horses and set off across the ice in the night. She was never seen again. One legend says that locals found her red cloak floating where the island is.

That's not science, Tim Butler interrupted. It's a story. He was the boy who'd said *Awkward* on Ruby's first day. He was new in the class too. He'd been held back a year and had to repeat third grade. His voice was raspy.

Miss Bukowski said we should research about what we see around us, said Sophie. I saw that island, and my mom helped me make the cloak.

Tim's presentation was on algal blooms on the lake. It was good and very scientific.

Nathan had forgotten all about the project. He kept turning his head, trying to look anywhere but at Miss Bukowski. She must have known he'd forgotten because she never called on him.

Ben Peters showed them the marine fossils on Isle La Motte. Everyone had seen them before and Ruby was relieved she hadn't done them.

Nathalie called hers Legends of the Lake, which was not typical stories like Champ the Loch Ness Monster of Champlain but a presentation of disasters and tragedies. People had just disappeared, whole planes. She'd made little models. A plane that took off from Burlington in a snowstorm and four minutes later just vanished. She flew a little plane over the crumpled-crêpe-paper lake in a swirl of paper confetti she tossed in with her other hand, then nosedived the plane into the middle of the diorama. She finished, whispering, Is it possible that we have our own Vermont Triangle?

Well, that was very dramatic. Great performance, Nathalie, said Miss Bukowski.

That was good, said Tim. But it still isn't science. He shook the hair off his face. His eyes were brown with dark circles under them. He was the only student in the class who Ruby could see might be like her in some way. He was taller than the rest of them and said stuff without thinking. He could sound rude. His hair was never combed, his clothes were wrinkled and didn't match and had holes in the knees. Ruby never came to school like that – her clothes were actually overclean and stiff; Clover hung them on the clothesline when it was too cold. But it was just a feeling she had about herself compared to everyone else. That her family didn't quite match up. That there was something to be embarrassed or feel bad about.

Sophie's friend Kelsey Hatch went next. The smallest student in the class, she barely reached Ruby's shoulder. Mostly she shrank into the shade or hid in corners of the playground with Sophie and didn't talk to anyone. She whispered her entire presentation to the floor while she rubbed her hands together. Kelsey had drawn a good likeness of a black bear, but Ruby wasn't sure what the presentation was about. She was relieved for her when it was over.

It was Ruby's turn. Her hands shook slightly as she propped her plywood against the easel. Lucas had said that if she felt nervous presenting to talk louder, speak over the nerves, get air in and get it out. Bigger gestures, he'd said. Stretch your whole arm out, not just your hand. Don't stay in the one place, move around. She stepped forward and extended her full arm toward her board, took a deep breath and began: Fungi In Our Forests. Kelsey flinched and Tim raised his eyebrows. Ruby had practically shouted. Nathalie sat forward. Ruby passed around the caps as she told them about how nutritious mushrooms could be, and how and when to forage. She saved the *Amanita bisporigera*, the destroying angel, for last. As she'd done with the other mushrooms, she passed it around in the clear plastic sandwich bag. Some kids were afraid to even hold it. Tim Butler wouldn't let go of it and Sophie in the next chair kept elbowing him to pass it on, but when she got it she held the bag with her arm straight out, her face scrunched in disgust, and passed it immediately to Ben. Miss Bukowski asked again about the prints, how Ruby had made them, said how they were like works of art, how she'd never seen a spore print done before. The destroying angel reached her, and she placed it on the table behind her instead of passing it back to Ruby like the others.

When Ruby finished it was recess time and everyone scrambled for the door. Ruby took down her board and put it against the wall. When she turned, Miss Bukowski was beside her.

Ruby, can you stay back just a minute?

Ruby fidgeted and watched the others line up at the door.

Go ahead, called Miss Bukowski. Slowly!

Something wasn't right. Miss Bukowski was uncomfortable, started her sentence twice. She said she was going to keep the destroying angel, just to be safe, and that she'd dispose of it properly.

Maybe it's better if we don't bring anything that's poison in to school?

Lucas had said not to bring psilocybin, the hallucinogenic mushrooms. They were considered banned drugs in the state of Vermont. But neither of them had thought about this. Embarrassment heated Ruby's skin. She had done something very wrong, she could see that now. It was like bringing in a knife or a loaded gun. Miss Bukowski was trying to be nice about it, but Ruby couldn't look at her. As she moved toward the door Miss Bukowski called after her so she had to stop. The project is amazing, Ruby, she said, and what makes it especially great is how you did it without the internet or help and found everything yourself and made your own images and used all recycled materials. It's really, really good. Maybe you could show our class how to do the prints?

In the playground, kids clustered around her by the jungle gym. Did she really find the deadly mushroom? Had she ever been poisoned? Did she actually forage and eat stuff from the ground that was fungus? Tim Butler pushed to the front of the group and faced her, tossing his head slightly to get the fringe out of his eyes. The other kids in the class said Tim had been held back because he'd missed so much of third grade last year, enough days that he didn't learn anything. Ruby was surprised they'd held him back because he was smart and she'd been allowed to skip the grades she missed. During recess he mostly hung out with the fourth-graders.

Did you really get those mushrooms yourself?

Yeah. I was with my dad. He saw it first, but I cut it.

He hesitated, as if uncertain what to say, then jumped to catch a rung above him that none of them could reach, shouting, Watch out! Fungus Girl!

He was swinging, trying to get momentum started. The others stood around, waiting to see what would happen. Ruby could see it, a glint of when they started to mouth that phrase, Fungus Girl. Then someone pushed past Ruby and lunged at Tim Butler's hanging legs. One second he was above the ground and the next he was in the dirt. Nathalie was standing over him with her Captain Jack headpiece. Miss Bukowski had asked her not to wear it in the classroom anymore, only at recess, because she kept swinging her head back and forth.

One speck of that mushroom and you're dead.

Fourth-graders had come over. Everyone was standing around Tim. He was still on the ground. Ruby was almost sorry for him.

Tim said, Yeah, okay. He got up, brushed off his trousers and shook Nathalie's hand. His response was confusing. Nothing happened and the kids watching just wandered off to other parts of the playground.

Nathalie turned to Ruby and said, Okay, you're still Ruby Chevalier because the name is so good, I'm Mary Read, we are captains of an all-girl pirate ship called *Destroying Angels*, and we are about to encounter another pirate ship that's all boys.

5

Ruby

2009

At the end of the lane the mailbox had disappeared. The pole was just a wooden stump, with hacked notches left in it. Ruby walked around it in a circle. The box was gone. She ran back to the house.

Clover, she gasped when she fell into the kitchen. Someone took our mailbox.

Clover turned off the stove and put on snow boots and a jacket over her flannel nightgown. She held Ruby's arm as they walked down the lane. She stood over the remnants for a few moments. The air was cold and Clover's eyes teared in the wind.

It's been chopped down. An axe did this.

Who would do that?

Clover said: Never mind who.

She drove Ruby to school still in her nightgown and mumbled to herself.

My mailbox.

Fifty years.

My house.

Snow still banked at the side of the road, weighed on branches, out-lined mailboxes – even coating the little red flags – and electricity wires. Daggers of ice had formed underneath the gutters. Lucas smashed them with a lump hammer while Ruby swept small drifts from the edges of the porch.

Hypothermia does weird things to people, he said. Mental fog, amnesia. There's a thing that happens called paradoxical undressing,

47

where people suffering from hypothermia start to take their clothes off. He wiped his nose with the back of his hand. Scientists don't know why. He paused. The problem with schools is they don't teach the important stuff, like how to survive.

Miss Bukowski teaches survival skills.

Does she? Like what? He swung the hammer and a shard of ice skidded across the porch.

Ruby shrugged. She didn't want to say things that he would pick apart. She didn't want to hear him say her teacher was wrong.

Well, like, sometimes it's better to undress in freezing weather. Miss Bukowski says if you get wet in sub-zero temperatures, it's better to have nothing on than to wear wet clothes. She also says to keep your head covered and that eating snow will make you dehydrate faster. If you can't heat it then wrap it in a cloth and suck out the water as it melts.

She couldn't say it to him, but she loved school. They had a new class aquarium with a brilliant-red betta fish called Flame. She had friends. Everything was better than she could ever remember.

She watched as Lucas swung the heavy hammer against the icicles. Some were as thick as her wrist. He kept talking about what was wrong with the school system. She wanted him to understand that she was learning stuff that wasn't boring and started telling him about the women pirates who dressed as men and fought alongside Calico Jack. Mary Read and Anne Bonny. Except Calico Jack hid with his men in the ship's hold and let Anne Bonny and Mary Read do all the fighting. They were all caught and sentenced to death. The last thing that Anne Bonny said to Calico Jack was: Had you fought like a man, you need not have been hang'd like a dog.

That sounds like fiction to me.

No, Ruby said, it's true. I read it on the internet at school. She realized as she said the word, tried to swallow her voice, but it was too late. She couldn't look at Lucas, only at the snow.

*

Miss Bukowski was coming across the parking lot in her pink snow hat and white puffy jacket. Which one is she? he asked. Ruby said nothing.

What's her name again?

Miss Bukowski, she whispered.

Lucas got out and they stood in front of the truck. He asked another parent walking past, Which one's Miss Bukowski, and they pointed. Lucas walked fast toward her, and right then Ruby couldn't see with everything so white all around them, like snow-blindness but different. Was he hitting Miss Bukowski? No. He was right up close to her, his face moving. Miss Bukowski stepped so far back she was out onto the road. Ruby couldn't hear. It was like someone had covered her ears tight with their hands so there was only a rushing sound from inside herself. Miss Bukowski's face turned red. Lucas was on the kerb above her. He looked very large. Ruby watched him speak. She saw his lips say Have I made myself clear? The same way he spoke to her sometimes. His arms were straight down at his sides, but she wanted to shout to Miss Bukowski, Get out, run. Miss Bukowski glanced over at her, and there was a look on her face like she was asking Ruby something, like there was something she didn't understand. Lucas was staring at her too and Ruby realized there was something wrong. All the people standing around were looking at her, not at Lucas, and she understood that she was crying uncontrollably. Nathalie was standing beside her. When did she get there? Lucas walked toward her, confused. Ruby stepped away from him, her back against the truck.

Her body was upset all by itself and wouldn't stop. She was seeing herself as if from the outside, her white woollen hat, red down jacket, the snow, the people standing around her. She was crying but couldn't feel it on the inside.

Nathalie, take Ruby to the classroom while her father and I go to the principal's office. Miss Bukowski was back on the sidewalk, in charge again. To Lucas she said, Let's go report what's happened so we know it won't happen again.

Nathalie took Ruby's hand and walked her into the school and down the corridor to their classroom, to the desk next to hers. They sat there and didn't say anything. Ruby listened for the filter in the betta tank. She didn't look anywhere but at her desk. The class shuffled in, hanging coats on hooks at the back, finding their seats. Tim Butler passed by her and stopped, then kept going. She knew it was him because it was his sneakers she saw. She was still wearing her coat and couldn't stop her legs from shaking. The tears kept falling. When Miss Bukowski came back into the room, Principal Clarke was with her. The principal stayed with the class and Miss Bukowski took Ruby down the hall. They sat on the beanbag chair Ruby had read in that first day. Miss Bukowski put her two arms around Ruby. Clover and Lucas didn't do hugs. Lucas gave her pats on the back or rubbed her head. Clover would get embarrassed and say, Enough of all that nonsense now. Miss Bukowski held her close and didn't let go until Ruby stopped and had those gasps that come after a long time. A heaviness was left inside her, above her stomach, a heavy, heavy thing deep down, pressing outward, pushing against her lungs and diaphragm, making it hard to breathe.

She began staying in every time it was recess. She read in the over-sized chair in the back corner, listening to the gurgle of the filtration system and watching Flame's flourish of red.

What's wrong with Ruby? Nathalie asked. Ruby sank lower into the cushion. She didn't want Miss Bukowski to say something was wrong with her but she didn't feel like playing pirates against the fourth-grade boys. She was tired. Some days she fell asleep in the chair and woke after class had started again. Miss Bukowski let her. One day Miss Bukowski stayed after the others had gone out for recess. She sat next to Ruby in the armchair and asked would Ruby like to talk to someone, that she'd like her to meet with a very experienced and kind person who could talk to her and maybe help her with being sad about the loss of her mother. Ruby stiffened, shook her head. No, please, I don't want to talk about that. She didn't say that if Lucas found out he'd probably take her out of school for good. She said, I want to keep coming to school, please don't, and she thought Miss Bukowski understood. It was strange that Miss Bukowski had said that about her mother because Ruby had never said she was sad about her mother leaving. She didn't think she was. It was the idea that something might happen to Miss Bukowski and Ruby might never see her again. It would be her fault.

Tim Butler also stayed in Miss Bukowski's room some days during recess. They talked about Flame, the weather or nothing at all. Ruby was reading in the armchair when she heard Tim say to Miss Bukowski that his anxiety was better. Miss Bukowski said she was happy to hear it. Ruby watched him, wondering about the anxiety that she could not see. She watched him doing schoolwork, pencil eraser against his lip, or while he was thinking, chin cradled in his hand. One recess, Tim told them he was leaving. He and his mom were moving to a town outside Boston at the end of the school year.

I'm going from a class of eleven to like a hundred.

Ruby wished he weren't leaving.

What will you miss about the Islands? asked Miss Bukowski.

The lake. My friends. Creemees. They don't have that. They probably don't even have good cows like us.

Maybe they have water ice in Boston, Ruby blurted.

What's water ice?

It's like coloured snow that's flavoured sweet.

Miss Bukowski said, I think that's a Philadelphia thing. You must remember from when you lived there . . .

Ruby said she'd lived here in Vermont all her life – but Miss Bukowski didn't seem to notice and kept talking to Tim about things

51

in Boston. She had lived there during college and was describing what a Celtics game was like.

Ruby half-listened. She was confused. *Water ice . . .* She was storing it in that place with the other shadows she couldn't make out. She could see water ice. Maybe she'd seen it on one of Clover's shows? But she could taste it, the cold suck of her cheeks. Why had that word come out of her? Why would Miss Bukowski say what she had? She couldn't ask Lucas. Or Clover. There were things they didn't want her to know.

At home she felt punished. Lucas was always somewhere else, out on the ice in the shanty, fishing without her. They barely spoke. Ruby found it hard to get her breath, like her whole body had to move through wet cement or thick, thick molasses. Everything slowed down. Clover said Ruby was so sluggish that maybe she was about to have a growth spurt, that her body must be busy growing.

From her bedroom she could hear the ice expanding, a rumbling like distant thunder. Then a few weeks later the crash of ice chunks colliding with the shoreline as they sped along the melting lake, pushed by winds. Sometimes ice crawled up ledges, uprooting and flattening trees, powerful and destructive as the lake level rose from the thaw.

One morning early in May, Lucas woke her and they went out at dawn. They headed for The Gut, the channel between the islands by the drawbridge. They fished for walleye, hooking nightcrawl-ers and live minnows for bait. That evening they cleaned the fish in the kitchen. Lucas asked her to identify the male and female. What made them different. She carefully laid a male and female out on parchment paper. She ran her finger along the male underside and watched the milt leak from the anal vent. Females were easy to identify: they were bigger, bellies swollen this time of year. She cut her from the anal vent up to the gills. Removed the organs. The two-chambered heart, the liver, the dark spleen, the air bladder. She held the roe sac; the skein was see-through, thousands of eggs in the casing. That was always the first thing you saw when you lifted the flap of flesh, a membrane of eggs that extended almost the full length of the female's body. Ruby punctured it with her knife and watched the eggs spill. They were soft. Ready for spawning. She dissected, cut, named. Lucas listened. Ruby knew being smart and attentive was how to fix things between them.

6
Ruby

2010

Everyone knew Dale Everett and his mail truck. He'd driven the same one for over twenty years. The steering wheel was on the wrong side so that Dale could drive right up to the kerb, lean out and put letters in mailboxes without ever getting out. In the school parking lot, he'd let Ruby's whole class sit at the wheel, take letters off the shelf, lean out like him and pretend-deliver them. Walking up the sidewalk to school, Ruby could hear Dale talking to parents as he passed them. Clover said Dale was a woodchuck that never shut up. He was sixth- or seventh-generation Vermont and never stopped talking about it.

He caught up with Ruby just before the school doors.

I have a package for you today, Ruby. Care of the school.

He handed her a large yellow padded envelope. *Ruby Lee Chevalier, c/o Middle Lake Elementary School* was written on it in thick black letters.

She'd never received a letter addressed to her. As they stepped inside the doors, she stopped and pulled the tab at the top and reached inside. There were notebook pages with writing. Her hand touched something at the bottom and she pulled out a small white envelope.

I have to deliver it to the office, those are the rules. Dale took the yellow envelope back from her. You know what they say? Know the rules well so you can break them effectively. He started to whistle. Ruby laughed. Dale was always quoting and saying things that made no sense.

Ruby followed him to the front desk. Principal Clarke put down the pen she was holding.

Morning, Dale.

Principal Clarke. I was just telling Ruby here that I have a delivery for her this morning. Arrived care of the school.

Principal Clarke's face brightened. How exciting, she said. She took the envelope from Dale and turned it over in her hands. Ruby, you come with me.

The yellow envelope lay in the middle of her desk; the white one was still in Ruby's hand. Principal Clarke hadn't noticed.

She searched a filing cabinet drawer. I'm just going to contact your father because this is addressed to you, not to us, and . . .

Principal Clarke didn't finish her sentence. Ruby sat in the chair. The big envelope was covered with hand-drawn ants and grasshoppers in blue and green. Her name, the sketched ants. She'd seen this before. Principal Clarke's back was facing her and Ruby fingered the envelope in her hand. In a flash of a second she had shoved it down the opening at the top of her Katniss Everdeen boot. It was like *The Hunger Games*, but in real life. One false move and she was dead. Principal Clarke turned around holding a file, pushed her glasses up on her nose and sighed. Had she noticed something was different? She picked up the phone and dialled. Ruby could hear Lucas say Hello? on the other end.

Mr Chevalier? Principal Clarke here at Middle Lake Elementary. I'm sorry to disturb your day but Ruby received a package today, sent care of the school. I decided—

Did you give it to Ruby?

Ruby could hear his voice clearly, distant but definite.

Principal Clarke stared right at Ruby as she spoke. No. I thought I'd call and ask before—

Ruby is not to see that package.

What he said next stopped Ruby's breath.

My daughter is at risk. You know that.

Ruby sank lower in the seat, the letter stuffed inside her boot hot against her skin. Her cheeks burned. At risk of what? Would her mother hurt her? She knew from the little things Lucas had said that her mother was *messed-up*, that she'd *lost her mind*. Was the package from her? Sometimes she thought she could remember her mother – a woman with stiff dark hair, a very red mouth that smiled but didn't move, the dark wide eyes like in the manga comics Sophie Dragan read. She tried to imagine that woman kidnapping her or drawing grasshoppers and ants like that – none of it made sense.

Principal Clarke resealed the yellow package with brown packing tape and said, There, like new. Ruby said nothing. She couldn't put the white envelope back in if she wanted to.

All day the envelope burned, the sharpness of its edge pushing into her skin, right through lunch and recess, every time she moved her leg. She couldn't concentrate. She was waiting for Lucas's truck to pull up, for him to drag her out of class, search her, make her take off her boots and discover what she'd taken. But the package had had her name on it. An hour before the final bell she asked to be excused to the bathroom. She closed the door of the stall, reached down and pulled out the envelope. A hand-drawing was sketched on the outside – a girl ant wearing a T-shirt with a big R on it, her foot on a grasshopper, pinning him down. Behind them was a row of little houses in pencil trimmed with icing, like the candy house in 'Hansel and Gretel'. Ruby studied the grasshopper. *A Bug's Life*. The memory came like that. Fish quick to the surface, and vivid. She could remember Flik and Hopper. Her mother must have watched it with her, a memory they had together, only she couldn't remember it. Her mother was trying to reach Ruby from wherever she was, reminding her of things they'd done together.

Inside was a photograph, a close-up of two people, a child and a woman. Squeezing their faces close together and laughing. The child was her. She knew it. The woman must be her mother. She is nothing like the way Ruby imagined her. Long dark wavy hair falls around her face. She is pale with freckles, like Ruby. Brown eyes. She is beautiful. Ruby turned the photograph over. In careful letters, *Deena and Ruby, January 2004*.

Ruby sat down on the toilet. Weak, as if the oxygen wasn't reaching the rest of her body. Her skin was cold and sweating at the same time. She wasn't sure whether she was fainting and put her head between her legs like Mr Henderson made Kelsey Hatch do because she was always feeling faint during gym class. In January 2004 Ruby turned four. She'd been with her mother when she was four and she couldn't remember. Lucas had told her that her mother left forever when she was two.

But here she was, her mother, holding her, Ruby. It was her. Ruby could see herself. The back of the picture was not a lie. She studied the faces, touched her own cheek in the photograph, then her mother's, then the place where their skin was the same. Sitting alone in the bathroom stall, she pressed her hand against her cheek. A rush of heat expanded in her chest, flooded up her throat, warmed her face. Her mother loved her. She was certain.

She stared at the picture and the drawing of her as an insect superhero until she knew that if she didn't go back the teacher would come looking for her. Miss Bukowski's third-grade classroom was empty when she passed it. On the far wall, between the classroom's two large windows, Miss Bukowski had hung the new third-grade science projects. Ruby's plywood with the spore prints was leaning against the wall further down the room, as if she were still part of it. Ruby went in and pulled strips of Scotch tape from the dispenser on the desk. Flame's tank hummed against the wall. She saw the swish of red near the cave. For a second she remembered the time she'd spent in the armchair looking at the tank when she was tired all the time. She shook the memory away. If she was caught she could just say she was looking at last year's projects, or that she'd come in to feed Flame – she was allowed to during recess. The tank couldn't be seen from the hallway. But it got moved for cleaning once a month, so it wouldn't do as a hiding place. Next to it was a bookshelf. She knelt on the floor and stuck the envelope to the underside of the bottom shelf. Her hands shook and wrinkled the tape on itself. If the envelope fell off it would get swept away, thrown into the trash. She heard the clicking of heels in the hallway. Ruby headed to the door and looked back again at the bookshelves. The envelope couldn't be seen. The click of heels was closer. She was afraid to turn, afraid that whoever it was would ask her, Where is the letter you stole?

Ruby Chevalier, why aren't you in class?

Ruby started even though she'd heard the steps coming. Principal Clarke was standing in the doorway.

I was on my way back from the bathroom and saw the projects on the wall. I remembered when we did it. I was just looking.

Well, get back to your classroom now.

When the bell rang, Ruby picked up her bag and walked toward the glass doors. Lucas's empty truck was pulled up along the sidewalk directly in front of the school, where the buses were supposed to go. *Bus Zone* was painted on the ground and a *No Parking Any Time* sign was directly next to the driver's-side window.

She sat in the truck and waited.

Lucas came out of the building, a satchel strapped across his body. When he sat behind the wheel he didn't take it off and it lay between them on the seat.

Good day at school? he asked.

By the end of the month the thaw was complete. It was spring. She paddled along the western wetlands and onto shore. Further into the woods there were vernal pools that time of year, mysterious land lakes that rose then disappeared. She sat beside one and watched several blue-spotted salamanders scuttle along the edge.

They had blots of blue that were the very best colour in the world. Their dark skin was dotted with a shade Ruby couldn't describe, a cobalt, glowing, like the enamel on Clover's oldest pot, only better, deeper. The salamanders were usually hard to find, except this time of year, when they came to these temporary pools to mate and then lay their eggs in the water. There were no fish this far in to eat them. Lucas had told her that the mother returns each year to the same pool where she was born. Like sea turtles that after thousands and thousands of miles and many years will find the shore where they hatched, the blue-spotted salamanders find their way back to the place they first came from. It can't be easy, Lucas had said, because the place they come from is a pool that only exists sometimes.

He'd also told her a weird fact about the blue-spotted salamanders. If attacked, they circle themselves with their tail and emit a toxin, so while the predator is holding their tail, and maybe gets stunned or weakened by the toxin, the salamander can just slip off the injured part, wriggle right out and run away. The predator doesn't have the heart of them, just a part of the body that will grow back anyway. It was the best survival story Ruby had ever heard. Their speckled blue was so blue it made her eyes water.

Ruby waited with her small net, scooping it low to net fairy shrimp, strange creatures with stalk eyes and prehistoric orange bodies. She bagged them in ziplock sandwich bags. Because Flame was a fighting fish, Miss Bukowski couldn't put other fish in the tank. Last year Ruby had brought in fairy shrimp so he wouldn't be lonely, and this week Miss Bukowski had stopped Ruby in the hallways and said she'd love some more. The fairy shrimp could be her excuse. She would be alone then and could look at her mother's picture.

7

Nessa

They bought several bundles of long black rubber snakes at the dollar store.

Ugh. It's like a nest. I think they're actually writhing.

Nessa pulled them out of the plastic bag and laid them across her lap. Deena sat on a low stool in front of her while Nessa coiled sections of her hair with a curling iron and then wove each snake through, head facing down, tail secured by bobby pins and barrettes. They slithered down Deena's back, over her shoulders, mouths open, ready to strike.

They're so heavy, said Deena, looking in the mirror and shaking her head back and forth softly to make the snakes stir.

Nessa dusted white powder across Deena's cheeks and swiped thick black liner around her eyes, then a deep-burgundy shadow. She painted Deena's lips the same colour. Her dress was three-quarter-length white jersey material that clung to her breasts and hips. Nessa had chosen it. They were night and day: Deena full-figured and tall, Nessa scrawny; Deena's dark wavy hair fell to her elbow, Nessa's blonde flyaway bob wouldn't grow as far as her shoulders; Deena's gentleness, Nessa's sharpness; Deena gullible, Nessa cynical. People loved Deena, Nessa not so much, not right away.

You're stunning for a Gorgon, Nessa said.

Deena gazed at herself in the mirror. God, I kind of am.

Nessa was going as the woman from the painting *American Gothic*, except she made it *Gothic Gothic*. Sunken eyes, white face, blood on her cheeks, her hands, her farming apron. The farmer's head she'd printed and impaled on her pitchfork.

They met Molly at the angel statue in 30th Street Station, the spot where Deena and Nessa always met. Their mother had started it. Meet me at the angel, she'd say if they were in the city for the Mummers Parade, shopping or whatever. The Archangel Michael, his vertical bronze body forty feet high, lifting a dead soldier from the flames of war. Molly was there leaning against the plinth, wrapped in a blue cape and a gold tiara made from cardboard.

You're a princess? Nessa practically jeered. Molly had just given them a lecture on sexualized Halloween costumes.

Amazonian princess, Molly corrected. My Lasso of Truth? She held out a yellow jump rope and opened her cloak. Nessa and Deena burst into laughter. Molly was dressed as Wonder Woman. Instead of just a leotard she had a gold silk skirt.

On the platform for the Paoli Local there were about twenty others in costumes along with a handful of regular commuters, holding briefcases, leaving the office late. There was a Bill Clinton who didn't look that different from those headed home. Three Monica Lewinskys. When they stepped onto the lit train car everyone cheered.

Awesome snakes! someone shouted.

Somebody else started singing the Wonder Woman theme song when they saw Molly.

See? Molly elbowed Nessa. I've been recognized.

One of the Monica Lewinskys, in a blue dress with painted white stains, handed out Jell-O shots. Someone started cracking jokes about Bill's lucky night.

Bill Clinton was seated across the aisle; the mask covered his whole head and was faced down toward his shoes. He was embarrassed.

He's really the shy guy from radiology, Molly whispered, and he has no shoulders, so it probably won't be.

Bill's oversized head turned toward them, as if he'd heard.

Ohhh. I feel so sad for him, Nessa whispered back. Do it for the unit, Molly.

Stop, Nessa. I told you. I don't do pity-sex anymore.

It was one of those nights. Brimming. Full. Expectant. A fat harvest moon hung over the village when they stepped off the train in Narberth; there was an autumn chill in the air. Packs of kids crossed the street in their costumes lugging their candy haul, older kids holding the hands of younger ones.

Deena linked Nessa's arm and squeezed toward her.

It's like our Halloweens.

Yeah, Nessa said. She felt the same stab of nostalgia. Walking down Montgomery Avenue, the black gates of the Catholic girls' school, the trees, the wide road. The space, and a hint of smoke burning – applewood or cherrywood, something good. Leaves sifting across the road. Carved jack-o'-lanterns, candlelit, traces of singed pumpkin in the air. A pang of loss. Beside her, Deena was radiant, the night dispelling that time in college when Deena had been depressed and unresponsive. Here they were, heading to a party, the night and everything ahead of them.

A long tree-lined driveway lit with candles in jars led up to the house, a stone mansion with a turret on the eastern wing.

Will we have to cross a moat? someone joked.

Inside, an elevated DJ desk took up the corner of a large reception room. Disco lights blinked colours across the wooden floor. A handful of people were already dancing. Molly got three margaritas and they went toward the music.

Nessa danced with one of the Backstreet Boys. He told her he was an investment banker. He had never seen the painting *American Gothic* or heard of Medusa but he knew Wonder Woman. When the DJ played 'Thriller' Nessa stepped to the side of the dance floor; Molly and Deena knew all the choreography. In the blur of disco lights, spinning, Jell-O shots and gins, she saw a man in the doorway, shoulder against the jamb, watching Deena. Something registered, the unabashed, shameless *looking*. His remove from others. No costume. Older. Something. But she turned away, forgot about it. Deena always drew looks.

At the bar, Che Guevara told her he was a Marxist.

What kind of nurse are you? he shouted over the music.

Nessa shook her head. I'm not a nurse.

Everyone here's a nurse.

But he didn't ask her what she was if she wasn't a nurse; he started on again about bourgeois ways of thinking and middle-class mediocrity, a category he dumped her into while he ranted. She said she was going to the bathroom and went back to dance.

Nessa didn't see Deena again until the end of the night. All the crowd that had come on the train was gathered at the front door pulling on coats. They had fifteen minutes to get back to the station. Molly wasn't there.

Have you seen her? Deena asked.

Not for ages, said Nessa. She was talking to someone on the stairs earlier. She was pretty wasted.

A man, older than them, was with Deena. Army-green cargos, hiking boots. Flannel shirt open over a grey T-shirt. Was he dressed ironically as normal? If he had a ten-gallon hat on his head, she'd think he'd come dressed as the horse whisperer. Nessa tried to place him; she'd seen him before: the guy in the doorway. Handsome. She was drunk but she saw the possessive man-hand he put against Deena's lower back, like protective but steering. Saw it and then forgot. He said he was heading into the city. He would help find Molly. Would bring them home.

Molly appeared, huddled next to them, was sorry, wanted to go to sleep.

Take the train, Deena whispered to them both. Deena liked this guy enough to ditch them and make Molly Nessa's responsibility.

Yeah. Okay, Nessa said. She'd get them a taxi at 30th Street. Molly could crash at hers. Deena seemed so happy.

Three weeks later Deena called while Nessa was picking through the trash in the kitchen to separate the recycling.

My fucking roommates won't separate the trash.

I'm moving in with Lucas.

Nessa dropped the recycling bag she was holding and stood straight up, a squashed plastic Coke bottle in her hand, the phone cradled on her shoulder.

Who?

The guy who brought me home on Halloween.

Nessa wanted to say But he's way older than you, you just met him, are you nuts?

What about Molly?

I'm going to pay rent until the new year. Deena sounded defensive.

But you guys rented that place together.

Molly knows everyone. She'll find someone.

Isn't it a bit sudden?

Nessa, why can't you just say I'm happy for you?

Nessa exhaled. Have you told Mom and Dad?

Not yet. I'm twenty-five years old. They'll get over it.

Molly didn't like Lucas. And she didn't want to spend time with Deena right now, she said.

Nessa held the phone away from her ear for a second. Deena and Molly were tight. They never fell out.

What? Nessa was confused. She'd called to ask when they were all meeting up before Christmas. Like they always did.

I don't like how he speaks for her. And I especially don't like how she lets him. And how I'm nothing since she met him.

Molly, you're her best friend. But it's a new relationship. You know.

It's not that. I can't put my finger on it. The morning he arrived at our house to pack Deena's stuff up, *he* gave me three months' rent and asked what furniture of hers I didn't want because *he* could put it on his truck and take it down to the Salvation Army store on Market Street. And I said to Deena, Aren't you keeping *any* of your furniture? and she said something about it being collegey or rag-tag, that it wouldn't fit in with his stuff.

Molly's voice rose in pitch. She was upset. Nessa listened. Molly had always been a bit possessive about Deena.

Deena and I have lived together for five years. I was there with her through everything. I mean everything. You know. When she was at her worst. And she barely spoke to me about leaving. I said to Lucas, She might want to hold on to the apartment, and her furniture, you know, in case living with *you* doesn't work out, and that I would wait and she could keep it here with me. He was pissed. He said, She's not coming back. So I said, Well, then I'll keep everything. And you always can come back, Deena. And Deena didn't say anything. We're standing there having a polite argument about everything she owns, the things in her life that she's collected from flea markets and thrift stores and trash-picking finds, stuff he has no attachment to, and she just pissed me off, how she was just willing to throw it out because he has some new matching shit in his house that someone picked out for him in Bloomingdale's home section or something because he can afford it.

It was like a floodgate on the phone.

Before Deena moved out, Molly said, like the first shift we worked after she met him, his truck was pulled up outside the back door of the hospital, waiting. She was excited – you know, the flush

66

of new love or whatever. But there are times since then I know she just wanted to get on the subway with me like we always did and talk about our day and the babies and the moms and some of the difficult cases or whatever. How we decompress. But he was there. Like every fucking night. They'd be back at the apartment before me, the truck parked outside. I don't know. We're all going to the same place but Molly you take the subway because she's with me and it's like exclusive. And the thing is I know Deena would have said Can't we offer Molly a ride? because she's considerate like that. So he must have said no and somehow she thinks that's okay. So, no. I just can't deal with her right now. And I hate how I am always walking on eggshells, afraid to upset her in case it causes another spiral of depression or whatever. Sorry. I know I shouldn't say that.

Nessa took the subway holding her VHS machine. Lucas didn't have one. She walked south toward Deena's new house. White Christmas lights were strung through the trees. Wreaths with red bows hung from doors. When she stood outside, she had that feeling of ringing someone's parents' doorbell.

Deena was still in her scrubs. She led Nessa into the living room. Sash windows overlooked the street. Inside, everything was cool and contemporary, like a furniture showroom. It smelled of new carpet.

Nessa poked around, curious what the house could tell her about Lucas. A collection of books: political biographies, history, two shelves on coding and software systems. Nessa pulled out one with an orange spine. *Applied Cryptography*. There was a watercolour painting on the front, bleeding off the edges, and a blurb from *Wired* magazine: *The book the National Security Agency wanted never to be published.* She slotted it back onto the shelf. Half a shelf of poetry and fiction. Deena's.

The kitchen was out of a catalogue. Nothing extraneous. Molly and Deena had always brought home kitchen kitsch – tea towels with cringey quotes, ceramic roosters, religious pamphlets about hell and damnation that they stuck on the fridge with goofy magnets – but this kitchen was curated, sterile.

Deena was standing in the doorway. What do you think?

Nice. She knew her answer was flat and half-hearted and that it disappointed Deena. She couldn't say It's bland and middle-aged.

While Deena plugged in the VHS, Nessa pushed open a door off the living room. An office. A computer with several monitors. Maps on the wall.

That's Lucas's office, Deena said.

Nessa didn't answer.

Nessa! I just told you. Get out. It's his office.

Deena had said he worked in security. No knick-knacks or photographs of family or graduations.

Nessa waited on the couch while Deena fiddled with the back of the TV. She felt irritable and almost wished she hadn't come.

Where's your stuff?

What stuff? Deena was kneeling on the floor with the VHS machine. She looked up, her face blank.

Like the collages I made you and had framed.

Deena turned her face away.

Never mind, said Nessa.

It was like her sister had squeezed herself into someone else's space and there was no mark of her existence here except a few novels. Where were her pictures of family? The prints she had bought?

Deena went upstairs to change into pyjamas and Nessa sat on the couch waiting, hugging a cushion that she recognized from the Pottery Barn catalogue. The house irritated her.

Deena came back down with a blanket. Nessa had opened her backpack. I've brought your three favourite things: Doritos original

68

flavour – Nessa shook two large blue bags – the *Babe* video and two bottles of Glen Ellen Chardonnay.

Deena smiled. I brought the blanket.

Inside the fridge, everything was healthy. Nessa had to move some yoghurts to make way for the bottles. Fresh vegetables and organic brands.

Oh my God, is he a health freak?

Deena laughed. Yeah, kinda. We eat really well. Every meal. No more junk.

Well, tonight we're poisoning ourselves. Give me glasses and a bowl for these. Where is he, anyway?

Out with some work friends; he's giving us space. You know . . . for a sisters' night.

Deena spread out the blanket on the couch and they pulled it under their chins, the bowl of chips between them, their feet on the glass coffee table. While the opening credits ran, Nessa said, It hasn't even started and I already miss it. Let's watch it again on Christmas Day.

Deena didn't answer.

Deena?

What she wasn't saying hung in the air between them, and Nessa knew.

You're not coming home for Christmas?

It's just that for years Lucas hasn't had a Christmas with his family, and he really wants us to be together.

Deena's voice sounded small.

So you couldn't get more family overload than ours at Christmas. Bring him to us. Mom and Dad will be fine with that. They won't be fine with you not coming home.

I don't think it would work.

Why? It's not rocket science. Just get in the car and drive, with Lucas, to our house.

Well, he's just not that comfortable in groups. He really wants our first Christmas to be just us.

He wants Christmas to be just the two of you? Everything else is just the two of you. Fucking hell, Deena, it's Christmas. None of us have ever been away before. You have to come home. Just bring him for the dinner part at least.

Deena scooched away from her on the couch, dropped the blanket to her waist.

You should be having Christmas with us, not stuck here with a guy you just fucking met. I don't get it.

Jesus, Nessa. We just want to spend our first Christmas alone. Please don't give me a hard time about it.

Nessa drank her wine fast. Maybe she was wrong. It was inevitable they'd start to spend Christmases apart. She was probably being unreasonable. She tried to watch *Babe* like it was old times. After a while it felt like it was. They recited lines together, Nessa as Fly the sheepdog, Deena as Babe. By the end of the movie she'd almost forgotten what Deena had said. They sat on the couch talking, the light still out.

When they heard the key turn in the front door Deena took her feet off the table and sat upright. Deena doesn't slouch around in front of her boyfriend. Nessa added it to the list of things that bothered her. She left her feet up, angry again about Christmas. They – well, mostly her – were halfway down a second bottle of wine and so she'd stopped caring about making an impression on Lucas.

He flicked on the light. Still in work clothes, the white shirt unbuttoned at the throat, his tie loose. He had steel-blue eyes and his gaze unnerved her. In a quick flash she saw him again in the doorway at the party. She concentrated on not dropping her gaze. He was tanned in the winter like people who ski. Deena had said he spent a lot of time outdoors, hunting and fishing. She remembered the way Deena had said it, like it was a morally superior way to live.

You must be Nessa, he said.

She stood to shake his hand, knocking the bowl over. Crumbs scattered over the table and floor.

Shit. Sorry.

And maybe because of the wine, or because it was so awkward, she started to laugh. And he did too. Deena started picking up the bigger crumbs between finger and thumb and cupping them in her hand.

We sort of met on Halloween, she said. Well, I saw you that night. I was at the party.

He sat down, so she did too. They made small talk about her course at Penn and the internship she had with the city next summer. She was working with six Philly-based artists on a project that explored how place can be erased or overwritten by the built environment, or nature, or dereliction. How one text gets overwritten by another.

Do you know the word *palimpsest*? she asked.

How had she got here, so suddenly, onto something so distant, so personal too. She was giving herself away.

I know the word in computing; it's when you erase memory and write over it.

Yeah, well, the artists in the project all are interested in places, like specific neighbourhoods, buildings, institutes, green spaces – whatever – that are disappearing or have disappeared. The thing their work has in common is how the past persists even though that text has been overwritten by something else. The traces could be physical things like foundations, a wall, a ruin, but also stories, music, memory.

This is part of your art conservation study? I imagined you preserving seventeenth-century paintings or something.

Yeah. But it's still sort of preservation work. For one of my classes I started interviewing artists about place and disappearance.

The project just got momentum and people were interested. There's some money for the artists too, which is good.

Taxpayers' money well spent, I'm sure, said Lucas.

Maybe he wasn't so bad. He went into the kitchen and brought back a bottle of Beck's.

She asked him what had brought him to Philadelphia. He told her he'd come for college, done a postgrad, got a job, stayed. He popped the lid on his beer. He liked Philadelphia even though he didn't love living in a city.

Have you tried the suburbs? Nessa asked.

For a moment things were normal, pleasant even.

I've been out a few times. Some hikes and paddling.

You should come meet my parents, Nessa said. They're in the suburbs.

Yeah, I will sometime. They sound like great people.

I have an idea. She said it too brightly. Why don't you come for Christmas dinner?

Nessa heard Deena exhale and Lucas glanced at Deena like he was trying to figure out what had been said, whether he was being set up. He put down the Beck's.

Didn't Deena tell you? We're planning to have Christmas together this year.

Oh, I meant Deena would be there too. It would be strange you spending Christmas with us, and her not there. She gave a fake laugh as if he'd really misunderstood her.

I meant Deena and I are doing our own thing for our first Christmas.

He noted the wine bottles on the table, picked them up, one bottle in each hand, held them up toward the light, caught her eye. She saw the assigned blame. He moved toward the kitchen.

Nessa followed him. Now he'd really pissed her off. Smug asshole. Don't take the bait, she repeated to herself.

72

Yeah, she said something about that, but the thing is, in our family we've always had Christmas together. It would be a real blow to my parents if Deena didn't come home. Actually, to all of us.

Nessa stood on the opposite side of the kitchen counter.

Lucas gazed directly back at her. So, you're your older sister's keeper? He laughed but it was edged.

Nessa fixed her eyes on him and tried to lose any hint of anger. On behalf of my parents, I'm formally inviting you and Deena to dinner on Christmas Day. Our house, Havertown, three p.m.

Please, Deena said to no one in particular. She was still outside the kitchen door.

Lucas just laughed.

Invitation accepted. What would be an appropriate house gift?

A bottle of Jameson does it for my dad.

It's a deal. We'll be there.

Good, said Nessa. Well, my work here is done. I better get home.

The oxygen had been sucked out of the night and Deena looked deflated.

Outside, Nessa dug her hands in her pockets and walked back toward the subway. What the fuck was going on? A few haphazard snowflakes floated on the air. She tucked her head down. She'd forgotten the VHS machine. At least it was a reason to go back again and see Deena.

What Molly had said echoed in Nessa's head as she rattled west along the Market–Frankford Line, toward home: I don't like how he speaks for her. He'd done it tonight. *We. Us. Alone.* And Deena had sat there saying nothing. It was like she wasn't really there, and it reminded Nessa of the way Deena had been when she wasn't well. Unreachable. Blank.

PART II

8

Nessa

2003

There were always Irish workers around. They'd been there as far back as Nessa could remember – in the trucks outside the house, over for Sunday dinners out the back, drinking beers, helping with the barbecue. They came and they went. Over on J-1 visas, students from villages in Galway near where her father had grown up. Names like Kinvarra, Cahervoneen, Carnamadra, men called John-Joe, Padraig, Micheál or Oisín. Cousins, friends of cousins. Her dad gave them summer work with his contracting business. They also did jobs at the house – tarring the driveway, slating the roof, tiling the bathroom. Her dad loved talking to them – blathering away about whatever, as he put it. They caught him up on people he knew that were still alive, told stories and made him laugh. There were snippets of gossip, jobs, difficult customers and jokes she felt outside of.

She always found it hard to understand them. *Howerya?* Which she realized was How are you? but all slung together like it was one word. How's things? they would ask, and Nessa didn't know what things until she realized they meant all things. Like, How's everything, as in life, the universe?

The lads, as Joey called them, were due to start work on the house a few days after she got the keys. Some of them were working for her dad for their third straight summer or were younger siblings of guys that had been before. Their fathers and uncles had spent summers working for John Garvey.

Joey had always hung out with them, going to the bars in Havertown and Ardmore and into the city. He'd even been to Ireland to visit them. Nessa's dad never went back. His brothers and sisters came over with their kids, Nessa's cousins, but he never went home. It's better to leave it the way it is in my head, he said. It helps me. It was a pragmatic kind of nostalgia, thought Nessa. He didn't want the home that was real to him, the way he remembered it, ruined.

Chunks of wall upended, textured wallpaper still attached, kitchen cabinets ripped off their hinges. On the street outside, the skip brimmed over with rubble. Nessa felt a pang of guilt; it was the remnants of someone else's hope for what their life might be in this house, and now they were gone and she was here smashing out the remains of how they had once existed.

Joey was alone inside, sweeping a pile of debris into a wide shovel. Dust floated through the room. Every surface was layered with a thick white powder. There was a slight breeze, and it moved against the transparent sheets hanging from the ceiling. A wooden frame with a door sheeted in heavy plastic separated the downstairs from the upstairs. Joey leaned on the shovel.

Well? He gestured around himself, proud of the demolition.

It's so open. Her voice echoed in the empty space and she started to cough, the dry particles catching in her throat.

Come outside, he said. He leaned the shovel against the bare brick wall they'd exposed and picked up a plastic bag.

They sat on the front stoop. Joey took off his dust mask and wiped his face.

Big change, huh? In their family they joked that Joey was the Italian. He was dark compared to Deena and Nessa, but it was also something in his relaxed attitude and easy-going confidence. Nessa couldn't help but compare the men she met to him. Their egos and self-awareness, the way their conversation wasn't talking but projecting a self. Joey was like a bullshit barometer in her life.

He pulled two spiral-bound booklets out of the bag.

Here. He passed one of them to her. *Nessa Garvey* and her address were typed in large font. She lifted the cover.

A table of contents?

Joey shrugged, smiling. He lit two cigarettes and passed her one.

CAD drawings mapped the ground floor, exactly how many square feet in the overall area and how much space each element took up. The drawings showed how the kitchen would get more light if she glazed the back wall and put the sink and stove top on an island between the kitchen and living areas. It could also serve as a breakfast bar on one side. Suggestions were made about where to position the refrigerator, the oven, where the sofas could go. There was a section on materials for flooring, kitchen work units, lighting. Everything.

What do you think about the glass onto the backyard?

Can I do that? On my budget?

Yeah, it's all costed. He flicked to the back pages.

Oh my God. I love it. I didn't know you could do this.

Joey turned sideways to look at her, puzzled.

You joking? I can barely turn on a computer. Working from the plans, yeah, but I don't know how to design them.

Who did them?

One of the Irish.

Really? When she was young she'd thought they were grown men, but she realized now they were only young, mostly students.

Ronan's almost an architect, an exam away or something.

Does he know what he's doing? I mean costings and all?

Yeah. He's the real thing. You know him. The tall quiet guy? He's come maybe three or four summers. He's working in Philly as like a trainee architect or something. But he still does design and project management stuff for Dad.

He made the little doorway to the upstairs?

Yeah. That's him. Joey stubbed out his cigarette on the stoop. So, what do you think of the plans?

Yes to everything. All of it, she said.

79

Nessa loved her new neighbourhood. Sylvia next door sat outside in the evenings smoking on a metal lawn chair set up on the side-walk. She was Italian, like Nessa's mother, and she wore the same gold horn. A cornetto, her mother had called it. An amulet. Sylvia loved to complain about the city workers and reminisced about the old neighbourhood, what it used to be like, before all these upstarts moved in.

Like me, said Nessa.

You're not half bad, said Sylvia.

Every few days the front doorbell would ring – the two little boys from next door holding their badminton rackets. They had a net in their backyard and kept firing birdies onto her side of the wall and had to come around to the front to ask her to retrieve them. Deena and Ruby were moving in. The boys were older than Ruby but kids she could play with.

In the mornings she left before Joey and the crew arrived. She stayed at work until she was certain they'd gone. It avoided the awkwardness of having to make small talk, that embarrassment she felt about people doing a job for her. It made her uncomfortable and was maybe the reason why she never talked much to the Irish students that came over every year.

In just a few weeks the downstairs of her new house was trans-formed. Everything was new and replastered except the windows onto the street and the art deco fireplace. Large windows ran across the back of the kitchen space, glass doors led out to her tiny back-yard. Sun streamed through both sides of the house and, even with the unpainted grey plaster, the house was bright.

The day Deena had to go to Family Court, Nessa left work early and walked home to get her car. Sitting in the driver's seat, she watched her house. The front door was open and two workers stepped out-side, holding flasks and mugs. It was a habit the Irish workers had that she loved. They sat on the stoop. The younger guy was ani-mated, telling a story, gesturing and talking non-stop. The older one was amused by him. He laughed a few times and Nessa kept watching as he poured his tea, then lit a cigarette. He was tall, his movements relaxed. She sat there for a few minutes, started the car and headed toward the suburbs to pick up Ruby.

Ruby was waiting at the door and ran down the sidewalk as Nessa pulled up, a large plastic bag of bread swinging off her arm.

Grandad gave me bread for the ducks! she shouted. Her long dark hair in thick braids thumped behind her.

Nessa waited at the car. Her dad waved from the doorway as Ruby climbed into her car seat in the back. Nessa buckled her in.

Okay. Let's go feed ducks. Haverford College ducks or Willows ducks? Smart or wild?

Wild, Nessa!

Ruby loved The Willows, a large park surrounded by willow trees with a pond in the middle of a meadow. Nessa, Deena and Joey used to sled there when they were kids. Ruby would ask Nessa to tell her again and again about the times they'd gone night-sledding, how there would be hundreds of kids spinning down the hills on snow saucers and garbage-can lids, store-bought sleds that could steer, plastic bags, anything – careening down, bumping into each other, landing face first in the snow. All in the dark.

Nessa parked and they walked along the path and then down the hill to the pond. Ruby set to work, reaching into the bag for bits of bread as a group of mallards cruised noisily toward her on the black water. There was something Nessa had read about ducks and quacking. The hens, she remembered, had a call for their young, a 'decrescendo call' that their ducklings could hear for miles.

Ruby threw bread as the mallards squabbled, and Nessa watched her, curious. What had Ruby seen? What happened to those memories? Those things Lucas had done, the times Deena had gone back, when Deena had been unwell, the nights he'd come to the house. What did Ruby remember? Had the memories just vanished, or were they buried underneath other ones? Ruby seemed untouched by any of it, running along the water's edge, a V of birds following, her bag of bread in her hand. Behind them, the field was empty. No one was here, just the trees and clear fields. They were extricating Lucas bit by bit. Deena wouldn't go back. He'd lost his grip on her. Nessa sat on the grass while Ruby ran alongside the green ducks in the greenest field amongst the willows.

When the ducks had eaten all the bread, Nessa took Ruby shopping to pick out sheets for her new bed. She chose a pattern with frogs. While they waited at the checkout Ruby spotted a hanging chair suspended by three hemp ropes and begged to sit on it.

It's adjustable so you can hang it at different levels, said the saleswoman. How old is she?

She's three.

Three and a half, Ruby said, grabbing Nessa's arm with both her hands and swinging it.

It's safe for her age. They can't flip it over.

Ruby sat and held two of the ropes, leaning back so far her braids trailed on the floor.

Sold, said Nessa.

At the house on Parrish Street, Ruby ran ahead up the steps and pushed open the front door. Unlocked. Joey must still be inside, Nessa thought; it was nearly six and the workers always left early on Fridays.

How'd you get here, you wee scut? said a voice beyond the plastic dust sheets.

Nessa froze for a second. Then relaxed. Lucas didn't talk like that, and he wouldn't dare put a foot wrong right now, when all the custody proceedings were going on. It was one of the Irish workers, the one she'd seen smoking on the step earlier. He leaned to catch Ruby, holding her up high before settling her on his hip.

You're Ronan?

I am.

I'm Nessa.

I know.

Um. I should have tried to meet you before – you know, to say thank you so much for all this, the plans, design, making decisions. She gestured around her. It's all just perfect. Really. I am so shit at all that.

Shhh, Nessa, Ruby said, disapproving.

Oh God, sorry. I've—

The mouth of a fishwife.

What?

Just a saying. Sorry. He was embarrassed and turned his attention to Ruby, still in his arms. Well, Ruby, what brings you to your castle today?

I'm here to see my room. Nessa got me a bed. And I got a new swing chair.

Nessa was holding the chair in its plastic wrap. It was in the display room and I couldn't get her out of it. They said if I hang it low to the ground it's safe.

Will I do it for you? He put Ruby down and reached for the package. I could do that now. Everyone's gone. Finished for the weekend.

Really? Would you? That would be amazing.

No problem. He was already looking at the hook.

Upstairs, Nessa covered Ruby's eyes as they went into the room.

Okay, open.

Is it my bed?

Yep.

Where's my mom's?

Her bed is in her room, next to yours. Mine is right below. I showed you last time.

Ruby turned in a circle.

It changed. I like it.

Nessa got Ruby to help her unpack the new pillows and comforter and they made the bed. Ruby lay on it, staring up at the ceiling. She looked like pictures of Deena as a child. The pale face and dark eyes, the cheeks flushed pink.

Ronan came in and the three of them walked around deciding where would be the best place to hang the chair.

I think it should be near this window, said Ronan, so you can swing in it and look out.

Ruby and Nessa sat on the wooden floor with their backs to the small bed and played I spy. Nessa watched Ronan for the second time that day. He was quiet and comfortable. Older than the other workers but younger than her. Joey had said he was still a student. She and Deena had grown up with men who worked with their hands and Nessa was convinced this had left them with some predisposition. Like they were attracted to guys who could do stuff. Lucas could do stuff. But Ronan was nothing like Lucas. She could see that.

Nessa, I spy with my little eye something green! Ruby shouted. Nessa laughed. She knew it was Ronan's top.

Is it the frog on your new sheets?

No. Ruby shook her head and looked furtively again at Ronan.

He was reaching upward to drill into the ceiling. His shoulder blades moved beneath his T-shirt as he worked, screws held in his mouth.

Is it the leaves outside?

No! Ruby screamed. Do you give up?

Is it Ronan's shirt?

Ruby scowled and didn't answer.

The chair was hung, and Ronan pressed down on it.

84

Now, he said. That'll do. Come up here.

Ruby scrambled up off the floor and flung herself into the seat. She leaned back holding on to the hemp, already swaying back and forth.

Ronan sat next to Nessa on the floor, cross-legged. He had cement dust in his hair, flecks of plaster on his clothes. His hands were paint-speckled. He watched her without shifting his gaze. It unsettled her a bit. They sat there without saying anything. She didn't know where to look.

How old are you? she asked.

Sorry? He seemed taken aback by the question.

Oh. That must seem rude to ask.

Twenty-four. Old enough. His voice was slightly defensive. I've been doing this work since I was young. Dozens of houses.

I didn't mean that. She could feel heat in her cheeks. She wasn't sure what she'd meant. I'm three years older than you. She said it more to herself.

We've met before, he said.

We have?

Several times, and I've seen you at your parents' over the years. I know all your family, except you, really. I went to that show you curated a few summers ago in West Philly. I came over for your mum's funeral before Christmas.

Those words, *your mum*, pummelled her. He'd come halfway across the world for the funeral and she didn't even remember him. The house had been so full.

Jesus. You're like a stalker. She tried to make her voice breezy over the emotion.

He laughed. It was a good sound. Small creases appeared each side of his mouth. And she thought how beautiful he was. He was about to say something and without thinking she reached and brushed the side of his face with the backs of her fingers.

85

He recoiled as if she'd struck him.

Nessa pulled her hand back and buried it in her lap. I don't know why I just did that. Shit. I'm sorry. I don't even know you. Really, I am so sorry.

Ruby had stopped swinging and was looking at them. Everything was suspended, excruciating.

Here you are!

Deena stepped into the room.

Mommy!

Ruby jumped off the chair and Deena knelt and hugged her.

Hey Ronan, she said, her arms still around Ruby. Nessa, I've been shouting downstairs for like five minutes.

Oh. We, I mean Ronan, hung Ruby's new chair for her.

Look, Mommy. A moon chair. Ruby back-stepped her feet to let herself swing forward. They all watched. She leaned back and pointed her toes.

That's just magic, said Deena, turning back to them. She looked at Nessa, then Ronan. Deena smiled. Is everything okay?

Nessa didn't know what to do with her face. Deena had sensed something was awkward.

How did today go? asked Ronan. His voice had shifted a gear. He stood up from the floor.

He knew that Deena was in court? Nessa stood as well.

Hard, Deena said. He was there. She glanced at Ruby swinging and humming in the chair to see if she was paying attention. I don't know what's going to happen. The psychologists gave their reports. That's a whole other story. So the actual hearing will be scheduled soon.

Deena had become thin; the elastic waist on her dress hung loose. The case weighed on every aspect of their lives. She was worn out but couldn't stop. It was essential that she didn't show any physical or psychological cracks. Lucas was going to use mental illness against her. Her suicide attempt in college, the investigation at work, the arrest. Even though he was the one who'd made her come off her meds. They had to be hypervigilant. She couldn't miss a day of work; wouldn't even have a drink; Ruby couldn't get a bruise or a scratch. Anything would be used against her.

We should head. Ruby, let's get in the car.

One more go.

We're all going now, you villain. Ronan scooped her out of the chair and Ruby laughed.

9

Nessa

2003

She followed Gabriel down the hallway, sidestepping heaped earth and stacks of broken tiles, glass, tin cans scorched in makeshift fires. The building was so vandalized that there was nothing left of the copper wire, windows, door handles, architraves. Some walls had blackened patches where there'd been fires, others were black with mould. Wet insulation sagged from ceilings. Despite the July heat, the interior felt damp, the air heavy with spores. There were dreadful stories about what had happened here to people: beatings, restraints and neglect. A disused psychiatric hospital. She'd been here before with Gabriel. *Philadelphia Palimpsests*, her first show. The building was scheduled for demolition now. The city didn't want it, a visible reminder of a terrible history, and the neighbourhood didn't want the antisocial behaviour it fostered. There'd been scrappers and squatters and, more recently, urban explorers. Gabriel had said at weekends there could be up to fifty a night.

They were looking for two rooms. What had been the female dormitory, and the treatment room. They had xeroxed copies of rough maps and had been given permission to film only in the specific rooms requested. Large red X's were drawn across the outbuildings with exposed asbestos. Behind them Jason struggled with the camera equipment and projectors. The building was more depressing than Nessa remembered. Maybe it was because they were here during the day this time and the decay was palpable. She didn't want to touch anything. Fungal colonies grew in the corners of walls. Satanic symbols and crude crosses obscured earlier graffiti and spray-painted tags. God, don't let there be rats, she prayed as they stepped through a hole in the wall.

They were in a long rectangular room. The windows just below the eaves let in light but the people who'd lived here hadn't even had a view of the outside world. A whirr of wings sounded near the ceiling as a flock of birds swept through a missing pane.

This is the dormitory, Gabriel said.

Gabriel's mother had been committed in the 1960s when he was a baby and he'd done a series of recordings with her about her time in this room. At the far end, three steel bed frames remained. Gabriel had already edited a video of her talking about the hospital, splicing it with footage of her as a child. He wanted to project the film in the space where she had been confined all those years ago. Jason was filming the whole thing for the exhibition. Despair still hung in the air, had seeped into the walls and floors. When they started the sound recordings, Gabriel's mother's voice resounded through the space, echoed and reverberated, came from everywhere.

They listened to Gabriel's mother talk about how difficult it had been. Not seeing her son. The filth and humiliations, but also friendships she'd made in this room.

The treatment room was still tiled in sections. In the video they projected there, Gabriel's mother told a disjointed narrative, her memory spliced, fragmented. She remembered mechanical restraints but that memory was overlaid with the memory that she had been drugged.

The acoustics are nuts, was the only thing Jason said.

Toward the end the space felt so claustrophobic that Nessa had to go and stand outside.

She and Gabriel drove back to the city together. They said very little. It was Friday afternoon and the rush-hour traffic was heading in the opposite direction, away from the heat and asphalt, toward the bridges, the shore, the trees, the suburbs. She wanted to tell him how powerful the work was – but didn't. They were both depleted.

Gabriel was meeting his partner for a drink. You want to come for one?

No. But thanks. Builders fitted my kitchen today, so I need to check in.

She wanted to shower the hospital rooms off her body and out of her hair.

Are you okay? she asked as she pulled over on Pine Street to let him out. That was pretty profound.

Yeah. I'm good. My mother wanted this. She wanted people to know.

Driving home, she worried about the ethics of it all. Gabriel's mother's stories from inside that institute would be superimposed on the walls of another, the museum. An official place of remembering. What about when his mother and others had tried to tell people and weren't heard? Was it okay to remember it on the walls of the museum? Was it sometimes better to just let the past be the past?

She turned her key in the door. The relative cleanliness inside the house was a kind of mercy after the dereliction of the day. It was still a building site: no furniture and the plaster skim still damp, but the afternoon light tinged the grey walls with warm golden-pink and it felt like home. In the kitchen all the empty spaces had been filled. Dishwasher, oven, stove top. The refrigerator hummed. She checked the kitchen faucet. It worked. Hot and cold. She opened and shut a cabinet door. She turned on the stove, listened to the ignition clicks, smelled the gas and watched the flame catch. Everything was here. She poured a glass of wine, sat on a crate, pushed off her sneakers and took it all in. Her house. Soon Ruby and Deena would be here. Drop cloths had been lined around the room to get ready for painting, and tubs of emulsion were stacked against the wall. Nessa and Deena had done sampler squares on one of the dry patches until they settled on a soft cream. Bright, warm and blank.

There were two knocks at the front door. The kids with the lost birdies. She went to the kitchen's glass door, looking out for the white shuttlecocks, but couldn't see them. She heard two more knocks.

Coming!

As she opened the front door she started to say You're really going to have to improve your game. But it wasn't the kids. It was Ronan, standing on her stoop in work clothes, the ones he must wear for the urban planners or whoever he worked for in the city – a crisp white shirt and dress trousers.

Oh, hi.

Am I interrupting? You were expecting someone else?

Yes. No. I thought it was the kids next door. You're back?

Yes? He said it like a question, as if he didn't know what she meant.

Do you need to come in? Did you leave something? She looked behind her as if whatever it was would materialize.

Can I?

Yes, she said, but didn't move. Did you put in the kitchen today?

Joey and the crew did. I came over at lunch just to check on them. I couldn't get away from work. What do you think?

I love it. Really. Everything works.

Nessa saw a flicker of something at the corner of Ronan's mouth. Had he come up to the house to see how she liked it?

That's good.

There was a pause. She needed to say something.

Look, I am so sorry for what I did last time. You know, touching your face. It was weird.

Could I talk to you for a minute?

Oh God, sorry. Yes, come in. She opened the door all the way.

He stepped in and shut it behind him.

You forget something?

I wanted to talk to you about, you know, as you say, the weird thing you did.

Um, okay. Do you want a beer first?

Yeah. He smiled and again something shifted inside her. That'd be lovely.

Lovely. She almost burst with relief. Everything was okay.

She got him a beer from the fridge.

Cheers, he said, and drank, wiping his chin with the back of his hand.

Nessa pointed to the crate she'd been sitting on. Please. She pulled over another one and covered it with a leftover piece of plasterboard. Now we have our seats. She picked up her wine glass and sat down opposite him.

They held eye contact and he started to speak but didn't. They'd done this the last time.

Sorry, he said. I was all set to do this and now I'm not sure. He exhaled and laughed slightly, took another pull of his beer. The touching-the-face thing, I wasn't expecting it. I was a bit bowled over. I'm not sure if I understood what it was. What you meant by it?

I don't know, she said. You came all the way for my mother's funeral. I was overwhelmed that you did that. And I felt bad that I didn't remember you.

Yeah. Okay.

He'd pulled back a bit and she could see his face strain with embarrassment. Why had she just made it sound like that, like he'd misunderstood. That her hand touching him had been a condescending thank-you, an apology. She was fucking this up.

Look, that didn't come out right. I touched your face because I wanted to. I didn't even think about it. I just wanted to. There isn't an explanation.

He dropped his head and ran his fingers through his hair. It was

93

a gesture that she would come to think was him – humility, a touch of shyness. He lifted his face and she could see his cheeks had reddened, but there was that little twitch again, at the corner of his mouth – he was pleased.

Since the first time I saw you, I was curious. You know – interested.

She kissed him first. She dragged her crate closer, leaned forward and kissed him, and his hand reached and held the back of her neck. She was making out with Ronan who came to her mother's funeral, designed her house, hung Ruby's chair and walked here to understand something she'd done in an unthinking instant. They kissed deeper. She felt like she was catapulting forward. Things were moving too fast, as if they might not stop. He'd said he'd been interested since he first saw her. Where? What had she been doing when someone like him saw her and felt something?

Wait, she said, pulling away. When was the first time you saw me? Seriously?

She went to lift her hand from his thigh, but his hand covered hers.

Wawa. Darby Road. Like four – no, three – years ago. A morning before work. We were sitting on the back bumper of Joey's truck having breakfast. You came out holding your coffee. You stood and talked to Joey for a few minutes and then got in your car. I don't know. I'd heard you were into art and restoration and was already interested in who you were, I guess. I just saw you there, in that light, with your convenience-store coffee, giving your brother a hard time, slagging him.

He smiled and added, And then I realized you were totally aloof compared to the rest of your family. You ignored me and the other lads. Yeah, and that probably made me more interested.

He reached his hand to pull a thread of cobweb from her hair and held it in front of her.

Ugh.

The smell of damp spores was in her hair, on her skin. She didn't want this to end but she felt grubby and unclean.

Would you wait for me to have a shower and change my clothes and then we could go somewhere and get food? Or drinks?

Yeah. That would be good. I think that's what I came here to ask.

Lynne's office had a glass wall and was on the twenty-third floor. The view faced north and Nessa caught glimpses of the Schuylkill and the Art Museum.

You can see the Family Court Building from here, Lynne said. She stood and pointed. There, on Logan Square. Nessa looked toward Vine Street in the distance, the grey neoclassical structure, then directly down. Cars and buildings rushed toward her, the room spun. She had to step away from the window.

Sorry, I'm not good with heights.

Deena wasn't fazed. She had her hand against the glass. It looks so different from here, she said. So dignified or something. It's not like that inside.

Lynne was in her early fifties and cool. Edgy in a way that made Nessa think she would be brave in front of Lucas and whatever judge they got. She didn't look like a lawyer. Her hair was short, raven-black, silvered through at the front and spiked. Her left hand was bare but on her right pinkie she had a long silver ring that went past the knuckle. Her voice was low, the cadence measured. She seemed like she wouldn't take shit from people, or be afraid to ask uncomfortable questions. Lynne had a long list of advice, which she introduced with a disclaimer.

I hate what I'm about to tell you but this is the system we're in. She leaned back in her chair, and listed things she knew by heart:

Wear something conservative, but not priggish.

It should be feminine, but not too much so.

95

No bright colours.

No make-up because several judges hate it.

No earrings that dangle; studs or pearl drops are okay.

Don't cry.

Don't get emotional.

If we're unlucky and get Judge Kavanagh, then don't make direct eye contact and don't use the word *professional*. Make your nursing role sound more like a caring one. He'll like that you have an income but won't like what he thinks is female arrogance.

Is this for real? Nessa interrupted. Seriously?

Unfortunately, this is the system. We've seen cases where the mother has not even been allowed to speak in the court because the judge took a dislike. Those cases are exceptional, but we need to read the judge.

This is a bit overwhelming, said Deena.

Look, Lynne said. We have a strong case. You have an extended family that spends time every day with Ruby. She doesn't know his family. You have job stability now and a support system. You've had primary physical custody, despite his attempt to undermine your credibility. Ruby is flourishing, she has an extended social group that you facilitate for her. These are the things we have to emphasize.

What about the restraining orders? Nessa said. The violence.

Lynne shook her head. I know this is almost impossible to believe but allegations of domestic violence have no demonstrated effect on the rate at which fathers are awarded custody of their children. She spun in her chair and opened a filing cabinet behind her. She handed a sheet of paper to Nessa.

A fact sheet with gathered data on custody and domestic violence. It's rather depressing.

Abusive parents are more likely to seek sole custody than the non-violent ones, Nessa read out loud. *They are successful about seventy per cent of the time.*

How is that possible?

Nessa scanned the bullet points and put it down. It would only stress Deena. She stood and walked toward the window; the street, thirty storeys down, pitched. Unbalanced, she gripped the back of a chair.

Lynne kept using a phrase Nessa hadn't heard before: IPV. Women who experienced IPV often presented poorly in court because they were still suffering from PTSD.

IPV?

Intimate Partner Violence, Deena answered.

The abbreviations bothered Nessa, their distance and disembodiment, how they almost normalized harmful behaviours. Abbreviations didn't allow nuance or humanity – it was as if the people who'd experienced these things were all the same.

Lynne was seeing Deena this way. Anxious, harried, the nervous twitches. Losing weight had made Deena's face angular, her eyes bigger, almost confused or stunned. She had developed a nervous habit of rubbing the thumb of her left hand rhythmically as if she were trying to squeeze out the remnants of a tube of toothpaste. Nessa was positive Deena was taking her meds but she'd noticed some of the tics from before when she'd come off them – muscle twitches and spasms, mood swings. The stress of everything. Maybe Lynne thought she was only just about holding it together.

Deena's ready to do whatever she has to. Tell her, Deena.

She's right. I hope. I mean, she is. I'm getting help trying to understand what happened. How I let it. I'm worried about them going on and on about me being unfit or bringing up the case at work. There was doubt in Deena's voice. Lynne heard it too. How would she cope if they drilled her?

It's my job to worry about that and to disallow that kind of harassment. We've practised this. You take medication like millions of other Americans. Millions of mothers. Your probation at work is resolved and you continue to be trusted to provide the best care for critically ill infants. You are holding down a job and giving Ruby a great life.

Nessa nodded, encouraging. And Ruby's better with you. Happier. You know that deep down.

Deena had talked to Nessa about the way Ruby was when she came back from her weekends with Lucas. Deflated. Quiet. It was always just Lucas and Ruby, except a few times lately with Tina and her daughter, but both Deena and Nessa knew those playdates were just a show for the hearing. He won't just let her be a kid, Deena had said. She always has to be exceptional. It's exhausting.

There's something I need to mention to both of you that involves Nessa, said Lynne. There's a letter from the court. Lucas has filed a complaint alleging that Deena has breached the separation order by allowing a third party to sleep over.

Lynne was looking at her. Nessa. Was she the third party?

I'm not allowed to sleep in my own house I share with them?

It's not you, said the lawyer. The complaint names Ronan O'Halloran and includes dates when he has slept in the house when Ruby has also been there.

Nessa sat back in her chair, brought her hands to her forehead. Oh my God, I'm so sorry.

Would this hurt their case? Was he watching them? How could he know Ronan's full name, dates? There'd been a beat-up white Honda parked across the street. It flashed through her head. Sylvia had asked her did she know who it belonged to. Nobody ever drove it. Maybe it was his. Could he have a camera in it watching them?

He'll do anything to discredit the mother, said Lynne. That's what they do. We see this all the time. And I hate saying this, but whoever Ronan is, he shouldn't stay the night when Ruby is there – at least for the time being.

I never even thought about Ronan staying or how it could look.

It had felt so easy, all of them together. Ronan was the eldest of six kids much younger than he was, and he was great with Ruby. The night before, they had watched *A Bug's Life*, again, the four of them on the couch, shouting out the lines. Deena laughing and animated like her old self.

It's technically not a breach of the sleepover rule because the person is not there with the mother, but there's a potential judgement regarding risk.

No, I get it, said Nessa. He won't stay again if Ruby is there. Definitely not.

She and Ronan had spent nearly every day together in the past two months. Ruby was a part of that and Lucas resented it. At the last visitation, when she and Deena brought Ruby to the bookstore, Ruby had run up to Lucas shouting that she had been to the ocean with Nessa and Ronan.

I was jumping the waves in the ocean! Ruby had shouted. Higher than my head. Nessa and Ronan held my hands.

Lucas hadn't liked it.

Stop torturing yourself, said Lynne. The complaint will work against him. He'd have been better off letting Ronan Whoever stay on and then bringing it up during the proceedings. But he's impatient. He can't help himself.

The researchers gave dogs random and inescapable shocks. The dogs could not escape because the grid floor of their closed cages was electrified. All efforts to avoid the pain were futile. When the dogs received the shocks – the unprovoked and random pain – they started to respond in a disturbing way. They just lay down and took it. Defeated, they cried, defecated, ate, did nothing. And when the researchers opened the doors of the cage, the dogs didn't even try to leave.

Nessa picked up the remote. Maybe I should switch the channel.

No. Don't. I want to see this, said Deena. She was sitting cross-legged on the couch in her pyjamas.

The researchers tried different variables. They put the dogs in a box where one side was electrified and the other wasn't. Escaping the shocks simply meant jumping over a small barrier. Unlike the fresh dogs, the dogs who had already experienced inescapable shocks didn't move. Again, they just lay down and took it.

The researchers dragged the inescapably shocked dogs to the doors of their cage; they carried them to the non-electrified side. But the dogs had learned they were powerless and that nothing they did would affect their outcomes. They had lost their sense of agency, their ability to control their destiny.

Deena watched Nessa watching. Her large brown eyes had smudged shadows beneath them. She was wiped out.

I don't know if this is good for you to watch right now, said Nessa.

He made me feel safe. That's the thing. I always felt safer with him than with anybody. The person who was most dangerous to me was the only person I believed could keep me safe. It's so fucked-up.

Nessa and Deena rarely talked about that time. Deena wrote in her journals every day, hours in her room, scribbling, her face close to the page. Sometimes Nessa wished she'd talk to her instead, other times she was glad she didn't.

I can't explain how I went back after you and Joey got me out the first time. I'm still trying to work it out.

That's behind you now.

The first night I met him . . . For so long I saw the lead-up to that night like a movie trailer, a sequence of scenes leading to that moment, and I associated its magic with him. I clung to that idea, of that night as proof of something inevitable or meant-to-be. It's only lately, like in the last few months, that I realize I was seeing the magic of my life then, my youth, of everything my life was up until that moment. I was seeing everything he took away from me. And I feel like I brought it on myself. Some vanity in me. I could sense him looking at me that night.

Deena leaned forward as she talked.

We were dancing and I sensed him on my skin, watching.

She brushed both her arms as if to chase away the memory.

It made Nessa sick. In that crowded party of all those people, he had picked Deena.

This is the hard part to admit to you – to myself. That night I was dressed up as a powerful destructive force. And it's sort of fucked-up but I was hyper-aware of my body as beautiful or desirable. This man seeing me and wanting me, my in-the-bones awareness of that, did something to me. Because he was older, maybe it was like sexual power I felt. Or something. I don't know.

Nessa listened as she talked. Deena was rubbing her thumb.

That first night we went outside. He told me this thing about the Pleiades in the sky – you know, that cluster of stars that's brightest or highest at Halloween. He said how in some mythologies they were called Seed Stars as a way to explain the birth of seasons, light and dark. I liked that he knew this. Everything that I thought was compelling then is creepy now.

Deena had double-crossed her legs and wrapped her own arms around herself.

I'm sorry, I know you probably don't want to hear all this. But I want you to understand how everything happened, the hold he had on me. Even from the very start. Why I found it so hard to leave. Even when I knew he would hurt me. I think about that night, how it unfolds: meeting Molly at the angel, the train, walking through Narberth in the dark, meeting the Halloween children, dancing to 'Thriller', him in the library talking to me, the backyard and the stars, him driving me home. How just one thing different could have avoided all that has happened. He wouldn't see me.

Nessa listened, afraid to say anything.

But now when I see those pictures it's like the images are burning, and there's this black undertow flooding and distorting everything. Distorting me and that picture and all the pictures of me ever, ever taken, even from before then.

Deena bit her bottom lip. Nessa could see she was holding back tears.

I can see the shadow of myself moving through the events of my life up until that night, but I also see the dissolve, how some other element engulfs me, is chemically disintegrating me, is burning me up.

Nessa tried to catch her breath. It was the most frightening thing Deena had ever said to her.

Mommy?

Nessa nearly jumped off the couch. Ruby was standing at the bottom of the stairs in her nightgown.

Come here, sweetie. Deena had instantly sat up, made herself look strong and gathered Ruby into her lap. Ruby's head relaxed against her chest. They rocked back and forth and within minutes Ruby had drifted off, holding a fistful of her mother's hair, a tether, the way she always slept. Deena laid her cheek on her daughter's small head.

This girl makes everything good again.

10

Ruby

Ruby and Nathalie stood in the hallway amid the wreckage of the sixth grade. The final bell rang. Crushed poster board, sandwich wrappers, waterlogged notebooks, dried-up markers, old apple cores – the debris of the past years – had been discarded on the floor around the overflowing trash cans. They had just emptied their lockers forever.

Wait with me for a minute? Ruby asked.

One of the first-grade teachers passed and said, Girls, hurry up. Outside for the picture.

We're coming, said Ruby. She waited for the teacher to turn the corner. I have to get something from Miss Bukowski's room.

Nathalie worried, looking up and down the hallway, checking all possible directions. Why are you going in the third-graders' room?

I have something there.

Nathalie kept watch at the door while Ruby ran in and peeled the envelope from the bottom of the bookshelf. She was out in seconds and handed it to Nathalie.

Can you hide this in your bag and keep it for me?

Okay?

On the steps they posed with the rest of the sixth-grade class.

Lucas's truck was parked out front. He leaned against it, arms crossed, a few yards from the other parents who had grouped at the bottom of the steps to take pictures.

What is it? Nathalie whispered.

Ruby looked straight ahead for the camera. It's a picture of me and my mother. She sent it to me in secret.

Later Ruby cut out the photo of the class and taped it to the refrigerator. All the graduating sixth-graders are looking at the camera, except Nathalie who has turned to look at Ruby. Her mouth is an open oval, the dark frames of her glasses half the size of her face, her hands raised wide like a question.

This feels like old times, Clover said one afternoon. They were at the kitchen table, Ruby shelling peas and Clover cleaning fish. Ruby didn't know what she meant but it was good, the time they were spending together. They cooked, fed the hens, watched daytime television and sat out on the porch while Clover smoked. Clover couldn't drive anymore and Lucas had started a job across the border in Montreal, still working on computers and security. He spent most weeknights away because it was almost a two-hour drive, so it was just the two of them. When middle school started at the end of the summer, Ruby would have to take the bus. She couldn't wait.

Clover's hair kept falling from its bun. She shrugged her shoulder against her forehead to push it out of her eyes because her hands were inside the trout, tangled in the pink-red entrails.

Wait, Ruby said. She wiped her hands on her jeans, took out her barrette and clipped wisps of Clover's white hair away from her face.

You look like a teenager now.

Clover laughed, which she didn't often do, a big laugh from her shoulders, and shook her head.

It's a long time since I felt like a teenager. And after a pause she added, Don't know that I ever did.

Ruby kept shelling, waiting for Clover to maybe say more. She seemed lost in the past and spoke as if to the air.

My father was a troubled man. I've always been around troubled men.

Ruby spilled the bowl of peas into a steaming pot of water on the stove. Clover hadn't moved, her hands still in the fish.

Nathalie's room was at least twice the size of Ruby's and was bursting with stuff. All the furniture matched and, like everything in the Hoags' house, was wooden or hemp. Natural materials. But you couldn't really see this underneath the clutter of everything Nathalie had ever been interested in. Life-size cardboard cut-outs of Shrek and Fiona, Beanie Babies and plastic swords and rifles. The shelves were crammed with photographs, ribbons for races, certificates and all the books she'd ever had as a child. The first time Ruby had gone to Nathalie's house, and then home to her own sparse room, she'd thought she might get swallowed by its emptiness. Nathalie's room was exploding with her, and sometimes, by comparison, Ruby's made her feel panic. She didn't know what had happened to the stuff from her life. Nathalie even had the foil dolphin balloon they had gotten when a group came to the school to talk about cetaceans during Science Week. Ruby had chosen an orca and left it floating in the kitchen. Later she'd found it deflated in the trash, punctured. Lucas hated fake-nature garbage.

Ruby sat on the floor with her back against Nathalie's bed. She held her mother's photograph and tried to filter out the rest of the room. She knew the picture by heart, the geometry of their faces, the map of freckles, the overexposed patch where they were one bright burn, the corners of their eyes touching. That summer after elementary school, Nathalie had started what she called the Memory Games, exercises to try to help Ruby remember. Nathalie played top hits from the early noughties on her iPod while Ruby closed her eyes, listened, and tried to grasp a feeling or an object. She still heard those songs on the radio now and her associations were driving with Clover or the kitchen at home while they ate cereal in the mornings. Ruby told Nathalie what Miss Bukowski had said about Philadelphia and Nathalie rented movies set there – *Rocky, Witness, Trading Places.* She would pause the DVD outside buildings, in the middle of street shots, train stations, and make Ruby look in case she recognized something, as if imagining being there would restore Ruby to her past.

It didn't work. But memories came unbidden anyway, all by themselves. She was throwing bread in the air. An onslaught of descending wings. A picture. Then it evaporated. Like that. There, and then gone. There was no focus, no vantage point, no common thread. The taste of Ovaltine, the scent of Pledge furniture cleaner. The texture of someone else's tumble-dried towel in PE. Mustard at the back of her tongue. They brought indistinct feelings that almost had a shape. Maybe they belonged to someone else. She wasn't sure. Maybe she had seen them on TV.

Ruby heard her name being shouted. Someone was walking fast toward her. Sophie Dragan.

Thank God you're here, Sophie said. I've been waiting for you. What took you so long?

They crossed the road together, kicking stones to avoid looking up. All the other kids were high-schoolers; Ruby and Sophie were just starting middle school.

Ruby and Sophie had been in the same class since third grade but had hardly ever talked. Now, Ruby was relieved to see her – the upcycled outfit, her spooky translucent skin. While Nathalie and Ruby had run around the playground at recess playing make-believe, Sophie had sat in the shade with her friend Kelsey, the one who was always passing out when someone asked her to physically exert herself. They liked to knit and sew.

Sophie was in a white T-shirt with a waistcoat and tie, a plaid skirt shaped like a cheerleader's, white sports socks that went above her knees, and Converse sneakers. Ruby was wearing a faded green T-shirt and shorts.

The chatter died as they got to the bus stop. One of the high-school girls called out a smart remark to Sophie about her outfit. The other girls laughed. Another said, Aww, leave her alone. Sophie's older sisters were there and Ruby envied her. She'd often imagined having her own sisters, one older and one younger.

Sophie and Ruby were the last to get on. The older ones moved to the back and Ruby slid in next to Nathalie at the front. Sophie took the seat behind them. There was cheering and booing when kids stepped on at different stops. Everyone was laughing. As they crossed the bridge coming off the Islands, some of the high-school students at the back of the bus started singing 'Firework'. Then everyone was. The morning light was shimmering on the water and the whole bus was singing about how powerful a person can be, and Ruby in their midst felt like she was being carried toward something elusive and bright.

Where's Kelsey? Nathalie asked Sophie.

She went to school in New York. Their house is right next to the ferry.

I am glad we're staying the hell in Vermont, said Nathalie.

Nathalie was like a little version of Dale Everett the mailman. One of those Vermonters always listing the great things about the state – the first to legally recognize civil unions, the first to outlaw slavery, only one of four states without billboards, the only state capital without a McDonald's.

I don't know who I'm going to hang out with here, said Sophie. Everyone looks normal.

Hang out with us, said Nathalie.

Sophie looked worried.

What's wrong with us?

Nathalie always said what she was thinking, a quality that stirred both admiration and embarrassment in Ruby.

I don't know. Wouldn't I have to like dress as a pirate or run around shooting arrows or something? Being in your friend group looks exhausting.

We don't do that anymore, said Ruby.

Well, mostly not, said Nathalie.

They left the house in the dark. A hard frost had settled on the fields and the road glinted under the headlights. They drove south down Route 7, past Vergennes, Middlebury, toward Rutland. Ruby drifted off and woke as the truck jounced over stones and small branches; they weren't even on a road, the woods all around them. Lucas parked and they trekked up a long logging track. The sun just touched the treeline to the east when they started searching. Scratchings or droppings. Evidence of turkeys feeding. Coming toward a small clearing under beech and oak, Ruby saw them. Two or three adult hens and a clutch of four or five jakes and young hens, about a hundred yards away. She stopped. Lucas saw too. Together, all at once, they raised their arms and started sprinting, yelling and shouting, crashing through the underbrush. Ruby roared. The animals bolted in different directions. Like that, they were gone. Ruby knelt on the ground and Lucas dropped beside her. They caught their breath.

Ready? Lucas asked.

Ruby sat at the base of a beech almost exactly where they'd scattered the flock. Lucas was just a few yards away. They settled themselves. Masks and gloves on. Fully camouflaged, guns ready. Lucas nodded and she picked up the box call and ran it, moving the paddle across the wooden container. The hen yelp echoed in the quiet woods. It was the part of hunting that made her slightly sad, how they separated the hens and their young and then drew them back by the mother's call. They waited. Patience was crucial. You had to be willing to sit for hours. She used the box call again. Nothing. She leaned back against the tree. Then she heard it: a raspy yelp. A hen calling. She replied on the box. Waited. The hen's throaty yelp again. She called back. Not too much, Lucas had taught her. Don't overdo it. Then the sounds were close. A shot of adrenalin went through her; she steadied the shotgun on her knee, leaned in, watched the bead. Listened. There were three rules of turkey hunting. Don't move and don't move and don't move. Turkeys were smart, could see even an eye blink. She sensed them before she saw them. First one, then two jakes. Maybe forty yards away. She held her breath. Dared not move. Thirty yards. Watched the bead. Waited. Twenty yards. The bead and the head were indistinguishable. She squeezed. Felt the kick from the 20-gauge in her chest as the turkey started and slumped. A hit.

They waited a moment while the other jake fled. Lucas called over to her and they stood, bagged the animal and carried its warm limp body back to the truck.

In the cab they drank thermoses of chowder and ate ham sandwiches they'd made while it was still dark. They talked about the day, how they'd charged the flock, how it had scattered, the calls, wondered if they should have done anything differently. Every hunt was like this, each with its own memorable details. They'd have the turkey for Thanksgiving, just a month away. Lucas had a saying: Give a child a meal, you feed him for a day; teach a child to hunt and you feed him for a lifetime. Ruby knew she couldn't repeat this to Nathalie or Sophie. They already made jokes about her being a homesteader. She couldn't tell them anyway. She had a licence but twelve-year-olds weren't supposed to hunt during this season. Lucas ran the engine to keep them warm. She couldn't explain the good feeling that she had after a day like this when it was just the two of them and he was proud of her. It made her feel capable of anything.

Miss Tierney put Christmas lights up in the English language and arts room; she said it helped to have extra light coming into the darkest days. The whole seventh grade had been assigned *Narrative of the Life of Frederick Douglass, an American Slave* and they discussed it while the lights twinkled along the walls.

Ruby had never read someone's real account of their own life and experiences. She hadn't been able to put it down and read all eleven chapters in one go. Frederick Douglass didn't know when he was born. Slave owners never told their slaves their birthdays. He didn't know any slaves who knew the date of their birth. Most didn't even know their mothers. He described how his had been taken away from him when he was an infant, a thing that was common practice in that part of Maryland, usually before the child was a year old. Douglass wrote that he did not know why they did this *except to blunt and destroy* the relationship.

Douglass's mother was sent to work as a field hand twelve miles away. She used to walk back at night to the farm where he was and hold him in the dark. Then she would get up and walk back the twelve miles to be working in the field on the other farm by sunrise. Ruby thought of the young Frederick Douglass, what that must have been like for him as a child, to have this person come and hold you at night, a body safe and familiar and so full of love for you that they would come all that distance to just have the opportunity to hold you while you drifted off to sleep. Douglass's mother died when he was maybe seven. Ruby's lungs ached when she read that, as if she had run a fast race in freezing air temperatures.

Miss Tierney asked what they thought of the reading assignment, and nearly everyone in the room raised their hand.

This is what oppressors do, Mia said. She was one of three black kids in the class. She and her dad had talked about it. Taking away birth dates and connections to family and parents was on purpose. It was so they could erase identities and make people feel like they were nobody. And if you made them nobody, it was easier to abuse them.

Someone else mentioned the way Douglass wrote, how easy it was to read and how emotional. The class had never had this much discussion. A boy behind Ruby said at least Vermont had always been anti-slavery from the beginning. We weren't like those other states, he said.

Mia's hand shot up. She turned around so she could look at him at the back of the class.

When Frederick Douglass came to Vermont in 1843 to speak against slavery he was heckled and a group of students threw stuff at him.

The class went quiet.

I'm just saying you didn't have to be a slave owner to support slavery.

Another student said how awful it must have been to see his aunt being tied up, stripped and beaten. He'd been so young. Ruby wanted to say her idea, that he had written the book for his aunt, but couldn't bring herself to. He'd left Maryland and told the world what was happening. He'd made everyone remember her and see her.

The December light was thin, the trees bare, the sky dull. In the bus Ruby pressed her face against the glass, watched the blur of stark trees, leaves stripped, fields shorn. They crossed the bridge back onto the Islands. She had started to cry. She couldn't stop. Everything was grey: the bare lake, the low sky, the road in front of them. She wished it would snow, something clean to fall on the earth.

11

Ruby

2012

The ice fog was so thick Ruby couldn't see the lake. For several days since Christmas, Lucas's plough had been scraping and rasping against the ground, pushing snow. The grating made her head hurt. She lay back down, tunnelled further under the comforter and fell back to sleep.

Hard rapping on the door echoed inside her skull. She tried to sit up but it was like her limbs couldn't hear her head.

Up and out, Lucas ordered. You're not spending the day in there again. We've a job to do up north today. You're coming.

Downstairs, Lucas was leaning against the sink drinking a mug of coffee. A puddle circled his feet on the linoleum, icicles dripping from the tips of his hair, his hat, his gloves, the snow melting from his boots. The room smelled like wet mittens.

You're already a teenage cliché with the amount you're sleeping.

Ruby didn't answer. She took half a bite of toast. Even her mouth was tired. New Year's Eve. In a few days she would be thirteen. So what? It wasn't like they were going to invite her friends over and celebrate.

They were picking up an old generator in Quebec from a guy Lucas worked with. He wanted to use it out in one of the sheds. Ruby balled her scarf up and rested her head against the truck door. She had bursts of pain in the sockets if she lifted her eyes up or moved them sideways. Her jaw and ear throbbed. It had stopped snowing but the roads were narrow, the drifts banked on both sides, sometimes too high to see over. They drove north and didn't speak. Crossing the border, Ruby stirred as Lucas rolled down the window to hand over their passports. The rhythm of slush under their wheels played on a loop, Lucas listened to talk radio, and Ruby fell asleep again.

When she woke they were on the outskirts of the city, near a bridge and old train lines. Shipping containers and billboards edged the road, their shapes softened by snowfall. Vacant lots hadn't been ploughed and there were no tracks. They passed a Costco and pulled in a few hundred yards down. A red pickup idled, its white smoke drifting across the snow. The driver's door opened as they approached.

Why don't you get out and say hello, said Lucas. Get some fresh air while we shift the generator. Move around to stay warm.

A man older than Lucas walked toward them. He had thick eyebrows and a grey matted ponytail held with purple elastic bands just visible at the base of his hat.

The man shook her mittened hand. I've heard so much about you, he said. Your dad's very proud.

Thanks, she mumbled. It made her feel sad.

She moved to the side of the pickup while the men opened their tailgates, manoeuvring the generator off the other truck with metal planks. The man didn't look like how she'd imagined her dad's colleagues. Lucas was clean-cut, but she remembered him saying that you met all types working in security; every kind of cyber-nerd headcase crawled out of the woodwork. When they had the generator hoisted on the back of Lucas's truck, the two men leaned against the bumper talking. Ruby stamped snow and made shapes in it with her boots. Small shocks radiated through her skull. The headache hadn't gone away.

My grandmother's from here, Lucas said.

Ruby stopped kicking and listened.

From Montreal? asked the man.

Well, from this part of it. Right here.

Victoriatown?

Yeah. She called it Goose Village.

Ruby looked around. Where could she have lived? There were no houses. It was just roads and bridges. It was depressing to think of being born here.

Before they bulldozed it, the man said.

Yeah, she never wanted to talk about home much after they did that. Said it was the best place to be from, back in the day.

Ruby had never heard anything about her great-grandmother. Neither Clover nor Lucas talked about family.

The men started talking about work and Ruby got back into the truck. She was freezing and her head was pounding. The passports were on the seat next to her. She remembered going to Burlington and getting her picture taken but had never seen it. She opened the one that looked like it had never been used. Hers. The picture was a few years old. Maybe when she was ten. Her name. Her date of birth. Just below was *Place of Birth: Pennsylvania*. She dropped the passport as Lucas came around the side of the cab and got in. He took off his gloves, then noticed the passports and slipped them into his jacket pocket.

Your grandmother lived here?

Yeah. Clover's mother. He started the engine and rubbed his hands together.

And you knew her?

She came to live with us when I was a teenager. For three years we lived in the same house.

Lucas pulled the truck back out onto the main road.

She lived in our house?

Yes.

Where?

What do you mean?

Like which room was hers?

The one you're in. Your room.

Ruby was stunned. Someone had lived in her room before her, slept in her bed, a great-grandmother she had never met. She'd never even considered Clover having a mother before.

How could she be from here? Ruby asked. Outside was bleak in every direction. Just snow, parking lots, metal storage containers and depots.

There's no houses.

There used to be a town here. Immigrants. Irish. Italian. By the 1960s I guess some people thought it was an eyesore and the city completely knocked it down; they just bulldozed the whole thing away.

Ruby shivered. She didn't like the idea of a whole town just disappearing.

Which one was she? Ruby asked.

Which what?

Italian or Irish?

Oh. Irish. You're Irish on both sides.

The mention of her mother's side took Ruby aback; it sat in the air between them. It was so rare that he said anything about her, and when he did Ruby got the feeling that he was trying to be careful because maybe there was something wrong or bad about her. But this was just a comment about who she was. It was vaguely familiar, like she might have known her mother was Irish but couldn't remember whether it was Lucas or Clover who had told her. Her mother must be from Philadelphia. It was in Pennsylvania. That's why Ruby had been born there. It was so much information in only a few minutes. Her head felt fuzzy, like she couldn't order it. Maybe he was going to say more. The pain in her ear and jaw had moved into her neck.

I'm going to pull in here for a minute. Lucas turned into another lot and shut off the engine. I'll show you something.

They got out of the truck and crossed two lanes of traffic to stand on the median. About thirty feet down Lucas stopped and started brushing snow off a black stone. Cars passed in both directions either side of them. Ruby read the inscription aloud when he had cleared it.

TO
PRESERVE FROM DESECRATION
THE REMAINS OF 6000 IMMIGRANTS
WHO DIED OF SHIP FEVER
A.D. 1847–48

Lucas told her that in Ireland there had been a Great Famine and Irish people had left in shiploads. Many contracted diseases during the passage to Canada and the United States. Mostly typhus. Thousands died on their way and thousands and thousands more in the camps after they arrived.

The ones who died here in Montreal are buried beneath us.

Ruby kicked the snow at her feet. Trucks and cars whizzed by, throwing up slush from their tyres. There were no graves or church.

Under the road?

Yeah. And a few years later, when Irish workers were building the road and bridge, they found the bones and refused to work any further. Even though they had hardly anything themselves, they paid for this stone. Like a grave marker.

They should have stopped the road or gone around it, said Ruby. It was sad how all of it – the bones, the town, the history – got bulldozed away and there was just this ugly pavement and emptiness here now. Lucas knew about the history, about the workers insisting the dead be remembered, and she'd liked hearing him talk about the past – their past. But she couldn't ask him about hers.

They stayed quiet driving home. It was getting dark and Ruby was preoccupied with the great-grandmother she had never known and the place she had come from. Ruby herself was from a place that had disappeared, that was lost to her. Her head was too heavy. Her pulse pounded in her jaw with every bump on the road. She couldn't get warm.

Crossing the border back into Vermont, Lucas tuned the radio to a Burlington station. Two guests were arguing about changes to the city charter that would ban firearms in places where alcohol was served. They kept talking about the Connecticut school shootings earlier in the month. Ruby's hand covered her right ear. The shootings made her think of Frederick Douglass's mother walking fields to hold her child, how all those parents could never hold theirs again.

You can't have individual boroughs overriding state laws, Lucas said.

It would be a good law, said Ruby.

Lucas made that laugh that's not a laugh but like a jeer.

They're just trying to stop open carry in places like bars and playgrounds, Ruby mumbled.

She didn't know why she was even speaking. Her head was thumping and she didn't want to set Lucas off. Thinking about what made Lucas angry exhausted her. Everything Lucas didn't like spun in her head: how other people fished, where they fished, the boats they bought, people who did water sports, people who didn't, flatlanders whose boats leaked oil, idiots who didn't know to be quiet around fishing lines. On land it was worse. Assholes who couldn't drive on ice, cyclists who rode in packs, cyclists who wore Lycra, actually anybody in Lycra, people who were into fitness, gym people who ran like gerbils on machines, unfit people, hikers, adults in Birkenstocks, especially if wearing socks, hippies, feminists, bigots, liberals too, women who carried yoga mats, women who drove SUVs, women in SUVs who tried to overtake him on Route 2, maybe women who drove, anyone who tried to overtake him, anyone who said *awesome*, people who whined, people who were too chirpy, volunteers, the unemployed, waitresses that tried too hard, waitresses that didn't try hard enough, people who looked bored, ugly people, beautiful people, people who read or wrote with their mouths open, children on Ritalin, parents with children on Ritalin, anyone who didn't know how to change a tyre.

She used to feel special, grateful to be on the right side, better than the others, but now she felt deep nicks of shame when Lucas began to rant. She also knew some of this was in her too, under her skin – the quick judgements she made about people at school. Until she'd become friends with Sophie, being physically weak had seemed like a moral failure. Not knowing how to do things or fend for yourself showed lack of mettle, was a character flaw. She'd disregarded opinions when they weren't the same as the views she and Lucas held. Nathalie had called her out a few times. Ruby had eye-rolled and made an exasperated sound when a girl in her science class said she didn't believe in parthenogenesis, that asexual reproduction was gross.

Why are you so harsh? Nathalie had asked her later.

I'm not.

You are. You do that thing where it's like you're angry that someone doesn't get what you get. And you're judgy about it.

It's just that she knows all the details of *Keeping Up With the Kardashians* but she doesn't believe basic life science.

There it is.

It was as if someone had opened a door into herself. And she'd recognized it because it was like Lucas. She knew what Nathalie had said was true. That undertone of contempt.

Lucas made his sarcastic laugh again and turned off the radio. She knew what was coming. He started into the arguments he always made. In Vermont over seventy per cent of the population own firearms. There are no gun laws. Yet we're the safest state in the country. This past year, only eight murders, and just two of these involved guns; yet we own more firearms per capita probably than any other state.

You've told me this like a hundred times. Then she repeated something Nathalie had pointed out. There is open carry not just for Vermonters but for anyone. No one needs a permit. They could come from anywhere and carry assault rifles around our state and no one can say anything about it. It's crazy.

We don't believe that, he said. For us it's a freedom and we don't need the state telling us what we can and can't do.

Who's *we*? she whispered. She wanted it to stop.

Us. You and me.

A ball of frustration had formed in her chest and she had that feeling of wanting to lash out and at the same time just lie down and say Whatever. Instead she muttered, Not me.

She couldn't help talking back. She was ruining this good day that they'd had together.

Lucas started driving faster. It was completely dark outside now and the roads had been reduced to single lanes each side.

The thing about here is you can do what you want to do, he said, his voice deliberate and slow, the way he spoke when he was angry, because people here will leave you the hell alone to do it. That's the culture. And the problem with outsiders like those Hoags is they think they're decent just because they grow their own kale and drive a hybrid, and they think they should impose their so-called morality on the rest of us.

Ahead of them on the road a small Toyota hatchback was piloting through the dark, going slow. Lucas started tailgating. They were so close Ruby could see the University of Vermont sticker on the back window. Lucas accelerated toward their bumper several times, then swerved to overtake, but the ice caught the back end of the truck and they veered wildly to the left.

Lucas hit the brakes and they started to skid toward the verge. Ruby pressed her feet against the floor of the truck as if to brake. They were out of control. There were no snowbanks here and she watched the metal guardrail rise toward them, the blue-grey valley of bare treetops visible in the wide white landscape below. She held her breath, waiting to sail through the barrier, into the enormous drop. But the truck righted as Lucas swung the wheel, grunting as the tyres gripped the road and headed back into the lane. Ruby moved her hands away from the dashboard and tried to stop her body bracing for impact.

Lucas started talking about driving on ice, how you should always steer into the skid, pump the brakes. He was acting as if he had just manoeuvred them out of a dangerous situation. He was a hypocrite. Tailgating and overtaking on ice, then bragging about his skill. She didn't say anything at all and the good feelings she'd had about him earlier evaporated.

He dropped her off at the end of their road and said to go straight up to the house. She watched his tail lights slash red through the white snow until they disappeared, and she started up the track in the dark. The air was cold and the sky clear. The moon was still full, casting tree shadows across their fields. A few days earlier had been the thirteenth full moon of the year. And now it was almost her birthday. Would her mother try to send her a package? Would Lucas intercept it? She held her hand against her ear. It was taking forever to walk up the lane. There was something wrong inside her head. Or ear. Her breath came in short bursts and her legs were heavy. The blue light of the television from the living-room window moved closer. Clover would be inside. She could lie on the couch. Clover would cover her with warm blankets. Ruby was so tired she didn't even think she could stay awake to watch the ball drop in Times Square. Or climb the steps to the porch.

Lucky you're turning into a giant. I might never have heard the thump when you hit the door. You could have froze to death.

Clover was fussing around her in the bed. Ruby couldn't remember how she had gotten here. Pain was shooting through her ear. She pressed her hand against it and held it there.

Good thing too that Adelaide was here and has arms as thick as trees to help lift you, or we might never have gotten you inside.

Am I falling? Ruby whispered.

The doctor's on the way. You're burning up.

Clover? My ear. Ruby pulled her hand away. A sticky brown liquid was all over her fingers.

Clover got a washcloth and cleaned each finger, then tried to wipe the thick liquid from her hair on the side of her face and around the ear.

The doctor will be here soon. I think it burst.

The doctor wasn't Dr Francis. It was a woman. Young. She was the one on call from the practice. Her hand was cool on Ruby's forehead and when she leaned over she smelled like lemons. When Ruby closed her eyes, tears started to stream down her cheeks. The new doctor listened to Ruby's lungs and heart. Her fever was high, almost 104. She needed antibiotics.

I know your ear is very tender but I'm just going to take a gentle peek.

She was gentle. Slight pressure. Ruby couldn't remember what she'd said her name was.

Perforated eardrum. Infection. There's a lot of scarring in the other ear too. You must have had problems as a child – perforations. Our records for you start in 2004. So maybe your doctor before that could tell you.

Clover coughed.

The doctor kept talking. Antibiotics. No showers, no water in the ear. Rest. Plenty of fluids.

Ruby tried to ask: Philadelphia? but didn't have the energy.

Later, when she woke, Clover was by her bed and she held a glass of water to Ruby's lips. Try to drink some. You heard what she said.

Ruby sipped the water and put her head back. Clover swiped hair away from her eyes and Ruby felt the touch of Clover's papery old skin against her hot cheeks.

Am I from Philadelphia?

You're from here. Don't be kicking up a hornets' nest. Go to sleep now.

Was this your mother's room?

Clover put the glass down next to the bedside lamp. It was, she said.

What was she like?

Clover shielded her eyes as if to see her mother more clearly. She worked hard all her life. Real hard. But she poked fun. Everyone liked her. A bit like you. I never learned how to do that. You know, get on with people that way. Clover stood up and brushed Ruby's brow. Go to sleep now. She switched off the light.

Ruby lay there watching the shadows on her ceiling and wondered why Clover wouldn't tell her about Philadelphia, why she didn't even want to talk about her own mother for too long. In her half-sleep she imagined her great-grandmother who'd lived in this room before her lying in the same bed, staring at the same pockets of shadow. Had she died here? In this bed?

Later, she woke to arguing. Lucas and Clover, shouting in the kitchen, like distant roaring in the dark.

Deena. Philadelphia. It was as if Ruby's ear had burst that night with all the history she'd never heard before, like it was too much. She was born in Pennsylvania, her passport confirmed it; she was Irish, *both sides*; Clover had had a mother who'd lived in this house. Ruby had a past.

Back at school, she considered asking Nathalie or Sophie to use their phones, but she didn't want them to see something first. She needed to know what she was before they did.

Getting on the internet was easy. The school login was your last name, a full stop and your first name. Ruby didn't have a login but Nathalie used the same password for everything. At lunch, Ruby said she had to meet a teacher and went to the computer lab, sat at a desk in a corner and logged in as Nathalie. She typed *Deena, Philadelphia* and *Lucas Chevalier* in the search bar, paused for a moment, then tapped the return button. Rows and rows of articles appeared. *Missing Mother, Fairmount Woman Disappeared, Missing Nurse Has History of Mental Illness, Estranged Partner Person of Interest in Disappearance of NICU Nurse Deena Garvey, Missing Nurse Was Investigated in Neonatal Intensive Care Unit.* Ruby put her head down and gripped the table edge. Her hand shook as she tried to scroll down further. *Nessa Garvey, Sister of Missing Woman, Appeals to Public for Information.* Nessa. A sob stuck in Ruby's throat. Nessa. Laughing. Driving the car. Singing. A field and ducks. She scrolled back up to the article *Estranged Partner* and clicked. Words swam on the screen, her heart pounded against her perforated drum and involuntarily her hand went to her ear, like she didn't want to hear this. *History of domestic violence. Lucas Chevalier. Custody dispute.* Ruby shook her head no, leaned forward and switched off the power at the wall socket. She shouldn't have looked. She'd done a terrible thing. She sat in the chair trying to catch her breath, as if she'd been running. The door opened and someone came in. Ruby didn't look up. She repeated the name over and over in her head. Deena Garvey. Deena Garvey.

12

Ruby

2014

An airplane carrying 239 passengers vanishes in the sky, leaving no trace. Less than an hour into the flight, air traffic control loses contact. The plane continues to fly, veers off its flight path, banks west, then south. Someone is in the cockpit, navigating. They fly until the fuel runs out. Then it's gone. People say a jet can't just disappear like that. But it does. A month later, almost three hundred schoolgirls in Nigeria are kidnapped and vanish into the forest. A few jump from the backs of trucks and make their way home. The others disappear, punished as infidels, for being girls who wanted to learn.

It seemed to Ruby that all the stories she heard these days were about things vanishing. Her mother included. For over a year Ruby hadn't told anybody about what she'd read. She tried never to think about it. She didn't want Nathalie or Sophie to look up articles about her father. Or her mother. The past that was bad. Maybe they'd already seen, and knew. She spent less time with Lucas and worried if what the articles said about him was true. Vanished. But her mother hadn't disappeared. She'd sent her the package with the picture. There had been other packages. Lucas was keeping them. Her mother was somewhere. Had Lucas told the police?

They didn't find the missing plane and there were reports on the girls. They'd been taken by Boko Haram. The kidnappers said they'd be made into slaves, that they had been given away to men. Clover shook her head and said it was hard for girls everywhere, no matter what country or culture they were born into.

Clover was smoking out the kitchen window because Lucas

wasn't there. Ruby watched her from the sink. She stopped washing their dinner plates. Then she spoke without even planning to.

My mother went missing in 2004.

Clover didn't turn. Her arm stayed out the window, her chin still tilted to the open air.

Who said that?

I read it in a newspaper.

Yes. Clover shifted on her chair, the cigarette in her hand.

Yes? Yes what? What happened? Did Lucas do something to her?

Clover leaned back to the outdoor windowsill and dropped the cigarette into a glass jar where she kept the butts.

Why on earth would you say that?

The newspaper said he was a person of interest.

Papers say all kinds of cock and bull. The police had to question everyone, even me. Your mother left. She had her problems.

The paper said there was violence.

What are you talking about? Clover was leaning forward, her shoulders hunched up, her eyes narrowed.

It said things like history of domestic abuse, and protection orders, and a custody battle? Ruby's voice broke. Both hands were covered in suds and she pushed back her hair with her forearm.

The colour had drained from Clover's face. She half-stood then fell back into her chair as if Ruby's words had pushed her.

What papers?

Ones from 2004. From Philadelphia. I saw them.

You listen to me. That's a bunch of lies. Do you hear me? There was no violence. Never say that. Ever. You were with your father when your mother left. She was living somewhere else. I was there. He had nothing to do with it.

In Philadelphia?

Yes.

Clover and Lucas had told her nothing. All these years.

What was wrong with her? What problems did she have?

Clover lifted her hand, palm upward. I don't know. Something with her nerves, I think. She was on medicine.

She stood and shut the window, staying there, her back to Ruby. No more about any of that. It will just upset everyone.

Something shifted in Clover. She contradicted Lucas more, listened less. Stopped setting her hair. Her arthritis made her irritable. She sat with a cigarette out in the open, smoked on the front steps whether Lucas was there or not, or out the kitchen window whenever she felt like it. She didn't get dressed anymore, just wore her housedresses and – between small chores and making food – sat in the chair, footstool in front, her legs jutting straight out, and watched TV with the volume turned up high so that she could hear it from every room in the house.

Adelaide Puckett started coming over more. In the past she had been a straw hat in the garden when Ruby passed in the boat or a flannel shirt riding shotgun next to Ethan in the truck. But she and Clover had found each other, had decided to become neighbours after all. She brought over dinners in foil trays and mopped their floors. She helped Clover cook and started doing things for Ruby like laundry and buying her pads or things Ruby didn't want to ask Lucas to get. Adelaide made Clover laugh, called her an old cow or an unlicked cub.

A what? Ruby asked.

She's rude, said Adelaide. Like her mother never licked her into shape.

Clover listened and laughed. They joked, whispered together and watched bad TV. In some ways Ruby preferred this Clover, the one who had sort of given up on pleasing Lucas and had a friend.

During the day Clover watched news channels and westerns. After dinner it was true crime. One night they watched a *Disappeared* episode about a young woman who had vanished from a nightclub. Ruby wondered if it counted as missing when you knew where you were but other people couldn't find you? Could you say her mother was missing when her mother knew where she was? She should have asked Clover about the envelopes. Sometimes she still spotted a yellow package in the mail Lucas collected from the post office.

Ruby heard the truck and saw the swipe of headlights across the kitchen windows as he pulled in.

He's home, she said.

But Clover didn't look away from the TV or change the channel, just shrugged and said nothing.

Lucas came in and said, Hey there, from the kitchen. Ruby could hear the microwave beep on and the vent noise. He stood in the doorway, leaning against the jamb.

How was school? he asked.

Good.

Any tests back?

Ninety-eight per cent on biology, Ruby said.

Turn that racket down. He picked up the remote from the arm of Clover's chair and reduced the volume.

What did you miss?

Eukaryotic.

Lucas stood thinking for a moment. He was wearing a blue button-down shirt with a small floral pattern and chinos. He dressed differently to what he used to when it had just been them on the lake. More like other dads.

It's a basic of cell theory, he said.

Yeah. I know.

On the TV the presenter was talking about the nightclub woman, the trauma for the family. Lucas watched it for a second.

Turn that shit off. I told you before. He grabbed the remote again and switched off the TV.

Clover didn't look up, just kept staring at the blank TV as if it were still on. He opened his mouth to say something to her but the microwave dinged.

Your dinner's ready, Clover said.

They were sitting in their new cafeteria, beige plastic trays in front of them, looking at the list in the Extracurricular Fair brochure. This year we're joining, said Nathalie. It's high school. We're going to be joiners.

Nathalie said she was signing up for the Diversity Club, the Gender and Sexuality Alliance and the Environmental Club.

Sophie gaped at her across the cafeteria table. There was a straw in her plastic bottle of Coke. You're gay?

Nathalie stared back at her with disapproval. No. I'm an ally. It's an alliance? She said it like a question, as if Sophie were slow. Unfortunately for you there's no K-Pop Club.

Ruby stayed out of it. Sophie complained that Nathalie always defaulted to moral posturing online. Nathalie mocked Sophie's obsession with Korean pop bands and online forums she was on with other K-pop fans, who were, as Nathalie pointed out, also white Americans, where they discussed groups like Girls' Generation and Wonder Girls.

Sophie was joining Art Club to work on life-drawing skills and Drama Club so she could make costumes. She designed and sewed outfits, and then posted them online. With four older sisters, she had a house full of clothes to restyle. She was against fast fashion and everything she wore had been altered in some way. Most of the high-school kids dressed casually in hoodies and jeans or sweatpants. Sophie wore second-hand saddle shoes with knee socks, high heels with ankle socks, and woollen skirts she'd shortened. She made what she called poodle skirts and wore them with Converse. Some days she wore flared jeans with big wide belts from the 1970s. She looked like she belonged to any time but the one they were in. One day she would arrive in a real cheerleading outfit, blonde hair curled and all, and the next day she dressed like a goth flapper in a vintage dress.

Ruby studied the list. Coding, cybersecurity, robotics and loads of other clubs involved computers. She didn't play a musical instrument and couldn't sing. The very idea of drama made her cringe. They'd done a workshop in middle school where they were told to create an avatar and act it. She'd performed as a clam and didn't move or speak for the entire session. She read further down. Rowing. She knew how to row. She'd never been on a team or anything, but she knew how to make a boat move.

Lucas got out of the truck in waders and waved. Ruby lifted her hand but stayed on the steps watching. She was uncertain whether to ask outright or wait. The sun was warm on her face, the last touch of summer. Lucas lifted a bag from the bed of the truck and walked toward her.

Fresh Chinook. He dropped the bag on the steps.

He'd been fishing on Lake Ontario on his way home from Montreal. A Saturday morning on a lake and a good catch made Lucas happy. Ruby spent the afternoon cleaning salmon and making his favourite marinade with maple syrup and soy. She dug out the last of the sweet potatoes and cut two perfect heads of broccoli. Clover sat at the kitchen table watching her and reading the papers Lucas had brought home.

What's all this about, then? Clover asked.

Nothing.

Over dinner Ruby rehearsed her speech for Lucas in her head. The importance of extracurricular for her college application.

Lucas said it was good to be home and that this was the best meal he'd had in ages. Nothing store-bought.

I want to join the rowing team. The words burst out of her before she had time to list all the reasons why.

Lucas leaned back in his chair, but before he could answer, Clover said, Ruby should do that.

I'll be working. How will you get home?

A few others from the Islands row and said I can ride with them. Most of the training is on Lamoille. The coach brings them after school. In the winter it's all on ergometers.

Lucas stacked his plate on top of Ruby's. Okay. Yeah. As long as it doesn't interfere with homework and grades.

Ruby wanted to catapult across the table and hug them both. She couldn't believe how easy it had been.

Lucas went in to watch the news. Ruby dried the dishes. She was going to row. Clover shuffled around, putting dishes away, wiping the table. She scooped potato peels left on the counter into the trash.

He used to wrestle when he was in high school. She paused for a moment, the flat of her hands on the table. I went to see him just once. Didn't like it. The smell in the gym, seeing him pinned down like that, all that struggle. She lifted her hands and swiped the last peels away. Anyway. We used to always feed the peels to the pigs.

On the water, the senior girls moved in unison, gliding up the slide to the catch and driving back with a strong, firm finish. Ruby was watching from the shore with a handful of other freshmen. The *swish* on the water, the chop from the spoons of the blade, everything moved together. Wind, water, sound, bodies, oars, boats. Ruby already loved it. The tempo, the soft splash, the memory of it.

Coach Morgan had a whistle around his neck and carried a clip-board. He gathered those on shore in a circle. A few of the others had rowed in clubs, knew each other and knew Morgan.

Ruby Chevalier, he called.

Ruby put up her hand. Me.

You've swept before?

Ruby shook her head no. She'd only ever rowed alone. Two oars unless she was paddling in the kayak.

Sculled?

Yeah, but not in a club or anything. Just by myself.

Coach Morgan talked about catch and release, feathering the oar, keeping pace. He put some of the club girls in a boat together. You and you, he said, pointing at Ruby and another girl with broad shoulders and two pigtails caught at the nape of her neck. Single sculls.

For the next hour and a half Ruby rowed, and for the first time since high school had started she was in an element she understood – the headwind, the slight spray on her face, the rhythm of catch and release, the sun on her shoulders.

On shore, Morgan coached them on how to carry the boats and secure them on the rack.

You'll be back? he asked Ruby.

Yes.

Chevalier . . . You anything to Lucas Chevalier?

He's my dad.

Morgan paused. Her dad didn't come up much, but there was always an uneasy hesitation when he did. In Middle Lake, years earlier, Ben Peters had repeated something his dad had said. That Lucas Chevalier was already a bad egg when he was in high school. She'd felt dirty ever since, whenever people talked about Lucas.

You've instinctive form. And the length.

Waiting for their rides, Ruby and the other ninth-graders

stretched their backs, said how good it was to stand up straight after that. They laughed about the blades digging too deep, being out of time, nearly capsizing. They all agreed to come back. A senior girl that Ruby recognized from the bus fist-bumped her.

Island girls can row, she said.

Ruby went home with a sophomore who lived in North Hero. She was tired and happy. Outside the car window the sun had fallen as low as the reed beds, igniting them an orange gold, turning clapboard barns pink.

Why do you think your dad has those everywhere?

They were standing on the road where the mailbox used to be and Nathalie pointed up at the cameras Lucas had installed.

I don't know. Ruby wasn't sure why. He'd gotten them in the last year or so. Around the house, at their stretch of shore, the sheds, where the driveway met the road.

Do you think he's watching us now?

Ruby shrugged.

Let's keep going, Nathalie said.

They walked further down the road that led to the Pucketts' inlet. Ethan and Adelaide didn't mind Ruby using their dock. She and Nathalie walked out to the edge and sat down, legs swinging above the water.

Below them, bands of yellow perch darted under and around the wooden beams beneath the water's surface. Ruby was quiet. She didn't like the cameras either, couldn't forget about them. Last year in her global citizenship class they'd talked about surveillance after the Boston bombing. One student had said that cameras in public places violated our civil liberties and had been shown statistically to have no impact on reducing crime. We're being filmed by the government all the time without our permission, he said. Others

133

had said it was un-American. Mr Polinksi had said, Well, those surveillance cameras helped them catch the bombers. About five hands had shot straight up in the class. He'd missed the point. The cameras hadn't prevented the bombings. Surveillance couldn't undo what had happened. Plus, all the media and sharing of people's videos in the aftermath of the bombs meant that innocent people had been put on trial by social media.

It was a feeling she'd had before, like a heavy hole in her seeping out, bleeding its dark numbing poison through her limbs, making it hard to move, to try to do chores or even talk. It was like being tired in every cell of her body and in every neuron in her head. She wanted to lie down on the Pucketts' dock and sleep.

Later she came home alone up Route 2. The road was dusty. Blue chicory bloomed on the verge, scraps of trash caught in its long zigzag stems. She was about fifty yards from her turn when she saw it. A green car on the side of the road just beyond her turn, a sedan. Her heart quickened. She'd seen it before, one of the mornings she and Sophie had been waiting for the bus. There had been nothing unusual about it except a strong feeling that someone in the car was watching her. She'd forgotten about it. Got on the bus with Sophie and fallen into her seat.

There was someone in the car. Pretending not to look. Ruby was doing the same thing – looking but not looking. Aviators, a pale-grey baseball cap, maybe dark hair. She wasn't certain. They slouched low and watched using the rear- and side-view mirrors. She could feel their eyes. Man or woman? Her whole body prickled as she turned the corner, ready to burst into a sprint. Without warning, a sound and shadow came at her from the left and blocked her view of the car. Ruby jumped back with the shock of it. A truck. The door swung open. Ethan Puckett smiled out at her from under his cap, patted the seat next to him and asked, You want a ride? Ruby looked back up the road. The green car had already started driving north.

How's the high-school girl? He grinned at her, his two buck teeth more prominent than she remembered. She wanted to hug him.

She's good, Mr Puckett.

She didn't tell Lucas about the green car. She didn't tell anybody. She convinced herself that she had imagined it, or it was only a coincidence. But then, coming out of school with some of the other rowers, she saw it at the stop sign. Was nearly positive. When she got dropped off on Route 2 that evening, she sprinted home.

What's the rush? asked Clover when Ruby came into the kitchen breathless.

Ruby shook her head. Nothing.

Clover was at the sink, canning jars lined up on the draining board. Ruby wished Clover could still drive and meet her with the Pontiac, like she had when Ruby was at Middle Lake, smoking her Marlboros, Blake Shelton or Garth Brooks playing on 98.9 WOKO country music station.

Clover, what colour was my mother's car?

Clover went still, didn't turn around.

What kind of a question is that? How would I know? She started arranging the jars, bigger ones at the back, smaller ones to the front.

Was it green?

Now, don't start in with all that again.

All what?

The past. I barely knew your mother.

Clover shook her hands over the sink and left Ruby in the kitchen. The television volume turned up high in the living room. Ruby swallowed the sob in her throat. She never started in on the past. They never let her ask anything. Maybe she should tell Clover about the green car.

Clover's Pontiac was outside the window in the yard. Even

though she didn't drive anymore, sometimes she went out there and started it up. Sat inside with the radio and heat turned on, smoking her cigarettes in peace. It made Ruby sad, Clover choosing outside, the white winter landscape and the bare trees. And the old Pontiac, white smoke puffing from the exhaust.

13

Nessa

2004

John Garvey was dying. Deena had probably understood this, but Nessa and Joey hadn't. A failing heart causes fluid to back up into the lungs, the doctor said. They'd been blindsided. Joey took care of his appointments and medication now, propped him up against pillows at night to help him breathe, listened in on the baby monitor they had used when Ruby was small, the receiver beside his bed. Joey told Nessa some nights he lay there listening until he couldn't take the coughing anymore. He'd go into their dad's room, walk around the bed, the bent shape in it wracked by spasms.

I don't know what to do. Pat his back, adjust pillows? I don't know. Joey's head was in his hands and he wiped his fingers under his eyes. Across from him at the kitchen table, Nessa saw for the first time how exhausted he was.

I just go downstairs then, and watch garbage on cable most of the night.

Nessa had ignored the strain on Joey. There'd been tension between them, but she'd blamed it on him. If she talked about Lucas or Ruby or the particulars of the case, Joey got irritated, said Leave it, or Can you just talk about something else? She couldn't. It consumed her, she knew that, but it was like he had just given up. He thought there was a possibility that Deena had just left. He'd nearly said as much. She had to be vigilant all the time. It was down to her.

Joey stared out the window.

I'll do weekends, Nessa said. Friday to Monday. You stay at Kate's.

Joey and Kate had postponed their wedding. It had been scheduled for July. They'd been together since high school, so what was another year or two?

Yeah. Thanks.

Nessa watched *Dateline* with her dad. Coverage of Ronald Reagan's funeral.

She made him chicken soup that he hardly touched. Joey told her apple tart and vanilla ice cream. It was really the only thing their dad ate – at least there were some calories getting into him. His hand shook as he brought the spoon to his mouth. That night she fell asleep in the room she had shared with Deena when they were children, the baby monitor beside the bed. She listened to her father's laboured breath as she tried to fall asleep. The monitor made it sound as if it were coming across an ocean, as if he was already far away.

She was hollowed out. Her father and her brother needed her, but she had nothing to give. The only thing that felt meaningful was the case: the ritual of calling Lucas's house every evening – he never answered but she could tell the court when the time came that she tried every day to phone her niece – talking to Lynne, calling the detectives and, last thing before she fell asleep, calling Ronan in Ireland, where it was early morning, to tell him about the investigation. She couldn't stop her thoughts and they frightened her. There was nothing on earth that was good. If she saw a doctor, Lucas would find out. He'd use anything and everything against her petition for visitation. She had the sense of being watched. He was waiting for her to make a mistake.

Frank Capione radiated health, like he should run marathons or cycle, one of a pack of men in bright Lycra. But he chain-smoked. He lit one cigarette from another while they waited for their coffees. He was one of the most serious men Nessa had ever met. Maybe it was because he was a homicide detective. Or maybe he'd been like that already. Everything about him was inscrutable – his impassive face, straight posture, the air of reserve. His clothes were always trim: fitted grey suits, neutral blue shirts, black shoes.

It's about fucking time, she'd said aloud when he first called, introducing himself as Detective Capione from the Philadelphia Police Department. She had just gone out the front door when the phone rang and she'd gone back in. It had been two days since Deena went missing. Stories had started to run in the papers and she'd heard the report on KYW News that they were looking for information on a woman missing from the Fairmount area since Sunday morning. But the investigation didn't seem to be underway and none of them had been interviewed. I've called the precinct like ten times already today, she'd said.

I'm not with the precinct. My unit will be handling it from now on, he'd said.

Your unit?

We're based in the Roundhouse. Homicide.

Homicide? She'd slid down the wall to the floor, her ears ringing. You found her?

No. We haven't. And we don't have any further information. We often take missing persons, especially where there's a history of violence.

I've been trying to say this.

He'd cleared his throat. I knew your sister. I knew Deena. From St Christopher's. She was three years below me, in my sister Theresa's class.

Theresa Capione?

Yeah.

Nessa remembered her. She'd played basketball. Long dark hair in a high ponytail that swung when she shot from the free-throw line. She'd walked like an athlete. The Capiones had lived the other side of the playground. Big Italian family.

Theresa contacted you?

Yeah. She heard it in the neighbourhood, but I'd already seen the report and recognized the name. I've spoken to the district detectives. They've begun an investigation of potential camera footage, phone records, that kind of thing. But we'll be doing the interviews and will lead on the case here on in.

Since then, Nessa had talked to Frank almost every day. He took her calls when no one else would. Just to tell her the same thing: still no trace, no hits on the car, nothing on credit cards.

Nessa fingered one of his cigarettes from the packet. Can I?

He flicked his lighter and she leaned toward the flame.

Lucas still won't let us see or talk to Ruby.

What does your lawyer say?

Legally he can do what he likes, apparently. We've filed for third-party visitation rights, but she's told us that he's going to block it at every step. It won't be easy.

Yeah. She was in touch, wanted to know if there was anything we could contribute about the father's fitness as a parent. She already has the Protection From Abuse orders and the statement from Deena's assault in November 2002. We can say he's a person of interest in the disappearance of your sister, but not much more.

It's such bullshit. There isn't ambiguity. You saw what he did. The pictures. You read her statement.

I know you saw what he did to your sister, but in a court of law that's just hearsay. And there's her previous arrest. Disorderly conduct, resisting arrest. So that might level it in their eyes.

He did that. She was arrested because she was distraught about what happened at work. That only happened because she was off her medication because he made her. Nessa's voice was too loud.

Frank spoke low. He's fought for joint custody all along and was already awarded joint legal custody and partial physical.

His index and middle finger drummed against the saucer of the coffee cup. She knew he was trying to be blunt and truthful about what was ahead, but she wanted him to be angry too.

Ruby saw it all. His violence.

But they will say it's never been directed against the child.

How is violence against the mother not violence against the child? It's so messed-up.

There's never been any indication of violence directed at his daughter. That's what they're looking at. His fitness as a parent, not as a husband or human being. And as the sole parent now he has all the decision-making power.

Lynne had explained this to her. Lucas was protected by the Fourteenth Amendment in raising his child free from unwarranted interference from the state. She kept citing Troxel v. Granville – how, after that finding, the courts acted on the assumption that the parent was fit and had the right to make the decisions they deemed best for their child. Even if it meant preventing any visitation by other family members. Lucas could argue that he didn't want Ruby retraumatized by having to see her mother's family. That it would just reinforce her feelings of abandonment.

Nessa watched Frank's face – the downturned mouth, the way he looked off to the side – and it felt like he was accepting it all.

What about families like us? We've been her caregivers, the family Ruby knows, and now we can't even lay eyes on her?

Nessa lowered the coffee cup because her hand was shaking. She saw Frank notice.

What about the psychological harm that's doing? This whole system is fucking pathetic. Police. Courts. All of it.

Frank stubbed his cigarette in the ashtray. He lit another and stared past her as he sucked on it.

Sorry, said Nessa. Sorry, Frank. I'm really tired.

It had been months of walking into dead ends. At every turn the state protected Lucas's rights: protected *him*. She was angry all of the time. Angry and empty and poisonous. People had started avoiding her. She kept Ronan on the phone for ages, forgetting that he still had study to get done for exams and his time zone was five hours ahead.

Lucas has never asked for her things. Nothing. Not her clothes, her toys, her bike, her books, her fish, the tank. Nothing. Who does that? You see what he's doing? Who will tell Ruby about her mother?

He'll say he's doing it to avoid further hurt for his daughter. He'll say it's in her best interest.

The bakery was busy now. Their cups were empty. An untouched blueberry muffin sat on Nessa's plate. Frank noticed.

Are you eating at all?

She shrugged her shoulders. I find it hard to do anything normal.

Sleeping?

I feel like I have to be on all the time. I think I will miss something, a chance, a clue, and that one little misstep, that millisecond where I relax, will mean we lose Ruby forever or that we never find Deena. She crossed her arms. Dad's just given up. His heart is literally dying and Joey's just bewildered. He wants me to stop talking about it all the time.

She caught a glimpse of Frank's discomfort. He shifted in his seat, sighed.

It's frustrating. I know.

Lucas does make mistakes, Nessa said, as if to encourage him. His temper. He loses control. We've all seen it – everyone in my family. Not just me. God, the week we moved Deena and Ruby out for good. I know he'll fuck up at some point.

I'll get this, Frank said. He picked up the bill and reached for his wallet. Nessa waited while he paid at the register. He had to get to work. So did she.

The morning Deena vanished replayed once more. It was habitual, a string of thoughts she fell into in any silence. Deena getting dressed for work, stepping outside and then the series of questions: Did he choose a Sunday morning because there would be no rush hour? Fewer witnesses? Did he call her that morning and say something was wrong with Ruby? Had he waited in her car? Outside their front door?

The white Honda parked across the street for months. It had disappeared. Maybe it *was* his. It had bothered Sylvia, a car that never moved. It must have been abandoned, she'd said. Nessa should have reported it. Why hadn't she?

Frank slid back into his seat. When does the petition get heard?

Two weeks.

She swallowed, tried to focus on commuters walking toward their jobs. Their purposeful lives.

I know you've heard this already, Nessa, but you are no good to anyone if you have a breakdown or get sick. If you don't eat or sleep, or find a way to manage yourself, that's going to happen.

Yeah, I know.

I asked to meet you about something other than the petition. He looked down at the table and Nessa knew he was going to tell her something she didn't want to hear, something he'd put off for the last forty-five minutes.

Lucas made contact a few days ago. He's leaving Pennsylvania this summer. Because of the ongoing investigation, he's informed us of a change of address. He's moving to Vermont. Him and Ruby.

She'd read that airports and train stations were perfect examples of extreme modernity, the travellers in them rootless, between places. Nowhere. But they'd always suggested the opposite to her: points where people touched down again, returned, came home, kids running to open arms, awkward teenage boys hugging mothers, adults suddenly shy at the sight of one another, goodbyes, 30th Street

Station, at the angel with her mother and Deena. All of it. She would have to hold back tears for the sheer beauty of humans meeting again. Now, standing in Arrivals at Philadelphia International Airport, waiting for Ronan, she felt nothing.

He had wanted to come back for weeks, defer his exams. She'd put him off. She hadn't seen him since a few days after Deena went missing. Ronan belonged to another world. Before all this. She didn't have that space left in her anymore.

She saw him coming down the ramp, dark-blue button-up shirt, dark jeans. Already a shadow on his face from a day of travelling. A tweed blazer that he wouldn't be wearing in the Philadelphia weather. She could see him searching the crowd and his eyes resting then on her. A twinge of worry there; maybe distress was written all over her, or maybe it was a sign of regret, as if he could see the world of pain he was walking into. He set both his bags down, wrapped his arms around her and held her. Nessa's face was inside his blazer and for the first time in weeks there was something like comfort. She couldn't speak. Gestured to try to explain her silence.

It's okay, he said, his head buried in her hair. They stood for a moment. You're wasting away, he said. I can feel the bones of you.

She wanted to stay there cocooned, the world shut out. For Christmas he'd given her a DVD of David Attenborough's *The Life of Mammals*. She watched it at night, unable to process anything that involved narrative or characters. Recently she'd seen a joey explore the world outside its mother's pouch, struggle, fall down a few times, then crawl back in, as if being in the world was too hard. She wanted to stay there in the dark of Ronan's blazer, the scruff of his jaw against her head, the breadth of him against her cheek. A distant smell of wool.

The petition for visitation was turned down. He's not going to let us see her.

144

Ronan held the back of her head, stroked her hair. I am so sorry. That's . . .

He trailed off, didn't know what to say. They stood there and she realized he would hold her in the middle of the Arrivals hall until she let go.

Ronan went shopping, cooked a roast for her the first night. Comfort food – something easy to eat, he said. Mashed potatoes. Mushy peas. A roast chicken. She lay on the couch and watched as he puttered around the kitchen he had designed only the year before. It felt almost like childhood, the clattering pots and pans, the hum of the TV, the smell of cooking. Ronan set plates down on the coffee table. You need a gravy boat, he said. This mug will have to do. Try to eat, he urged. She did, but even the potatoes, well mashed in milk and butter, were like pasteboard on her tongue. She struggled to move the muscles of her mouth, to swallow.

Later, when they were lying in her bed, she told him she didn't think she could have sex. My head is so so fucked-up right now, and I can't control the thoughts that come in. It's not just Deena – flashes of her dead somewhere in the woods, unburied, looking up at me, or in a shallow grave or a dumpster or an abandoned lot somewhere – it's thoughts about how she died. How she might have suffered. Her scared or terrified cuts me up like a hundred times every day.

She could hear her voice in the dark, Ronan's breathing beside her. She knew he was scared by what she had become. So was she.

It's other stuff too, she said, like those pictures from Abu Ghraib on the news. Or the guy that they filmed being decapitated. I keep seeing the very worst things in my head. The pictures just come in. I can't stop them.

She didn't know why she was like this or how to explain it to Ronan. It was as if everything had been ruined and degraded. She would never be normal or touchable again.

145

It's why I didn't want you to come. I feel like I'm poison right now. Just toxic, dirty poison. To myself. Others. You.

The first morning, Ronan came back with a month's supply of protein drinks for Nessa to fatten her up, and a bag of old DVDs. He drew her a bath in the middle of the day, cooked for her and played *American Graffiti* and then *When Harry Met Sally*. She watched him move around her house. He would make a great husband and father; he nurtured without even thinking. These weren't things that could be hers.

The night before he left they had sex. In the middle of the night, unthinking, almost half-asleep sex. When it was over, Nessa faced the wall. She couldn't stop crying.

Jesus, Nessa. What's wrong? I'm sorry. I thought you wanted to.

I did. It's not that.

Ronan didn't say anything. Pulled her body closer to him. Rocked them both gently. His bare thigh over hers, the warmth of his damp skin, his chest still pounding against her back. She knew this would be the last time. She wasn't capable of receiving all that he had to give. She didn't understand how someone so good and beautiful wanted to hold her. At the same time part of her resented his wholesome goodness, his gravy boats and roasts. His conversations about his younger brothers and sisters, when everything was so fucking shit in the world. She couldn't stop coughing out sobs.

It was like he heard her thinking. Nessa, please. Please don't say anything yet. It's not time to decide things. Honest to God, I'm here. I'll wait. We can do this for years to come. We can always do this. When you're ready.

Nessa said nothing. It was already over.

14

Nessa

2004

She'd been in a meeting all morning with the graphic designers about the layout of a catalogue. There was a line of Post-its on her desk.

> Call Molly ASAP.
> Molly said call her back now.
> Molly again.
> Molly.

Nessa picked up her cell.

Nessa. I am about to burst. I've been trying you for hours.

What's wrong?

Did you see it?

What?

You won't fucking believe it. There's a front-page article about Deena in this month's *Philadelphia Today*. About the NICU probation, her mental health. Like stuff as far back as college. Everything. They couldn't know all those details unless someone gave them information.

Jesus. Lucas. But Frank said he didn't think Lucas would be stupid enough to talk to the media. Did the hospital release it? A surge of panic went through her. People would have the wrong idea about Deena.

Everyone here is saying absolutely not. He must have. Who else would? It doesn't quote him. But how would they have all this information? It mentions her suicide attempt in college. Her going off her meds. The baby with the wrong syringe. The breakdown. The arrest.

All of it. So either the Police Department released all that or he did.

The catalogue proof Nessa had been working on all morning was still in her hand, Artemisia Gentileschi's painting *Judith Beheading Holofernes* on the cover. She dialled Frank's number and concentrated on the image while the phone rang. Gentileschi had been raped by a painter friend of her father's and there'd been a trial. She'd described how she fought him. When he was finished, she said she wanted to kill him and he mocked her. She threw a knife. He said he would marry her because he'd taken her honour, but then refused. Nessa imagined the courtroom. The teenage girl in the stand. Her rapist, who called her a whore and who had plotted to have his own wife murdered, in the same room.

No answer.

Nessa ran down to the Wawa, bought a copy of *Philadelphia Today* and sat outside to read. It was all about Deena's mental health and the investigation that had happened at work. It had to be unethical. There had to be a way to make them retract it. She wrote down the reporter's name. How could they disclose that much of Deena's history and not mention the PFAs and beatings, the insane things that had happened to her? The mistake at work was because he'd made her come off SNRIs cold turkey. There was no mention of that fact.

She tried Frank again. No answer. She tried Lynne and left a message with her secretary.

Back in her office she sat at her desk, studied the catalogue she was supposed to be working on without registering any of the words. She looked up the number of *Philadelphia Today* and called. She wanted to scream. She asked to speak to the reporter who'd written the article. She was transferred to the editor.

How could you publish this? Do you understand the damage it's doing to my sister's investigation? To my family? This is defamation. My sister is missing. Something happened to her and you dig up her use of antidepressants as a story?

She wanted to scream You monsters. You unethical fucking monsters.

The editor was calm. He said he was sorry she felt that way. They were committed to fair and balanced reporting.

Everything we published is factual and can be verified. We invited your family to contribute.

We are in an ongoing investigation. There's a constant media circus. We're not doing interviews because we aren't allowed to say anything, to name him. Nessa was shouting. We are going through hell. Where's your decency? She slammed the phone down.

She stood and kicked her desk hard. A shock of pain shot up her shin.

She left another message for Lynne and tried Frank again.

During the rape trial, Gentileschi had been tortured using thumbscrews to make sure she was telling the truth. It's true, she'd repeated over and over. It was hard not to look at the painting of Judith without thinking of her trial, the rage and the pain she must have felt. She was tortured. Not him. Her. A teenager. Artists had always depicted female anger as ugly. The Furies, the Gorgons. Gentileschi painted a picture that imagined women working together to pin down their oppressor and slit his throat, cut off his head.

Nessa left work in the early afternoon. Neither Lynne nor Frank had called back. She walked to Center City, went by Lucas's street, still imagining she might see Ruby out on her tricycle coming up the sidewalk. She couldn't pass a playground in the city without searching for her. She found a bar and ordered a shot of whiskey. Then another. She drank three beers. Took two Xanax that Molly had given her because she'd been too afraid to ask a doctor for a prescription in case Lucas found out during the application for visitation. It was late afternoon and people started to spill in. She forgot it was a Friday.

A guy in a blue suit that was slightly too bright or shiny, or both, sat on the stool next to her. When he flashed a smile, which he did a lot, he was handsome. Perfect white teeth. But something about him was off.

It might never happen, he said.

She wanted to punch him. But just said, Whatever.

He bought her a drink. A double whiskey. She bought him one. It went back and forth. He did something in finance, had one of those big gold college rings with a green stone. Bunches of dark hair sprouted from his knuckles and she almost felt sorry for him. He was talking about his life. She wasn't listening. The day darkened against the windows. That time on a Friday when one type of person went home to their families, and the others, like her, stayed on.

The guy in the suit had coke. In the bathroom he and Nessa did lines off the catalogue proof. They had more drinks.

Coke always gets me going, he said.

You have more?

The bathroom light was dim. She cut lines across the catalogue, on Holofernes' red velvet blanket, on Judith's skin.

You know, Gentileschi's painting is different to Caravaggio's, she said. In his it's as if the knife just falls through his neck without any physical effort. Judith and her nurse are practically several feet away, not even really holding the sword. Look. She pressed her finger on the catalogue. In this one the maid pins him down, the blood spurts. Judith has the fistful of hair for leverage, so she can really sever his arteries. It's hard physical work but they're so calm. Resolved. They're doing what has to be done. See?

Are you talking about the picture? The shiny-suit guy leaned over and did his lines.

Never mind, she said. What the fuck did he think she was talking about? She snorted the coke and saw her face in the mirror as she lifted her head. I look jaundiced. She wiped her nose.

He stood behind her at the sink and rubbed his horrible hands down the front of her shirt. His wet mouth slurped at the back of her neck.

She ducked her head and bent over, trying to stop him.

Get the fuck off me.

You came in here with me.

Because you had coke.

She put her back to the sink and shoved him.

What the . . . ? His face morphed from startled to angry. Crazy bitch. He pushed open the bathroom door and left.

Alone, she looked again at her cloudy reflection. She must have been crying at some stage during the night – mascara sediment clumped beneath her eyes. Like a painting of a deranged woman. She pitched through the noisy bar and stumbled onto the sidewalk. At the corner of Broad she hailed a cab.

She told the driver where she lived. As they drove up her street she asked, Can you wait for me here? Just a few minutes. I'll be right back.

At the top of the steps she had to lean against the door while she took out her keys. Get the right key, the house key. *Focus.* She dug the key into her wrist as hard as she could. *Fucking focus, Nessa.* She had a purpose now. The kitchen knife from the good German set Ronan had said she needed. On the way out the door she saw his wooden Irish bat thing. She'd never mentioned to him that he'd left it there. Back in the taxi she gave the driver the address and they drove back toward Center City, down side streets.

Here, she said. The Nissan Frontier. She paid and stood next to the truck, waiting for the taxi to drive away, turn at the stop sign. She had the knife in her bag. Held the stick. All day she had wanted to puncture or wound something, someone. Lucas, the reporter, the self-satisfied editor, the judge who'd denied her third-party visitation, the guy in the bar. She staggered alongside Lucas's Nissan, the knife in her hand digging a line through the paint from bumper to bumper, a white seam in a smooth black surface. Not perfect anymore. She pushed hard, making the cut deep. Fuck you, she whispered. Fuck you, fuck you, fuck you. At the front bumper, she stood beside the tyre, gripped the knife with two hands and stabbed backward. On the second thrust it went in properly and she tripped forward, falling onto the street when the blade came free. She went for another wheel, lunging. The knife stuck this time. She fell against the truck and the alarm went off. Of course he'd have an alarm.

Fuck, fuck, fuck. She picked up the stick off the ground and started swinging. She smashed a headlight. Was she actually shouting or shouting in her mind? The other headlight. The chrome grille. The shock reverberated through her arms. Lights flicked on. Lucas's doorstep lit up. She kept going, round the back, smashing the tail lights. It took five or six blows before the driver's-side window shattered into thousands of tiny pieces held together as if there were an invisible wire running through them. Smithereens. An Irish word, she remembered Ronan telling her.

She was everything she wasn't allowed to be: ugly, enraged, violent, drunk. Faces behind curtains watched her. Shadows in windows. Crazy, hysterical, fucked-up. That's what they saw. He was probably watching from a window. Still in control. She wished right then that he would just come out and shoot her with his gun. The knife stuck in the tyre, if she could get it out and slice herself, just get it over with. It wouldn't budge. Defeated, she knelt in the glass on the street and managed to ring Frank's number. This time he answered.

I've smashed his truck. I'm here on the street. People are looking.

Kneeling there in the dark, she had one terrible thought: What if Ruby was watching? What if she was at a window and saw Nessa, deranged, smashing and violent. Like him. Her knees were bleeding. Her hand had a deeper cut.

The Roundhouse. Fluorescent lights, a ripped faux-leather black chair, ink on her finger, the flash of the camera. A female detective repeating I hear ya or You can say that again as if she agreed with Nessa who kept crying that there was no justice, not for women, not for women anywhere. She knelt on the floor of the women's restroom and threw up, a uniformed cop the other side of the door. The linoleum layer had missing bits, as if someone else had crouched there and clawed at the ground. The stench was unbearable. The seat up. A man thing.

The worst thing, she told the guy outside the door coming out, is you let men piss all over the seat and floor of the women's bathroom. We don't do that. Nessa stumbled, pointed at herself. Why can't you just get the men to use their own? Tell them to stop, just stop taking over every fucking bit of everything. Just get back. Jesus.

The room spun. She fell asleep on the floor. Someone moved her to a chair.

Frank must have pulled strings; it was him that brought her home the next morning.

No more avenging, he said. And whatever you were on last night, you need to cut that crap out. Immediately. And eat.

Yeah, she said. She had never been so tired in all her life.

She was served with a restraining order. At least they did it at her house and not at work. A bill for criminal damage arrived in a certified letter; she had to sign for it at the post office. Lucas and Ruby had already moved to Vermont.

You know her first steps were in this room? John Garvey had barely any breath left but he spent his final days talking almost non-stop. Hospice care had set up an adjustable bed in the living room.

Your mother steadied her over there by the sofa. I was on the chair. Just there.

He had to pause. Nessa watched the cage of his ribs move up and down beneath his undershirt. He had gotten thin and bloated

153

at the same time. His stomach swelled, and his ankles, but his arms and chest were wasted. Against his pallid skin his silver medal. *St Christopher Protect Us*. A gift his mother had given him when he'd left home.

I held my arms out and she wobbled over to me. Pudgy little legs. All by herself.

It wasn't really even a story, but he told it on repeat now with other memories. Deena's first steps. Her first day of school. The time she hid the hair she'd cut off Nessa's head. Deena singing. Sometimes he confused her with Ruby.

He wheezed and Joey leaned forward and wiped his mouth with a Kleenex.

At least Maria didn't have to live to see what happened to our girl. He cried, and drifted to sleep. Their father was dying and he could only talk about the dead. It was just a matter of days. The hospice nurse had told them they knew by his blood markers.

Outside, the backyard trees had started to change colour. Their dad had planted saplings when each of them was born. Deena beech, Joey maple, Nessa cherry. On this little plot of land, in this little square of America, so much had happened. Every summer all the Irish that came through, the barbecues and stories, their childhoods, the business, romances and grief.

If she could listen to my heart now, he said, but it was in his sleep and Nessa didn't know which of them he meant.

He woke suddenly, gasping for air.

I met your mother at the Irish Club, he said when he could speak. She'd come with a friend. I was forty-five. I never expected I'd meet someone at that stage of my life. An Italian, fifteen years younger. She made me laugh. She made me feel young. She should have lived longer. And then he remembered and said, Thank God you didn't, Maria.

He talked until he fell asleep again; the sleep lasted a long time and neither Joey nor Nessa was certain at first whether he was dead. They waked their father in the house that night, just the two of them, because he'd said that was what he wanted, and called the funeral home the next morning.

They buried him on a beautiful fall day. They stood together outside the church where they had been baptized, made their confessions and communions, where they'd been confirmed and where they'd said goodbye to their mother. Next door to the church was the elementary school they had all gone to; across the street the graveyard. Less than two years earlier when they'd buried their mother, Ruby and Deena had stood there with them in the bitter cold, circled by Joey's friends in case Lucas showed up.

The line was long. People liked John Garvey and everyone had something to say. Nessa and Joey shook hands and listened. Nessa hadn't broken down. She didn't feel capable of it. To the right of the hearse a group of the Irish had gathered. Some of them had stayed on in the area. Standing to the edge of them, Nessa saw a familiar shape and her heart faltered. Ronan had come from Ireland for her mother's funeral. Now he was here for her father's. She'd told him there was nothing to salvage. She listened as a woman from Donegal told her a story about meeting her father in 1950. Over half a century ago, at the Irish Club, when she had just come over. What a gentleman he was. Nessa shook her hand and received her hug. Ronan shook hands with Joey first and Joey broke down, putting his head on Ronan's shoulder. Ronan hugged him, patting his back. She'd forgotten what good friends they'd been before she even knew who Ronan was. Her father had loved and trusted him, asked him to do her house.

She went to shake his hand when he stood in front of her.

Ah, Nessa. Not today. Again she felt a pinch of shame and dropped her hand to hug him.

You shouldn't have come, she said.

Why?

I don't know. Distance. Expense. A card or whatever would have been enough.

He tilted his head, a question or disbelief. You know I'm here, don't you?

What?

Here in Philly?

No. It was as if the ground beneath her was moving. Joey knows?

Yeah. I've been to see your dad several times the last few weeks. I thought you knew.

Why? Don't you have the exams?

I sat them already. Got an offer from my old job here. They organized the work permit and everything. So.

You weren't going to tell me?

Nessa, did you even read my emails? I told you. I've been working here.

She nodded. Yeah. Yes. I see. Joey was no longer beside her; he'd moved across the lot to Kate and her family.

I heard you were arrested.

Joey told you?

Yeah. Ronan shrugged. He was wearing a soft brown sweater over a dress shirt. Part of her just wanted to fall into the safety of him. He seemed so good.

You'll be happy to know you supplied the weapons.

What?

The Wüsthof, that quality kitchen knife. *When over two hundred years of knife production meets the modern home kitchen?* And your sport stick thing.

You used my hurley?

I guess. That. They didn't return it.

Ronan shrugged and gave a half-laugh. I don't use it here anyway.

I was pretty out of it. It was really fucked-up. All of it.

She could see Ronan wanted to say something more but the undertaker was at her elbow.

It's time for us to go across, he said.

Okay.

She watched as Joey, Kate's brother, Ronan, two of her cousins and another of the Irish workers hoisted her father's casket on their shoulders, the old-fashioned way – how her father would have wanted it – and carried him across the road to the plot he had pre-paid for. Where their mother was waiting.

Lying on Ruby's floor, Nessa gazed up at the glow-in-the-dark constellations they had stuck to the ceiling, the streetlight glancing off Ruby's moon chair, Ruby's picture wall, her bookshelves: *Frog and Toad, Guess How Much I Love You, Olivia*, and Ruby's favourite, *Sharing a Shell*, a gift Ronan had sent from Ireland; she'd insisted they read it every night. Three times. Ruby even started to talk like the book. One of the last nights before Deena disappeared, the three of them had been in Nessa's car and Ruby had said, from her booster seat in the back, Three friends, driving along, under the night-sky blue. Nessa had nearly driven off the road. It was a riff on the *Sharing a Shell* book.

You've spawned a poet, Nessa had said.

And Deena had beamed.

Lying on the floor of Ruby's room, Nessa started to sob. The need to hold Ruby overwhelmed her.

She left for Vermont at two that morning. John Garvey's Rand McNally *Road Atlas of the United States* was under the seat of her car. She knew the town where they were living, where Lucas was from on the Islands in Lake Champlain, but not the exact address. She didn't check if a restraining order was valid across state lines or not. She drove anyway. A few miles before the New York border she pulled into a twenty-four-hour rest stop on the New Jersey Turnpike. Outside, she sipped her coffee and smoked a cigarette. At four in the morning people were already milling around, ready to start their working day. Mostly labourers, men in steel-capped work boots, paint-splattered trousers, men like her dad and brother.

After Albany, on a section of road they called the Northway, she watched the sky change. A dark line of blue in the east was visible as the road rose, below it a deep indigo sea of trees; even the road beneath the headlights shone blue. The blue hour – she'd read that somewhere. The silhouettes of forests, the dark hulk of mountains took shape as morning broke over the Adirondacks. By the time she crossed into the state of Vermont, the sun sat on the fields ahead like a burning red ball. She was further north than she'd ever been. Cow fields, clapboard houses, rust-red barns and blazing trees, the whole world vibrant in death: burning hickory, amber beech, red maple. Just before Burlington she could see the lake on her left. She pulled in off Route 7 and smoked a cigarette. Deena had come just once, when she was pregnant, had wanted to see everything. Went up there like a tourist with her guidebook and camera and came back quiet, with no pictures to develop. The trip had unsettled her.

Did you know Robert Frost is buried there? she'd asked. Nessa hadn't. She didn't know anything about Robert Frost or Vermont, or poetry for that matter.

He is, Deena had said. His gravestone inscription says *I had a lover's quarrel with the world.*

Don't we all, Nessa had said. Like so many other fragments of memory, she tried to mine the moment now for what it had meant, what had drawn Deena to that poet or his grave. Later, after Deena went missing, she'd found a Frost quote in one of Deena's journals. *My Sorrow, when she's here with me, thinks these dark days of autumn rain are beautiful as days can be.* It was dated November 2003, a year after she'd left Lucas and a few months before she disappeared. Had she been depressed? *My Sorrow.* Nessa had never even asked whether she got to visit the grave. They never got back the missing years, the journals Deena had kept when she was with Lucas. Everything she had recorded about Ruby those first years. About him.

Nessa rolled the window down as she crossed into Grand Isle County on the Sandbar Causeway. Fishing boats lingered to the north, lines drawn in the still silver water. The road fish-hooked north and she pulled in at what looked like a general grocery store. The edge of a town. Large cardboard boxes packed with pumpkins caught the midday sun. A hand-scrawled sign read *Homegrown on the Island: $3 each.* Nessa picked one out of the box, full, unblemished and bright. A gift for Ruby if she got to see her. Inside, she gave three dollars to the man behind the counter. He wore a lumberjack shirt and a camouflage hat with fishing lures hanging from it. She tried to sound casual.

By any chance do you know the Chevaliers? Clover and Lucas?

He didn't say yes or no, just walked out to the front. Outside, he pointed north. A few miles and you'll make a right turn. You'll know it because there's a red barn on the corner, Holsteins grazing the field in front.

Nessa looked at him, puzzled.

Cows. Like the ones on Ben and Jerry's.

Black and white? she asked.

That's them, he said. Turn right when you see 'em. Go down that road a stretch until it forks. Keep left. It's only a side road heading to the lakeshore. The Chevalier place is up there on the left. He's out on the lake a lot with the young one but Clover should be there.

Nessa thanked him, her heart starting to pound. She hadn't worked this through.

Help me, she said out loud as she put the car back in gear, not sure if it was her mother or sister or father she was asking. She drove slow, followed the directions, saw the faded red barn, the cows' slow ambling out front, and turned. The road was grit and bordered by dying grasses, goldenrod and aster. If she met another car she would have to back up. Does Ruby walk down this road, reach her hand out to brush against the wildflowers? Is she happy enough to pick them? Does she like Lucas's mother enough to bring her a bunch? She stayed left at the fork in the road. The lake came into view, brief shimmering glimpses. There was a break in the hedgerow ahead, someone's property. She could see a mailbox and slowed to a crawl. C-H-E-V-A-L-I-E-R was spelled out in squares of stick-on gold letters. She lifted the camera from the passenger seat and took a picture of the mailbox, of the lane, the lake. Kept going up the drive. Vegetable beds in small square patches, and beyond them rows of corn, the stalks golden and dry. The gable of the house on the hill above blended into the grey trunks and the sky surrounding it. It reminded her of an Andrew Wyeth painting, *Autumn Cornfield*. Rural. Austere. An old tyre swung from a branch. Maybe something he'd put up for Ruby. She took another picture. A blue Pontiac was parked on the grass in front of the porch, at least thirty years old. Nessa pulled in behind it. Lucas's truck wasn't there.

A two-storey farmhouse. Weathered clapboard with peeling white paint, forest-green shutters and a wraparound porch that sagged at the front. Wide steps leading down to the lawn. She stepped out, took a photograph, then put the camera back on the seat and closed the door. It was like a postcard of Vermont, one faded with age. The house faced the lake and along the treeline there were several sheds, cords of neatly stacked grey wood at the side of one. Machinery in an open barn – a tractor, a plough, lawnmowers. Canoes and kayaks stored on racks.

Before she'd put her foot on the bottom stair, an old lady appeared at the top. Maybe late seventies, her flowered housedress like the one Nessa's Italian grandmother wore in South Philly, every single moment of every day except when she was leaving the house for Mass or bingo. This woman was smoking. The dainty flower pattern on her dress was incongruous with the bulk of her. She was wide, support hose rolled down to swollen ankles, her hair in a flat bun at the top of her head, like it had been slept on. Her face was wrinkled but Nessa could see Lucas. The steel-blue eyes, the set jaw. She must be Clover. Deena had described Lucas's mother as cowed, but this woman looked formidable.

Yes? she asked, taking a drag on her cigarette, her eyes narrowing against the smoke. No Hello or Can I help you.

Is Lucas here?

Who are you?

Nessa hesitated, was going to lie about being a colleague from work or that she was a friend of his from Philadelphia. She hadn't resolved on what to say.

I've driven from Philadelphia. I'm Nessa Garvey. Ruby's aunt.

Clover's hand reached to hold the banister.

Please, Nessa said, taking a step forward. I just want to see her. She could hear her voice thin as she lost her breath. Please.

You're trespassing. You have to leave. The girl's fine. She's happy.

Please. I only have her.

Clover repeated, You're trespassing; I've asked you to leave. I'm calling the police.

Lucas wasn't home. He'd have come out. She looked up at the house. Dark windows reflected back the outside, sky and trees. On the porch, metal chairs with cushions and a side table. She considered shouting Ruby's name to bring her to a window.

Where's Ruby? she asked.

She's with her dad.

Wait, Nessa said, but the woman shuffled back to the door and closed it.

Nessa sat on the bottom step. The lake glistened before her, edged on the far shore with blazing foliage. She wasn't sure what she should do. She searched for traces of Ruby, or her life here. But, other than the tyre on the rope, there was nothing. No little wheelbarrows or building blocks or plastic playhouses. No evidence of childhood. She remembered how Lucas had always wanted Ruby to be like a little adult. Precocious. No childish language or babytalk.

A few minutes later the old lady was at the top of the steps.

I've called the police, she warned.

You're Clover. You met my sister. You never saw her with Ruby. She would never have left her. She's all I have and he won't even let me see her. Please.

She was pleading but the woman wouldn't look at her.

They're on their way.

Clover waited at the top of the steps. Here, she said, holding out a sheet of paper. Take it. Just leave her be. She's happy here.

A siren wailed in the distance. A breeze blew and a scatter of leaves moved together, falling over themselves, tossing along the lawn toward the lake.

Nessa looked at the sheet. She recognized the Ruby people straight away. Unfinished circles for faces. The three of them holding hands, an image repeated on her picture wall on Parrish Street. Purple marker, those three familiar outlines. In the distance a house with circles all along the edge. Nessa knew. Ruby was drawing home. It had been eight months since Deena disappeared and Lucas took Ruby, but she was still trying to imagine them, make them visible. The boathouses trimmed in white lights along the Schuylkill. Ruby was here in Vermont drawing pictures of them. Her mother, herself and Nessa – together in Philadelphia.

Clover must have assumed this was Ruby drawing them, Ruby, Lucas and Clover. Nessa turned to say, It's us – it's us she's drawing, not you. Not you and your monster son. You don't even understand her, or what she's trying to say in her pictures. Clover was gone, the door was closed. Nessa watched the white patrol car glance through the trees on the dirt road below and then emerge, crawling up the dirt lane.

PART III

PART III

15

Nessa

2008

Look at you. You're bone-thin and exhausted. And, quite frankly, you've become isolated and odd. You need help. Like, from professionals.

Thanks, I think? Nessa tried levity but Molly didn't laugh back.

We have to make these referrals every week in the NICU, she said. There's a lot of suffering out there.

In the restaurant the drone of conversation was broken now and then by laughter. People living. Linen tablecloths, the clink of cutlery on plates. She wanted everything to stop.

Molly kept talking. Nessa, in the course of two years you lost your mother, your father, your sister and . . . Ruby. You've also pushed away a boyfriend who loved you and most, if not all, of your friends. Your sister isn't here to say it, so I will. You need help.

She pushed a leaflet across the table.

This isn't therapy. It's a group of people who meet every two weeks and they have artists who do work with them. I think it would help.

Molly was always the one to call it. She'd said from the beginning something was wrong with Deena's relationship with Lucas, that she didn't like what was happening. She had never stopped being Deena's best friend. Nessa loved her intensity and candour, her thick eyeliner and bright-red lipstick and her ability to always be herself. Being with her was as close as she could get to being with Deena.

There's something else, Nessa. David and I have been talking about the stuff with Ruby, and he has a suggestion that would at least help you know what's happening in her life.

Molly had married a lawyer. David was straitlaced and quiet. Nessa liked him, loved watching him watch Molly. He hung on her every word, revelled in her, especially when she was being irreverent or outrageous.

What?

A private detective. David knows a really good one. If it's ripping your heart out that you don't know what's happening to Ruby, this way you can still be sort of a guardian. At least from a distance. You'd know how she is, if she seems okay, if there's anything you should be concerned about, like abuse or neglect, her living conditions.

Molly took a card out of her purse. David knows this guy. He was a few years ahead of him in law school.

Talking about Ruby still made Nessa feel like she couldn't breathe in, as if someone had stepped off the see-saw and dropped her to the ground.

Something has to change, Molly said. These are two things to make a start. Help her, even from a distance, and please, for God's sake, help yourself.

Henry Crofton opened the glass door into his office. He was wearing a pinstripe suit, cufflinks, designer glasses. His law degree hung on the wall alongside his membership to the Pennsylvania Association of Licensed Investigators.

Henry put out his hand: David and I spoke. I am so sorry for the loss of your sister. Nessa wanted to hug him. People tended not to mention Deena to her at all because they didn't know what to say.

Have a seat.

He gestured toward two dark-blue armchairs away from the desk, beside the window. A coffee pot and two cups in saucers sat on a table between them.

Why don't we get started? he said. I've read all the paperwork. Your sister's history with Lucas Chevalier, the PFAs and reports. I've reviewed your applications for visitation and access. I've seen the restraining order against you and note you now have a criminal record.

The way he said it didn't feel accusatory. It was like he understood.

The first question I ask clients is: What do you want from this process?

David had told her she would be asked this, to go in prepared.

In the big picture, I want to know about her well-being. Is she being looked after? Are there any signs of neglect? Does she have opportunities to socialize? Is there anything that might help us if we renewed our application for third-party visitation? I want this to be long-term. If it's the only way I can watch her grow up, then so be it. I've made a list. Nessa took the sheet of paper she had prepared out of her bag and read out what she'd written:

I want to see her. Photographs.

I want to know if she's still living in the same house with Lucas and his mother.

I want to know what school she goes to.

If possible, I want to know how she is doing in school.

I worry about her socially. Ruby was gregarious and outgoing. She was part of a large extended family. I don't know what she'll be like after all this time with people like Lucas and Clover. People who don't mix.

This is Ruby's world now, so I want to know if she has friends and maybe even a little bit of information about them, you know, but not anything that violates their privacy or rights. I mean just general stuff.

She held Henry's gaze. Do you think I'm awful to suggest spying on children?

169

We wouldn't call it spying. Information about someone's well-being is vigilance. It is a duty of care that has been denied you by the commonwealth. We do custody work all the time. We'll be co-ordinating with another office in Vermont so that we can use someone who is there, someone familiar with Vermont legislation, who will become familiar with Ruby, her friends, Mr Chevalier and his mother, will recognize them and reassure you or alert you and the authorities if there is reason for concern.

It won't be you?

No. I'm not licensed there. It's better for us to work with a person on the ground, especially if it's long-term. They'll know the area, the state law, get to know the subjects. Someone experienced in surveillance.

Nessa hadn't asked him yet about his fee. She wanted the arrangement to be long-term but had no idea how much it would cost.

Nessa watched him as he spoke. He was maybe just a few years older than her, earnest and upright, sitting forward in the chair.

Is there anything else?

Oh. Yeah, sorry. I want to know if he has friends that come to the house. Anyone who might put Ruby in danger or be a potential ally. I want to know if he has a girlfriend and, if so, who she is, so we can warn her about him and what he's like. It's not to be vengeful. If someone had told us that he had a previous history – you know, before my sister – it might have persuaded Deena to get out earlier.

Before they finished, Henry brought up the costs.

We do long-term contracts, and it does help mitigate the fee. There may be times when you want us to do an intervention, make an application to the state or county. Those are additional costs if we have to involve a legal team in Vermont. But for surveillance, to see her four to five times a year, not just in photographs but substantive information about contacts, activities, memberships et cetera, it will be a flat rate of approximately ten thousand dollars per year. We can make a payment plan.

Nessa calculated in her head. Ten years until Ruby was eighteen: $100,000. When their father had died, Joey had got the business and the house, and paid out $75,000 to be split between Nessa and Ruby, who would also share the assets of John and Maria Garvey. Nessa had been executor. The total each was approximately $125,000.

The service the agency provided was more than just checking up on Ruby; it included continuous checks on Lucas Chevalier, document retrieval and so forth.

That's fine. I can pay that, she said.

Leaving Henry's office, she felt good for the first time in as long as she could remember. She was doing something. Henry Crofton had made it clear that this was the right thing for Ruby's well-being. She was doing it because Deena couldn't. She had no choice.

Joey and Kate lived in the *home house*, as their dad had called it, the house they all grew up in. Before they got married, Nessa had cleared out the room she and Deena shared growing up. She couldn't bring herself to look at individual things. She just put everything in boxes and suitcases and dragged it all into the garage. At some stage she would look at everything, all the photographs, certificates, drawings, ticket stubs. She would keep it all for Ruby. Now Joey had asked her to collect the boxes. They were renovating the garage and maybe it was time for Nessa to sort through things. She wasn't sure if she could tell Joey that she'd hired a PI. He only wanted to talk about Deena before she met Lucas, from school and the neighbourhood. He got agitated when Nessa brought up the investigation or Frank Capione or Ruby. When Nessa pulled into the driveway, Kate was kneeling by a flower bed across the lawn.

Nessa parked and walked over. Kate stood, her T-shirt stretched outward by her expanding belly. She pulled off pink gardening gloves.

I know, she said, laughing. Joey insists I wear them. He's convinced that all the neighbourhood cats are going in our garden. Letting him read pregnancy books was a mistake. He worries about soft-serve, mercury in fish, cheese. Everything.

Kate rolled her eyes but was obviously elated. For a flash of a moment Nessa remembered Deena pregnant with Ruby here on this front lawn, laughing.

Nessa hugged her. You're really showing now. How're you feeling?

Yeah. Good.

How was Ireland?

Beautiful. Except Joey driving. All those turns.

Nessa remembered the trip she'd taken with Ronan, how only one car could pass on some back roads and they'd had to reverse.

Plus, Joey insisted on renting a manual transmission. Like he would lose face with the Irish. So basically Joey was learning to drive stick with me nauseous beside him.

Where'd you go?

Oh, you know, different places. You should ask Joey. He's inside.

Kate put her gloves back on and Nessa realized she was saying: Talk to your brother about Ireland, not me. Why?

Joey was sitting at the kitchen table with a pile of envelopes and papers in front of him.

Hey Joey.

He stood and gave her a big hug that lifted her feet off the floor.

What's up, girl?

How was your trip?

Good. Good. How'd you survive the heat?

You know me. Just stayed the hell out of it.

Did ya see Kate?

Yeah. On my way in. Again Nessa had the feeling that questions about the trip were being dodged. Where'd you go in Ireland? You never really said.

Loads of places, you know. Touristy things, like the Cliffs of Moher. What did you get up to?

You were in Clare?

Yeah, and in Galway and Dublin.

Did you stay in Clare?

Joey didn't say anything for a second. Did Kate say something to you?

What the hell, Joey? Why are you being so goddamn cagey? It's just a question.

Joey looked away.

Okay, so you saw Ronan. Is he there now or something?

I didn't want to say.

You didn't want to say that Ronan lives in Clare?

No. He doesn't. He lives here still, in the city. We went over for his wedding. He asked me to be in it.

What? There was sudden pressure in her forehead. She couldn't think.

Yeah. I know. I should've told you.

Why didn't you?

I didn't want to get you upset – you know, the way you've been.

What way?

Nessa. Don't. I don't want to get into this.

No, Joey, you said it. What way that I've been?

Like this, Nessa. Just weird and insane about everything.

I'm being insane right now? Seriously?

Shit. No. I didn't mean it like that.

Show me the pictures.

No. Nessa, just leave it.

Is it that architect he used to live with? Aisling?

What? No.

Joey. Please just let me see the pictures. Did Ronan say not to or something?

Ronan has never mentioned you to me since Dad's funeral. Not once, ever.

When he said it, the finality of it hurt her. As if the sun had just clouded over, a chill went through her.

I'm asking Kate . . . because you're a fucking asshole.

She was sure now she wouldn't tell him about hiring Henry. He'd say it was more evidence of her being crazy and obsessive.

Outside, Kate was still weeding.

Nessa shouted from the porch. Kate. Can I see the photos of Ronan's wedding?

Kate didn't seem surprised.

Yeah. Okay.

Nessa flicked through the pictures. The green landscape, the grey of the sky and stones, the sea in the distance. She tried to feel jealousy, wanted to say something mean, but instead she looked at Ronan in his black suit, his younger siblings surrounding him, the smile that lit his face, his tenderness to those around him, and she just felt overwhelming loss. She tried to focus on the bride but couldn't assemble her features into a coherent picture. She could see that she was beautiful, dark hair and eyes, but couldn't see her. Not properly.

Where in Ireland is she from?

Kate laughed. Sinead's from Morristown, New Jersey. Her parents are Irish – the mother's also from Clare. That's why they did the wedding there. Plus all the little ones in Ronan's family. It would have been a lot to organize them to travel.

Yeah, said Nessa, and felt a stab of regret. She remembered Ronan's siblings, that Christmas before Deena disappeared. Their adoration of Ronan, who had a different father and was years older.

How they kept getting out of bed to sit on the sofa with him, sit in his lap. He'd want kids too.

They met here?

Yeah. Sinead does something in financial services, like investments or lending or something. She did an MBA at Wharton.

It was hard to imagine Ronan with an investment banker type. Wealthy. Nessa just about met her mortgage each month. Joey had told her repeatedly to clear out Deena and Ruby's rooms and rent them. She couldn't. She vacuumed them once a month. She'd even replaced Nemo after he died. Their rooms were spaces where she could be with them. And what if Ruby came back?

Do you like her?

She's nice, Kate said. But different. Different to us, anyway. Me and Joey. Sort of socially or something. We don't really fit in with all their friends. Ronan and Joey are still tight, but it's like we'd want to get a few master's degrees or something.

It didn't seem like Ronan. Are they pregnant or something? It seems a bit sudden.

It's not, really. They've been together for like two and a half years. I doubt they're pregnant. I was the only one not drinking at the wedding. Kate took the photos out of Nessa's hand and slipped them back into the envelope. Anyway, they're the type that plans. You know. Have everything in place first.

Yeah, Nessa said, as if she knew them as a couple. An ache deep in her sternum pressed outward, crushing across the cage of her ribs. Ronan was married.

Nessa had expected to walk into something like an AA meeting from a television drama – a dark and dingy basement room, thick bitter coffee from Styrofoam cups, metal chairs arranged in a circle with a bare bulb swinging above them. Instead, the room was upstairs.

It had bright, high ceilings with full-length windows overlooking a garden on Penn's campus.

It's the geology garden, said a woman standing beside her, offering her a coffee in a blue-green glazed mug.

Nessa thanked her. I went to college here and never noticed it.

I worked here twenty-two years. Maintenance and grounds. I could walk around that garden in my sleep. Ten boulders, one for each geological period.

I'm embarrassed I don't know that.

They should make it mandatory for students to know that stuff. I could give the tour. I'm Jessie. I lost my son a few years ago. She reached and squeezed Nessa's forearm. It's good you're here.

The writer was Southern. His words slow and unhurried. Nessa was so used to how people in Philly spoke, her family – fast, blurted out, unconscious. This man weighed each word. He was early forties, maybe. Handsome. He read some of his poetry. It was about his brother. Why couldn't Deena have met someone like him? After the reading he introduced the workshop. They talked about memory. What we remember, what we forget. A woman, younger than Nessa, said she felt like she wasn't allowed to remember her son. She worried that people were sick of her talking about him. It was all she wanted to do. Nessa could feel herself nodding. Their writing task was to list specific details from before, things they wanted to hold on to about the deceased, things that made them feel good. They were going to begin each item in the list with *I remember* . . . For this exercise, the writer said, maybe avoid the remembering that is too painful.

He read several pieces that previous groups had wanted to share with others in grief. Nessa listened. They were poetic; the writer read them slow, lists and lists of ephemeral moments. The repetition of I remember, the specific details. Nessa looked around the room at the others and wondered if she was the only one without a body to grieve. She thought how strange it was that she envied them their

176

finality, the irrevocable deadness of the body they mourned. After the article about Deena's mental health, she'd stopped telling people about what had happened in case they thought what it had said was true, that Deena had just left of her own accord and that Nessa was a grief imposter or something.

It was hard to think back to the time that pre-existed Lucas, the memories that he could not ever touch, the things that belonged to just her and Deena. The writer had said to take half an hour. Nessa pulled her chair to the window and concentrated on the bare branches, the clumps of leaves gathered at the base of the trees, the autumn light hitting the side of a grey boulder. Deena was all her earliest memories. Around her she could hear pens and pencils against paper. She had to start somewhere.

I remember there were leaves on the ground and you were holding hands in a circle of friends across the schoolyard, and I was happy just to know you were there in the distance.

I remember that I had a mullet in all my kindergarten pictures because you gave me a haircut before my first day. I remember that you hid the hair cuttings in your bottom drawer.

I remember you buried me in the sand in Ocean City and you put seaweed around my head for long hair because I wanted to look like you.

I remember the glow of our room at night when you read under the covers with your flashlight. I remember that sleeping between you and the wall was comfort. I remember now that it is you I have slept beside more than anyone else in my life.

I remember you shaved my legs first for practice and took a strip off my shin. I remember you bandaged me with gauze like I was a wounded warrior.

I remember you loved Bon Jovi passionately and then later passionately denied it.

I remember hot days when we got water ice from Rita's and sat on the swings in the park, the red colour dripping down our hands.

I remember you cried when Mom said it was time to wear a bra.

I remember when you laugh how the sound bubbles and that you bend your head to the side as though shy to have revealed that part of you.

I remember the weight of your hand on my head, French-braiding my hair, and I remember its grip walking up the steps to the first day of school.

I remember you sewed handbags for me and my friends from old jeans with beads and flower patches stitched on.

I remember that for every photograph of you there is a photograph of me in the same outfit a few years later.

I remember when I got drunk at Anna Murphy's house you came and got me and brought me to the park until I was sober enough to sneak back inside the house.

I remember the first time I saw you holding Ruby and when I think of that I remember that I have two griefs.

I remember the three of us together driving in the car along the river, windows down, singing 'Kiss Me' by Sixpence None the Richer, and Ruby knew the words, or her version of them.

I remember I can't get you back, or her.

I remember every fucking day, forever, that I must help her to remember you.

Nessa put the pen and paper down and held her head in her hands, concentrating on not tearing up in front of people she did not know. She was biting her bottom lip so hard she could taste blood.

Late that afternoon, Henry Crofton called her at work. He had pictures, he said, and information.

Ruby isn't enrolled in school. By law she should have started at age six.

She turned eight in January, Nessa said. She should be starting third grade.

There's more. Lucas Chevalier has not filed his curriculum with the State of Vermont for home-schooling. This is where you exercise due vigilance. We report this to the Department for Children and Families and help ensure she is either enrolled or that a curriculum is registered with the state that meets the official criteria. There is further scope here to report concerns about her social and emotional development and opportunity to mix with peers.

She needs us, said Nessa. Whatever we have to do.

Okay, said Henry. We can start that process straight away. There's two parts. We file a complaint with the claim of educational neglect and then we also file a complaint with Family Services about Ruby's right to play and socialize that's not being met. The latter complaint might impinge on the first and force his hand a bit. If she goes to school, he kills two birds with one stone and in the long run it's probably best for her.

Yes, Nessa said. I want to do this immediately.

Okay. We'll need to make an appointment to get you to sign the paperwork.

Henry?

Yes?

Can I see the pictures?

They were put through your letterbox at home earlier today.

Oh my God. I'm kind of overwhelmed. I haven't seen her in over four years.

I know.

Nessa hung up and walked back home. Ruby hadn't been in school. What had been happening to her during that time? She had to see her, hold the tangible proof that she existed.

Two large photographs were in the envelope between sheets of cardboard. One looked like it had been taken at a traffic light: Ruby, in the passenger seat of a car – Nessa recognized it as the old Pontiac she'd seen parked outside the house – the grandmother driving, but in shadow and hard to see. In the picture the windows are rolled down, the shot in profile, as if taken from another car. Ruby is talking, her face animated, her mouth wide open, a gasp of breath or a smile, or both. Her hand is out the window. She is tanned and looks just like Ruby from four years ago. Spirited and chatty. The second photograph stopped Nessa's breath. Ruby and Lucas, in a boat, Lucas's back to the camera as he steers the boat away from what looks like a gas pump at a pier. Ruby is staring toward the shore, toward the camera. She looks older than her eight years. The eyes are shadowed. Hair loose. Face serious. Pensive. Something care-worn or resigned, like the expression of an old woman.

16

Ruby

2016

What was your mother's last name? Nathalie whispered to her at the lockers.

Ruby froze. She'd avoided talking about her mother to Nathalie since she'd googled her. It had been three years, and she'd hoped that not talking about her had made Nathalie forget.

Why?

Google.

Don't.

Was it Chevalier?

I don't think they were married.

Ruby's heart raced. She didn't want Nathalie to look her mother up. Instead of saying that, she turned and walked away.

Every time she thought about it for the rest of the day, a surge of terror squeezed her chest. Nathalie was going to read all that stuff about her mother and Lucas. And more. Ruby hadn't looked further. What if there was even worse stuff she hadn't read. She didn't want to know. What if Nathalie found her mother? Knew who she was now, without Ruby?

Nathalie wasn't on the bus the next morning. She wasn't at the lockers at first period. When she came into language arts class late, she didn't take the seat next to Ruby, where she always sat. At lunch Ruby sat on a different side of the cafeteria from their usual seats. Sophie and Nathalie were together at the hot food counter but Ruby pretended not to see them. Sophie spotted her anyway and slid her tray next to Ruby's. Nathalie sat across from Sophie and mumbled, Hey.

Sophie was oblivious to it all.

Nathalie, look. Sophie squeezed Ruby's bicep. Ruby's become an athlete. She said it as if it were a disappointing thing. There was hardly a day since high school started where Ruby didn't do something connected to rowing. She was on the river, and when the river was too cold and the water rough she rowed on ergometers and did weights. She'd started running. She's even sitting on the jocks' side of the cafeteria today, said Sophie.

Blame Nathalie, said Ruby. She made us be joiners.

Nathalie didn't laugh or add anything. She and Ruby ate in silence while Sophie talked. Ruby pushed back her chair from the table and lifted the beige plastic tray. She said something about getting her books and left. Nathalie followed.

Ruby spun around when they were in the hallway. What?

Here. Nathalie unzipped her backpack on the floor and pulled out an envelope. I'm giving this back to you to keep. I can't keep it in my room anymore.

You can't keep my mother's letter anymore?

No. It shouldn't be in my house. And anyway, it's not a letter. It's a picture. Anybody could have sent it. Her tone was defensive, as if Ruby had asked her to believe a lie. Nathalie wouldn't look at her.

Ruby said nothing, just took the envelope and slipped it between the pages of her chemistry book.

That afternoon, walking alone across the football field toward the gym, Ruby turned several times, certain someone was behind her. Maybe Nathalie, coming to apologize, but there was no one, just cropped grass, and a plume of birds rising out of the brambles that edged the school. Her chest ached. It seemed unfair. She'd said not to look her up. She hadn't said her mother's last name. Ruby didn't know what Nathalie had read but she knew she'd looked her up and didn't want to have anything more to do with her because her mother was sick or because there were things said about Lucas.

182

It was Nathalie who had started the Memory Games, had pushed Ruby to try to remember.

For several days Nathalie sat separate from Ruby and Sophie on the bus.

What's wrong with the two of you? Sophie asked.

Ruby shrugged. I don't really want to talk about it.

Yep. Fine with me, said Sophie. You know how I hate drama.

Ruby almost smiled. Sophie thrived on it.

Lucas was relentless. Ruby's driving test was in a week and it didn't matter that she had driven since she was young – in fields and on logging roads, round and round parking lots on Sunday afternoons – they'd still look for reasons to fail her, he said. Not stopping long enough at a stop sign, not checking your rear-view mirror, tailing a car in front; the slightest thing that will give them an excuse so you have to pay the government for another test. They had practised parallel parking, changing lanes, and four-way stop signs. Ruby begged for a break. He cracked a smile and they stopped for pastries and coffee. Then it was straight back to three-point turns, parallel parking and merging into traffic. Ruby had just pulled onto Route 2 when Lucas's phone pinged. He bent over it, lifting his hand to try to block out the light.

Christ, he spat. Christ Almighty. Drive, Ruby. Step on it. Home.

Is Clover okay?

Someone's outside the house.

And Ruby knew that the cameras had alerted his phone. Nathalie had told her that's how they worked.

Ruby pushed the gas. She was already going forty, the speed limit. She watched the speedometer crawl up to fifty.

Faster, Ruby, faster. I said step on it. Lucas was pushing the heel of his hand against the dashboard, as if it would make the truck accelerate harder.

She was going sixty. Then seventy. Her hands started to feel slippery on the wheel and she had to slow down.

Fucking bastard!

Ruby turned onto the road toward the house, checking her mirror as she cornered, though Lucas wasn't watching her anymore. His eyes were fastened to the phone. Dust rose in her wake as the engine geared up again and she pushed the pedal toward the floor. Lucas turned to the rack behind their heads and took down the rifle.

Faster, he said.

Ruby's vision started to waver on the periphery. She could feel panic building up, like she would crash if she turned her head or loosened her grip on the wheel. He reached under the seat and pulled out a box of rounds and loaded three.

What is it? Ruby said. What?

Just drive.

She turned onto their road. Was something happening to Clover? They were a few hundred yards from the house.

The truck was bouncing around the road. Usually Lucas would say something about the axle. The rifle sat in his elbow, the barrel pointing toward the floor. Ruby's foot hovered over the brake; she'd have to slow down soon.

Stop! Lucas shouted.

Ruby slammed the brake. The truck fought on, crunching in the dust and cinders until they came to a final halt, skidding sideways.

Out. Get out, go into the woods and stay down. Do you hear me? You stay down until I tell you to come out.

Ruby opened the door, stumbled through brambles and down a small embankment into the trees. Lucas slid over to the driver's seat and accelerated forward.

Ruby staggered about a hundred yards through the undergrowth and crouched down, her breath ragged. She couldn't be seen here. All around her were sprouting jewelweed leaves. In late summer they would bloom in fiery tangled thickets. Her heart pounded and she pulled her T-shirt over her knees, trying to make herself into a small ball. She touched a leaf. Her first week in Miss Bukowski's class at Middle Lake. A nature walk to Champlain down a side road brimming with jewelweed. October. Miss Bukowski had told them it was called touch-me-not, because the seedpod exploded when grazed or brushed against. They'd all scrambled through the hedges, torn pods from pale-green stems, laid them in open palms and pressed stubby fingers against the casing, watching the seeds hurtle out of their hands. She rubbed her open hand, her chin on her knees, and rocked slightly.

A car was speeding back up the road. Was it Lucas? She huddled lower. It was close, driving fast, a flash of green in the haze. She stayed perfectly still. Heard it take the turn on the second road. She didn't move until Lucas called her name. Her legs were scratched and small streaks of blood trickled from her thighs to her ankles. They were shaking. She walked toward his voice and met him coming, still holding the rifle.

Did he see you? Lucas grabbed her elbow. Did he see you? Ruby. Answer me.

Ruby was trying to say no. She'd lost her breath. Lucas was angry. The veins on his neck bulged and moved under the skin.

No. Ruby shook her head and tried to say the words, He didn't see me. But they were swallowed by the black hole rising from her stomach. Lucas was furious. His face thunderous and dark. No, she tried to say again.

Have you ever seen him before? A green car anywhere near the house? Lucas was shouting.

No! came out as a choking sob. She could never tell him.

Lucas let go of her elbow. Brushed his shirt with his hand. Wiped his forehead.

Ruby took several steps back from him, her arms crossed.

185

Stop it. Stop. He's gone. He was annoyed with her for being upset. He stepped toward her. She flinched. He exhaled and took a few steps back and reset the safety on the rifle. Calm down. It's nothing, he said. Just some out-of-towner tearing up side roads. I'll talk to Ethan and we'll watch out for him. I don't think he'll be back here anyway. If you see that car or any car around here you let me know straight away.

She shook her head yes. Lucas kept looking at her as if checking to see that she meant it.

I'll have to get you a phone. After lunch we'll head to Burlington. You drive and we'll get a phone. That way, when you're away rowing or if you're out driving and have car trouble, you can call me. And if you see someone around here who shouldn't be.

Okay, Ruby said.

Okay, then. He patted her back. You better get up to the house. Don't worry Clover about this.

Lucas dropped her to the high school at five in the morning. When they pulled into the parking lot there was a coach waiting, its undercarriage open. The students were loading their bags.

That's a pretty big bus for a small team, Lucas said. Where's the minivan?

The swim team are travelling with us. They have a meet in Boston.

The swimmers were loud. They told stories, shouted, sang, made jokes, showed each other stuff on their phones. Ruby knew some of them from classes but had never really talked to any of them. Wyatt Smith was sitting a few rows back; he had been at Middle Lake, a grade above her. One of the boys who had played Destroying Angels and Hunger Games with her and Nathalie.

The bus dropped the rowers at the lake in Worcester and went on to Boston. Ruby raced late that afternoon. She could never really remember details, what she did or didn't do. At the stake boats she concentrated on the space just in front of her. Then the adrenalin surge in those first few seconds, quick out but measured, nothing crazy, and then into the rhythm, watching buoys, ensuring she was steady on the course. In every race she counted strokes because it calmed her and helped her manage oxygen. But the details floated past. The shell beside her, people shouting from the riverbank, a bird. She knew when she was sculling well, when everything was fluid and not separate – catch, drive, finish, recover – like one sweeping motion and one stroke into the next, with no beat between. She could see she was putting distance between herself and other scullers but she didn't notice how much. She didn't know she'd won until she looked around and someone said it.

That night she was in the hotel room alone, half-watching a sitcom from the nineties she couldn't name, when the bedroom phone rang. She wasn't sure she should answer it.

Hello?

Hi. Yeah, is Ruby there? It was a boy's voice. Familiar.

This is Ruby.

It's Wyatt. You know, from Middle Lake? The swim team? There's a bunch of us in my room and we think you should come over.

Oh.

Yeah, you should come out and celebrate your win.

I'm not sure, she said.

Ruby never went to other people's rooms, although she knew some of the others did. It was nine o'clock, half an hour past the curfew. She was about to say she couldn't, but changed her mind. She never did anything. Never went to parties. Nathalie barely spoke to her anymore. Lucas was far away. He would never find out.

You should come. Just for a little bit.

What room?

187

Two-oh-three.

Okay.

Wait, Ruby. Uh, can you bring your own glass from your bathroom? We don't have cups.

She changed out of her pyjamas into jeans and a paisley-green halter-style top that Sophie had made from scarves. Her nose and cheeks were slightly pink from being outdoors all day. She wore her hair down and put on the choker Sophie had crocheted.

She took the stairwell in case she met Coach Morgan or chaperone parents, sliding one hand along the banister, holding the glass from her bathroom in the other. Outside 203 she could hear talking and laughter. She knocked. There was no answer. When she knocked again, it went completely silent. Someone was scuffling on the other side of the door and she stood back from the peephole so they could see it was her. Then the door swung open and Wyatt was standing there with a bottle of vodka in his hand.

Quick, get in.

There were five people in the room. No rowers. Ruby recognised one of the girls as a sophomore but didn't know her. There were two double beds. The others were sitting or lying on them, except one guy at the window. A small speaker on the bedside table was playing music low. For an uncomfortable moment everyone was looking at her.

You look so different like that, said the girl sitting on the bed closest to her. With your hair down and not in gym stuff.

Ruby didn't know where to look.

Fill her glass, someone said. Let her sit down.

There were three girls, including her, and three guys. Ruby remembered everyone from the bus except the guy by the window. He was looking at her as if expecting something, like for her to say hello or recognize him. His hair was longish compared to everyone else's. He was tall, maybe six foot, and pale. He had a black stud in each ear and a thick silver chain around his neck. He didn't look like Wyatt or any of his friends. He didn't look like he'd hang out with the swim team.

Great race today, Ruby, he said.

Thanks? She didn't know how he knew her.

You don't remember me?

She shook her head. Sorry. Are you in one of my classes?

No.

Butler, give her a drink, said Wyatt.

Butler . . . She was trying to think. Was it Tim Butler from Middle Lake?

You're Tim Butler?

Yeah. It's me. He laughed. Uncertain. She remembered that about him. Assured and funny but not too much.

God. Hi. You left in third grade. You look so different. Wait, actually you look the same. Just older.

He did look the same. He was wearing faded jeans that hung loose, a Green Day T-shirt. That thrown-together, almost negligent look, like when he'd come into Miss Bukowski's class with sweatpants several inches too short for him and a sweater that obviously belonged to his mother.

Yeah. You look different too.

Why are you here?

I live here. Like less than a mile away. I went to see Wyatt swim and then we went down to the rowing.

It was awkward talking in front of everyone and Ruby sidestepped the beds and stood beside him at the window.

Do you want to have a drink? he asked. Or just soda? Seeing as you're an athlete and all that.

Yeah. She held out her glass. Vodka and Coke.

The bathroom sink was full of ice. A fifth of vodka and a plastic bottle of Coke were lying on top.

Tim poured the vodka first, about a third of the way. He filled the rest with Coke. Just go slow, you know . . . if you haven't drunk before.

Does it seem like I haven't?

Maybe?

They sat on a wide windowsill leaning against the glass and reminisced about Miss Bukowski's class, the wars they'd fought. He told her about high school in Massachusetts, how big the school was. Bands he liked. Concerts he'd been to. He played the guitar.

Ruby took a swig of the drink in her hand. Her eyes smarted for a second but it didn't taste bad. She liked the trail of heat it left in her throat.

I go to the Islands every summer for a few weeks, Tim said, and during vacations to see my dad. He still lives there. I've actually seen you a few times.

Ruby thought he must be wrong. She didn't ever hang around with Wyatt's crowd and she and her group of friends barely did anything.

Where?

On the lake. A few times by yourself. I saw you once in the co-op in Burlington.

Oh. Wyatt was kissing the girl who was a junior on the far bed. The other two were showing each other stuff on their phones and laughing.

Had they been paired off or something? She had a flash of discomfort and finished the rest of her drink. Tim noticed.

Sorry. Like on behalf of Wyatt. Do you want another?

Yeah, please.

They went back into the bathroom.

Is this awkward?

Sort of. I don't know anyone.

Me either, he said. Except Wyatt. He poured her another drink. Let's talk in here.

She lowered the lid of the toilet and sat down. He sat on the floor with his back to the sink. He told her about Worcester and Boston, what he missed.

Vermont. Not my dad or anything. Just being on the Islands. The remoteness. Being one of the few that winter it out.

Rugged and rude. That's us. It was Lucas's phrase and saying it made her think of him. For a second there was a flicker of guilt.

Tim laughed. Yeah, that's what flatlanders say about you. Us. He took a drink from his glass. I don't know. I liked that feeling of belonging there. I've never had that here as much.

Ruby listened. The vodka had warmed her chest and stomach. She didn't feel self-conscious. She liked this.

What time is it? she asked when she knew it must be late.

He checked his phone. Almost midnight.

How will you get home?

Walk. Uber.

The hotel phone rang and she could hear Wyatt answer it. Then he said loud enough for them to hear, Party's over. The chaperones are back.

By the time Ruby came back into the room, the other two girls were gone.

I'll go with Ruby, Tim said. Thanks, man. He gave Wyatt a tap on the shoulder.

See ya in a few weeks, Wyatt said.

Ruby walked down the corridor with Tim. He stopped at the elevator.

No, the stairwell, said Ruby. Chaperones won't take the stairs. They reached the landing and stood at the door for a second. She could feel the effects of the vodka, but just at the edges. She wasn't drunk. Maybe you shouldn't come into the hall in case someone sees you.

Yeah. You're right.

191

Okay, then. Thanks.

Do you think we could meet up this summer? When I'm back at my dad's?

She dropped her gaze to his T-shirt. The red heart grenade gripped in the white hand.

I don't know, she said. Lucas probably wouldn't let her hang out with Tim Butler; she was barely allowed to hang out with the friends she'd been with all along since third grade. She felt both good and like she might burst into tears. Maybe?

Yeah. Well, you've had a stellar day.

I guess, she said.

Would it wreck it if I kissed you?

It took her a second to process what he'd asked.

No? She lifted her face and Tim Butler's lips touched hers, gently. He held both sides of her face. She closed her eyes, thinking he would keep kissing her the way couples did at the back of the bus, how Wyatt had with the girl on the bed. But he pulled back.

Well, he said, see you sometime in the summer.

Yeah, like maybe at the co-op.

And that was it.

17

Ruby

2016

Chemistry was last period on Thursday. Ruby double-checked the lever to the gas line on the Bunsen burner and dropped her lab goggles in the box. She was putting her lab book into her backpack when she saw Nathalie through the window, then pretended she hadn't, concentrating on her books, rearranging them in the bag. The room had emptied but she sensed Nathalie there beside her table.

Hey.

Ruby zipped the bag. Hi.

I'm sorry, Nathalie blurted out.

Ruby didn't look at her. She tugged on the zipper of her bag, which had caught on the material.

I'm not supposed to talk to you about your mom and my parents have said I am not supposed to tell you that I looked up your mom or what I read.

Ruby felt prickly all over her body. There was an announcement on the intercom, something about soccer, but the sound was swallowed by the whooshing in her ears.

What?

I had to tell them. I'm sorry but I didn't know what else to do.

Tell them what?

About your mother missing.

But they know that already.

No. Really missing. I did google her. Deena Garvey. She went missing in February 2004. The eighth of February. She didn't leave. She disappeared. Everyone was looking for her. *In Philadelphia.*

Nathalie blurred standing there in front of Ruby, her dark hair pulled off her face, her eyes made big by her glasses with the thick lenses. Like looking at the bottom of two Coke bottles, that one, Lucas had said. Ruby focused on the Periodic Table posted on the wall. *Boron family, Group 13. Ga – Gallium. An element that looks like metal but melts in the heat of your palm or in lukewarm water.*

I told you don't look her up. I already knew.

I'm sorry I didn't tell you and have been avoiding you. I didn't know what to do. My parents will kill me if they find out I told you.

Why would the Hoags be so upset if Nathalie told Ruby something she knew already? Her mother left or her mother went missing didn't seem that different.

They don't want me involved. They're scared of what your dad could do, and they don't want your dad to know I've been talking to you about it.

The Hoags being so weird about Lucas gave Ruby that crawling, grovelling feeling of being dirty.

Nathalie looked in both directions, even though they were the only ones in the room, and then whispered the last bit. There was stuff about your dad in some of the articles.

Nathalie held out her phone.

Ruby could feel the heat in her cheeks. I don't want to see them. I already know. My grandmother was there with me and my dad when my mother went missing. He had nothing to do with it. My mother's alive. She sends packages all the time. Not just that picture. Lucas keeps them. Plus, she's been watching me.

Nathalie stared at Ruby as if she had just said *I see dead people.*

It's real. Not in my head. She's been following me. I mean, someone she knows is. For two years at least. This green car. I wasn't sure at first but now I am.

She was about to say that Lucas knew about it too but she didn't want to tell Nathalie about Lucas chasing him with a gun.

Nathalie didn't believe her. She could tell. Nathalie was about to say something but then decided not to. She kept adjusting her glasses, a fidgety nervous tic she'd always had. Ruby knew Nathalie already regretted telling her anything. Ruby wished she hadn't too.

Okay. Whatever. I just don't want things to be bad between us. Don't tell Lucas I told you this. Or anyone.

I won't.

Promise?

Yeah. Ruby meant it. Why would she? The Hoags' reaction stung her, Nathalie's too, and she remembered that Lucas didn't like them that much. Bumper stickers and placards so everyone knows their politics and their virtue. His instinct was right, really. They did think they were better. The bus is about to leave, said Ruby.

They walked outside toward the pick-up zone. Nathalie had always been her best friend, but Ruby hadn't even told her about Tim and Worcester. Everything had been so weird with her lately. Plus, she didn't want to have to defend herself for going to Wyatt's hotel bedroom or for drinking. Nathalie would moralize, say something like Haven't you seen enough after-school specials to know better?

The sun cast their shadows to the side. Long and short. Ruby's stretched and exaggerated. Seeing their shadows move together on the ground, sometimes overlapping, then separating, made her sad, like she was seeing their past projected at the very same moment they were falling apart.

The early weeks of June had been unusually cool, too cold to seed in the ground. After a stretch of days when there was some heat in the sun Lucas said it was time to set the garden. It was a job Ruby could do the next day. The weather would be good.

Okay.

I've the seeds all labelled, said Clover.

That night Tim Butler sent her a text. *Here in Vermont. Can you kayak to Knight Island tomorrow? Meet N. Hero @ 1?*

She didn't know how to answer. *Okay*, she texted back. She'd get up early and get the garden done. She wasn't sure how to ask Lucas, but when she woke he was already gone. She was digging by seven thirty, turning the soil, mulching, then sowing seeds taken from little brown envelopes, each one carefully labelled in Clover's shaky scrawl. Carrots, bush beans, cucumber. In the final rows she planted the seedlings they'd started in boxes a few weeks earlier. Just before midday she finished. In the shower she scrubbed the dirt under her nails. She put on swim shorts with the high-neck bikini top she wore for training. She pulled her hair into a loose bun on the top of her head and grabbed a backpack. Clover was in the living room watching television.

Clover, I'm going on the lake. Did you have breakfast?

I did.

Don't burn the house down.

Go on, you. And bring that phone like your dad tells you.

She got to the slipway first. A few boats drifted on their lines, the water making gentle slaps against the hulls. It was the first hot day of the summer. Ruby waited in the kayak and tried not to stare when a white SUV pulled into the parking lot. A woman got out and stood on the pier looking over at Ruby, pushing her sunglasses to the top of her head and holding her hand over her eyes to get a better look. Tim was taking the kayak off the roof. The woman waved and Ruby half-waved back, then concentrated on a scar halfway down her shin.

Text me when you're on your way back, the woman called as Tim walked down the ramp.

My dad's girlfriend, he said when his kayak was alongside Ruby's.

He was wearing cut-offs, his legs pale and thin. She looked at her own legs, the bulky muscles. She thought about covering them.

She seems young for a stepmom.

I never really think of her like that.

They paddled toward the island. Ruby fell slightly behind him, watched the shape of his back beneath his shirt, his profile when he went to say something to her over his shoulder. Sometimes they just coasted, letting the kayaks spin slowly in the current.

At Knight Island they pulled the kayaks up toward the trees and threw in their lifejackets.

I have to swim right now, she said. I'm going to pass out.

Me too.

At the water's edge Tim kicked off his sliders and walked with his arms out for balance, dipping and nearly falling. Ruby walked barefoot, straight out.

Show-off, he said.

City boy.

Tim laughed. It's true. This is killing me.

Swimming slowly out of their depth, they treaded water, floated on their backs. Ruby breathed in. All the sounds of the world were muffled. Weightless. The strain of the morning's work lifted away, and all the worry about Nathalie and Lucas and the green car seemed distant.

Tim tugged her foot. I'll race you to that buoy, he said.

About a hundred yards out was a small orange marker.

Okay?

She let him head off. He swam wildly, splashing all around him. Ruby swam a slow breaststroke in his wake. He stopped at the buoy and held on to the base. She reached for it too.

Why aren't you racing? He was out of breath and gasped the words.

You know I'm way faster? she said.

197

Yeah.

Back on the shore Tim picked up pieces of bluestone as they talked, his head bent. He told her about his parents' break-up and leaving Vermont.

My mom's been a mess over it. I guess maybe she was already. It's more in my head that there was this cause and effect.

He skimmed the stone he was holding across the water's surface and it skipped twice.

When I'm up here I stay with them in our old house.

Do you like her?

Sarah? She's okay. Actually, yeah. I like her a lot more than I like my dad. She's the one who invites me up, which is weird, her inviting me to the house that used to be ours.

She looked at the tufts of hair against his neck, his jawline. She was sad for him and yet drawn at the same time. They sat in the sun saying nothing at all, just letting the heat dry them. After a while Tim spread a towel and opened his backpack, taking out a plastic container wedged with wraps, small pitas and crustless sandwiches.

It's like an episode of *MasterChef*, said Ruby.

Sarah. She tries really hard.

I don't even know what's in these, Ruby said, taking a bite.

I don't either, said Tim. But everything she makes is good.

After lunch they lay in the sun for a while. Tim nudged her.

Do you want to go for a walk?

Yeah. She picked up her shoes and followed him. They walked further north along the shoreline.

You've been here before?

Hundreds of times, she said. I've camped here too. Loads.

With friends?

No. With my dad. When I was younger.

That sounds good. I wish I'd done stuff like that.

Yeah, she said. It was.

A speedboat passed dragging an inner tube and made a wide swoop. The passenger screamed as the tube left the surface of the water for an instant.

I've never done that, Ruby said.

I have, said Tim. It's exactly the kind of thing my dad likes to do.

It's exactly the kind of thing my dad hates.

They sat down on a giant piece of driftwood, almost silver in the sunlight, and stared out at the water.

You know I got Wyatt to invite you to his room in the hotel?

Okay?

I'd seen you up here a few weeks before that. In the co-op. I was with Sarah and she wanted me to pick out food I like. My mom doesn't cook, not properly. We'll make stuff from a can, but Sarah makes everything from scratch. My mom says my dad has always wanted a Martha Stewart and that he got one, which I guess he has.

Ruby nodded but had no idea what this had to do with her.

She kept asking me what I liked, and I didn't even know the name of the stuff in front of us. She was getting upset so I said something like pasta with a can of tuna mixed in would do me. It was as if I'd said Let's be cannibals. She thought I was being sarcastic.

Tim was peeling thin strips of bark from the branch beneath them. Ruby watched his hand.

We were standing there in the vegetable section and she was having a meltdown because she's insecure and I was about to have a panic attack because I was asked to name a meal that I liked. It was just a coincidence. Right then I saw you. Pushing your cart, picking out fruit and vegetables, literally knocking on stuff, like you knew what you were doing. Your hair was down. I knew who you were straight away. I wanted to ask you: Tell me what I should say I want to eat. I'm not kidding. You just seemed wise and calm. I thought if I just told you, you would know what I meant.

Snowflake, Lucas would say. When someone said the word *anxiety*

199

or *panic attack* or anything that suggested being psychologically vulnerable, he would say Snowflakes. And she was sure there was something about her mother in there when he said it. Tim was still looking straight out at the lake. He had just been honest about himself, and she felt ashamed that Lucas's word had intruded into her head.

I remembered things about you in the third grade. How your mom was gone. How you were sad. I didn't – I don't – even know you, but I just thought you could keep me breathing or something. It was only recently, like the last year or so, that my dad said your mom went missing when you were little. I never knew that.

There it was. Everyone knew. Sophie probably knew. Ruby and Nathalie had probably been the last to find out. The Hoags definitely must have known, which was why Nathalie wasn't allowed over. *How you were sad.* She hadn't thought about that time when she just slept in the chair. Maybe she'd been missing her mother then. Everyone else knew. Even Miss Bukowski must have. Tim was still talking.

Anyway, I forgot all about it, he said. I told Sarah food decisions stressed me out and I'd eat whatever she made. I didn't even see you leave the co-op. Then Wyatt mentioned you rowing when they were down, and I got him to call your room.

Tim stood up and reached his hand down and pulled her up to standing.

When we did actually hang out that night, it was easy to talk to you. Like from the moment you came into the hotel room.

His hand was holding her wrist. She heard a motorboat in the distance. He'd told her everything he knew about her, and it didn't make her feel ashamed. They kissed. Different to the last time, a real kiss; his tongue pushed against her lips, her tongue. His hand moved to the outside of her swimsuit top, skimmed against the fabric. A rush of heat moved through her lower belly. His lips were on her neck.

The motorboat was closer.

Shit, Tim said. He stepped back.

No one can see us, she said. But the boat came into view and stuttered to a stop. Lucas? She ducked involuntarily. No. The people who'd been tubing.

Come on, he said. We'll go back to our stuff.

They dipped in the water again and sat on their towels. A beetle made its way through the stones, slowly managing all the obstacles in its path. Ruby wanted to kiss again.

Are you okay? Tim asked. Should we go?

Not yet. She moved the edge of her towel out of the beetle's way. Have you had sex before?

What? He started to laugh. Seriously?

Yeah.

Okay. Yes.

Lots?

What does that mean? Like how many times?

Yeah, and like how many people.

Two. The first was a girl I went out with for a year. Until recently. With her a few times. Not that many. The other time was just once. I was drunk. It was embarrassing.

So you were fifteen the first time?

Sixteen. Held back a year.

Same age I am now.

Yeah.

Tim lay on his stomach and turned his face toward her. She lay down and let her cheek rest against the warm stones.

You have freckles across your nose, he said.

Like my mom.

She didn't know why she'd said that. It just came out. She never mentioned to anyone other than Nathalie that she knew what her mother looked like.

Tim started to say something but didn't.

Ruby closed her eyes. The water lapped gently at the lake's edge. A motorboat grumbled far in the distance. The heat of the sun warmed her bare skin. She wished they could stay right there.

It was dusk when Lucas's headlights glanced off the kitchen window. The tyres skidded on the gravel, and even before she heard his feet heavy on the porch steps she knew he was angry. Ruby's insides tightened and the good of the day squeezed out of her. Clover concentrated on stirring a pot, the gas switched off already.

Lucas used silence as punishment; they ate most of the dinner without saying anything.

Ruby waited for it to drop. Whatever it was.

He pointed the fork toward her in his right hand. Where were you today?

Here. Helping Clover, she said. I did the garden like you said then I paddled a bit because it was hot.

Where? The fork was steady in his grip, his body tense; he didn't take his eyes off her and she knew that he knew she'd gone further on the lake.

A flash of panic ripped through her. Someone must have seen her. The boat with the inner tube?

She tried to sound casual. I kayaked up to North Hero.

Where else? He knew.

Knight Island.

By yourself?

Yes, she lied, and held her breath.

Lucas lowered the fork. I gave you that phone so you can ask me when you want to do something like that. So I know exactly where you are.

Ruby exhaled. Clover chased peas around her plate with a spoon and said, We didn't have phones when we were young.

Lucas ignored her, his attention still completely on Ruby. *Do – you – understand?* His words thumped.

Yes, said Ruby.

After dinner she went down to the hens. It was pitch-black and the night crackled with the sound of cicadas and katydids, the call of frogs. Lucas knew she'd gone beyond North Hero. But they hadn't met any boats on the lake. Lucas definitely didn't know Sarah. Ruby hadn't known the people on the inner-tube boat. She bent to lift a Rhode Island Red that hadn't roosted yet and the phone in the front pocket of her shorts dug into her leg. She pulled it out. Would Lucas use her phone to track her?

Earlier, when she'd been in the water with Tim, not long before they'd got out, she'd suddenly swum into a cold patch in the lake. She'd laughed and shouted, Watch out, cold patch, but something had washed through her. Stopped her. An invisible gloom had touched her. She felt it again now: despair was a physical place.

18

Nessa

It's the male seahorse who gives birth. The female deposits her eggs into his brood pouch and they gestate there until he expels them. In one labour he can give birth to over 1,000 fry.

Nessa was about to show the magazine article to Deena but decided against it. Deena hadn't spoken to her since they'd sat down. A lamp on the low table between them cast an amber glow across the walls. There were no windows and nowhere to look, so they both pored over the magazines. Nessa didn't know how to shift the silence. They hadn't had an argument, but the rift was there.

How's work? she asked after a while. Just to say something.

Fine. Busy. Deena didn't look up.

Lucas? Deena knew she didn't give a shit about how Lucas was doing. She paused as if to measure the level of hostility. Nessa tried to look like she cared.

Fine.

Every time Nessa tried to say something real to Deena about Lucas, Deena was defensive and patronizing, as if Nessa would only understand when she had a partner. She couldn't know what it was like between a couple, how they made sacrifices for each other. Every time Deena said *we* or *Lucas says* . . . Nessa couldn't help but eye-roll. He was so obviously a dick. Deena had literally thrown her previous life into a dumpster because he didn't value it. She didn't understand how this man had pushed something between them. They wouldn't even be here now, in the same room, only their mother had asked them both to come with her.

She wanted to go for breakfast after, *just the girls*.

Nessa kept reading. Seahorses also mated for life and woke every morning and did a dance with their partner that could last hours. She checked her watch and let out a loud sigh. Deena didn't even look up.

I'm pregnant, Deena said, her face still in the magazine.

Nessa's chest tightened. She had that teenage feeling like they were in big trouble.

Are you sure?

Of course I'm sure.

What are you going to do?

What do you mean, what am I going to do?

I guess I mean are you keeping it? Nessa was counting. Deena had only known Lucas six months. What was she thinking?

What kind of question is that?

Like, a legitimate question?

I can't believe I tell you this and you can't even say you're happy for me.

I didn't say that in case you *weren't* happy about it. I was trying to figure it out. Jesus. Congratulations, then. I'm happy for you.

I'm not telling anyone for another month. Until I'm twelve weeks. To be sure and everything.

Thank you for telling me. Nessa tried to sound sincere.

I'm only telling you because I'm still getting sick, not just in the morning. In case I have to get up and go to the bathroom suddenly.

Okay. Nessa's head was racing. Deena was young, was relatively new at her job. She barely knew Lucas. How much did he know about her?

Does Lucas know what you went through, the depression and everything?

What do you think? I live with him. I'm about to have a baby with him. Of course he knows. Why would you even bring that up right now?

206

Nessa tried to look back at the magazine. This wasn't how she should have reacted. She tried to restart the conversation on a better footing.

Are you feeling sick all the time?

Mostly.

Is it hard at work?

It's not that bad.

Deena kept reading.

Were you trying to get pregnant? Nessa asked, even though what she wanted to ask was Are you fucking nuts?

Well, I stopped taking birth control. Lucas wanted to start a family. He felt ready.

Did you? Nessa couldn't help herself.

Of course, Deena snapped. We both do. What is wrong with you?

A nurse stepped into the waiting room. Are you here with Maria Garvey? She's awake now and would like you to come back.

Nessa couldn't help watching Deena as they stood, her stomach flat underneath her jeans. A baby growing inside. The first grandchild in their family. Deena had lost weight since she'd moved in with Lucas. She said it was all the walking at the job, that she probably walked seven or eight miles a shift minimum, usually with no proper break to eat. But Nessa blamed Lucas, imagining he was regimental about food. Maybe it was from throwing up with pregnancy. She wanted to whisper to Deena, Oh my God, a baby. Your baby. I will love it like my own, do anything for either of you. But Deena had already walked past her, following the nurse.

Maria Garvey smiled at her daughters. In her blue paper hospital gown she seemed small, diminished. Deena sat next to her on the edge of the bed when the doctor came in to speak to them. They'd found a large mass, he said. It would require surgery. He believed it was cancerous because it had grown so aggressively, but they would have to wait for lab results. Either way, she had to have it taken out.

What? Nessa said. The doctor's voice sounded far away. She sat down on the other side of her mom and put her arm around her. Maria squeezed her hand. But my mom's so healthy.

The symptoms she's been having are consistent with what we found, he said.

What symptoms? Nessa had never heard her mother complain about anything.

Blood in the stool. Bloating. She should have gone to her primary-care physician a long time ago.

For the first time that morning, Deena looked at Nessa directly. She shook her head slightly. She hadn't known either.

The doctor gave Deena cards with the names and numbers of two surgeons he'd recommend. Maria sat there listening, bewildered and a bit frightened, but working hard on smiling. Trying to make it easier for the doctor and for them.

Outside, the sun was blinding. Maria was still groggy from the anaesthetic but she hadn't eaten for three days and said she'd kill for a cup of coffee and a full breakfast.

Somewhere quiet, Deena said.

With good coffee, said Nessa.

No, said Maria. The diner. I want to go somewhere that's noisy and bright and full of people. She didn't want to talk about what was further ahead. We'll figure out the surgery and have breakfast and then you can drop me home. I'll tell Dad and Joey.

They sat in a booth overlooking Route 1. Deena was already on her phone trying to get an appointment with one of the surgeons. They had so many memories from the diner – Sunday mornings after Mass, late nights after a school show, eating bowls of ice cream, their costumes and make-up still on. Nights after being out drink-ing, coming in to sober up on hash browns and toast and coffee before going home. The way it never changed. Her mother's news seemed impossible.

By the time the food arrived Deena had already made an appointment for the surgery. She will be a good mother and this child has been sent now to help us, Nessa thought. Something they could all look forward to together. They barely touched their plates. Nessa studied their six hands on the Formica, hers included, and she had an urge to grab her sister's and mother's, to tell Deena's news, to say how another pair were growing to help them carry this load, and she knew already that there was nothing in this world she wouldn't do for that baby.

Nessa was at her parents' house, downstairs in the basement doing the laundry. Deena came in, her scrubs on, ready for her night shift. Despite the loose top, Deena was starting to show.

She's asleep now, she said. The chemotherapy was proving harder than any of them had imagined and the steroids didn't seem to be helping their mother enough with the nausea and fatigue. Deena picked up a shirt and started folding it. They stood together making the piles. Joey's, Dad's, Mom's.

Vermont was strange, said Deena. She and Lucas had gone up for a week. Nessa was still annoyed. The timing hadn't been good; their mother needed Deena. But Lucas wanted to visit his mother and so that's what Deena did. It pissed Nessa off but she was trying hard not to fight with Deena, not now, with everything that was happening. Deena kept folding, talking to Nessa without looking at her: His mom, Clover, was in the house all the time but they didn't talk or reminisce together, the way we would if people came over and Mom or Dad were there. You know how they'd be gagging to tell stories about us, would be reminding each other of things . . . exaggerating, laughing and contradicting each other. Being loud. In Vermont it was just – I don't know. Quiet. Empty.

Maybe, because she's been alone so long, she's not used to company? Nessa was careful to not say anything to shut the conversation down. It was the first time Deena had ever said anything negative to do with Lucas.

I don't know. The quiet . . . The quiet was oppressive. Like something else. It wasn't me. I think his mom liked me. Something between them. Or maybe she doesn't have the social skills or something for guests. There was just no . . . joking or teasing.

Maybe it's a New England thing – like their Puritan austerity, said Nessa. She didn't know why she was making excuses. Lucas was so obviously just like his mother.

Deena shook her head. I think it's the way they are. There was no one else. No friends came over, no other family. We saw one neighbour drive by in a truck.

She didn't say anything for a few minutes. Nessa set up the ironing board and Deena kept folding.

Something weird happened when I was there. Or I don't know if it's weird or I just feel weird about it. I wasn't feeling good. The whole time I was still getting sick. The wristbands weren't helping. Deena held out her arms. She had red elasticated bands above both wrists that pressed down on a pressure point that was supposed to help with nausea. It was all getting to me, the way the house was, the heat. I don't know. Lucas needed to put up some new fencing down the side of one of the fields that a neighbour was grazing. He needed help. Someone to help steady the posts while he drove them in. It was hot, unusually hot for Vermont, like low nineties.

Deena stopped folding and leaned against the washing machine.

I had to kneel on the ground and hold the posts in position while Lucas stood up on the bank above. He was hitting them hard, swinging the sledgehammer from behind his head, throwing it forward with all his weight. I didn't like it. We had driven five posts and I began to feel really unsettled, and I wanted to stop. I said, I don't want to do this, and he said, What do you mean? I'm not going to hit you. We're nearly done. There's just a few more. I regripped the pole. Like I knew I was being stupid. But when he swung the sledgehammer back again over his shoulder, I let go of the post and screamed, I can't do this. It just came out of me and I jumped back and the metal head of the sledgehammer sailed past my face and hit the ground with a thud where I'd been kneeling. I looked up and Lucas was holding the broken wooden handle.

Oh my God, said Nessa.

I understand what happened. It wasn't like a premonition – it's explainable. Lucas said they know this from hunting, trusting your sixth sense. My sixth sense protected me and the baby, you know, that I had heard the changes in the wood as it started to weaken, but at an unconscious level. My body knew something was wrong even though my head didn't.

That's a good thing, isn't it? Nessa asked, though it didn't sound good at all. She felt there was something she urgently needed to do to help, but what?

Yeah, said Deena. She picked up one of their dad's shirts and was hugging it to her chest. It's just that the whole trip, being in that house, I had that feeling.

Like foreboding?

I don't know, Deena said. She shook out the shirt and laid it on the ironing board. I think I'm just really tired. Anyway, let's get this done. I'm on night shift in a few hours.

Yeah. Nessa picked up a laundry basket to take upstairs.

I told Mom, Deena said as Nessa was about to walk out.

About the sledgehammer?

No. The baby. Just now. I told her.

Nessa put down the laundry basket. What did she say?

She cried. Like happy crying. She asked did I think she would live to see the baby.

19

Nessa

2000

With a newborn, the house was like a cocoon. Everything modulated to a hushed rhythm of feed, change, sleep. Ruby had transformed it, made it feel like a home. In those early days, Lucas was at work and Maria came several times a week, keeping awed vigil over her granddaughter. Nessa visited less often, between classes and whenever she had time. But when she was there she was transfixed: the quiet breath, a stretched limb, a sigh, the flutter of thought under closed eyelids.

The baby had come early, just a few days after New Year's, when Lucas was away in DC. Nessa, Maria and Molly had been in the room with Deena. A girl for the new millennium, said the midwife. They all cheered. Here we are. Us. Welcome. All these women, said Maria, looking around.

Ruby, said Deena, her arms reaching for the body they'd laid across her belly.

Nessa never asked her why the name Ruby and what did it mean. It was just right. Something vibrant nestled deep in the heart of them. Deena held Ruby naked against her bare chest – Let her feel your skin, the midwife said – and Molly snapped a picture.

The miracle was that the baby had arrived when Lucas was away, as if she'd chosen to give them that time together. Deena said Lucas would bring it up after, like she'd conspired to do this with her mother, her sister and her friend. Have the baby without him. Like they were witches that could control a thing like that.

Maria held Ruby on the couch. Deena had nodded off, worn out. How would she cope when she went back to work?

Are you getting any sleep? Maria asked when Deena stirred, yawning and stretching her arms up.

Yeah. Some. I find it hard to fall back asleep after the feeds. Ruby cries.

Maybe she's still hungry?

No. She's full. She doesn't want to be put down.

Even when you lie down with her?

She sleeps in her own room.

Maria was kissing Ruby's fingers. She turned toward Deena.

What? She's only a few weeks in the world; she needs her mother. All of you were in the bed with me.

Lucas has read a lot about it. Researched. It's good for babies to learn to self-comfort. They do better in the long run.

He read that in a book? Maria shook her head. What other species does that? Has a baby and then leaves it in the cave or the burrow next door? And then says, Aren't we great that we've taught it independence at such a young age, just days old.

Deena shrugged. Nessa could see she didn't want to talk about it, like with all things Lucas.

What do *you* want? Maria asked. Deep down, what do you want? Tell me. Maria was looking at her eldest child and she spoke as if she would accept whatever the answer was.

I want her in the room with me. Her cot next to my side of the bed.

Deena just said it out loud. Her honest answer. Nessa looked at her mom, the baldness of her bent head – her earrings, the pencilled suggestion of eyebrows, the mauve lipstick – and the baby in her arms. All that effort, even when she had no hair and the treatment had zapped everything out of her. Her mother had elegance and wisdom and courage. She had just got Deena to admit something, to break ranks with Lucas.

Maria burrowed her face against the baby and Nessa took a picture of their two bald heads, Ruby's small hand cupped against her grandmother's naked scalp; it was as if Ruby's small hand was holding her grandmother's head, reassuring her.

The key turned in the front door and Lucas came in wearing his snow hat and down jacket. He had grocery bags under each arm.

Maria. Nessa.

Nessa said a half-hearted hello and Maria kept her attention on Ruby and said, Now here's your daddy home. Is that your daddy? She murmured in that sing-song voice she used with children.

For a second it annoyed Nessa and then she realized her mother wasn't able to speak to him directly just yet. She was gathering herself after what Deena had said, speaking through Ruby.

I'll just put these away, he said.

Wait, Maria said, her voice commanding.

He stopped.

Lucas, I was just telling Deena that she works with babies, knows all the statistics, the importance of touch. All that experience. She knows what she's doing when it comes to newborns. It's her profession. And she's also a mother. Both she and the baby are stressed when the baby's crying in a separate room at night.

Lucas glanced at Deena. Deena looked toward the hallway.

We're trying something out, creating a safe routine for Ruby, Lucas said. I know it's not everyone's parenting style but we believe it's best.

Maria nodded her head as if she were considering the merits. Lucas was uncomfortable. He shifted the groceries in his arms, as if to say he had to go.

Maria ignored him and started speaking again. It's not best for either of them, though. Is it? Ruby is crying and her mother can't sleep from the ache to hold her. They are both awake in separate rooms wanting each other. She's just days old. Deena's a new mother. It's instinctual. It's natural. Don't come between that.

215

Lucas clearly didn't know what to say. He was always careful around Maria.

When he spoke, it was calm and polite, practically scripted. Thank you for your advice. We want what's best for our daughter and we'll certainly consider what you've said. I better put these away now.

When he left the room, Nessa exhaled, only realizing then that she'd been holding her breath. Their mother could be a force of nature when she felt strongly about something. In her own way she was telling her daughter, in front of Lucas, Never mind what he says. You know better. You're a mother and your instincts are right. For a brief moment Nessa felt like, together, they had taken him down a notch.

I wish this chair was by the window.

Ruby had nodded off while feeding and Deena was rocking slowly back and forth; she spoke absent-mindedly, breathing onto the baby's head.

Nessa stood in the doorway of the little nursery, holding the glass of water she'd brought up for Deena.

Then put it there. I'll move the changing table for you.

No, Deena said, still swaying gently back and forth with Ruby. It's more complicated than just switching them around.

How?

Never mind.

No. How is it complicated? It's straightforward. I'll do it in two minutes.

Lucas doesn't want it like that.

So what?

I already tried. A few weeks before she was born. Lucas was working late, and I put together all the flatpacks. The crib, the wardrobe, the changing table. I had the chair by the window, the chan-

216

ging table over there where the wardrobe is. It was just right, and I sat in the chair and looked out the window. I could see myself there, feeding the baby, watching the world. Anyway, I went to bed and when Lucas came home I heard him at the top of the stairs. He went into the baby's room instead of ours. Like he knew. Like he knew that I'd done something without checking with him first.

Deena stood, took the glass of water from Nessa and handed her Ruby. She fixed her bra strap back on her shoulder.

That night he undid everything, changed everything around. He never said a word. Got into the bed next to me and I lay awake until it was time to go to work.

Nessa could feel the heat flushing into her face.

That's nuts. Seriously, let's just move the furniture.

But it was the wrong thing to say and she could see Deena retreat.

It's important for fathers to feel part of it, said Deena, that they don't feel shut out.

Lately Nessa had tried to keep quiet and neutral when Deena said these things. It was hard for men, Deena explained, they were excluded from so much. It had hurt Lucas to have missed the birth, and it meant a lot to him to be included in decision-making.

Nessa tried to hold her tongue now but couldn't help herself.

So you consulted together and came to the conclusion that his way is best? She couldn't keep the sharpness out of her voice.

Relationships are about compromise, Nessa. You can't always get your own way.

Nessa wanted to roar Well, fuck you. When you were upset about it like two minutes ago, then you were real, and I could deal with you. But this couples-and-relationship slop? Are you kidding me? She wanted to shout it at Deena, but Ruby was there, her small body against Nessa's, her eyes closed, her mouth open.

*

217

Days when Deena wasn't working, she sometimes brought Ruby over to Nessa's, a studio apartment on Pine Street. They sat on the green velvet couch that had been in their living room all through childhood. Nessa held Ruby for hours. She had started to smile. Unexpected bursts of joy and recognition seized her little face and Nessa could not stop gazing.

This may sound weird but sometimes I think Lucas is jealous of me and Ruby, Deena said.

He's jealous because you spend less time with him?

No, not that. The breastfeeding. That my body can do this. Like I'm undermining him.

Well, that's fucked-up, said Nessa.

I don't know. I'm tired. I think I misinterpret things.

A few weeks later Deena heated the kettle on Nessa's stove and scooped powder into a bottle. She poured the hot water over the formula, screwed the nipple top on and started shaking it.

Oh. So you've gone over to the dark side?

Deena slammed the cutlery drawer shut, clattered the spoon into the sink, took a glass from the draining board and spiked it into the sink. The glass shattered.

Nessa jumped.

Jesus, Deena. What the hell. She turned to check Ruby in the buggy beside her. She was doing her baby squirming. Oblivious and bubbling.

Deena turned around and faced her. I'm sorry. I'm so sorry. I'll clean it up. Replace the glass. She started picking up shards off the floor.

Deena, leave it. I have a dustpan and broom. I just made a joke. I don't get what I did. Nessa swept up the glass.

Lucas had started Ruby on bottles of formula. Didn't use the frozen packets of milk she'd been stocking up.

I'll be bursting to feed her. Like, early in my shift, I'll use the hospital-grade pumps. Save every drop. By the time work is over I'll be out to here I'm so full. Soaked milk pads. Everything. I won't even speak to people on my way out. And I fall through the door, like Give her to me, and he'll have just fed her a full bottle. But not my milk. Not all the milk I've been fucking killing myself to store up. Formula. Some organic shit he mail-orders. And then I have to hand-pump to take the pain away because she's full and won't feed. Then he starts getting up to feed her in the night. Waking her for a feed. Doing it quietly, sneaking, and fucking pretending it's so I can get some sleep.

Nessa had never seen Deena this angry. She didn't know what to say. Anything she said about Lucas always backfired.

I'm just so fucking tired, Deena said.

Didn't the doctor say the sertraline was safe for breastfeeding? Is that what he's worried about?

Well, he doesn't agree with me taking anything, especially feeding Ruby.

Nessa tried to speak carefully. But everyone agreed. The obstetrician and the primary-care doctor, that you should keep taking your medication. It's really important. She tried to keep the anxiety out of her voice. You are taking it, right? She'd stopped sweeping and stared at Deena.

So now I'm not allowed to be angry, like deeply legitimately angry, without it being that I'm insane and possibly off medication? She paused. Of course I'm taking it.

Nessa didn't tell her mom because she didn't want to upset or worry her, and she didn't say anything to Molly because Molly hated Lucas and would escalate things. Joey couldn't handle a conversation about whether his sister was breastfeeding or not. Nessa let it go. She was angry at herself for mentioning the medication. It wasn't until much later that both the cruelty and the pathology of what Lucas had done hit her.

Deena changed. She lost all the pregnancy weight and more. She was jittery. She started smoking, but weirdly, like a teenager, hiding it, stashing packs in Nessa's bag, changing her shirt and rinsing her mouth with Listerine before she went home.

It was adolescent and sad. But Deena was talking to her. Being honest. And she was taking her medicine.

They had drinks. It seemed like a way to defy Lucas. Deena would come over a day she didn't have work and say, Open a bottle. They weren't getting sloshed or anything. Just a drink or two late afternoon, with a dose of junk food. Reese's Peanut Butter Cups. Doritos.

My milk's gone; it doesn't matter anymore.

I'm starting to feel like Pine Street is your tour across America and you go home a few blocks to the Betty Ford Clinic, Nessa said.

Once, when Ruby was sleeping in her stroller, they did a line of coke each. One line because Nessa had some, mentioned it and Deena wanted to. It was almost nothing and Nessa forgot about it. Maybe a week or so later Nessa walked over to get Deena. They were going to meet Molly. She rang the bell and when no one came she used the door knocker. Nothing. She heard Lucas's voice. Raised. When she rang the bell again, he opened it. Deena was behind him in sweatpants and an old sweater. Nessa started to ask Why aren't you ready? when she saw Lucas's face.

You are not welcome. He wasn't shouting. It was all in the tone. Seething. You are forbidden to come here. You gave her cocaine? While our daughter was sleeping in the same room? You are banned from our house. You stay away from my daughter.

Deena just stood there. Apathetic. Not upset. She looked like she'd been slouching around all day. She hadn't showered. There was no *sorry* on her face, no effort to catch Nessa's eye. She was completely expressionless and Nessa saw what was happening: they were closing ranks. She'd become the enemy. Deena was trying to realign with him and she'd thrown Nessa under the bus.

A few minutes later she rang Molly from the street, still shaking, her entire body drained of blood. It wasn't Lucas or what he said that had shocked her, it was Deena's impassive, pliant face.

Betrayal bonding, Molly said. She's so completely under his thumb. I don't know if we can ever get her back.

20

Ruby

Ruby's mother leans down to kiss her and says, Goodbye, Ruby, in a very formal way. She wears white gloves and a travel outfit like she is in one of those movies Clover watches from the 1940s, when clothes were tailored, hair was set and voices strangely clipped. Ruby's mother smiles and lifts her hand like the mannequin in the store window in Burlington from years ago, the one that used to wave out at the street, fixed in that position, all the time smiling. But she looks like someone else Ruby has seen. In fourth grade Ruby watched a programme about John F. Kennedy that showed his wife, Jackie, in the motorcade in Dallas, and her mother looks like Jackie Kennedy waving from a convertible, a crowd thronged either side of her. Maybe that's why her mother is wearing a Chanel-type outfit with gloves. Her mother is leaving, but in the memory she sits on top of the car facing Ruby, smiling, driving backward, waving good-bye, or maybe beckoning, in a pastel outfit like she is in a parade, except it is the dirt-clogged track to the house. Ruby feels nothing. She stands there and watches even long after the car is gone.

Had someone given her the wrong memories? Ruby had always believed that the first thing she ever remembered was her mother leaving. It happened outside their house, at the bottom of the steps.

She kept the memory long after she should have known it wasn't real. Had Clover or Lucas given it to her? She watched *Blade Runner* with Sophie because Sophie said it was a classic and she felt burdened with, as she put it, building Ruby's dismal cultural references. The memory implants in replicants didn't seem like science fiction. It was easy to make someone believe something had happened in their past. She knew Lucas had lied to her about where she was from, how and when her mother had left. Everything before she could properly remember was potentially an implant. Nothing was real. She knew he must be the one who had given her a memory of her mother that made her empty and mechanical like the mannequin. In her real picture she looked nothing like that.

Once, a few years earlier, Ruby had come into the kitchen with her hair down after a shower and Clover had stepped back from the sink, still holding a scrubbing brush, and said, Girl, you're like the ghost of your mother. Ruby wished she hadn't said it like that. When Ruby asked How am I like her, Clover clammed up. She pressed her lips together and banged the pots she was washing. Ruby knew to stop. She'd thought then that maybe Clover was protecting her. Clover had said her mother was taking medication. The things written in the papers. The small bits Lucas had ever said. But now she wasn't sure. She wanted to know what was in the envelopes. What was her mother saying that she wasn't allowed to hear?

Ruby was pouring milk into her cereal when Adelaide said to Clover, I always thought you were a cross bitch.

Ruby's head shot around and milk sloshed onto the table.

Adelaide!

Both women burst into laughter.

I might have been, said Clover.

Adelaide was always with Clover now, shelling peas, talking, drinking coffee. The Pucketts had never had children. It made Ruby sad, in case it was something they had wanted. Adelaide and Ethan would have made good parents. They liked looking after people.

You should watch the slurping, Adelaide said to Ruby.

Ruby stopped reading the back of the cereal box. Adelaide was wearing a man's denim shirt and hunting trousers.

You dressed up as Ethan again today?

Adelaide laughed. I always like a bit of backtalk, she said. Ethan buys multiples of everything. He likes a shirt and he buys five of them. These suit me fine.

They do, said Clover. You carry it off.

Even though she was brusque and liked to have her hands in mud, Adelaide had elegance. She caught her silver hair in a short ponytail and she always wore a pair of drop turquoise earrings.

It's not coffee without a cigarette, said Clover, and she stood to go out to the porch. Adelaide and Ruby stayed together at the table.

Oatstanding! Ruby said out loud. *A bowl is so much more than cereal.* Adelaide kept reading her newspaper. *A shared moment across generations.* Nothing was shared at their table. She looked at Adelaide concentrating, Ethan's drugstore glasses on the tip of her nose. Ethan's family, the Pucketts, had lived here for generations. They'd lived here forever. Adelaide must know something.

Ruby's heart quickened. She would just ask.

Adelaide, did you know my mother?

Ruby didn't take her eyes off Adelaide's face, saw her flinch ever so slightly.

I never met her. I saw her once, the time she came to visit. I passed her on the road. Before you were born.

Ruby's thoughts flew. She nodded, like she understood about that time.

Didn't she ever live here with me before she disappeared in Philadelphia?

Adelaide leaned forward, her large hands around the coffee cup, and spoke clearly, as if she couldn't understand how Ruby had this wrong.

You and your mother never lived here together. You came with your father after.

Adelaide shifted in her chair, looked toward the door.

I think you should be talking to your grandmother about this. Not me.

Ruby wanted to scream that she'd tried with both Clover and Lucas, that they'd tell her the wrong thing or nothing at all.

They sat and didn't speak.

Clover lumbered back in and sat down at the table. She sensed the change of mood.

Who put the cat among the pigeons? she asked.

Ruby heard voices from the lake and sat up on her elbows to look out the window. Lucas was several yards out, in waders, opposite a man on shore; between them a long black tube snaked across the surface of the lake. They were working on the water line. Clover was already up. Ruby could smell bacon frying. In the hallway passing Lucas's room she tried the knob. It turned.

Since Ruby could remember, Lucas's room was always locked and she and Clover didn't go into it. His room had his bed and clothes, but it also had a desk, shelves, filing cabinets and computers. She'd hardly ever stood in it except to bring him a cup of coffee and the time he'd had the flu, when she'd brought him glasses of water and chicken soup. Lately, she tried the knob whenever she passed. She knew the yellow envelopes were inside.

She paused and listened to the drift of voices outside. She stepped into the room. A long white curtain lifted with a slight shift of wind, then settled. A triangle of light rippled over the wooden floorboards.

The shelves were ordered. Spiral-bound documents arranged in tidy stacks. He was the same in the tool shed. Everything in its place: claw hammers, screwdrivers, nails by size, power drills, spades, shovels, gloves. Here, reports and manuals were alphabetized, spines out. A cybersecurity and computer language Ruby couldn't decipher. Three black monitors stared back at her, caught her reflection in their dark surfaces. Could he look at his phone down at the lake and see her here, in his room where she wasn't allowed, peering out at him? She backed toward the hallway and again listened for voices, scanned the room for a pile of padded yellow envelopes. Nothing. She tried a filing cabinet drawer. Locked, all of them. She turned full circle in the room and then squatted down on her hunkers and peeked under the bed. Several large plastic storage containers were lined up. She reached for one. Her breath constricted. She pulled the box toward her and lifted the lid. It was full of spiral-bound notebooks. She pulled out one on the top and flicked through it, the pages falling against her thumb. Blue ink in writing she did not recognize. Cursive. It wasn't Lucas's. He always wrote in block letters. She tilted her head toward the door again, listened, started turning pages. A list of things to do. A page about a sick infant full of medical terms and dosages. *The mother has not visited. No dad.* Pages where the writing got messy and bigger, the connected letters broken. She stopped on one.

Night shift. Work in three hours. No sleep. Lost it when I said about the shore in June with my family. Smashed picture. So fucked-up. Still bruised from before. So tired. Mom so sick.

Every muscle in Ruby's body tensed and a dread cold coursed through her. The doorway was still empty.

Ruby!

She nearly jumped out of her skin, but it was only Clover calling her from the kitchen. Ruby put the notebook back in the box, clicked on the lid and pushed it back under. In the hallway she pulled the door as slowly as she could, and then gently released until she felt the soft click. At the top of the stairs she had to sit down.

Clover came to the bottom of the steps to call again and saw her sitting there.

What's wrong with you?

Just light-headed for a second. Her voice was small.

Come down and get some breakfast into you. The morning's half gone.

She needed to get back into the room. Every time she passed she checked the handle. It was always locked. The first day after she'd been in his room she froze every time he looked at his phone, convinced he was seeing her crouched over the box reading whatever it was under his bed. She couldn't make sense of any of it. Was it her mother's?

Can you look up how to pick a lock? Ruby was looking at the ground through the slats of a picnic table. Across from her Sophie slathered sunscreen on her pale arms and face. She had a wide-brimmed hat and large black sunglasses.

Who are you planning to rob?

Seriously. Can you look it up? It's for a room in my house.

Let's sit in the shade, Sophie said, so we can see.

Ruby sat with her under the apple trees at the far end of the parking lot of Schneider's General Store. Sophie found videos on You-Tube.

What kind of lock is it? A privacy lock or a locked entry?

Her door and the bathroom door had privacy locks. She wasn't sure if Lucas's was different.

They watched the privacy lock video, which made it look easy. Ruby went back into the store to buy a pack of bobby pins.

When Lucas left for Montreal, and she was sure he was gone, and Clover was in the living room watching a western, Ruby knelt in the hallway and unfolded two bobby pins. One for tension, the other to pick. But Lucas's lock was different from hers or the bathroom's or Clover's. He'd had a different lock put on his room.

She was still crouching outside the door when her phone pinged. A message from Tim. He had to go back home. His mother was unwell. *She suffers*, he wrote. The closed door was not going to open. She read Tim's message again. Cold seeped into the pith of her. She didn't know what to text back. She didn't know what the right words were. She couldn't think. And she didn't text then, or the next day, or the next. She kept thinking about the locked door and all the information about her on the other side of it. Then she had left it too long. A week later he texted again. *Ruby? Txt or call or smthng*. Thinking about it all – her mother, his mother, Lucas – made her feel like she couldn't breathe. She didn't reply.

That summer before junior year felt like the world turned upside down. Trump became the Republican nominee. Everyone talked politics. She hardly saw Nathalie anymore. Ever since they'd spoken in the chemistry lab, there'd been distance, and Ruby spent more and more time with Sophie.

I asked Nathalie what's up with the two of you, Sophie said to Ruby when they were walking back from swimming in the lake. And she said, Just drift, you know. Ruby shrugged and didn't say anything.

Nathalie and her mother were volunteering for the Clinton campaign, even though their first choice had been Bernie Sanders. The campaign took up her time and they hardly saw her. Lucas wouldn't say *Hillary* or *Clinton*. Just *Mrs Clinton*. Ruby felt the festering contempt. The yellow envelopes, the hidden notebooks, all the secrets became a heavy weight she dragged around every day. An invisible gravity pulled her toward the ground. She never messaged Tim. She didn't know why. She spent days with Adelaide and Clover in the kitchen and worried about what they knew and weren't telling her.

They'd been back at school a few weeks when Sophie said something. Ruby was outside her locker getting books when Sophie put her shoulder against a locker nearby and faced her.

If you want to talk, we can.

Talk about what?

The way you've been. The weirdness. Crying?

Ruby didn't answer.

Ignorant of what thou art, Cody Evans shouted at Ruby. She sank in her seat, could feel the whole class watching her.

Before Ms Barrett had assigned the parts, Ruby knew her name would be called to read Miranda. A girl growing up on an island with her father and no mother. She saw the words but when she went to speak found it hard to make their sounds. She could barely whisper, *More to know did never meddle with my thoughts.*

Hearing her own voice – whimpering and passive and ignorant – she was angry. Fucking Miranda who thinks nothing for herself, only wants to know what her father can tell her. Obediently forgetting. The others would be thinking it – she was empty, the gangly puppet of her weird father. Her missing mother.

They read on, Cody hamming it up with dramatic arm gestures and a big booming voice. She knew it wasn't true but she felt like Cody was talking directly to her, that the whole class knew this, was in on it. He was looking straight at her, mocking. *Canst thou remember a time before we came unto this cell?* Prospero doesn't wait for her to answer. He tells her: she can't. She was only three. Ruby wanted the floor to swallow her.

At the end of their scene, Prospero just puts her to sleep; *Thou canst not choose*, he says. Ms Barrett interrupted.

Thank you, Cody and Ruby, she said. She turned to the class. So, let's discuss.

Caliban and Miranda are the two children of the island and are opposites. Good and Evil. Somebody else said no, it was Prospero and Caliban that were opposites. Prospero was art and culture and intellect and Caliban was body and appetite. It was the same stuff written in their introduction. They were just repeating it.

Miranda's innocent, someone said.

Miranda's boring, said Cody. Ruby shifted in her seat. He turned his head away. Had he been looking at her when he said it? She'd heard the contempt.

Nobody questioned what Prospero was doing to his daughter. Ruby listened to their responses, how they just took for granted that Prospero was a force for good. He controlled everything, her story, her body, even her memories. Ariel was like his cameras. Prospero's surveillance system.

Ruby? Ms Barrett was looking at her. Do you want to weigh in?

No, she mumbled.

Nothing? Ms Barrett asked.

Not really.

You agree with the others?

No.

Tell us, then.

Well, I don't agree that Prospero is those things. Look what he's doing. Spying, making slaves, making people think they've lost their family, knocking his daughter out when her being awake or aware isn't convenient. He keeps telling her and others to shut up. He controls what she knows. Who she marries. And no one is saying he's even a bit off?

Everyone was looking at her. Had she shouted? Sneered those last words? She'd made it emotional. She could feel the well of tears building and she kept her head down long after the bell rang so she wouldn't have to face anybody.

21
Ruby

2017

It smelled like Shake n' Vac and urine. There were possibly fifteen people in the room; the two single beds had been pushed to one side. Worcester. The same two-star hotel the rowing team had stayed in the year before. She was doing tequila shots with the stroke on the team from Virginia that had won earlier that day. Handsome and knew it. She'd placed second in her race. He licked his hand between his thumb and index finger, spilled salt across it and Ruby licked it before she took the shot because he said that was how to drink them; it would take the burn out. She did it but then he made it weird by pointing at her and nodding his head.

She'd had too much to drink. Vodka and Coke and then shots. How had she not noticed how ugly the room was, how ugly she was in it. Its wall-to-wall carpeting, blue floral polyester bedspreads, plain brown curtains. Her in it pretending to be someone. Rowers from her own state were taking pictures of themselves and everyone started to look hideous to her, posing and making weird shapes with their mouths. She didn't feel good. Her keycard was somewhere in the room. But she needed air. People blurred, their forms indistinct, fuzzy, and then they split into two, doubles of themselves. She might throw up. She had to get out. In the hallway, her back against the wall, she tried to catch her breath.

The door opened and the guy from Virginia stepped out.

Nice one, he said, and he faced her, pressing the flat of his hands on the wall either side of her head.

Then he tried to kiss her, his tongue straight in.

No. She wrenched her face away.

He pushed himself against her and tried again to kiss her.

Get off me.

Come on. He smiled and kind of elbowed her as if she didn't really mean it. You just licked my hand.

You said that's how people drink tequila shots.

You licked me like you liked it. I didn't tell you to do that.

Ruby couldn't think. She remembered wincing at the salt and lime, but somehow she had looked as if she liked it? That's what he thought.

I didn't. Get off me. She pushed against his chest with both hands. Hard. I will scream if you touch me again.

The skin around his lips lost colour, turned almost white. She suddenly saw how absolutely ugly he was.

Stay away from me.

Fucking headcase. He went back into the hotel room.

She focused on the busy patterned carpet and her stomach heaved. At the bottom of the stairwell she found the exit door. Outside, the air was chilly and her top was thin. At the far end of the parking lot she stood by the dead shrubbery, uncertain if she was going to throw up or not. She realized she was crying. Over at the fence round the empty swimming pool, she sat on the ground cross-legged, looking through the chain links at the hole in the ground with leaves and some trash lit by a spotlight.

She couldn't go back to the front door. It was way past curfew and she was drunk. But she'd have to ring at reception to get some-one to give her a keycard. She checked her phone. Eleven thirty. She called him even though she knew she probably shouldn't.

Hello?

It's me. Ruby Chevalier. From Middle Lake School.

I know who it is. There was a pause. And where you went to school.

Can you come get me?

234

What's happened?

I'm really drunk.

You want me to drive to Vermont because you're drunk?

No. Here. Worcester. I think. Please, Tim. I'm stuck.

Where? Do you know where you are?

The same hotel as last time. Outside. In the parking lot. Near the pool.

Jesus, Ruby. I thought you were like lost on a road or something. Go back into the hotel.

I can't. I'll get expelled from school.

He paused. She heard the exhale, like she was a bother to him.

I'll be there in ten minutes.

Everything about him was the same but different. Earrings and chain. The way his eyes were tired. He'd lost weight. He had two thick silver rings on his thumb. They were new. She remembered that he had turned eighteen in February.

You're eighteen, she said.

Yeah.

Seventeen. She pointed at herself.

I know.

On the passenger seat was a pile of spiral-bound notepads and textbooks. The *SAT Prep Black Book*. Tim moved them to the backseat then reached across to buckle her. She handed him her phone.

Can you take out the battery? Make it go dead so my dad can't track me?

The following morning there was little traffic. Worcester early Sunday looked like any town in Vermont. They didn't speak. She'd slept on their couch and Tim's mother had said hello when she passed through on her way to work. Ruby had been embarrassed, couldn't even remember coming into the house. Tim pulled in a few hundred yards before the entrance to the hotel.

You might not want your coach to see you getting out of a car.

No. Thanks for helping. Ruby wiped her nose.

Ruby. Maybe you should get help. Like the counselling service at school or something.

It was the most he had said to her and the way he said it made her feel judged.

Okay. Thank you, I guess, even though I didn't ask for your diagnosis. Her voice was angry and sarcastic. This won't happen again.

Well, probably not in Worcester.

She'd made him angry.

She tried to say something but she knew a sob would come out if she did. She pushed the door open, stepped out and slammed it.

Your dad has a girlfriend.

For a moment everything swayed. They were standing at the bus stop and Ruby put a foot forward to steady herself.

What?

She could hear the irritable snap in her voice, like she was disagreeing. Sophie tucked her hair behind her ear and looked around to make sure the others couldn't hear. Her 1980s outfit included oversized eyeglass frames with no lenses. They were gigantic on her tiny pale face.

My mom saw him in Montreal.

Heat flushed Ruby's neck. She stared at the road. Another thing she wasn't allowed to know.

The words under her father's bed reverberated – *lost it, smashed, fucked-up, bruised.*

There's women at his work.

Together together, Ruby. A restaurant at night.

Sophie was staring hard at her, like Come on.

The bus doors swished open in front of them and Ruby started. She hadn't seen it coming.

Maybe they did it to improve people's moods but the bright lights made Ruby feel overexposed and disoriented. Everything in the room glared: bright couches, fluorescent cushions, posters, smiley faces. She sat in a chair and wanted to leave.

Are you here for an appointment?

The woman at the reception desk was talking to her.

Do you have an appointment?

Ruby shook her head no and stood. The woman twirled a pencil through her fingers. Her eyebrows were painted, not real.

Who would you like to see?

A counsellor?

Academic, college, career, stay-well group, mental health matters . . . She rattled them off.

Ruby went closer. Tried to speak. The woman's fingernails were green acrylic. Tears had already started. She turned to leave.

Hold on right there. Don't take another step. Give me one minute. Helen's here for walk-ins. She clicked a button and spoke into her headset.

An arm moved around her waist, a voice said, Okay, okay, okay, you'll be just fine. She was guided into a room where she sat for a long time. Ruby cried and cried, avoiding eye contact with the woman across from her.

Sorry. She blew her nose again.

Not a problem. Take your time.

Okay. I'm okay now, Ruby said.

She recognized the woman from the hallways. Sometimes she was outside the school talking to students on the steps. She was young.

Her hair had long braided extensions held in a loose ponytail. Her suit was deep navy with thin white stripes. No make-up or jewellery. Everything else was minimal too. No motivational posters or glaring overhead lights like in reception. Just books on a shelf, a desk and a large open window overlooking a tree-lined field. In her room you couldn't hear the hallways or cafeteria.

I'm Helen.

Ruby.

Helen passed her a wastebasket and Ruby scooped all the tissues from her lap into it.

Sorry. That's actually gross.

It's fine. Helen sat forward in her chair. Before we start, I want to reassure you that whatever you say here is completely confidential, except if you disclose that you are in danger or that you have been abused. Then I'm legally obliged to report it.

Ruby said she understood. She found it hard to hold eye contact so she looked at the window. She started talking, first about nothing. Like I don't know why I'm here, why I'm even crying, it's stupid and embarrassing. Helen didn't try to contradict her. Just listened, saying nothing. Then everything poured out, in one extended gush. For the very first time in her life Ruby spoke to someone other than Nathalie about her mother, her uncertainty about why she'd left, her inability to remember. The article headlines she'd seen. She told Helen about the yellow envelopes, the photograph, how it had all created a rift between her and her best friend. Her leg jiggled as she talked and she tried to still it with her hand. She told Helen about Lucas's girlfriend. She didn't tell her about the notebooks under his bed. It still sent a shock of fear, like a blow, just under her ribs. *Bruised*. She remembered what Ben had said about Lucas at Middle Lake, *bad egg*. She tried never to think about that.

Helen sat in her chair, legs crossed, hands in her lap. She didn't take notes or interject. Just listened, her head tilted slightly to one side.

It's like I'm not allowed to know who he is or who I am. I just washed up to Middle Lake School with amnesia or something, like in a movie. And I feel like nothing. Everyone will eventually find out that I'm empty. No personality, no history, no stories about family. I am nothing except what I've been told I am.

Ruby paused, took a long breath, then exhaled. She suddenly had nothing to say. Helen leaned forward, her hands wrapped around her knee, and asked: Who's telling you?

I don't know. My father, I guess.

Helen started to ask another question but the final bell rang. They made an appointment to meet in a few days.

Outside, the sun was shining and Ruby felt good. Lighter, like she could finally get fresh air. For the first time in months and months she believed things could get better. Helen would help her.

Mr Schneider had had two hip replacements and he walked up and down the aisles like the cowboys in Clover's movies, knees bent and waddling as if he had to swing each leg to propel forward. He managed to be all over the store and up ladders even with the arthritis and bionic hips. Schneider's was his store and they did a bit of everything – gas, groceries, tackle, bait, souvenirs, hardware, deli, garden and soft-serve. Ruby was a full head taller than him and tried to make herself smaller as they talked about a job.

Helen had suggested that working would give Ruby freedom and time outside the house: Ruby had immediately thought of Schneider's. It was close to home and even Lucas liked Mr Schneider. Having responsibility was good, Lucas said, and it would be up to her to manage her time. Rowing and schoolwork had to come first. Mr Schneider said Ruby could start that Thursday afternoon to get trained in. It was Memorial Day Weekend and he was going to need help. Tourists. Mr Schneider showed her how to work the register and make creemees. The art of soft-serve, Vermont-style, he called it.

Wyatt came in for ice cream.

The future you can expect now that you want to be an English major, he said when she handed him the cone. This or Starbucks.

Fuck off, she muttered under her breath, pretending to serve him with a smile. She pulled cones all day, sprinkled and poured toppings and did the register. By late afternoon, when business slowed, she was sweaty, loosened strands of hair stuck to her face, and her feet ached. She smelled like sour milk. The atmosphere in Schneider's was easy and laid-back. Not like at home, walking on eggshells around Lucas or thinking about all that was kept from her behind his closed door.

There were sisters, dogs, clothes everywhere. Ruby loved being at Sophie's. Sisters sitting in armchairs, legs draped over the sides, with headphones in. Sisters at the kitchen table with friends. In the bathroom doing each other's make-up. Sisters shouting room to room, teasing Sophie. Dogs were on couches, on Sophie's bed. Sophie's walls were covered in posters and textile projects she had done in art. She shared a room with one of her four sisters and it was like a tornado had whirled through. Sophie's mom was divorced. Her dad lived in Burlington so the house was all women.

Even the dogs are female, said Sophie.

Sophie's sisters took over when it was time to go out. They sat Ruby in front of a vanity mirror. Sparkling-gold eyeshadow. Thick welts of eyeliner and mascara. Shimmer powder. They played music and oohed and aahed. Ruby wore a crop top with a pair of flares that belonged to one of the sisters.

The jewel neckline suits you, said Sophie.

Ruby didn't even know what that was. She looked in the mirror and didn't recognize herself. Her lips were dark. Lucas had a phrase about women who wore too much make-up: Painted corpses.

Sophie passed her a joint between her thumb and forefinger and Ruby hesitated for a moment, then took it. Lucas was in Montreal and Clover would be asleep when she got home.

'Crank That' blared at top volume on giant speakers as they walked across Wyatt's lawn, and Sophie had started dancing before they even reached the crowd. Within a few minutes they were in the midst of a hundred other teenagers.

Ruby! You came! Wyatt shouted when he saw her.

She laughed and they kept dancing. Everything was better than itself. The sky, the night, the air, the music, the people.

Ruby stood outside the house for a moment when Sophie dropped her off. The noise of the lake rose up as the car drove away – katydids and frogs. The counting clicks of the katydid against the higher trill of the frogs. Spring peepers, said Ruby to herself. They had a piercing call. She pushed open the door and walked into the kitchen. Before she'd flicked on the light a voice whispered out of the dark.

What did I tell you about this phone?

Lucas. She hadn't seen his truck.

What did I tell you?

Everything about him was taut, his voice, his effort for control.

I forgot it this morning. I called Clover from work and explained. Clover said it was okay for me to go out with Sophie.

Stand at the sink, he said.

She stood shivering, the dark window beside her.

Breathe out.

She blew air out of her mouth and thought she might gag as Lucas breathed in the air she had exhaled. The joint earlier. She couldn't see his face in the dark but she could feel his breath.

I haven't been drinking, she said, and she started to push past him for the door.

He gripped both her arms above the elbows. Hard. Her breath tightened. She wanted to scream *Stop!* but no sound came. She couldn't pull her arms away while his fingers kept crushing.

Don't you ever leave this house without that phone. I have enough in my life to worry about without having to wonder where the hell in the state of Vermont you are.

He tightened his grip.

And you ask me, not your grandmother, if you want to do something. Do you understand?

Yes. Her voice was a whisper and a choked sound followed.

Stop it, he sputtered. I didn't hurt you. I didn't do anything to you. Ever.

He squeezed even harder, and she could feel rage in his fingers, nails biting into her skin. She could only see the dark outline of him, but she knew what his mouth looked like, tight, thin. She'd seen Lucas like this before.

You're hurting my arms. She gasped it. Said it too loud, and maybe Clover would hear. Lucas dropped his hands and stepped back.

I forgot I was holding them.

She stood waiting.

Go to bed, he said.

PART IV

22

Nessa

2000

Molly told her to come straight away. It's about your sister, she said. It's fucked-up.

Nessa catastrophized the whole way there. Deena had made a mistake with a baby, an intubation had gone wrong, a baby had died . . . All the things that could happen in a NICU. All the things that could happen to Deena if she wasn't holding it together.

Dante's was dark, Goo Goo Dolls' 'Iris' blasting on the sound system. Nessa elbowed through the people crowded at the bar, mostly grad students from Penn and Drexel.

Molly was in a booth at the back, still wearing her coat, badges pinned to the front: *Gore 2000* and, beneath it, *Bush Cheated*. The election had been almost a month ago. Molly's parents still had *Bush/Cheney* placards stabbed into their front yard. Nessa slid into the seat opposite; a pitcher of ale and two glasses were waiting on the table.

What's happened? Nessa took off her jacket and rubbed her hands, stiff from the cold outside. Molly was visibly upset. White streaks tracked down her face through her foundation. You're scaring me, Molly.

Deena needs help. I'm not messing. Really. She needs help.

What happened?

An hour ago we were changing out of scrubs in the locker room. We've had a long day. A hard shift. Understaffed. I had two inconsolables.

Nessa knew the shorthand Deena and Molly used. Inconsolables – addicted newborns who cried and cried no matter how much you held them, rocked them, fed them. They couldn't get comfort.

I've been asking Deena for months to go for a drink and because it's Friday I knew Lucas could stay home with Ruby. She agreed earlier in the week to come here tonight. Like old times. It's so close to the house as well, you know, so Ruby wouldn't be far.

We were changing in the locker room and we were both in bad moods. Me because of the shift I'd had – morphine weans, one baby alarming all day – and Deena because she didn't really want to go anyway; I was making her. She kept hinting about being tired and run-down, but I wasn't letting her off the hook because she does this any time we're supposed to meet. It pisses me off. You know how Deena always changed in the closet when we were in high school? She's like that at work too. Changes in the cubicle and the other nurses tease her, flash her – you know, mess around because she's so easy to embarrass. But tonight it was just us and we weren't talking. The lockers are under construction, so there's no doors to change behind. I was by the benches and her back was to me. I was looking at her because I knew she'd lost weight, but with just her bra I could really see it. Her back looked like my grandmother's when she got old, that way the vertebrae protrude.

Molly paused and Nessa nodded. It was true. Deena was skinny.

She has this yellow-and-black bruise on her arm. A big one. I pointed at it and asked What's that? and she covered it with her hand and turned away. And on the other arm was the same exact bruise. The *same* one. How do you get matching bruises? Molly's eyes widened. How, I asked her. Deena, what the fuck is up with the bruises on your arms? I said straight out: Did Lucas do that? She got annoyed. She said, I just told you, nothing, it was nothing. Then she made up some shit about a new dresser in Ruby's room that she keeps bumping into going in and out in the dark to feed her. And I said, I think your story's bullshit. I said, If Lucas is hurting you then you and Ruby have to get out of there. You can come to me or your parents. Or go to Nessa . . . And she just turned on me and said the weirdest thing. She said, If all of you would leave me the fuck alone, this wouldn't happen. She was angry. At me. Like I had done this to her. And then she just screamed, at the top of her lungs, I don't want to fucking go anywhere with you. Why won't all of you just leave me the fuck alone? She was crying, and she put her jacket on over her bra. She had no top underneath, still in her scrub bottoms, and she threw all her other stuff back into her bag and left me there in the locker room naked, wondering what the fuck just happened.

Molly's eyes filled with tears. She pushed her finger under her glasses and slowly wiped them away.

There is something seriously fucked-up going on in that house.

Nessa waited until Deena's day off and asked if she and Ruby would come over to their parents' to make Christmas-tree decorations. She'd bought copper wire, ribbon and sheet music to make tree angels. She'd already finished one for Ruby. They were sitting on the floor around the coffee table, Ruby on her under-the-sea play-mat, swatting squid and dolphins with her little fist. Nessa showed Deena how to shape the wire, and brought up, casually, what Molly had seen. She'd practised it.

Molly mentioned you had some bruises.

There was a slight pause, but the second Deena started answering, Nessa knew she had prepared her answer. She laughed slightly and shook her head.

I bumped off the bureau by the door in Ruby's room. It's wide and I keep hitting it on the way in and out. Little bruises on my arm.

She dangled the bare wire angel she was working on to show Nessa she'd done it right.

Molly's never changed. Her imagination's wild and it's always against men or against the system – fuck the patriarchy. You know how she is.

Deena sounded almost disdainful. Like, Our silly Molly.

Nessa kept talking, concentrating on her own angel, not even looking at Deena. Keeping it casual so Deena wouldn't feel attacked.

Molly was pretty certain that the bruises were inflicted by Lucas and, because you got so upset, she was sure she was right.

Deena's voice stayed calm. She wasn't rattled. I was upset, she said, because Molly was completely off the mark and out of line. She's always insinuating things about Lucas. The stuff about the bruises was just complete projection. It's like she wants there to be something bad between me and Lucas.

Nessa knew nothing she said would change anything, but she couldn't help trying: But Molly's been your best friend since like third grade.

I know. And I'm tired of her shit. It's been the same for years. I'm cutting Molly out of my life.

Deena began another angel, carefully turning the scissors as she shaped the head.

Nessa should have said more. Sixteen years later, sitting on her Parrish Street stoop, she pieced over that conversation with Deena for the thousandth time and questioned whether it would have made a difference if she'd said or done something then. She had been sent photographs taken that month in Montreal. Lucas Chevalier with a woman. A girlfriend had been mentioned in previous reports but this was the first time Nessa had seen her. Long auburn hair, a pale face, almost pudgy in a pretty way. A gentle expression. Something in her demeanour like Deena. That first time she'd asked Deena about the bruises, she'd been afraid that, if she pushed, Deena wouldn't let Ruby come to the home house for her first Christmas. Or that she would pull even further back from Nessa. Withhold Ruby. Withhold herself. They'd all begun tiptoeing around just to have Deena and Ruby in their lives. Nessa especially, since she was the one banned from their house. Even back then she'd worried about whether Deena was taking her antidepressants. That night in Dante's, Molly had said, Do something. She'd done nothing. Why? She could have told Joey. Her mother. If she'd organized an intervention straight away things might never have gotten so out of control.

Across the street a black SUV was parked where the white Honda had been that summer, the one before Deena disappeared. She hadn't done anything about that either. Or not enough. She studied the picture in her hand; she should do something. The door opened to the house next door and a woman stepped out in a cream linen dress and oversized black sunglasses. Nessa had only seen her a few times. She started to say hello but the woman didn't acknowledge her at all, went down her steps and clicked her car lock. Another SUV. The tiny street was flanked both sides with them. Weird to have these tanks, seeing as they all lived in a city. When Sylvia next door had died, her children had sold the house. No one sat out on the sidewalk anymore and talked to each other. Nessa missed her. Her metal chair and her golden jewels. The houses had all doubled in value but the old people were gone and it wasn't a neighbourhood anymore. Not really.

So much had happened during those weeks after Molly saw the bruises. Maria's cancer came back. Her hair had grown in, wiry and greyer, but full; her cheeks had colour. Nessa had gone with her for the scan. The previous day, Maria had swung Ruby around the kitchen, made them all dinner, exuded health. But the scan said different. A lesion on the liver. She had surgery in the new year. The day they left the hospital, George W. Bush's inauguration was being broadcast live on TV. Maria sat on the bed, hands folded in her lap, her packed bags on the floor at her feet. Deena sat beside her. Nessa leaned on the windowsill looking out at the city. The Philadelphia skyline was chalky in the January light. When the discharge nurse walked into the room it was Deena she spoke to. More chemo. They were all tired. Dick Cheney's face, close up, filled the television screen.

Nessa hadn't mentioned the bruises again. Molly had said their family had avoidance pathology.

Nessa scrutinized the photograph in her lap again, Lucas's profile, the same hand on the lower back, that I-am-in-charge-here gesture, and this beautiful young woman. *Mathilde Lavoie* was written in neat handwriting on a white sticker in the corner of the picture. Someone had to warn her, tell her. Nessa couldn't let what had happened to Deena happen again. Why hadn't she done something?

But she had – she had done something. Hadn't they? They'd done what they could.

It was the spring after Ruby's first birthday. Nessa had been working on a site-specific exhibition in West Philly. The day the calls came she was on location. The artist she was working with had chalked portraits on buildings zoned for demolition. The portraits were from the old neighbourhood: a young man who'd been shot, a teenage girl who'd died of an overdose, a woman who'd fought for her community all her life and been like a mother to many. Large-scale, the portraits took up entire gable walls. They didn't last. That was the point. Nothing does. The chalk faded in parts, especially after rain. Like the buildings, all traces would be gone as the gentrification continued. They walked around the houses, took pictures. The phone in her purse kept buzzing. She ignored it, trying to give the artist and photographer her full attention. She assumed it was someone back in the office.

By the time she pulled it out to see who had been calling, she was back on the subway, heading east on the Market–Frankford Line. Five missed calls.

Deena.
Deena.
Deena.
Deena.
Deena.

She called her back. No answer. She tried again.

Hello?

It's me. What's up?

Oh. Hi. It was Deena, but a kind of public or polite Deena, acting as if she didn't know it was Nessa.

You rang me like five times in a row. Is everything okay?

Gosh, I'm sorry. I don't think I can switch shifts. I already have plans.

What? You know it's me – Nessa. Right?

Yes. Of course.

Is Lucas there with you right now?

I'm afraid so.

Deena? What's going on?

That's right. She's almost one and a half now.

Nessa tried to think. She had to ask the right questions.

Deena, are you okay? Are you safe?

There was a pause. I think so now. She's growing so fast.

Is Ruby okay?

Yes.

Should I call the police?

Oh no, don't do that, she said, and sort of fake-laughed in their fake conversation.

I'm coming to get you and Ruby right now.

No. Definitely not. But thank you so much for the offer.

Deena, I'm going to come over.

I don't think you should do that. Why don't you try the night shift people?

You want me to call you tonight?

Ah, thanks. Okay. Bye. Bye.

She hung up. Nessa remembered the passengers near her that day: a young man, hoodie up, a man in a suit nodding off, a small girl sitting next to her mother looking back at Nessa as if she knew the subterfuge that had just gone on, the desperate thinking. She'd been concentrating so intently she had no idea where she was or if she'd overshot her stop. It was three o'clock. The train braked and the woman and girl stood, the nodding man stood. Center City. She got off there. Rang Joey.

She told him about the phone call, what Molly had seen, the way Deena had been acting.

Joey said nothing at first. Just listened.

Then: I'm going over there.

I don't know, Joey. She made it sound like I should just call her tonight. But if she didn't want me to do anything, why was she pretending it wasn't me? She didn't want Lucas to know she'd called me, obviously. But I said repeatedly I would come get her and she said no.

I'll go check.

I'll go with you.

I thought you weren't allowed in their house.

I'll stay in your truck. Please.

Yeah. No matter what she said about not coming, I have some stuff for her backyard that Dad ordered. I have to drop it off anyway. Garden furniture and a playhouse for Ruby. I can just stop by unexpectedly with it.

The magnolia trees were in bloom and three petals fell against

252

Joey's windshield as she sat and watched him carry each box over and then knock on the door. Lucas probably wouldn't answer. He'd pretend they weren't home. Joey sat on one of the boxes and started digging dirt out from under his nails. He was trying to look casual. After a minute the door opened. Lucas. His normal self. He greeted Joey, stood on the doorstep. Joey took a step down and gestured toward the boxes, was explaining but not looking up. Nessa knew by Joey's manner that he was nervous. He and Lucas each took an end of a box and went into the house. The door was left ajar. She wasn't sure what to do – stay in the truck or go inside while they were out back? She got out and started running, terrified the door would slam shut. She heard Joey and Lucas outside in the backyard. Joey saying something about their dad spoiling Ruby. The kitchen and living room were empty. She ran upstairs.

Deena? She whispered it; the house was so quiet.

No answer.

Deena? She spoke aloud, but her voice cracked.

Ruby was asleep in her cot. Nessa lifted her and she stirred, cried for a second and fell asleep again on Nessa's shoulder. In the hallway she stood outside the master bedroom.

Deena? she whispered as loud as she could, praying that Ruby wouldn't wake up.

Downstairs, Joey and Lucas were inside again, their voices moving through the house as they went to get more boxes.

The bedroom was empty. The bathroom door shut. She tried it. Locked. She knocked lightly.

Deena, it's Nessa, open up. I have Ruby here. Open the door.

Fuck, Nessa. I told you not to come. What are you doing? Does Lucas know you're in the house? Her voice was muffled and Nessa knew she'd been crying.

Open the door, Deena. Joey's with Lucas, moving boxes. He doesn't know I'm here.

Go away. You're making things worse.

Deena, open the fucking door or I'm walking out of here with Ruby. I don't know what's going on, but, trust me, I will call child protective services.

Deena unlocked the door but didn't open it. Nessa did.

Deena turned away, her back to Nessa, her face framed in the mirror. She had a bloody nose. Her top lip was purple and distended grotesquely.

What the fuck?

It looks worse than it is, Deena said. Don't make a big deal, Nessa. I can't do your drama right now.

Let's go.

Nessa, it's nothing. It's fine. Lucas wouldn't hurt me.

Deena. Come with me to the truck. Joey's here. It's okay. Lucas hurt you. This is fucked-up. We're leaving.

Nessa was still trying to whisper. Deena was crying, fresh blood trickling from her nose.

Jesus. Deena, please. Look at you. Look at your baby girl. If you don't leave I'm calling the police anyway.

The front door clicked shut. Nessa froze. Had Joey left? She heard his voice, louder, for her to hear.

Last box, man. Promise.

Now, Deena. Nessa touched her shoulder.

My bag. Deena's voice wheezed.

Nessa saw it on the bed, grabbed it, Ruby still in her arms. She left the room first, Deena behind her. Down the stairs, out the front door. When they reached the sidewalk Deena hesitated.

Deena, just keep walking. Please.

You go in first, Nessa said when they got to the truck. Hold Ruby. Sit in the middle.

Deena climbed in and buried her face in Ruby's neck, rocking back and forth. Nessa shut the tailgate, got in the passenger door and locked it. Joey would see the closed tailgate and know to get in and drive.

Joey came out, moving at his own pace, trying to look casual. Deena hadn't stopped rocking. He raised an arm as if to wave goodbye as he walked toward them, away from Lucas in the doorway.

Keep your head down, said Nessa, sliding down in her seat. Joey jogged the last few paces, got in, shut the door and drove.

They went down to the end of the street, Nessa looking in the side-view mirror to see if Lucas was chasing them. Joey turned right.

Take the expressway, said Nessa. In case he follows us. We won't be stuck at a red light.

Oh my God, oh my God, Deena kept saying. He'll kill me. I'm in so much trouble.

When they went inside their house, Deena couldn't lift her face to look at their mother.

She'd had five months of chemo and was weak, her head bald again, her skin pasty-white, but nevertheless Maria took charge. She put Ruby on a blanket on the floor, led Deena to the couch, murmuring to them both. Okay now, okay now, you're home. She asked Deena had she been hit anywhere else. Deena shook her head.

I don't want Dad to see me.

He's not home.

She made Deena lift her top so that she could see her front and back. A bag of ice for Deena's swollen mouth. A warm cloth to wipe the blood dried under her nose. Nessa found it hard to watch. Her frail mother ministering to her bruised daughter.

Lock the doors, said Deena. Please.

Nessa checked the kitchen door and went to the front. Where was Joey? He hadn't come in yet. She stepped out onto the front lawn. His truck was still there, parked in the driveway. She looked closer. Joey was sitting in it, his head on the steering wheel, sobbing.

23

Nessa

2017

In the photograph three children in the sand squint against an August sun. Behind them waves break and a body, arms always reaching up, is caught mid-jump. The distant outline of a sail is visible through the summer haze. The children are the foreground. They have dug a hole, the water has not come yet. The two older children, almost teenagers, a boy and a girl, hold shovels; the youngest, between them, has her arms flung around their shoulders. She looks like she is shouting Ocean or Ice cream. Not old enough yet to be self-conscious, whatever she is saying she's shouting it. Nose scrunched, eyes squeezed almost shut, all smile and teeth. She believes in this, is smack in the moment. The others, the older boy and girl, are different; they aren't looking at whoever is taking the picture, but off to the edges, toward the outside. It's 1988, Ocean City, New Jersey.

Nessa sat cross-legged on the floor of Deena's room holding the picture. She saw herself, aged eleven, in her orange-and-pink striped tankini, at a time when having just them, Deena and Joey, on a sunny day at the beach was world enough for her. Her desperate arms around them, trying to hold on before they slipped off into their separateness. The photograph seemed to reveal everything ahead of her. Nessa was stuck there, the child in the middle of the scene trying to hold on.

Around her were boxes of loose photographs, documents, papers, drawings, ticket stubs, letters. She hadn't made albums or photobooks. She hadn't been able to start telling a story of all of them. She curated visual narratives all day every day, but could not begin on her own. This letter she was about to write to Mathilde was the

257

closest she had come. She set the Ocean City photograph aside to make a copy. She would include it.

She still combed through Deena's room meticulously, as if all these years later there might still be something encoded here that would unwrap the mystery of what had happened. It had become a cypher, a space holding secret information. Every object was like a clue, but she didn't even know what the questions were anymore. Against the wall Nessa had stored the boxes from her parents' house. Joey had let her take it all. The family photographs, everything. The room itself had been left exactly as it was that day. She had memorized every object, knew the texture of each item hung in the closet, could recite the books in order on the shelves, had read Deena's journals. Lucas had kept the ones she'd written while they lived together. Four years of her life. Deena had panicked.

Him having all my thoughts – it's worse than getting punched or kicked, she'd said.

Lynne had written to Lucas's lawyer on Deena's behalf, formally requesting the journals. He'd claimed he didn't know what they were talking about. Nothing of hers had been left in his house.

Well, he can't use them in the custody case if he doesn't have them, Lynne had said.

Deena continued the journals when she moved in with Nessa. She wrote what she'd done, what she was thinking about, what she was reading. She included stanzas from poems she liked. And Ruby and Ruby and Ruby. What Ruby said, what Ruby did, how Ruby slept, laughed, ate, ran. She transcribed Ruby conversations, glued in Ruby drawings.

The meaning of everything in the room was heightened by Deena's absence. The last place she'd been. For years Nessa had obsessed about the book Deena was reading when she disappeared. An Adrienne Rich collection. The one book lying sideways. *Dark Fields of the Republic.* The very first poem in the collection had been transcribed into Deena's journal. 'What Kind of Times Are These', a poem about disappearance, purges. Deena's last entry ever. Like an imperative to Nessa. Listen. Remember. Speak about it. Don't accept that people just disappear.

Did Mathilde have brothers and sisters? Nessa knew nothing about her, really. For over a year she'd known of her existence but now she had pictures and the concrete image of Lucas's hand on her back, the way he'd had of walking with Deena that had always bothered Nessa. The private investigator didn't think Ruby and Mathilde had met. Lucas was keeping his worlds separate.

She couldn't tell Joey what she was doing. He'd say, Don't start up with all that again. You need help. Don't do crazy shit. We've all had enough. When she had shown him the first photographs of Ruby in Vermont and said how she'd got them, he'd called her creepy. Spying. I don't want to be involved, he said.

They'd had a fight after Deena's death certificate was issued. After the hearing they'd gone for coffee, Joey, Kate, Molly, Lynne and Nessa. They'd all given statements and the petition for the death certificate on the presumption of death had been granted. While they were waiting for their coffees, Nessa mentioned that Frank Capione had been in touch. Deena's case might be opened again.

Joey exploded.

Are you for fucking real? We are all sitting here having just declared her dead and we are trying to process that, and you're still banging on about the investigation and Lucas and Ruby. Fuck's sake, Nessa, you are fucking wrecking my head. As far as I'm concerned, I just buried my sister. It's over. Have some respect. Just shut up. Be fucking normal. Get your own life. I can't take it.

Joey— Kate tried to interrupt, but he cut her off.

No. I don't want to hear it. We're leaving. Joey picked up his coat. Don't ever, ever mention Lucas or Ruby to me again. He stormed out of the coffee shop. Kate mumbled Sorry, and followed him.

Well, he's right about the part where you should get a life, said Molly.

Lynne hardly knew Molly and narrowed her eyes.

It's okay, said Nessa. She's allowed to talk to me like that.

She was trying for levity but it broke her – how Joey saw her. She wasn't loyal, she wasn't vigilant; she was aberrant and embarrassing. Disrespectful.

Nessa was mortified. Lynne tried to say something helpful like That's about how your brother is coping. Not you.

Don't, Nessa said. She didn't want kindness. Didn't think she deserved it.

If he knew. Writing to Lucas's girlfriend would be off the scale, as far as Joey was concerned. She'd wrangled with it for weeks and was now convinced it was the right thing. Whether it was to punish Lucas didn't matter. This woman had to know what he was. She had Mathilde's work address and found a courier that would hand-deliver and wait for proof of delivery. The courier explained that this meant they would wait while the recipient opened and read the contents. They'd have to sign a form to say they'd read it and this would be sent back to Nessa. She had talked to the private investi-gator about it and what was legally allowed.

She had written the first few sentences:

Philadelphia, May 17th, 2017

Dear Mathilde, I am writing to you because my sister is Deena Garvey. Deena disappeared thirteen years ago. We are convinced, and always have been, that Lucas Chevalier is responsible. I am sure he has told you a story where she was depressed, suicidal, unstable. He has probably told you that she took her own life, that she disappeared voluntarily. No one who knew her thinks this. The police don't think this. She and Ruby lived with me at the time of her disappearance. She was terrified of Lucas and believed he would hurt her as he had threatened. She would never have left her daughter. I have enclosed photographs, hospital reports, police reports, Protection From Abuse orders, third-party applications for visitation with my niece Ruby Chevalier, and complaints filed over the past ten years to ensure Ruby's welfare. I want you to know who my sister was and who the person you are involved with is.

Nessa flicked through hundreds of photographs. Christmases, sacraments they all went through, baptism, communion, confirmations, summers at the shore, school pictures from St Christopher's. Her eye fell on one photo.

This is second grade when Deena was in Mrs Mueller's class at St Christopher's. She is seven and still missing a front tooth. Her freckles are more pronounced, her hair lighter than it would be later. I remember those plastic butterfly bobbles holding her pigtails. The yellow school shirt, the red tie. There is a wild confidence about her in this picture. Something she lost later. In high school she became shy. I think he saw her vulnerability. I want to explain this to you. I have included a copy of Deena's arrest report. I want you to understand what happened and why the media pounced on issues of her mental health and an investigation at work when she disappeared. Remember that despite all that happened, the court still gave her primary physical custody of her daughter two years later. It's true Deena had a history of depression. In 1995, while in college, my sister took an overdose. Her roommate found her and thankfully she was resuscitated. She got help. Her depression had been undiagnosed. She started on medication and it rewrote her reality. She went from being almost catatonic to high-functioning. She finished nursing school at the top of her class. And she got a NICU job, something she had always wanted and a job she was very very good at. For Lucas, antidepressants signalled weakness. He needled my sister for years about coming off her medication. He knew better than all her doctors. He would help her. She had to change medications during her pregnancy and breastfeeding, but she stayed on them. She knew. But in late 2001 he talked her off them. At that stage she was on SNRIs and abruptly stopping can be physically harrowing. She had brain jolts and muscle spasms and crushing despair. She was distracted and she made a serious mistake at work. Wrong syringe, wrong baby. The baby, only 1500 grams, was given a dose of morphine intended for a much bigger baby going through withdrawal. The baby stopped breathing, the morphine inhibiting the respiratory drive, the ability to breathe. The baby had to be intubated. It was a serious med error and it was Deena's fault. There was an investigation and she was put on six months' probation. In the immediate aftermath of the incident she went off the rails. She was found in her old college neighbourhood near Drexel. She was drunk and incoherent and alone. She resisted assistance and was arrested for disorderly conduct. She called me, not Lucas, from the precinct. Still she went back to him.

Nessa picked up an envelope of pictures she hadn't seen since 2004, when she'd made copies for the investigators. Mathilde needed to see.

This photograph was taken the night of November 28th, 2002, while we sat in the emergency room waiting for an X-ray of her jaw. She is missing a tooth, Mathilde. It is hard for me not to compare it to her second-grade picture, her tooth proudly lost, when all her life was still in front of her. Lucas Chevalier's fist did this.

Nessa pressed her palm against the wooden floor. She was here on the painted white floorboards of Deena's room in her own house. The physical surge of dread was the most real memory she had of that night, more than the sequence of events. She remembered disjointed details but couldn't assemble them. Deena's phone call from the street, Ruby in the background: Mommy's hurt, Nessa, Mommy's hurt. The journey to the hospital, Nessa driving. She must have parked the car but had no recollection. In the emergency room someone kept asking for their mother, except it was an old woman's voice, maybe in the room next to them. Please get my mother, and My mother won't be happy about this.

Later Deena was on the phone to their own mother's hospice nurse, talking about moving from oral to parenteral dosing of opioids. Maria Garvey was dying. Nessa could still hear Deena's voice, hers but not hers because of her swollen jaw and missing tooth, arranging their mother's care. Her tongue lisping against her broken teeth. Someone, maybe a nurse's aide, brought Deena something cold in a Styrofoam cup. Ice-cold Jell-O or something, to get sugar into her, or to help with the swelling in her mouth. It was red and there was a spoon and even though she seemed to be holding it together her body couldn't get the spoon to her lips. Her hand jerked wildly. The small trickle from her nose. Deena would not file a statement against Lucas. He'll kill me. Just get us out, she said to Nessa. Help us.

This is Deena and Ruby on Ruby's 4th birthday, exactly five weeks before Deena disappeared. Look. The two of them hugging the good of each other. If Lucas has said things about my sister that made her out to be sick or if he told you she just walked away from Ruby, look at this picture.

263

She included the petitions for third-party visitation she had made and the complaints she had filed about Ruby not being in school.

In 2008 we learned through the private investigator that Ruby was not enrolled in school and if she was being home-schooled it was unofficial. She was not involved in any activities that brought her into contact with other children and gave her opportunities to play. From a distance, I have tried my best. I want to add that it concerns us that you don't seem to have any contact or relationship with Ruby and we wonder why? She needs support.

Joey and Molly said Nessa had no life. Maybe it was true. Her life was stuck in these images she'd put in random heaps on the floor. She hadn't moved on. On top of the pile of Nessa and Ruby pictures was one of herself, Ruby and Ronan the day they went to the shore. Ruby had found a horseshoe crab in the tide. Ronan had never seen one before, couldn't believe that this prehistoric tank was there on the Jersey shore in the midst of beach chairs and umbrellas and plastic buckets and pails. Nessa told him they were older than dinosaurs and had nine or ten eyes. She had handed her camera to a woman sitting near them on the beach and asked her to take the picture.

Ronan and Nessa are kneeling in the sand and Ruby is holding the horseshoe crab up toward Ronan, who is acting terrified. Nessa is bent over laughing. Her face turned up to the camera. Blonde strands stick to her tanned face. Her hand is on Ronan's arm. They are all beautiful.

24
Ruby

2017

Clover was cooking maple syrup sausages. Ruby could smell them from her bed, momentarily cocooned. Then she remembered the night before – Lucas at the kitchen sink in the dark – and a gloom fell over the room. Why had he come home early? She looked out the window. His truck was there, parked by the trees. Why hadn't she seen it?

Morning, said Clover, turning to face her from the stove. She scanned Ruby, reading her. Had she heard something last night?

Morning.

I made some breakfast seeing as you have a lot of brainwork ahead of you. Clover hadn't changed into her housedress or tidied her hair.

Ruby turned on the tap at the sink to fill a glass and pulled her hand back, splashing water across the floor. There were deep purple bruises on both her arms; blood had pooled and speckled under her skin.

Sorry, she mumbled, and got paper towels to wipe up the spill, trying to stay out of Clover's line of vision. I don't know what made me do that. I'll be right back.

She rummaged through her drawer and found a cotton shirt with sleeves that went to the elbows.

Clover never mentioned the party or asked her if she'd had fun. Had Lucas been angry with her for telling Ruby it was okay to go? Why had Lucas come home in the middle of the night?

At the table, Lucas sat beside her and rolled up his sleeves, his laptop open. It was time for the college applications. She gave him the online address and they set up her account. Ruby had to list all the places she wanted to apply to on the form.

Okay, let's research first. Division One teams for women's rowing, Lucas said.

They were pretending that nothing had happened, and Ruby was part of that camouflaging. She was making it easy for Lucas. Clover was too. Maple syrup sausages. Lucas found a list with rankings, divisions and SAT points. Ruby sat with her notebook and wrote down the names of potential schools. She felt uncomfortable in front of a computer with Lucas. It was the main thing she wasn't allowed to do and now it was weird to have him scrolling up and down, clicking on sites, acting like it was something she did every day.

Lucas wanted her to apply to Ivy League schools; Ruby didn't think she'd get in. The one or two students at her high school aiming for that level spent summers doing Model UN, working for congressmen and going to accelerated learning camps. They were always comparing marks and saying things like, God, I'm barely scraping a 4.3, or humblebrags like, I could barely figure out how to hit a nail with a hammer when I was building houses for the homeless all last summer. She didn't want to go to college with them. Connecticut and Massachusetts had loads of good schools. She wrote their rankings and SAT scores in her notebook.

Lucas stood to refill his coffee and Ruby continued the scrolling. Pennsylvania. University of Pennsylvania. Philadelphia. She'd met some Penn girls from rowing and liked them. And she'd be in Philadelphia, where her mother was from. It was Ivy League and Lucas would be happy about that.

Lucas sat back down. What's the highest-ranked college you've listed so far?

Ruby ran her finger down the list. I think University of Pennsylvania. Their general ranking is like six or seven.

What?

Yeah. Six, actually. She moved the mouse and pointed to the screen.

Penn?

Yeah, in Philadelphia.

Who told you to apply there?

It's right here on the Division One list. I know girls from competition who row there. It's a good school. Ivy League, like you said. I doubt I'd get in.

Lucas stood. Did someone tell you to try there? He was leaning over her.

What? No. It's on the list you just found on the internet. I wrote it down.

Lucas! Clover's voice was sharp. She was standing in the doorway. That's enough.

Lucas stood. Take it off, he said. He stormed outside and moments later Ruby heard the truck's engine.

Ruby put her forehead down on the table, her breath ragged. He didn't want her near where her mother was from. Why?

You apply wherever you want, Clover said. Do you hear me? You apply to that school. Never mind him. It would be good for you. I won't be here forever.

Ruby stood and hugged her, something they never did. Clover patted her back with soft thumps.

Later, she heard Lucas's truck return when she was closing up the coop. His and Clover's voices carried through the open windows as she crossed the lawn toward the house. They were arguing. Ruby was at the bottom of the steps when she heard Clover speaking over Lucas. Angry. Ruby had never heard her speak like this.

You stop it. You are in my house and I won't have it.

Lucas's voice was low. She could hear the spittle in it. Someone was interfering. She heard snatches: A grenade . . . My relationship. She's thrown a goddamn grenade . . . Someone following Ruby.

Then he bellowed at Clover: Don't you ever talk to her on the phone. She is not allowed near this house. Never. Do you hear me?

Ruby ran back down and sat in the dark coop. The soft murmuring roosting sounds reassured her. Was he talking about her mother? What if it was true that her mother had disappeared for real? Was maybe even dead? Who would try to make contact through Clover?

Mathilde was waiting for them at a table in the corner. She stood then, unsure, sat again. She was beautiful but on edge and nervous. Her hair was auburn and went halfway down her back. She was younger than Lucas. She wore gold hooped earrings and when she smiled she had double dimples in both cheeks. Her eyebrows were the same colour as her hair. She was not what Ruby had expected. Before Lucas could introduce them, Mathilde reached for Ruby's hand and held it with both of hers.

Ruby, I'm Mathilde. I've heard so much about you.

Lucas looked away. Ruby didn't know what to say. She'd never even heard Mathilde's name.

Me too, she lied.

Lucas had only given her an hour's warning. He'd been pacing on the shore when she paddled in after training with Coach Morgan and some others.

There's someone who wants to meet you, he'd said. We have to go to Montreal, so can you shower and all and be ready in an hour?

Who?

Her name's Mathilde. She wants to meet you. A woman I've been seeing.

Why doesn't she come here?

He hadn't answered and they'd made the journey in silence.

They all sat. Made small talk about the restaurant and then read their menus. The lights were low. A waiter lit the candles at their table.

268

Your hair is beautiful, Ruby said.

Mathilde smiled. Thank you. So is yours. I actually can't get over how much you look like your mother— She stopped, and in the instant must have realized the shock she had created. Sorry. Maybe I shouldn't have . . . Again she stopped and let the sentence drift off.

Had Mathilde said that on purpose? Lucas was agitated, shifting in his seat and trying to get the attention of a waiter.

Did you know my mother? Ruby asked.

Mathilde looked at Lucas while she spoke. No. No. I shouldn't have said that. I'm so sorry. I saw a picture.

Ruby was finding it hard to breathe. Lucas had never shown her a picture. He'd said her mother had taken them all when she left. Ruby went to lift her water glass and had to put it back down because her hand was shaking. Mathilde saw. She put her hand on Ruby's.

Are you okay? she asked. Ruby pulled her hands off the table and held them both in her lap.

There was something going wrong at the table between Lucas and Mathilde. Ruby wanted to disappear. Lucas was angry. She could feel it, but he was trying to keep the conversation going about their life together, his and Ruby's on the lake.

Did you like growing up on the lake? Mathilde asked.

Ruby didn't know how to answer the question. Well, I haven't known anything else. So. But yeah. The things most important to me are all connected to the Islands and growing up there. Rowing, swimming, Vermont, camping, fishing, the woods. Lucas added something about growing up connected to nature being healthy, and how well Ruby was doing in school.

Ruby couldn't concentrate on the menu. She was reading the words describing the dishes but they wouldn't sink in. When the waiter came to take their order she got flustered and Lucas ordered for her. Beef fillet, medium rare, just water is fine.

Mathilde asked what colleges she was thinking about.

Ruby told her how she and Lucas had been going through a list. She would probably apply to six. Two long shots, two that she had a good chance of getting into and two back-ups. She didn't mention Penn.

They talked about college and the adjustment. How Ruby would be eighteen in a few months. How much change was ahead. Their food arrived. The beef sat in a pool of blood, the way she usually would have liked it. She cut a small piece but found it hard to chew and swallow. It all felt like an interview and Lucas was using her. She had to pass some sort of test for Mathilde because he needed her to.

And your dad home-schooled you until you were eight? That must have been something.

Ruby tried to take deep breaths. She couldn't really remember that time in her life. She was uncomfortable. It was as if she was here to endorse Lucas as a father or something.

Yeah. I was definitely ready for mainstream, and I'd benefited from my dad's schooling by knowing the weirdest things.

Oh, like what? Mathilde was delighted by everything Ruby said.

Ruby told her about foraging, growing their own produce, rearing chicks, hunting, fishing. She told her how Lucas used to plough paths on the lake in the winter so she could ice-skate. He'd made her read articles from *Discover* and *National Geographic*. Lucas was pleased. This was making him very happy. This was what they were supposed to be doing.

Is that what you want to study in college?

What?

Environmental or natural sciences?

Ruby had never discussed her possible major with Lucas.

No. I'm thinking about being an English major.

Mathilde nearly jumped out of her chair. *I* was an English major!

Well, my friends keep telling me that with my English degree I can look forward to a career mopping floors or pulling soft-serve. Both of which I already do.

They're not wrong, said Lucas. You've plenty of time to change your mind.

Mathilde's laugh was edged. Funny, she said, then looked back at Ruby. Your dad told you I'm an editor?

Ruby almost burst out laughing. The whole thing was such a farce. She wanted to shout I didn't even know you existed until a few hours ago. It bothered her that Mathilde knew about her, but she hadn't been allowed to know anything about Mathilde.

I forget, said Ruby. What kind of editor again?

After their plates were cleared, Ruby excused herself. She was splashing cold water on her face when Mathilde came into the restroom.

Ruby, I am so sorry I mentioned your mother. Your father has said how painful it is for you and you don't like talking about it. I don't want to make the wrong first impression. She handed her a card. *Mathilde Lavoie*. Put that in your pocket. If you ever need anything, anything at all, you can call me. Your dad doesn't have to know. Just between us. I promise. It really is so so nice and reassuring to meet you. He's raised you beautifully.

Ruby tried to speak, to protest, shook her head. But Mathilde mistook it for modesty and before Ruby could say anything she had stepped into a stall.

When the truck pulled up outside the house, Ruby got out and slammed the door. She had performed for him, told lies, and it made her feel sick. For as long as she could remember she had wanted to talk about her mother. She had been desperate for any fragment of information, any detail of her. He'd kept her own mother's picture from her but shown it to his girlfriend?

*

Sophie and Ruby sat in Sophie's living room with two of Sophie's sisters, watching episodes of *Breaking Bad*. The sisters had all seen it before. Ruby hadn't but she couldn't concentrate and wasn't really following the plot. She was thinking about Mathilde seeing a picture of her mother, and the yellow envelopes that must be inside Lucas's room. She still hadn't gotten in though she had tried everything from paperclips to micro-thin screwdrivers.

Sophie, can I borrow your phone to send a message?

Sophie rolled her eyes and tossed it to her. Your crazy dad still tracking your phone?

Mathilde believed she didn't want to know about her mother. It was the one lie she'd gone along with that she couldn't let go of.

She was going to send a text message but first she googled her mother's name and clicked *Images*. Her mother's picture was there. Over and over. Sledding. A teenager holding a basketball. A graduation cap and gown. Nursing scrubs. On a swing in a park. Her mother was beautiful. In a pile of raked leaves, throwing them over her head, the whole picture golden. Her mother looking down, her expression happy, and Ruby knew that what the viewer couldn't see was her. Her mother was looking at her.

Mathilde's card was hidden in her wallet, and she took it out and put in the number, and then a message that she hadn't considered at all until she wrote it:

Mathilde, we met several weeks ago. I'm Ruby Chevalier. It does not upset me to talk about my mother. I am desperate to know about her. I always have been. My father doesn't let me talk about her and has never shown me the picture he showed you. I haven't seen any pictures except online and one that was sent to me. You said I could contact you. That it could be just between us. I want you to know how much I have wanted to know about her.

She punched in the letters, one after another. Her fingers could be angry too. She didn't even read it over: she hit *Send*. She felt detached from everyone in the room, listening to them laugh and talk. In Sophie's house everyone was at ease, bodies draped across each other. In Ruby's house they were each separate and rigid on the edges of chairs or behind locked doors. She wished she could stay here in the living room with them. Her own phone pinged repeatedly. Probably Lucas. She didn't even look at it.

Later Sophie said she'd drive her home. They sat in the car waiting for it to heat up, listening to Lorde's 'Writer in the Dark'. Sometimes just single piano notes.

Well? Sophie asked.

Yeah, Ruby said. It's good.

Sophie's neighbours had Christmas lights on the trees outside, the ones with large bulbs that Ruby loved. Sophie put the car in gear and sang along as they drove down the driveway. Lorde was singing about mothers and daughters, that connection. Ruby was thinking about all those pictures of her mother, row after row. They'd only gone a few yards when headlights came up toward them from the road several hundred yards down.

Maybe that's Cecilia home from work.

The car was coming fast.

Sophie blinked her high beams. Why isn't she pulling in?

The oncoming lights flooded into Sophie's car, blinding them.

She's driving so fast.

Ruby's hands went forward to the dashboard as if she could stop what was about to explode into them. Sophie accelerated onto the front yard, bouncing over the kerb. The wheels bumped on the frozen ground. The other car swerved also.

They're *trying* to hit us! Sophie shouted.

Ruby screamed as the headlights in front of them swerved sideways.

Sophie slammed the brakes. A truck was blocking them.

Lucas. Oh my God. It's my dad.

Before Ruby could open the door, Lucas was pulling her out by the hood of her jacket. She fell on the hard ground and he dragged her.

Sophie was out of the car, shouting for her mother. Some of her sisters were already on the lawn.

Get Mom. Call the police, Sophie shouted.

No! Ruby cried. No. Don't.

Where is it? Lucas shouted at her.

Ruby just stared back at him.

Where is it? He grabbed her bag and turned it upside down. Picked up the phone he had given her and spiked it back to the ground. He grabbed at her jacket pockets, patted the back of her jeans. Ruby stood there while he searched her whole body for another phone, staring back at Sophie's sisters watching.

Stop that. Stop! Get off my property now. Mrs Dragan's blonde hair was lit by the porch lights. Lucas had bent over to pick things up off the ground and swung around to face Mrs Dragan just as Ruby bent to get her bag. Both his arms collided with the side of her face.

Ruby was on the ground.

Sophie's mother was standing over her. She was telling Lucas to leave.

Sophie was kneeling.

She was repeating You're okay . . . but it sounded very far away.

Sophie's neighbours' outdoor Christmas lights blinking.

The shape of a cloud in the sky even though it was dark.

It was an accident, Lucas said. He crouched down, trying to haul her up.

Don't move her. She needs to stay still. Call an ambulance. Mrs Dragan's voice was in charge.

Please, Mrs Dragan, Ruby said. No.

Sophie was picking up Ruby's things off the ground and putting them back in her bag.

274

Lucas grabbed the bag from her and clicked the torch on his phone, shining it onto the ground. He went over to the open passenger door and shone it inside.

Get out of my car, said Mrs Dragan. Her voice was shaking with anger. And get off my property now.

Ruby sat up.

Easy, said Mrs Dragan. Just give it a moment.

Please. I'll just go home. Please. I am so sorry.

Lucas walked back. He wasn't wearing a jacket even. He leaned down and lifted Ruby to her feet.

Get in the truck.

Mrs Dragan held Ruby's arm and put a hand on her waist. Ruby, stay here with us. Stay the night until everything calms down.

Ruby looked at Sophie's face in the headlights of her mother's car, her eyes huge in the dark. Sophie's sisters were there on the porch. Sophie was crying. Ruby had done all this to them.

No. I want to go home.

Ruby limped toward the truck, still dizzy. When she got to the passenger side she knelt down in the grass and threw up. She didn't even wipe her mouth, didn't have the energy to fight with anyone, didn't want the police, or other people to get hurt. She wanted to go home to Clover and Adelaide, and to sleep for a very long time. She heaved herself into the truck and put her forehead on the dashboard.

They stopped at a store and Lucas went in and got a large bag of ice.

Rest your face on this.

She put the ice against the window, eased her face onto it and closed her eyes. At their turn off the main road Lucas pulled in and rang Ethan.

Ethan, can I ask a favour? Could you collect Adelaide from my house? I'm almost home but if you could go up and get her now, that would be great.

They sat for a few minutes.

Lucas said, Ruby, we have to get the story straight because we know it was an accident. We have to cover what happened. I had no idea where you were and you hadn't come home from work and you weren't answering your phone. I was worried and angry. I went to the Dragans' and you got out of their car and your bag spilled and unfortunately you stepped forward as I was standing up.

Ruby was only half-listening. It all seemed pointless. She could feel the ice melting to the shape of her face, a few drips escaping down the back of her neck.

25
Ruby

2017

Ruby knelt at the side of the bath and Clover scooped measuring cups of warm water over her head, squirted the shampoo and gently washed the vomit out of her hair, careful not to touch the right side of her face. Her grandmother's fingers on her scalp, the warm water, her bent head, her hair a liquid veil. Almost like a memory. Someone washing her hair long ago. Her head was spinning and her face throbbed. Clover led her to bed, wrapped a dry towel around her wet hair and put packs of frozen peas against her cheek. Ruby shut her eyes, everything clean now. She slept in snatches, sometimes waking and the dream still unfolding around her, someone on the ceiling talking, a forest in the corner of the room, shadows, whispering. When she opened her eyes Clover was beside her watching, asking her questions, facts, math equations.

I'm okay, Clover. I don't have brain damage.

You could be concussed. Or a bleed.

You watch too much TV.

Ruby didn't go to school. The side of her face was bruised and swollen, and she had a black eye, two wide swipes of deep purple below the lid. Lucas couldn't look at her and Ruby almost felt sorry for him. He didn't go to Montreal. He said he'd told Adelaide they all had stomach bugs. In case she showed up, Ruby guessed she was supposed to act like her stomach hurt. He did Ruby's chores for her and, again, none of them ever said anything about what had happened. He sent Ruby a picture of the hens from the coop to her phone but neither of them spoke.

The week passed in a stupor. Even the weather seemed dazed.

Sunless days and ice fog crawling into the shortest days of the year. None of them went beyond the property line; Ruby and Clover barely left the living room. They spent days in their pyjamas watching old movies and Lucas said nothing about it.

Ruby was at the sink when she heard a car door slam. A man and a woman were stepping out of a small car. Everything was grey and brown and hazy, the stark branches, the frozen ground.

Someone's here, she called.

Ruby went back to the living room and sat with Clover. The doorbell gave her a jolt when it rang; she'd forgotten they even had one. Clover didn't get up. The bell rang again when Lucas was halfway down the stairs.

He shut the door between the living room and the kitchen and then changed his mind and left it slightly ajar.

The woman introduced herself and the man. Lucas Chevalier? Family Services Division. Clover and Ruby sat very still, listening. There had been a complaint and Ruby Chevalier had been out of school all week.

Oh, said Lucas, she's been sick. I should have contacted the school. We can send a doctor's note after the vacation. My bad.

Ruby couldn't see him but she knew by his voice that he was being casual and friendly, the Lucas people couldn't help liking.

No, the woman said, it's not about the absence. A report of suspected child abuse and neglect has been filed in relation to Ruby Chevalier. We're here to complete an assessment.

I can assure you that's not the case. Can we schedule an appointment with you next week and Ruby can tell you herself? As I said, Ruby's not feeling a hundred per cent.

Ruby's chest tightened. Clover's face stayed blank. She was listening but saying nothing.

This is an assessment, not an investigation, Mr Chevalier. We'd like to do the assessment today. If it is obstructed, we'll then undertake an investigation. The assessment is just a tool to ensure the minor's safety and well-being.

Ruby had been worrying about what Sophie's mother and sisters thought of her. She had brought all that trouble to them, to the Dragans' house. She worried Sophie's mom wouldn't want her there ever again or that her sisters wouldn't like her anymore, but she hadn't considered them reporting it.

The woman wanted permission to talk to Ruby without Lucas. They would interview him separately, and the grandmother. Lucas didn't seem to have a choice and he let them in. When they stepped into the living room, Clover spoke first.

Can you get my neighbour Adelaide Puckett? I would like her to be with me. She's just down the road. Ruby has her number.

Ruby kept her head down, her hand covering the side of her face. She and the woman sat at the kitchen table.

Ruby, can you let me see your face?

The woman's voice was gentle. Her dark hair was undercut at the back and sides, her nose pierced. She didn't look like someone who worked for the State of Vermont. The woman waited.

Ruby lowered her hand, and the woman wrote notes down on her form.

Can you tell me what happened to cause those bruises?

Lucas had told her what to say and mostly it was what had happened. Lucas had swung around just as she was bending down to pick up the things that had spilled out of her bag.

When you fell, were you unconscious?

No.

You didn't black out?

I was dazed for a moment but not knocked out.

Did you throw up?

Yes.

Did your father take you to a doctor?

No. I was fine.

The woman went through a list of questions on a form. Was physical force used against you that night on the driveway? Were you physically restrained that night? Has your father ever hit or restrained you before?

He's never hit me. This was an accident.

Are you afraid that if you talk to us there will be repercussions? Will your father punish you?

No.

Are you in danger? Do you feel safe?

After the social workers left, Adelaide and Clover sat at the kitchen table and Lucas went upstairs. Ruby went back into the cocoon of blankets on the living-room sofa and pulled them over her head. She'd said everything right. Lucas couldn't be mad. She heard his shoes on the stairs and knew he was in the same room when she heard a sigh. She stayed under the blanket. Then Adelaide's voice from the doorway.

I'm heading home now, Lucas. I will be back in the morning, first thing. Clover has asked me to come. She needs help. She is my neighbour and she's asked me.

There was an edge in Adelaide's voice. When Ruby thought about it, Adelaide was there mostly when Lucas wasn't. She'd started coming *after* the job in Montreal. She'd known Lucas his whole life.

Bad egg.

That crawling, vile feeling. She held her breath. Lucas didn't say anything back but she could hear him breathing.

And Ruby . . . Adelaide's voice was still stern. Tomorrow you get dressed.

Sophie's sister Cecilia had a vanity in her room surrounded by round white lights. It reminded Ruby of backstage dressing rooms in 1940s films. There were tubs of brushes, powders, foundations, fake eye-lashes. Tubes of shimmer and pencils for highlighting, contouring, outlining. Ruby didn't know what half of it was. She was so happy to be there again. The sisters had flocked around her when she came through the door with Sophie and hadn't pretended that her face wasn't bruised. They'd murmured sympathy and said, Ouch. It had been easier than school, where people stared but then pretended they hadn't noticed. Cecilia had held Ruby's face to the light and said, Come to my room. The bruising on her cheek had faded to a yellow with hints of purple but there were still dark streaks under her eyes. Nobody will notice a thing.

Cecilia dotted Ruby's entire face with foundation using her fingertips and then blended it gently with a brush.

Does that hurt?

No. Not at all. It just looks like it might.

It was Ruby's eighteenth birthday and the Dragans were throw-ing her a party. Sophie said her mother had insisted, even though it was only two weeks since she and Lucas had had the scene on their front lawn. Nathalie and Wyatt were coming. The juniors and seniors from the rowing team. Friends from school. Sophie had practically body-tackled her at the bus stop two days ago.

You can't say no. Nathalie and I've invited everybody and my mom's already bought the ingredients for the cake.

One of her sisters was going to DJ.

Ruby's hand covered her right eye and cheek. I can't.

Yes, you can. Make-up will cover that. You're celebrating your eighteenth.

Isn't your mom mad?

Like a Fury. Oh my God, Ruby, not at you. Your dad was way

out of line, patting you down, dumping your bag.

Does Nathalie know?

Yeah. I told her what happened. Not like the specifics about the phone but that your dad lost it and there'd been a scene.

Those words. *Lost it, smashed, fucked-up, bruised.*

When Cecilia had finished she told Ruby to turn and look in the mirror.

God, I look better than the real-life me.

There wasn't a blemish on her skin. Cecilia had given her thick black lashes, shaped eyebrows, everything.

Wait, said Cecilia. Since you're the birthday girl. She stuck two small rhinestones at the inner corner of each eye. Ruby touched one with her finger, expecting it to fall.

Eyelash glue, Cecilia said. You are gorgeous.

In Sophie's room they drank vodka and Cokes.

We better down them before Nathalie gets here, said Sophie. The morality police.

Ruby started to laugh and her hand went to her cheek. It still hurt.

She was staying the night. She'd simply announced it to Lucas: Sophie is throwing me a party for my eighteenth and I am staying the night at her house on Friday.

She knew that he wasn't going to object. It was her first day back at school, her face was still bruised, and she was eighteen. It was Sophie's mother that had reported him, and Ruby knew he would see this as disloyal but that he wasn't going to say anything.

The girls from rowing gave her a framed picture, black and white, taken at the end of a race. It had been in the sports section of a Burlington paper: her, turned toward the camera, smiling, relief in her face.

Nathalie gave her a boxset of *Game of Thrones* books.

Since it was always mine you were reading.

Aww. Thank you. I will read them every year.

Nathalie hovered near her all night and Ruby knew she was sorry for the past year and a half, the distance that had wedged between them. At one point when they were dancing Ruby hugged her. I'm fine. Stop worrying. Nathalie looked like she might burst into tears.

Sophie gave her a hand-knitted sweater, the same colour as the choker she had made her sophomore year.

You're forest-green. That's always the colour I see.

I can't believe this is your first sleepover, Sophie said later when they were lying in bed.

Me either.

Sophie's King Charles, Lola, was snoring on her own little bed between theirs and they both started to laugh.

Lola's my ASMR soundtrack.

I find it comforting too. You could record her for me.

Is everything at home okay, with your dad and everything?

Ruby pulled the comforter up to her chin. I guess. I don't know. None of us have mentioned it. Lucas is around more, working some from home. He's only in Montreal like two nights a week, so I guess he and Mathilde broke up.

She shouldn't have shown him your message. She said you could contact her and then the very first thing she does is show him and doesn't even message you back.

I just don't think she'd do that, said Ruby.

She had to have. How else could he have known?

In a chilling instant it was clear to Ruby how. She knew she was right and she couldn't say it to Sophie. He spied on Mathilde too.

When the temperatures plummeted below minus fifteen Ruby worried about letting the chickens out. Adelaide told her to put petroleum jelly on their combs and wattles to keep them from getting frostbite. Sophie and Nathalie said it was hilarious when Ruby told them on the bus. They started a list of Adelaide's Life Hacks, which included bouncing batteries to test them and putting pantyhose over the vacuum cleaner head to find a dropped needle. Adelaide was in the house most days, sitting in the kitchen with Clover and doing more and more of the cooking and washing.

Did you notice Clover sleeps more than usual? Ruby asked her.

Your grandmother's tired. She wants to see you go to a good college and have a life away from here.

Is Clover sick?

No, she said. But she's old and she worries.

Adelaide's answer seemed slightly catastrophic.

Lately Clover would sit down in the middle of chopping carrots or stirring a beef stew, rest her elbows on the table and say, I am wagged out, or I am beat. Adelaide said Clover had been cooped up too long in the house. She never got out. This was true and it made Ruby sad. She could drive but she was always at school, rowing or work. And, anyway, Lucas had the truck. Adelaide started bringing Clover on short trips. Just for a spin to look at some scenery or to go shopping, and sometimes to have a coffee in Burlington. Lucas didn't like it. He said Clover shouldn't be walking sidewalks with all the ice. It was dangerous. Adelaide ignored him.

She doesn't even ask me – she just takes her. Lucas said it like Can you believe that? Ruby didn't say anything. She concentrated on her history book. Why should women in their seventies and eighties need to ask for his permission?

Two outlaws are watching a woman comb her hair, a profile shot that emphasizes her curves. Her husband has just died. The older outlaw tells the younger one that she'll find another man. He says something about her being the kind of woman who has a need so deep and lonely that only a man can fix it.

Clover, come on. Ruby raised her two palms upward. Seriously?

It was so bad Clover started to laugh. Then Ruby. Clover really laughed, so much it scared Ruby; she never laughed like that. She couldn't get her breath and she was clutching at her middle. Was she having a heart attack? But then Clover was blowing her nose and wiping her eyes, righting herself in her chair and chuckling.

The kitchen door slammed.

They hadn't heard him.

Ruby, get in here. The atmosphere deadened. He was angry.

Lucas was holding an envelope and a letter. Did you apply to Penn after I specifically told you not to? You did this behind my back?

She'd applied using the school's address. How did Lucas get a letter?

Answer me! He banged his fist on the table.

That letter is for me. I should have opened it.

You are in my house and while you're in it you'll do what I say.

She's in *my* house, said Clover. She was standing beside Ruby now. I told her to apply.

Don't interfere, said Lucas. I am talking to my daughter about discipline, respect and doing what she's told. I won't be paying for it and I won't be giving them my financial information.

You would prevent her from going to college?

I'd prevent her from going to *that* college. She went behind my back.

She's eighteen. Leave her.

Stay out of it, Clover.

No. She will make the decisions about her future, this house, everything. Not you.

I'm her father. I make the decisions.

In this house, she makes her own decisions.

Not while she's under my roof.

My roof. Then hers. This house goes to her.

Ruby gasped in air, felt the blood drain from her face. Why would Clover do that to Lucas. To her? Lucas took a step back, crossed his arms, cocked his head as if to call her bluff.

Did that old bat put you up to this?

I made my will long before Adelaide Puckett came visiting.

Clover, stop, Ruby said. You're scaring me. Please.

Lucas looked from one to the other, turned around and stomped back out the door. Ruby collapsed in the chair. Clover hesitated beside her for a moment, then left. Ruby could hear her slow steps on the stairs.

In the morning Ruby got up early. Lucas still wasn't back and she cycled to the post office in town. She had her school ID card. Dale Everett was at the desk and she showed it to him. From now on I'd like you to hold my mail care of General Delivery, Middle Lake. No one else, not my father or grandmother or anyone, is authorized to collect my mail but me.

Understood, Ruby, Dale said.

Outside, she rang Lucas.

Ruby, I'm not angry with you.

I want you to know that I've told the post office that my mail should be separated into General Delivery, and I've instructed them that it can only be collected by me. No one else is authorized to collect my mail. I told them not you.

Lucas didn't say anything for a moment. Did someone put you up to this?

Put me up to what? Asking to receive and open my own mail?

I can't talk to you when you're like this, he said. You're completely hysterical.

The call went dead. She hadn't even got the chance to say she knew the yellow envelopes he had always taken were for her.

The ice was still melting from the trees and ran in rivulets down to the lake, making a sound like rain. Ruby cycled to Schneider's for her Saturday shift, grateful for a reason to leave the house. The snow had dissolved and her wheels swished through the slushy road, adding to the sound of rushing water all around. Soon they would be out on the lake again and in the next month she would know which colleges had accepted her. She'd left early to go to the post office first to see if any mail had come for her. Back on Route 2 she cycled carefully because of the slush and the heavier traffic. A truck slowed behind her. She gripped the handlebars. It overtook her then pulled in abruptly just ahead. Lucas. He walked to the back of the truck and put down the tailgate. She got off the bike and without saying anything pushed it toward him and he put it in the back. She knew something was wrong.

Something's happened. Clover collapsed. She's on her way to the hospital.

I was just with her. Sitting at the table with her and Adelaide.

A stroke, they think.

Ruby felt like her insides had been scooped out.

Is she going to be okay? Do you know?

I don't know anything yet.

Lucas was upset. He tried to speak but couldn't. Everything had been going wrong in the house. It made Ruby sad. She knew he loved his mother.

In the emergency room, Lucas spoke to the people at the desk and Ruby went to find Adelaide in the waiting room. She was sitting alone in the far corner near the vending machines. She saw Ruby and patted the seat beside her. Ruby sat down and Adelaide took her hand.

I don't know anything yet. I was making us coffee and she was in the middle of a story and she just lost her speech. One side of her face dropped. Classic symptoms. I called 911. They got there fast. She has a very, very good chance. With strokes it's always about time.

Adelaide rubbed Ruby's arm as if to reassure her and squeezed her wrist.

She's tough. You know yourself.

Ruby nodded.

They waited hours. Lucas was restless and wouldn't sit near Adelaide. He jiggled his leg impatiently, went back and forth to the desk, paced the corridor.

Eventually a doctor came out. Are you Clover Chevalier's family? she asked.

Lucas stood. Yes. We are. Me and my daughter. He took Ruby's elbow and stepped forward, excluding Adelaide.

Why don't you come with me, the doctor said.

They sat in a small room with bare walls and the doctor explained Clover's situation.

She's not out of the woods. The next few days are critical. With stroke there can be confusion, memory loss and fatigue. She will need a lot of support when she leaves here, whether that's at home or in a facility.

Clover was asleep and didn't look like herself. The left side of her mouth sagged open. There were machines hooked up to her, beeping and pulsing, and an IV dripped down a tube into a cannula. Lucas stayed at the foot of the bed but Ruby went closer and touched her bare arm.

It's me, Ruby.

Clover didn't stir. Ruby wished she could close her mouth for her, pull her hair back into its bun. Why had they taken it out? She leaned to whisper in her ear.

Even though you'd tell me this is horseshit, I'm going to say it anyway. I wish I told you more that I love you. I'll come every day. My school's close by.

Clover was exhausted. She could sit up and talk but not for long. Her speech came in slow slurs but each day she sounded more herself. Adelaide was there most days too and Lucas would come if Ruby was there, as if he didn't know how to be alone with his mother anymore.

Do something for me, Clover said one time when she and Ruby were the only ones in the room.

Okay.

Tell no one. Understand?

Yes?

Not Lucas.

Okay.

In my closet. The bureau. Third drawer down. A bag. Beads. Clover gestured with her right hand as if to say Beads all over it.

She had to pause. Gather her breath and energy.

Inside the lining, a slip of paper. With a number. Bring me that.

Her head fell back against the pillow and she closed her eyes. The effort had exhausted her.

Clover, is this about your will and the house?

Shut up about that. This is important.

26

Nessa

The chairs in the Roundhouse were so low to the ground it was hard to get comfortable or feel dignified. She'd forgotten that about them. The carpet hadn't changed either, worn to a flat sheen after decades of feet – witnesses, drunks, families, suspects – spilled coffee, grease from hoagies or whatever. Filthy. The night she smashed Lucas's truck she had lain on the carpet, curled in a ball; she hadn't noticed or cared. She'd heard someone say, Leave her. She remembered the click of the door and being alone. When she'd finished crying, Frank had come back and coaxed her off the floor, into one of these chairs. Put his woollen coat around her shoulders. Her lungs wouldn't expand, making her breath shallow. She had never cried like that again. She wasn't inside herself anymore. The worst was already behind her and there was nothing to look forward to.

Joey was with her this time, waiting in a faux-leather chair beside her, checking the time every few minutes. He was uncomfortable, wanted this to be over. The plastic skin had been torn off the armrest; everything in this building was worn and tired. Developments in the case, is what Frank had said. *Developments.* He never used words like that. There had never been anything to give them hope. Or to let them give it up. Years of nothing.

You okay? Joey asked. The way he said it annoyed her. She was angry still that he'd refused to talk about Deena and Ruby. Concern creased his brow. He was dressed in his work clothes. He'd get back in his truck after this and head to the suburbs and his contracting business, collect his children from school at three, make them grilled cheese sandwiches with glasses of milk. Kate and Joey's house was always loud with the clatter of family. His five kids went to St Christopher's just like Deena, Joey and Nessa had. Joey had filled his life; she'd emptied hers.

Yeah, she said. She was too tired to feel much, but she still had to tamp down the surge of hope, prepare herself for disappointment.

The door opened. Joey stood up to shake Frank's hand. He looked like he'd lost weight, or maybe he'd just aged.

Nessa, Frank said. He'd made lieutenant a few years earlier. Nessa had sent him a card to say well done. He had never looked like he belonged in the Roundhouse, with his barbershop shave and crisp starched shirts. His formality and ordered care were out of place here, where boxes were haphazardly stacked, and shelves sagged under the weight of files that had never been digitized. Nessa liked this about him. He sat on a chair opposite, a low coffee table between them. He'd never made her feel that her anger was disproportionate and ugly, the way Joey had. And she knew he had never been able to give up on the case.

Look, he said, I wanted you both to hear this from me in case there is any media coverage or speculation. We hope not. We've tried to do this quietly.

He looked at Nessa.

We think we found her car.

Joey dropped back in the chair. Nessa's face tingled as if it was going numb. This wasn't what they'd expected.

Where?

Here. Philly.

Her car's here? It's been here all along?

For a brief moment she had a rush of Maybe, maybe there's an explanation.

Where?

He didn't answer.

Frank?

In a reservoir.

It took her a moment to process the word, what this meant. She swallowed. Something was stuck in her throat.

Reservoir, she repeated. Is it hers, Frank? Are you sure? You said you *think* you found it.

Look. It's a Corolla . . . just like your sister's. The right model and year. We're floating it this morning. The Marine Unit's on site. They're lifting it in the next hour or two.

Joey stood up. We should go. We should be there.

Nessa nodded. We can drive right now.

Frank tugged the cuff of his shirt as if to straighten it.

No. I wouldn't. It's difficult to watch.

She'd seen this process before on the news, a car on a hook dredged off a riverbed, all the silt and weeds, how it seemed both sentient and monstrous. Maybe it would be best she wasn't there.

It was as if she were floating in the room, watching from outside. She pinched the skin on her forearm and held it. The feeling was far away.

We acted on new information we received, Frank said. A unit has been mapping the terrain over the last few days. New side-scan sonar equipment. We sent in divers. We're pretty sure it's hers.

Is . . . she . . . in it? Joey could barely finish his sentence.

Oh God. Nessa hadn't thought of that.

My honest answer is: We don't know yet. I suspect that she is. The car has been there a long time and is covered in silt. The side scanner does not give interior details. The visibility is poor. We only know the make and year because the dimensions from the scanner were matched by the software.

The fluorescent light buzzed and flickered above them, making it hard to focus. He'd said there'd been new information.

Frank, did someone tell you to look in the reservoir? Someone knew?

Yes.

Who? She could hear the plea in her voice.

You know I can't say. But I want you both to know that the investigation has accelerated. We have an entire team working on it.

Frank explained the importance of the investigation over the next few days. No media. No interviews. Say nothing to anybody that could potentially be used. *No comment* to anything about the car. At the moment, it's better to know as little as possible and let the police do what they have to do. No contact with anyone you believe may be a person of interest in the case or who's connected to a person of interest. For the next week or two, *nothing*.

We get it, said Joey. Right, Nessa? It felt barbed but she didn't rise to it.

Yeah, said Nessa.

The catalogue proof for an exhibition scheduled for December sat on her desk. She could feel the start of a migraine, dull pressure at the base of her neck. The pain was building behind the right eye, knifing her from the inside. The words on the document were visible but she couldn't arrange them into meaning. She rubbed her fist in her eye socket, put her head in her hands.

Nessa?

It was Catherine, an intern working with them for six months. Nessa had forgotten she was in the office. She lifted her head.

Are you okay?

Tired, said Nessa.

She hadn't slept. She was afraid now to shut her eyes, afraid that if she closed them she would see submerged cars or bodies bogged down in water, chained, attached to stone, trapped. She didn't know how to still these thoughts. If she did sleep, she woke in her bed after nightmares, gasping, desperate for light and air.

She turned her attention back to the catalogue, concentrated on trying to read the words. The artist quoted Walter Benjamin's 'Theses on the Philosophy of History', a despairing analysis inspired by a Paul Klee print – *the angel of history*, Benjamin called it. Nessa knew it, an abstract monoprint of a scrawled angel, large head and teeth and spread wings. Benjamin saw an angel caught between the past and the future. The angel is looking toward the past, appalled, his mouth open. His back is to the future, where he is being propelled by a storm. Beholding the wreckage, the angel wishes to resurrect or wake up the dead and fix all that has been destroyed. Nessa understood Benjamin differently now. He couldn't move on. Neither could she. There was nothing she could experience except through the lens of what had happened to Deena. Nausea surged up her throat. Her right eye pulsed with the momentum of pain.

Sorry, Catherine, she mumbled. Really feeling like I might be sick. I need to step out for a few minutes.

She walked along the Schuylkill, the museum and the city behind her, and kept going until the arches of the Strawberry Mansion Bridge were visible. When they'd driven over it as children their mother used to tell them how she had taken a trolley across it many times as a young girl. On the water between the trusses a lone rower glided under the bridge and disappeared. For the moment, Nessa was alone. She turned around and headed back toward the city.

She'd always believed Lucas had killed Deena. Could she have been wrong and it was someone else entirely? Could Deena have driven into the reservoir? Nessa had been through every scenario. Could Mathilde have discovered something? An anonymous person who had information and had been brought in for something else? In TV procedurals there was always someone bargaining with information to get a charge reduced. Ahead of her along the river, more angels. Three tall slender pillars held up childlike figures, each bronze body balancing on a single foot as they played instruments against the open sky. *The Playing Angels.* Every day they were there, forever about to totter to their deaths. Instead of exuberance, lightness or heavenly bodies flying against an open sky, Nessa had always seen an act of endurance. The exhaustion of being on display, always keeping balance. Watching them from underneath gave her vertigo, as if she were the one falling.

The blaze of the sun was reflected in Philadelphia's silver skyline. More rowers appeared on the river, clusters of boats, probably college teams, the coxes hunched low but saying nothing, the rowers keeping beat as their blades silently swept through the water, just the sound of the oars against their locks. They held time beside her for a few feet, before pulling ahead. Ruby rowed like that, at that kind of level.

Ruby, a fleeting picture, a toddler. After a day at the shore, the coconut smell of sunscreen, sand caked in all the creases of her naked body – neck folds, underarm crevices, gaps between fingers and toes. Ruby, hoisted above her, one hand gripping Nessa's, the other outstretched. Nessa lying on her back, her legs and feet under Ruby's stomach, holding her weight.

And Ruby laughing deep from the belly.

Ruby shouting, I'm flying, Nessa. I'm flying.

27

Ruby

The lane was in bud. Green shoots, small spurts of growth lit by the late-afternoon sun. Her face smarted from hours on the river. First day back on the water and her whole body held the good of it. Sophie had given her a ride as far as the post office after rowing and an envelope was waiting for her. Penn had said yes. She didn't know how she would get there but she would figure it out. Clover would help. Philadelphia had become a lodestar, like if she returned she could resolve some mystery within herself. Beside her the bloodroot's first blooms in small patches, clusters of white unblemished flowers, upright and alert. In freshman biology they had cut the stems wearing gloves. The flesh had bled a deep-deep-red poisonous sap. The flower had one leaf like a parent that went to sleep at night, closing in around the flower when the dark came. There was a word for it: *nyctinasty*.

A car was parked at the end of the lane. Ruby stopped walking, a surge of fear flooding her stomach and chest. It was green. What would Lucas do? She took a few further steps and saw that it was the Vermont State Police. She approached cautiously. *Criminal Division* was written on the door. A trooper sat inside, the window down. He saw her but didn't move. She turned to walk up toward the house and took a step back. A whole line of cars was blocking the driveway. Police. State police. Other cars. At the top of the drive, vans. Clover? She started to sprint but stopped about a hundred yards away. Clover was sitting on the porch, staring back out at her. A stranger in a suit was coming out of the house carrying a computer.

Wait! Ruby shouted. Just next to her something moved. Lucas. He was sitting in the backseat of a dark-blue car. She banged on the window.

Lucas!

He didn't turn. Stared straight ahead. She banged again and again.

She hit the window with her school bag. He didn't move. Ruby wiped the window with her hand. It was as if he were underwater; on the surface of the glass she could see the reflection of the trees, the sky, herself, but her father was submerged. He was only shadows, like fish, and he didn't seem to see her.

Lucas!

Dad! she roared.

He put his head in his hands and she saw then that they were cuffed.

At the bottom of the steps a woman introduced herself. She was not in uniform but had surgical gloves on and what Ruby assumed was a bulletproof vest. A detective, she said. Philadelphia Police Department. Ruby started at the mention of Philadelphia. What did this mean? Ruby was not allowed to enter the house. They had search warrants and were authorized to remove material important to the investigation.

What investigation? Why is my dad in the back of the car?

A liaison officer is here for you. She'll explain.

Ruby dropped her bag and sat on the ground next to Clover's chair on the porch. Clover was zipped up in a green down jacket that belonged to Lucas and a pink snow hat. A blanket was thrown across her lap. Since she'd come home from hospital she found it hard to get warm. Her lips, still not their own shape, looked blue.

Clover, what's happening?

Clover's good hand went to her mouth, as if to stop herself from speaking, and like Lucas she just stared ahead. Strangers were inside their house, ransacking their rooms. A procession of boxes, filing cabinets, laptops, cameras and electronic devices came through the door and were packed into car trunks.

Beyond the cars someone was walking up the lane. Blue denim overalls. Adelaide. She came up the steps and sat in the chair the other side of Clover.

When did they get here? I went up to St Albans to see my sister this morning.

Four or five hours ago. Clover's voice was just a whisper.

Okay, it's happening, Adelaide said. She took Clover's hand. I know this is so hard.

What? Ruby straightened. Alert. What's happening?

A man came up the steps. He was tall, clean-cut.

I'm sorry, Mrs Chevalier. We thought we'd be finished by now. I know this isn't what you wanted. He glanced at Ruby and Ruby knew he meant before she got home.

Clover lifted her shoulder and let it drop but said nothing.

Someone called the man over. Frank.

Ruby started to ask how did Clover know this man, but a woman was introducing herself. The liaison officer from the Criminal Division, Vermont State Police. She explained that she was here to support them, that multistate agencies were cooperating today.

I know you must have some questions . . .

No, said Clover.

Yes, said Ruby, standing up. Why are you here? Why is my father handcuffed in the back of a car? Why are you taking our— Wait!

A uniformed officer was carrying a milk crate filled with the large yellow envelopes. Ruby followed him down the steps, pointing.

Wait! Stop. Those are mine.

The liaison officer followed her and took her by the elbow. You need to come back up and sit on the porch with your grandmother.

They're my letters. Addressed to me. They're from my mother.

Clover looked distressed, her mouth open now. What did you say?

299

My mother.

Everyone was looking at her and Ruby suddenly saw how implausible it seemed to them.

Please sit down. The liaison officer gestured to one of the chairs. It's important you understand. I need you to listen. Your father has been arrested today on suspicion of a serious charge.

Clover wouldn't look at her. Adelaide started to say something and stopped.

Is it something to do with my mother? Clover, tell them what you told me. Tell them you were there and you know he didn't do anything.

The detective with the vest and gloves stepped onto the porch carrying one of the boxes from under Lucas's bed, the ones with the notebooks. Now she would never get to see what they were. They were taking them away.

Adelaide always had something to say, but now it was only a single word; she held Clover's hand and kept repeating it: Okay. Okay. Okay. Ruby thought her head was going to explode. She wanted to scream Make them stop, somebody make them stop. She stomped down the steps but the driveway was full of police and people carrying boxes. She turned and raced across the lawn, toward the shore. Two men were crouching in Lucas's boat, searching. She ran back up toward the sheds. The door of the tool shed was open. Lucas always kept it closed – she shut it behind her. The police had rummaged through everything. Toolboxes were flung wide, seed bags emptied, bait boxes taken apart. Even the camping equipment had been ransacked, the tent left in a heap. It needed to be folded and precise. For a moment she worried Lucas would see it. Then she thought she might laugh, or that maybe she should laugh. She sat on the floor and waited. What were they looking for?

It was getting dark when she heard engines start. Outside the dusty window, the dark car Lucas had been sitting in was moving down the driveway, following a line of vehicles, their headlights glittering in the dusk. It was like a distorted version of her first memory of her mother leaving. A motorcade. She watched the line of receding cars, her cheek against the glass.

Adelaide and Clover were in the kitchen. Mugs of coffee in front of them. Ruby didn't know who to trust. They had done something. Ruby hesitated in the doorway.

Ruby, why don't you sit down. Adelaide said it.

No.

Ruby, I think you should hear your grandmother out. Listen to what Clover has to say.

Ruby. Clover's new stroke-voice dragged her name.

No.

Adelaide stood. This isn't just about you. Or Lucas. Her voice had sharpened. Your grandmother has been through hell and she's trying to do what's right. Before she . . .

Adelaide trailed off. Crossed her arms. She was upset.

She did this for you.

Ruby pushed past her and went upstairs. Lucas's door was wide open. It wasn't like their house anymore. Everything was gone. The shelves were empty. They had even sliced open his mattress. The stuffing was pulled out in multiple places, white explosions where the incisions had been made. The doorknob and lock were missing.

The police had been in her room, through her drawers, had moved the mattress against the wall. She lowered it back onto the frame and saw that they had cut hers open too. Four diagonal cuts and the foam pulled out. She flipped it over and went and got a sheet from the closet in the hall. They'd been there. She covered the mattress. She didn't want to sleep against where their hands had been rifling. In the closet her old school notebooks and textbooks were still stacked in the corner. In the middle of these were the Memory Games notebooks. Untouched. She lay on the sheet under the comforter but couldn't get warm. She put on a hat and scarf and thick bathrobe and burrowed under the covers again. A chill had seeped into her marrow. She lay there without moving all night, her head spinning.

At six thirty her phone pinged. *Ruby, this is Suzanne Meyers, your father's attorney. I am messaging on his behalf. Can you take a phone call?* Ruby sat up. Texted back: *Yes.* She turned off the ringer and held the phone in her hand, waiting.

Hello?

Suzanne said she had to be brief but that Lucas had been brought to Philadelphia and he wanted Ruby to come straight away.

Your father says you know where the spare key for the truck is hidden? The police took his set. In the lockbox there is money. Take it. You will need it for gas and food. And, Ruby, your father said he'd prefer you don't talk to your grandmother and her friend. Just come to Philadelphia and he will explain.

Suzanne had made a reservation for her at a hotel in the city, near where he was, and would meet Ruby when she arrived. Ruby had never gone anywhere except for rowing and was unsure what to pack. She tried to move silently. Toothbrush. She picked up the toothpaste; it would serve Clover right not to have any. Then felt bad and put it back. She'd buy some when she got to where she was going. Shampoo. Hairbrush. Pyjamas. Change of clothes. Phone charger. She put everything into a backpack. She lifted her school bag and then put it down quietly. What was the point?

Adelaide was asleep on the couch in the living room. Ruby tiptoed past and went outside and down toward the shoreline, stopping at the American beech. Lucas had fitted a small lockbox in a tree cavity that faced the lake. Nobody would ever think to look there. Ruby pushed the combination numbers and opened it. There were several keys and a ziplock bag of cash. She took everything, put it in the front section of the backpack and walked back up to the truck. She unlocked it, sat inside and started the engine. From the rear-view mirror she could see Adelaide standing on the porch as she drove away.

Ruby walked across the marble floor, past the fake waterfall, to the check-in desk.

A reservation for Ruby Chevalier, please.

Ruby?

A blonde woman was standing at her elbow. I'm Suzanne. I've already checked you in and your room is ready. My assistant Carlotta and I are just over there. She pointed to a circle of overstuffed chairs around a low table with two sodas on it. A woman with very red lipstick was working on a laptop. Your father's arraignment is in the morning so we need to get to work.

Ruby hadn't slept and had just driven seven hours on highways that sometimes had eight lanes.

Okay. She didn't even know what an arraignment was.

The two women started talking about the other side.

What other side? asked Ruby. What does that mean?

Well, your mother's family. Your aunt. Suzanne paused. And I suppose your grandmother and her friend.

I don't even know my aunt. I don't know my mother's family. But my grandmother? I live with her. She's not the other side.

Just until the arraignment. That's all.

They didn't want her to talk to anyone until after she went to court. It was really important. Ruby saying a few words about her father tomorrow might really help him.

I don't understand why they arrested him. How can they prove my mother is dead? How can they charge him if she's just been missing?

Suzanne's arm lifting the soda stopped in mid-air. She put the drink down. Started to speak. She paused, smoothed her skirt, then leaned forward.

Ruby, I am very sorry to tell you this, but your mother passed away a long time ago. Her body was found. Several weeks ago. She has been positively identified. There's no uncertainty that it is her. She's been dead for a considerable time. Since she left you.

Air squeezed out of Ruby's chest as if she were in a vise. The room tilted.

What? she said; her hands gripped the sides of the table, trying to not pitch over.

I'm sorry, said Suzanne.

But there were letters sent to me.

The two women exchanged looks.

Maybe they were from someone else and your father was trying to protect you.

And Ruby knew for sure then, probably had already known deep down, that someone else had sent her packages all those years. The person Lucas was angry about. *Interfering bitch*. Her aunt Nessa.

Suzanne said, We believe your mother left voluntarily, that her death was a tragic accident, and that your father is innocent.

Ruby nodded. She was trying to absorb it all. Her mother was dead. She had felt her all these years. The words Ruby had read in the journal came back to her. He *smashed* things. Her mother *bruised*. Maybe Lucas had done it.

From now until the arraignment, don't make calls or answer your phone, unless it's me or Carlotta, said Suzanne.

It's best for us to stay put in our room tonight, Carlotta said. The way she spoke bugged Ruby – *us?*

Carlotta is going to come back later with an outfit.

You mean clothes?

Yes. And shoes.

Carlotta looked at Ruby's feet. What size shoe are you?

Um. Nine. I brought clothes, she said to Suzanne.

Well, there's a kind of uniform for these proceedings.

No television. No newspapers. In cases like this there's always trial by media – lies and exaggerations – and it's important that we don't look at that. Carlotta again with the *we*.

They didn't want her to see the news or talk to anyone. Even now Lucas was controlling what she knew. Suzanne handed Ruby a bag.

It's a portable DVD player and some DVDs for tonight as there's no television in the room.

Ruby looked inside. Seriously? she said, looking at each of them. They had just told her that her mother was dead and then handed her a bag of romantic comedies.

Suzanne was uncomfortable but didn't lose composure.

What Ruby could say – they'd written some ideas down. Suzanne pushed a piece of paper across the table toward her.

You need to prepare tonight so your testimony sounds authentic and from the heart, she said. Ruby read the sheet:

Try not to cry.

Look at your father as much as you can when you are on the stand.

Tell the judge what a good father he's been. You could give examples. How you need him. That you are still in school.

Let the judge know that you were too young to remember your mother before she left. Let the judge know that your father is the only parent you've ever known.

It might help to practise it, Carlotta said.

Remember to look at him, Suzanne said.

Your father says you're very smart.

Carlotta was saying all the wrong things. Ruby didn't like her.

Right now you are all your father has, said Suzanne. And Ruby felt a wrench then, because she probably was.

She lay foetal on the hotel bed holding her knees. All she wanted to do was sleep but it was still only late afternoon. She wanted to hear Sophie's voice, Lola and her sisters in the background. To call Nathalie and say, The Memory Games are done, the quest is over because she's dead. We failed. She switched the phone on and wished she could call one of them – Sophie or Nathalie – and say, My mother is dead. Help me. Tell me how to feel. She had been told not to. *Your father needs you*, Suzanne had said. She wanted her friends but couldn't talk to them. None of them had ever liked Lucas.

Carlotta held up a hideous floral dress that fell above the knee. Ruby sat on the bed in disbelief. It would suit a child, a scrawny pre-teen, but not a five-foot-ten eighteen-year-old with significant muscle mass.

Have you seen my thighs? Ruby patted her legs. That dress will only reach halfway to my knees. It's way too short.

Carlotta knew she'd made a mistake. Look, she said, can you show me what you have? Like try it on.

Ruby had brought a knee-length patterned skirt and a cream blouse. When she came out of the bathroom Carlotta shook her head.

You look like you've just dropped your kids to day care and you're on your way to the office. Plus you're so . . . well, muscular.

I can't shrink into a little girl by tomorrow, if that's what you want.

No make-up, Carlotta said. No jewellery.

See Philadelphia and other tourist brochures were on a small coffee table in the hotel room. Ruby sat in the chair and flicked through them. The Liberty Bell, the LOVE sculpture, the Betsy Ross House, the Art Museum, and then a picture she recognized. A row of houses along the river, each one outlined in lights. She knew these. Houses along a river, lit up. *Boathouse Row* was printed underneath. Something she loved. Something she'd loved seeing with her mother. She grabbed her bag and went downstairs to the street. A couple were getting out of a cab and Ruby showed the driver the picture.

Can you take me there? Can we drive past them?

They drove in a loop. Ruby with the window rolled down, looking, taking pictures. On the fourth loop the driver said he'd pull in. She stood against a railing and looked across the river at the little lit houses that her aunt had drawn for her on the package she'd got all the way back in fourth grade, trying to help her remember. She needed to tell someone. Not Nathalie. Not Sophie. She rang Tim.

God. Ruby?

When she heard his voice, she started to cry.

She's dead, Tim. My mother's dead.

I know. I'm so sorry. I just saw it on the news.

She was thirty. She was only thirty years old.

I know. It's so sad.

Behind her she could hear the noise of the expressway. In front of her the lights from the boathouses moved on the surface of the black water. A light breeze blew.

I remember the feeling of her, Ruby said.

28

Nessa

2018

At the corner of Broad and Spruce she stopped. City Hall was straight ahead, the tower blinding white, the bronze William Penn magnified by the morning light and clear blue sky. Nessa's dad had always mentioned Penn's hat whenever he came into the city, how it had been understood that nothing should be built higher than its brim, and that ever since One Liberty Place had been built, a skyscraper taller than the hat, all of Philadelphia's teams had been hexed. He'd said it every time. The night the Phillies won the World Series she wished she could call him and say, The spell's been lifted! The builders of the new Comcast building had placed a replica statuette on top of the final beam, making Penn's hat the highest point again. Then the Eagles won the Super Bowl. She'd wished he was there.

The City Hall clock beneath the black eagle read eight thirty. She'd walked to Center City early that morning, afraid to miss anything, and had wandered. It was time now. She smoothed her skirt, took a deep breath and walked back north. Outside the Criminal Justice Center on Filbert Street, Frank was waiting. He saw her and held up a cup of coffee.

Flat white?

Thanks.

Your brother didn't come?

He'll wait for the trial. It's hard for him to get a day off. And you know Joey. He can't do all this.

Frank nodded.

She and Frank drank their coffees outside. One of the investigating officers pulled him aside for a few minutes. Around them, people gathered in small groups, talking and smoking.

All set? Frank asked, coming back over.

As I'll ever be, I guess.

They signed in and went through the metal detector; Frank joked with the security cop about someone they knew. She scanned the room, hypervigilant. Frank noticed.

You won't see him until his case is called and he's brought in. He's being held in a separate part of the building. The only place you could ever see him is in the court.

They walked down the hallway and past wide pillars, the hint of classical grandeur depressed by suspended ceilings and fluorescent lighting. She kept looking for a child even though Ruby was a teenager now, a young woman, who wouldn't recognize Nessa. They stopped at the elevators and waited. A large group of people passed, flocked together, yellow tags on their shirts marking them out.

Jurors have their own elevator, said Frank.

They moved as a unit, like a Greek chorus, eyes averted, afraid to look at anyone.

Could they be ours?

No. There's no jury in a pretrial. They're kept separate because they can't be mixing with the prosecution or the defence witnesses or families. Although they're not really kept apart when you think about it, said Frank, lowering his voice. They can walk out with the witnesses or families, stand together at the traffic light, discover they're on the same subway, same stop, parked in the same lot. Plenty can happen.

Are they here?

He hesitated. Pressed the up button for the elevator again.

We have Clover's deposition. She's unwell. She's not fit to travel and why would she want to be here? Ruby is on their list. She's their only witness. Our affidavits are procedural – medical, phone records, ballistics, that kind of thing. Today is just a formality where the judge says it goes to trial or doesn't and whether he'll get bail. Having Ruby on their list is sort of a decoy. His lawyer wants her to come to be seen by the judge, to present a particular picture of him as a father and all that. Anyway, there's nothing to worry about. He's out of state. There'll be no bail.

For fourteen years, more than anything, Nessa had wanted to see Ruby. It was a desperate visceral need to hold Ruby's little body – an assertion of Deena, them, their mother, their past. Everything. She had become everything. Now Nessa wasn't sure she could cope. She was as terrified of not seeing her as she was of seeing her and having to acknowledge that the rift was too great. The elevator opened and they stepped in, everyone suddenly quiet as the doors shut. When they got off on the third floor Frank said, It's funny how they put the jurors in a separate elevator, but they don't separate victims' and defendants' families.

Nessa was half-listening. Ruby would be here. With him, on *his* side. She wanted to scream She's ours. She belongs to us. The injustice of it all tightened in her chest, and deep down she knew that Ruby belonged to herself. It was too late. They had missed it all.

Here we are. Frank put his hand on her elbow to steer her left at the end of the hall. She started to feel like she couldn't get her breath and wished she had taken the just-in-case Xanax in her wallet. She had waited so long.

Ready? he asked.

Yeah.

Frank went in first. Rows of benches lined each side of a central aisle and straight ahead was a Perspex wall. Beyond it, the court. Frank led her toward the front of the gallery. It's like a wedding, he whispered. Plaintiff to the right, defendant to the left. You know, groom's side, bride's side. They sat. The wooden benches did remind her of church pews.

Three uniformed officers huddled around a small thin man with tortoiseshell glasses. He was looking at a file open on a table. The DA. She had met him briefly during the week; he looked like a college student. Up there amongst grown men he seemed even younger. The judge's bench sat empty. Beyond it, an armed deputy stood outside a door. On the left, a woman, forty-something with a blonde bob and powder-blue suit, everything muted and soft, like Grace Kelly in a Hitchcock film, was flicking through files. She must be Lucas's lawyer. In the gallery there was only one person on the other side. A woman, maybe late-twenties, was highlighting a document. Power-dressed. Bright-red suit, dark hair pulled tight into a stiff bun. She turned and stared straight at Nessa. Thick lipstick matched her suit. Nessa sensed this woman already knew who she was. She practised her bitch face in case the woman looked over again.

Frank leaned toward her and gestured with his chin. She's an assistant to the defence attorney.

Lucas had hired a two-woman team. He'd managed to get two presumably intelligent women to support and defend him. How did men like him do this? Nessa wanted to punch the young woman in her bright-red lipsticked mouth, shout Wake the fuck up, do better.

She took one more furtive look over her left shoulder to see if Ruby had arrived. Empty. They waited. The case was called. The judge came through a door. A woman. They stood, then sat. Frank had said that if they got her, they'd be on solid ground.

The Commonwealth of Pennsylvania versus Lucas Chevalier was announced. The defence attorney shot a look toward the back of the gallery and Nessa saw the woman with red lipstick do the same. Were they looking for Ruby? The case number was called. Where was Lucas? Nessa stared at the closed door straight ahead where the deputy was positioned, but then on her periphery a uniformed officer stepped out of a doorway to the side of the courtroom near the defence table, and behind him was Lucas, handcuffed.

She hadn't seen him in fourteen years, had forgotten that in-charge and controlled aura he practised. He was doing it still. Deena had said she'd found this attractive. They'd teased her about the alpha-manly-man, all Vermont-and-hunting thing at the beginning. He hadn't really aged. A bit of grey at the sideburns. White dress shirt, a glimpse of a pale-blue tie, grey cashmere sweater, slim-cut dress trousers. No suit jacket. Maybe he looked more sophisticated because he had ditched the jacket? Had the woman in pale blue made this decision, selected his clothes for him? Or maybe Mathilde. He looked like he'd stepped out of a Brooks Brothers catalogue. He was better-dressed than the prosecutor and appeared younger than fifty-two. Clean-cut and tanned in that outdoorsy way. There he was, feet away, cuffed and yet presentable, his attitude and look curated. His calm, steady air when it was required, as if there had been a mistake and he didn't belong here. She wanted to claw his face, to hammer his head, to feel the force of her anger against his body, to feel it give. The prosecutor's introduction hummed in the background; she couldn't hear the words. She didn't take her eyes off Lucas.

Called to the stand, he listened to the charges read against him. His face, posture, hands, his whole body: inscrutable. She promised herself that should his gaze meet hers she would stare him down. But it never did. He directed all his attention toward the judge and prosecutor as they spoke, nowhere else. Nessa allowed herself another quick look over the shoulder. Empty rows on the defence side. Her leg had started to twitch and she pressed her hands down on her knee. The prosecutor's questions sounded tinny and high compared to Lucas's replies. He spoke clearly, occasionally deferring to his lawyer at the table. She nodded or shook her head; the intimacy of their unspoken understanding made Nessa sick to her stomach.

The blonde lawyer signalled to her assistant to make a phone call. Subtle, but Nessa saw; a lifted hand to the ear. Nessa watched the furtive texting across the aisle. The prosecution had concluded. The assistant stood and walked to the back of the gallery. Nessa heard the door open. Maybe Ruby was in the hallway, waiting.

The defence lawyer stood and asked Lucas questions. They repeated what had already been established. Was his lawyer stalling for time? The door opened at the back of the gallery, a creak and footsteps. Was Ruby behind her? Nessa held her breath, watched Lucas. His gaze flicked beyond his attorney, past Nessa, to the door. And she saw a singular moment. A crack. His eyes lowered. He swallowed. Nessa felt his skipped heartbeat. Ruby hadn't come.

The questions that weren't really questions ended. Lucas was led to the defence table and seated. The judge asked if the defence witness was present. The lawyer in the blue suit asked to approach.

Bail was denied. The trial would proceed. Nessa watched Lucas disappear through the door, a uniformed police officer behind him. Her head dropped into her hands.

The very first night she'd met him, she'd asked him did he know the word *palimpsest*. He knew it from computing. He'd said, It's when you erase memory and write over it. She'd understood it in the opposite way. The impossibility of erasing what had been there before, how something persisted, refused to disappear, whether it was the trace of another text, a ruin, a memory. Her whole body flooded with relief. Ruby hadn't taken the stand to try to overwrite the story of Deena and what had happened to her. Frank nudged her. The court was being prepared for the next case. They stood and turned. Directly behind her, several rows back, was Molly. Ronan was next to her. They were here.

29
Ruby

She hadn't slept in three days and the dark road and woods threw shapes and shadows that she swerved around or drove straight through. Trees morphed into murky dancers, then dissipated to nothing under her headlights. Her eyes burned. The testimony she was supposed to have given on repeat all the way home. She saw it as if she were looking through a fish-eye lens in a peephole, herself in the foreground, elongated and grotesque, the panoramic court-room warped and disproportionate. Look at your father, they'd said. Look at him when you speak. It's important. She couldn't. She didn't want to see him. She didn't want to say the things they were asking her to say. His lawyer had told Ruby that she was all he had. She'd abandoned him.

Day was breaking when she crossed the bridge back onto the Islands. She would be home before the court even convened. She hadn't texted Carlotta or Suzanne, didn't want to have to justify herself. The glow from the porch light was visible as she drove up toward the house. Clover must have left it on just in case. She climbed the steps and pushed open the door. Adelaide's lumpy shape beneath blankets on the sofa. Ruby wished she could wake them both and say, I'm here, I've come home and I've done something terrible. I betrayed Lucas. But so had they.

Upstairs in her room the mattress was bare. The gashes had been stitched back together with pink embroidery thread. Like fixing a wound. Adelaide's careful hand, her neat even stitches. A fresh set of sheets and pillowcases were folded at the end of the bed and her comforter was on a chair. Everything washed. Adelaide had tried to scrub away all the strange hands in their space. Ruby lay on the bed. Her mother was dead, her father was in custody, she was legally an adult.

She slept. When she woke and went down to the kitchen Clover said nothing. Adelaide welcomed her then said she was heading home for a few days, was giving Ruby and Clover space. She would keep dropping off food but the two of them needed to talk.

The days that followed blurred together. Sleep, avoidance, chores, lethargy. After a flood of messages from Carlotta asking *Where are you?* Suzanne texted: *Your father did not get bail.* An accusation, but Ruby was relieved. For days, Clover sat stunned at the kitchen table, distracting herself playing along to *The Price Is Right* and *Wheel of Fortune* while Ruby curled into a ball on her bed, plunged deep inside an eddy of bad thoughts. She had let Lucas down, and her mother. If her mother had been bruised, Ruby must have seen it. Why couldn't she remember? Why couldn't she remember her mother?

Then Nessa's phone call. *You were her whole world. We've waited.* They wanted her at her mother's funeral. After she'd hung up, Ruby sat on the steps looking at the lake. At the end of their dock, Lucas's boat was sitting lower and lower on her lines. She was sinking. He had neglected her the past few months and it wasn't like him. He'd been agitated and distant even before Clover's stroke. He must have known things were falling apart and maybe a part of him had given up. She got the bilge pump from the shed and went down to the water. Lucas had told her at least a hundred times that most boats sink at shore, not at sea. She thought, Maybe if I do this for him, I'll feel that little bit better. There was nothing else she could salvage. She manually pumped the water out and brought down the power washer and scoured her.

Then she cleaned the coop, shovelling out thickened layers hardened in sheets of pine shavings and excrement. Heaped wheelbarrows of it onto the compost pile. She moved the fencing. She remembered the day they'd received their first shipment of chicks through the mail. The trembling thrill of it. Lucas scooping the dead chick out, trying to protect her from death. Showing her how to bring them to water. Wiping their vents, *gentle gentle*. Could he have killed her mother? Denied her a mother for all her life?

She arranged the hens' eggs in a basket with the dishes on the bottom step. She took her first shower since Philadelphia, rinsed off the bilge, the chicken-coop grime, the filth and crud of the past week of her life. She scrubbed harder and harder until her flesh was raw and pink. She'd done the right thing. What she'd wanted, not what Lucas had ordered. She needed new skin. She dressed in clean clothes, brushed her hair and went into the kitchen and said to Clover, I'm ready to talk.

Lucas called me and asked me to come to Philadelphia to help out with you for a long weekend. Early February 2004. I'd never met you. I took the train and got there on a Wednesday. He told me I needed to rent a car because he might need me to take you to your playgroup because it was too far to walk. He brought me to a place in New Jersey and I rented a car. I didn't want to do it. I was very nervous driving to the city.

Clover sat at the head of the table in her chair, Ruby beside her. Clover's speech was slow and laboured but better than it had been. She'd lost weight and the skin dragged off her face in folds.

The Thursday night he asked me to follow him in the rental car. He had to leave his truck for loggers to load it with wood. I don't know where we drove. Maybe an hour away. I focused on following his truck. I couldn't tell you whether we went north, south, east or west. We drove deep into the woods, where he parked, and then he drove me in the rental back to the city.

Clover paused for breath.

You came to the house on the Friday night. You were something else. All chat. A firecracker. On Saturday we went to a park, the three of us, and then to a diner. You'd been there before and told me what I should order. Bossy.

Sunday I slept in. I didn't get out of bed until nine but I was awake before that, maybe even an hour or so. I could hear the shower running. And the thing is, I thought he must have been out fishing or for a run or something because I'd heard him come in from outside and come up the stairs to the bathroom.

Clover had been his alibi. She'd told the police he hadn't left. She'd said that to Ruby. Ruby could feel pressure against her diaphragm; for a moment she wasn't sure she even wanted Clover to keep talking.

That evening you and I said goodbye. You shook my hand, like I was a stranger you had just met, which I guess I was. You left to go meet your mother but half an hour later you were back. Your mother hadn't come. Lucas acted like this was a regular occurrence. He made it sound like Deena wasn't reliable. I came back to Vermont the next morning. Lucas never said anything to me. Nothing at all. Then I got a phone call from a detective. Philadelphia Police Department. Your mother was missing and Lucas had told them that I was there in the house with him that weekend. They interviewed me up here in the police station. They asked me had Lucas left Sunday morning. I said no. I said I was there and awake and he hadn't left. They said I was his alibi. I signed my statement.

You lied?

I didn't want to believe that he would do something like that. I didn't believe he had. And I wasn't exactly sure what I remembered. I didn't want trouble for him. He told me your mother did this kind of thing regularly.

In June you came to live here. You were four and a half. Lucas said it was best if you had no contact with your mother's family.

Anything that was a reminder of her would be painful for you. He wanted to give you a new start.

Clover found it hard to get the next words out. She sat in her chair staring at Ruby, her bottom lip shaking.

You cried for them. For months. You cried for your mom at night. I couldn't comfort you. You cried for Nessa. Your grandfather. Lucas wouldn't let me call them so you could at least talk on the phone. Every time you asked about your mother, we ignored it or Lucas ordered you to stop—

Ruby's chin was on the table, her arms over her head as if shielding herself from her own story. She hadn't forgotten them.

Clover stopped talking. Covered her face with her good hand.

And you stopped asking for them then.

The year you started middle school, the detective from Philadelphia came to the house when Lucas was at work, the one who had interviewed me before. He was in the Homicide Unit. He said he could subpoena me to come to Philadelphia to be interviewed or talk to me right there and then. Your mother had been legally declared dead and he believed that my son knew something about it. I repeated what I'd said before. Lucas hadn't left. I didn't know anything. He did say those words – Protection From Abuse – but I didn't know exactly what he meant, and maybe I didn't want to hear it. It wasn't until you said it, that you had seen newspaper articles. Violence in the house.

Clover had to stop again.

Maybe I knew all along. The rental car. The truck. The fact that he had been out. I had lied. Perjured. I had interfered in an investigation. I knew they would take you away. And what would you do without either of us?

The detective left his card on the refrigerator, under the Champlain magnet, in case I remembered a detail or wanted to say anything. He wasn't gone ten minutes when your dad barrelled through the door. Back from Montreal. Interrogated me about what the detective had asked. Made me repeat over and over what I had said. And I knew then that he could watch the cameras. And I thought about how he'd chopped down my mailbox. And I remembered that he was angry.

Clover cleared her throat. I made a will. Spoke to an attorney about how to cash out life insurance policies to put money aside for you. I didn't know what was ahead. Maybe a year ago or more, I told Adelaide. She found news articles about the case for me. We were both sure. Then he hurt you.

That was an accident, Ruby interrupted.

It was and it wasn't, Clover said. And it was all I thought about. How the truck was at his house on that Sunday and the bed was empty. No wood. One morning I was sitting out there looking at the lake, smoking, and I was driving down that road behind his truck that night again, like a thousand times before, but this time I saw a sign. A road sign: *Laurel Wood Reservoir*. I had seen it just before we turned onto the dirt track into the woods.

Ruby had already read the papers at a rest stop on the way back to Vermont. Her mother's body had been found in her car in a reservoir. Listening to Clover, she knew. He'd done it.

I'd burned the card the detective gave me but had written the number on a slip of paper and hidden it. You brought it to me in the hospital.

Clover exhaled and her breath was short. She was exhausted and, despite everything, Ruby helped her to the sitting room to her chair. She fell asleep instantly. The doctor had said no stress, but Clover was trying to set things right, like Adelaide had said. Grey strands of hair were stuck to the sides of her face. Her woollen cardigan was buttoned to the chin. The enlarged fingers and one hand that didn't work. How had she even buttoned it? Ruby watched her breath move in and out. Her own body was struggling, each breath like trying to lift a cinder block on her chest. Clover had told her the truth. Ruby stood up and put a blanket across her.

She sat by the window and counted off towns. For a long time they were poised on the lake's edge, the fishing boats in the distance, the contours of the earth against the blue lake, the bays and the Green Mountains – our mountains, as Lucas called them – in the far distance. The train moved backward away from the lake, moving backward toward the past, and she watched everything in front of her, the familiar lake, the life she had always known, recede.

After New York they travelled through a tunnel, underwater, into New Jersey. Newark, Princeton, Trenton. Then 30th Street Station. Philadelphia. She was here. Nessa had said to meet her at the angel statue. Ruby knew it already from the movies Nathalie had made her watch. *Angel of the Resurrection*. In *Witness* she remembered the little Amish boy gazing up at it. A tall angel, high above, raising a fallen body in its arms. She came up the stairs from her platform, into the main terminal, and felt like she had been there before. Commuters bustled all around her. She turned in a full circle, then started toward them, at the far end of the concourse, the angel's wings raised high.

Acknowledgements

I have been helped by so many while writing this book. I am indebted to everyone at Faber: Louisa Joyner, Libby Marshall and especially my editor Sara Helen Binney, who steered the manuscript to completion and buoyed me when I most needed it. Thank you Lauren Nicoll for your generous effort to get this book into the world; Josephine Salverda for guiding the manuscript through all the steps; Silvia Crompton for your invaluable copy-edits; Jane Barringer for your forensic proofreading; and Arabella Watkiss and Mollie Stewart for your marketing creativity. Thank you Pete Adlington, head of design at Faber, for the beautiful cover.

Thank you Noah Eaker, my editor at Harper Books, whose insights and editorial suggestions helped me reimagine how things might end.

I am blessed to have Peter Straus as my agent. Thank you all at RCW, especially Stephen Edwards. At Gill Hess, thank you Declan Heeney and Simon Hess.

So many people helped with the research for this book. Thank you Lizabeth and Joe Macoretta, Deirdre Cosgrove Andrews, Deirdre Mannion Tükel and the Pergolini family for your guidance on everything from legal process, NICU protocol, memory studies and family services to Philly idiom. Thank you Joseph McDermott, former homicide detective, who generously gave several days of his time taking me around Philadelphia, including visits to the criminal court and the Roundhouse. Thank you Dave Greenough and Lawrence 'Lucky' Pyne for your intimate and passionate knowledge of Vermont's woods and waters and for generously sharing it. Thank you Alannah Donohoe in Sligo for your rowing expertise and your close reading. Any mistakes or missteps on any of these topics are mine alone.

I am especially grateful to Elske Rahill and Séan Farrell, who read as I wrote. Séan went through every draft, every paragraph, every word and offered robust and conscientious edits. I imagine that he despaired almost as much as I did but kept going. Séan and Elske, you made this book, and Sligo, better. Thank you, thank you, thank you.

Sinéad Gleeson has been a mentor and friend and I try to imitate her generosity to others. In Sligo, Tara McGowan from the Cairde Festival as well as Patricia Keane and Michelle Brennan from Sligo Central Library have continuously supported me and other writers. I thank my colleagues and students on the Writing + Literature and Performing Arts Programmes at ATU Sligo. It is genuinely an honour to work with and learn from you. Thank you Emmet O'Doherty and David Roberts. Thank you also to all at Liber Bookshop, Sligo.

I am infinitely grateful for space to write: Paul at the River Mill, PeeWee Stapleton and his humans in Tennessee, and the Model Arts Centre in Sligo for my yard studio, a haven without which this book would not have happened.

Everyone who read, shared and recommended *A Crooked Tree*: book clubs, bloggers, reviewers, interviewers and podcasters, thank you all, especially my NDA high school classmates who with Susi McKernan gave me the in-person launch that never happened initially because of lockdown.

My mother, my five sisters, two brothers, in-laws, nieces and nephews anchor me, as do Thérèse O'Loughlin, Lisa Johnson Viveros and Isabel Grayson, my friends for all these years.

Louise Kennedy, I don't know where to begin. You've kept me in the world, fed me, reminded me that there should be joy. I am beyond grateful to have you as my friend.

Michael, thank you. Dúaltagh, Brónagh and Aoibhín, this book is for you because you are the heart of everything.